THE KEEPER

Also by Gareth O'Callaghan

Dare to Die

Published by Poolbeg

THE KEEPER

GARETH O'CALLAGHAN

POOLBEG

All characters in this publication are fictitious and any resemblance to real persons, living or dead, is purely coincidental.

Published 1999 by
Poolbeg Press Ltd,
123 Baldoyle Industrial Estate,
Dublin 13, Ireland

Reprinted May 1999

A catalogue record for this book is available from the British Library.

ISBN 1 85371 732 0

Cover design by Slatter/Anderson
Set by Poolbeg Group Services Ltd in Palatino 10/13.5
Printed and bound in Great Britain by
Cox & Wyman Ltd, Reading, Berkshire.

Acknowledgements

My special thanks to my parents, Eileen and Joe. To Pat Henry and Patricia Scanlan. To everyone at Poolbeg, especially Nicole Hodson and Paula Campbell: Trojans in their fields. To my editor, Gaye Shortland, for the care she has taken and the interest she has shown.

Someone who deserves my heartfelt thanks for all she has done for me, and who is never far from my thoughts, is Kate Cruise O'Brien. Kate had just started working with me on this novel early last year, two weeks before she collapsed and died. Kate loved to write. That was why she loved being up to her neck in other authors' convoluted plots and literary dilemmas. From page one, she almost seemed to become another character in your story. I know she would have enjoyed this one.

My foremost "thank you" goes to my wife, Jacqui, and to my daughters, Kerri, Katie and Aibhín: your love and inspiration and enthusiasm have been my strength and the most important driving force in my life.

Finally, to the individuals who talked but asked not to be thanked.

A Note on the Author

Gareth O'Callaghan is one of Ireland's best-known broadcasters. During the eighties, he spent five years working on radio in Britain where he trained as a journalist with the BBC. He is currently hosting the 2FM breakfast show. His first novel *Dare to Die* was a bestseller in 1996. *The Keeper* is his second novel. He lives in Dublin.

For Jacqui, Kerri, Katie and Aibhín,
As always, with all my love

– *n* keeper: *an attendant in charge of animals in captivity;*
a custodian of a museum or gallery;
a prison guard;
The Chambers Dictionary

"A man who has not passed through the inferno of his passions can never overcome them."

Carl Jung

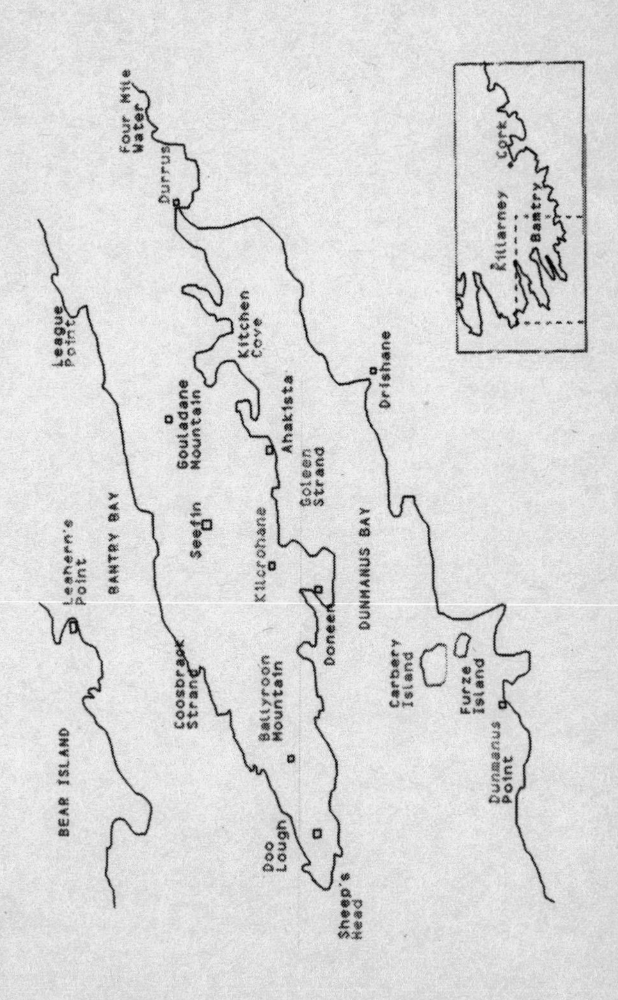

Durrus, West Cork, Ireland.

1

Durrus, West Cork – 12.10am, Sunday, May 5th.

Happy birthday, son.

Adam Roper imagined his father's words as he tried to focus on the wristwatch he'd received less than twenty-fours earlier for his seventeenth birthday. He was sure his father would ring any minute to wish him a happy birthday. By then it might be too late. *The police have recovered the bodies of three young teenagers from the wreckage of a stolen car*, the headlines would say. Stealing a car in a small town in the middle of nowhere was a bit like walking into a police station carrying the crown jewels. He tried to fill his mind with nice thoughts: the girl in the pub, Cindy. His father's new job at the car plant. He couldn't concentrate. He wasn't, by any means, a good back-seat traveller. His head was burning up. His eyes ached in their sockets. His mouth tasted of a mixture of bile and too many pints of lager. He'd begged them to stop the car so often he'd given up pleading with them miles back. He was petrified now, toying with the idea of throwing himself out onto the narrow road. But he was too sick, too dizzy, to find the door handle in the pitch darkness of someone else's car.

Death felt closer than the branches whacking the sides of the car.

It was difficult to make out the time. Ten past twelve, he reckoned. It was difficult to see anything inside the car now. Just the orange-tinted lights of the dashboard instruments and the two heads bobbing about above the tops of the seats in front of him. Beyond them, through the windscreen, the narrow road with its grassy banks and wild hedges and trees with their ghostly, overhanging branches seemed to be screaming towards them out of the jet-black darkness, sucking them in faster and faster. The writing had been on the wall ever since his two mates started to drink cider earlier in the afternoon. Occasionally Kevin Canning switched off the headlights completely and the three boys would count pluckily to see how far the car could travel in blind limbo, flat out, without hitting anything: *Three . . . Four!*

Beeping sounds were coming from somewhere in the car; somewhere close to him, it seemed, in the back seat. Then he remembered. His mobile phone. He had set it for 12.10am to remind him to ring his father and thank him for the watch. He tried to manoeuvre the phone out of his pocket with two of his fingers but it seemed to be caught under his jacket. He had it in his hand. Then it fell. He could just barely hear the beeping now, the flashing green light of the display difficult to focus on as it lay on the floor. He reached down just as the phone got swept away under the seat in front and out of sight. He was about to fish for it when the car hit something extremely hard, head-on.

The impact brought the Vectra to a sudden halt. Adam put a hand to his ear. His head had thumped against the sharp window frame and the ear was bleeding heavily. Kevin Canning and Ronan Murray, ignoring his begging to stop clowning about, laughed hysterically as the mighty 2.5 litre engine screamed and begged to be driven in anger, the back wheels of the car stuck now in a deep gully beneath the huge oak tree that had just claimed most of the rear end.

"Let's get outta here!" Adam pleaded again, not wanting to sound too childish.

The two boys ignored him, busy urging the car forward, as Kevin threw it into first gear and revved hard. It bucked and jumped, first up and over, forcing the front of the car nose-downward sharply. Then, with a loud thump, it was back on the road, swerving and ricocheting against the low mounds on either side, oversteering aggressively as four hands fought to find a straight line.

"Shit! Clutch is gone," roared Kevin above the deafening squeals and whirrs of an engine cooking in low gear.

Ronan Murray kicked the dash and screamed: *"Go, go, go!"*

The blaze of sparks lighting up the road behind them told Adam they'd lost a wheel, completely shorn off by the impact with a two-hundred-year-old tree. His friends ignored the jettison, pushing the car harder into the sharp bend ahead. To get through the hairpin at this speed was going to be a miracle. To get out of this debacle was going to be even tougher.

Adam Roper was spending the first ten minutes of his seventeenth birthday in the back seat of a stolen car. A *stolen* car. The word bombarded his brain. He'd tried to tell them they were stupid to even contemplate it. He really believed they'd never do it. Sense would prevail, he told himself. Then a moment's weakness on his part, the thought of having to walk back the three miles to the campsite, made him sit in. All he could think of now was his father and mother sitting in the public gallery, watching as a grey-haired judge sent their son down for six months.

They'd been drinking heavily, celebrating Adam's birthday and the end of the exams. The weekend was a gift from Adam's father. Adam had suggested a camping holiday in West Cork to coincide with the annual music festival. Just the three lads, Adam, Kevin and Ronan, drinking, hanging around and chillin' out. That was all.

And that *was* all. Until after ten that Saturday night, when Kevin broke a glass and spilled drink all over two locals in Hannon's pub. The owner, a fat, balding man with a gruff voice, asked them to finish up and leave.

"Just like in the movies," Kevin slurred sarcastically.

"Ye'll be gettin' no more drink here, lads. Finish up an' off with ye," he called from across the counter.

Adam had left at that point . . .

With the sound of an engine revving he'd heard Ronan's voice.

"Come on!"

He stepped into the carpark.

The black Vectra pulled alongside, the back door half open. *"Get in, quick!"*

"No!" Adam backed off.

"We're only taking it up the road a bit, to the crossroads. Then we'll leave it there and walk the rest of the way. Come on," he urged, "we're too pissed to walk. An' it's gonna rain. This way we'll be there in ten minutes."

Adam shook his head.

"Right then, *walk!* And you're not gettin' into the tent if you're wet."

He sat in and banged the door.

They'd passed the crossroads at least a mile back now. Adam knew they were on the wrong road. *"This isn't the right road!"* Talking to a stone wall. It was half twelve now. They had been in the car for almost half an hour. Travelling at this speed, he reckoned they'd driven twenty miles at least. The narrowness of the road, and the rough, gravelly sound of its unsteady surface, told him they had strayed well off the beaten path miles back. The hedges and mounds were gone, replaced now by huge straight lines of pines. They were on a forest road, most likely driving round in circles.

"We're runnin' outta fuel!" Kevin shouted.

Adam said nothing, determined now to stay calm and conserve whatever energy he might need for whatever might lie ahead. Up the road he noticed the flickering glow, a revolving blue blush which seemed to become more intense as they drove closer to the hilltop. The road suddenly started to widen, as if it was heading towards a forest exit, preparing to meet a main junction. As the car bounced over the peak, Adam's stomach crumpled into a small, painful ball. He gripped his left hand, covering his watch, and squeezed tightly. Then he started counting the blue flashing lights.

"Four cars!" screamed Kevin, his voice almost giving way to tears. *"Shit!"*

"It's only two, I think," replied Adam, trying to remain calm for the others who, he'd just remembered, were older than him. "Slow down."

"No way!" chirped Kevin.

"Do what Adam says," called Ronan.

"We'll crash through them. They'll never catch us in this!" He was starting to accelerate again.

"Don't be stupid, Kevin. We've only got three wheels and we're running out of petrol. Anyway we're in enough trouble as it is." Adam's mind had started to concoct excuses. Anything that was mildly plausible would do for the moment. He tried not to think of what the long-term consequences of their mindless pratfall might be. He was in the back seat. Often the repercussions for the passengers within a stolen car were serious.

The car was slowing, almost to a halt now, as Kevin moved closer to the two vehicles, one a jeep, the other an estate. He sniffed hard, trying to disguise the tears.

An *estate*? Adam sat forward, rubbed his head and studied the scene unfolding in front of them. A man in an oily-looking reflective raincoat held his hand up high in front of the Vectra. Kevin stopped.

"The police don't drive estates," Adam muttered.

The other two seemed to ignore his remark, busy preparing their own stories, occupied with a multitude of excuses, failing to notice for a few moments – unlike Adam – the balaclavas. Adam counted them. Three in all, each peering through the tiny slits in the black headgear, each cradling what seemed to be a long baton or walking stick.

Kevin grunted, "What the hell is *that*?" He nodded to the small illuminated red dot – afraid to put his finger near it – like a small florescent bulb flickering beneath his jumper, wavering about mid-point on his chest.

Adam looked back across the clearing, past the flashing blue, and spotted the fourth man, crouched stealthily at the side of the jeep, his high-powered automatic rifle locked on Kevin.

"No silly moves, boys. Outta the car slowly." The man had a deep, keen tone and an unusual, rare accent. He stood well back from the other men who were now training their weapons on the three boys. *"Over by the big spruce. Shoes off. Trousers round your ankles. Hands high above your heads. That's the good boys."*

There was a playful sound in his commands now. His accent was strange. Definitely not like the locals.

Adam looked around as he unbuckled his belt, trying hard to stop his hands shaking and his teeth chattering. The damp, freezing cold couldn't match the sheer terror he was feeling right now. Dark night against the flashing blue, so dark he almost lost his balance, a blackness he'd never seen before, and up above a billion stars. Yet he couldn't understand why there was no light. No sound. Just the three men huddling and discussing, and the fourth with his weapon pointed.

But who were they?

Adam knew he was in the deepest possible trouble.

2

"God gave us a second chance, Jack Buckley!"

Maggie lay on her side in the bed, her hand resting under her cheek, watching him as he dressed in his sergeant's uniform.

"Thank God for AA," she muttered, in the same worshipful way she always did just when he least needed to hear it.

"To hell with AA!" he muttered as he danced on the toes of one foot, trying to find his right trouser-leg with the other. He wanted to say: *And to hell with you too, Maggie!* But he would pay dearly for being so thick-headed. Anyway he never meant it on either account. They'd gone to bed at half ten the night before and were enjoying passionate sex for the first time in three weeks when the phone rang. If he hadn't answered it they could have fallen asleep in each other's arms, exhausted and happy, and he would still be dead to the world right now. Instead he'd spent over two hours sitting in the freezing kitchen, only to find Maggie comatose when he returned hoping to take up where they'd left off. He cursed her for not fighting the tiredness, and his anatomy for being so single-minded and frustrated. He wasn't a morning person, plain and simple. The early hours made the cravings for a cool, icy, lemon-tinged vodka difficult to tolerate. But at least he had his mornings back, he reminded himself, which was a partial compensation.

And he had Maggie. She looked beautiful from where he stood, buckling his trousers. A long strand of blonde hair hung down across her eye, her bare neck and shoulders, soft, down to where the white sheet came up to cover her breasts.

Any time after eleven, he'd jokingly tell the folks of Sheep's Head if they came looking for him about a sick heifer, or burst heating pipes in the old schoolhouse, or storm insurance, or a tree down blocking the entrance to someone's drive. That was the sum total of life on the peninsula.

It got busier during the summer months. Tourists would call to the small police station, or to their house next-door, asking directions from a French-English dictionary. The teenagers would return from boarding-school, sleep till eleven, then congregate in Ahakista, or Durrus, or further out in Kilcrohane. Occasionally, if there was a disco, Jack Buckley would take a spin across to Drishane Bridge, just to make sure the kids weren't drinking too much, and that the young girls weren't going home to their fathers "in an interesting condition", as he'd describe it to Maggie before leaving the house late on a Saturday night.

He'd never say "pregnant". It saddened her, Jack thought, and made her moody. They had never been blessed with children in twenty-two years of knowing each other. He had come to accept it for himself now, but Maggie still pined the odd night when she was alone in the house. "The sound of little voices squabbling would be lovely," she'd often say to Jack.

He maintained, to himself, that her saving grace was that she was a fatalist. She explained to him matter-of-fact, time and time again, the doctrine that all events were subject to fate, and happened by unavoidable necessity. Jack wished so often that he too could have accepted life as a mapped-out linear calendar of pre-arranged kismets. But it didn't make sense. "Sure, yeah," he'd argue with her, "barns blow down, and the post gets delayed. But, *unavoidable necessity*?" he'd haggle. But you couldn't win in an argument against Maggie. That *was* unavoidable.

He looked at the reflection in the mirror for a minute, partially shading the early-morning sunshine, his face slightly side-on. That way, at that angle, he reckoned, he seemed much younger, more his real age. No one believed that Jack Buckley was only forty-three. "You're fifty-five and not a day younger!" Leo Hannon jeered one night below in the pub. Jack laughed off the snub in company but took it home later and slept on it, tossing and turning, damning and cursing, eventually deciding that he wasn't going to drink ever again. Two bottles of neat vodka every day for three years had made him look ten years older than he was. And he *was* only forty-three. He calculated that night that another six years at this rate, equating to four-thousand-three-hundred-and-eighty bottles of vodka, and he'd pass for an eighty-year-old. *If* he lasted another six years. And there wasn't a turf accountant in the country who'd take odds on that.

Three years before, Jack Buckley was one of the county's most distinguished detectives, lean and fit, eager for promotion, hell-bent on getting to the top. Until that fateful day, as Maggie called it, in Macroom. The call for assistance mentioned a car acting suspiciously outside the old, red-bricked bank in Castle Street. Jack answered and told control they were no more than two minutes away. His partner, Tony Young, swung the Carina around, handbraking slightly to save time on the narrow road. They arrived outside the main entrance just as one of the robbers opened fire with a sawn-off shotgun from the top step, at what he thought was another pair of armed detectives sitting in a car immediately beside where Tony had stopped. Tony Young died instantly in the hail of bullets. Eight people were injured. Jack Buckley took three hits, two superficial, the third to his right leg. His days as an armed detective ended at 11.07am that morning as he cradled his dead partner and screamed for an ambulance.

The police commission decorated him with the Scot Medal and offered him a choice. He could retire on full pension or go back into uniform and take up a position in the peaceful surroundings of West Cork. He chose the latter, knowing that retirement meant listening to Maggie all day long, and her ramblings, and her news, and her bawling him out for not getting off his backside and doing something useful with his life.

She had her own life. No children occupied her time.

She applied for a job with the local health board as a district nurse and was accepted within a week of consideration. They were mostly elderly – her patients – living in remote, hilly areas on the two peninsulas, some without phones, one or two without electricity. Eighteen in all – there were originally twenty-three but the bad flu two years before had claimed five of them. Generally her work, although fully qualified to RSN standards, was spent getting in their weekly shopping and doing the odd spot of housework.

Faced with the lonesome prospect of nothing to do all day long, if he retired – after all, there was only so much fishing a man could do during an afternoon; and dogs, no matter how frisky they are, don't necessarily need to be walked twelve hours a day – Jack Buckley became the new sergeant of Sheep's Head, with responsibilty for the twin-peninsula jurisdiction on either side of Dunmanus Bay, soon to be followed – out of sheer boredom, thanks to zero-crime – by the need to drink whenever he got the chance. A chance he'd relinquished three years ago.

"What time did you come to bed?" Maggie called from the bed.

"Nearly one," Jack replied, stretching his jaw while he shaved, careful not to nick his chin.

"Why do you have to get up so early?"

Jack glanced at his watch, recalling the previous night's marathon phone conversation. It was quarter to seven. "Superintendent says the Commissioner's pissed off with all the publicity these missin' teenagers are getting. He says it makes the force look bad. Like we're not doing anything to find them." He tapped the shaver against the enamel and dunked it in the warm water. "Seemingly one of the kids' fathers is a big-shot businessman with loads of money. Took out separate ads in each of the national papers asking people to help find them, half a page each."

He towelled off slowly, running the tips of his fingers across his face, pretending to himself that his skin was smoother now.

"What could have happened to them?"

"The superintendent thinks they may have just travelled on to somewhere else further up along the coast and not bothered to call home. Maybe they ran out of money and couldn't afford to get home when they planned. Maybe they met three young wans! That's what I think happened."

Maggie was standing in the bathroom doorway now, wearing one of his old work-shirts. She reached out and stroked his back. "Is it?"

He liked her hand there. It was warm. He studied her in the mirror. "Is it *what*?"

"What you think?"

He shrugged. "Don't know yet." He turned to her. She'd known him long enough to recognise when he was holding back from her. "Super says the rich kid's father's plannin' on comin' down here to do a bit of investigatin' himself."

"There's nothing wrong with that, Jack. If my child went missing I'd never stop looking for him."

It was always a boy she'd wanted. "Yeah, well, I just want to make sure I have all my facts right before he arrives next week. Maybe even see if we can arrange to throw up a five-star hotel for him before he gets here. The Sheep's Head *Hilton*? Nothing less than he's used to, I suppose, eh?" He smiled at her.

Maggie laughed back at the notion and kissed him on the neck. She could tell his nose had been put out of joint. He was clearly miffed at the notion of a stranger walking on to *his* patch, trying to do *his* job. "Be nice to him, Jack. He could be OK. Remember, *he'll* be relying on you."

Definitely an unavoidable necessity, Jack thought. She kissed him again. He could tell by the way she looked at him that she would have preferred to take him back to their bed and make love, and then lay out, sprawled across him, her cheek beside his neck, till eleven. He would have preferred it too. Knowing his luck the phone would ring again.

"Will I make you up an egg sandwich?"

"No thanks. I'll get coffee in town. I gotta drop in on Leo Hannon. His car was stolen on Saturday night. Stupid dimwit only reports it yesterday."

"Did he get it back?"

Jack nodded. "Found it outside town. One wheel missing . . . a lot of panel damage . . . pretty messed up, he was tellin' me. Probably some of the kids coming back from the Drishane disco. How that place is still open I do not know." He returned the kiss, but her mind seemed elsewhere. "What's wrong?"

"I was remembering those three kids I passed on Saturday evening hitching a lift."

"Where was that again?"

"Out near Holy Well. Looked like they were hitchin' a lift into town."

"Ollie Jennings lets groups of kids camp in one of his fields out there, doesn't he? I'll take a look." He attempted one last kiss, trying to make it long and passionate.

Maggie pulled away. "That's all for now, Sergeant. I gotta get my beauty sleep. Then I gotta go visit my Golden Oldies. So on your way."

"See you later." He walked slowly towards the patrol car, studying the clear blue horizon, etched darker into the landscape where the sea meets the sky, and breathed deeply the ice-cold, exhilarating Atlantic air.

As he turned the key in the ignition at exactly 7.00am that Friday morning, it never occurred to Jack Buckley that he was about to trigger a series of events which, had he foreseen the consequences for himself and for a number of people, whose lives would be changed irrevocably, might just have given him the perfect excuse for staying in bed.

3

Jack Buckley cursed his little Astra. No comfort, no power, no maintenance. He'd requisitioned a new model, preferably an off-road 4x4 for the mountainous terrain. The officer in the traffic division balked and then laughed timidly, as if Jack had just asked for the head of the commissioner on a plate. He was told his order for a new car was programmed and he'd have it within a month. That was two years back, he reminded himself.

He enjoyed the early morning drive. Often he'd just drive to the north side of the peninsula for the sake of it. Time to think about nothing in particular.

He stared out to his right, across the choppy bay towards the two big mountains, Knockaughna and Coomfarna, permanently soaked in soft grey cloud, and back across his shoulder towards Carberry Island, barely visible in the misty swell. Two small trawlers raced against time and each other to get their catches in to Durrus for the vans that would take them to the shops in Bantry and Glengarriff and Skibbereen and a dozen other little towns dotted across the giant peninsulas.

He'd accepted long ago that the world had forgotten about the people on Sheep's Head. Life in the great big fast-moving world next door just seemed to pass them by, along with all its horrible crimes and wonderful technological advancements and famous people. He didn't care much for all that. In fact he didn't care at all.

The journey to Alex Kline's house, barely a mile outside Durrus on the R591 Bantry Road took twenty-five minutes. He would have driven it in fifteen if he hadn't got slowed up along the narrow road close to Doneen Pier behind Oliver Jenning's creamery tanker. He'd bought it from his lotto win the previous March. Jack tooted his siren briefly to alert Ollie. He waved to him as the elderly farmer studied his huge wing mirror, signalling to him to pull over. He pulled in behind the lorry and left the engine running. It was a fresh morning with a bracing south-westerly breeze blowing in across Bantry Bay. "Morning, Ollie."

"How's it goin', Jack? What's ailin' you?" Ollie turned off the engine, and lowered the volume of the traditional hornpipe music on the radio.

"Searchin' for three young lads. Had you anyone staying up at your place last weekend, Ollie?"

Jennings turned bright red, despite the biting cold gusts. He knew the sergeant didn't condone his makeshift accomodation and the money he reaped.

"You been chargin' kids to stay in that oul' shitty field of yours again, Ollie?"

"No one stayed last weekend. But I did talk to three kids. Lads about seventeen. They called about four. Asked if they could stay. I told them I'd need a deposit before I'd take their bags to mind, like." He saw the frown on Jack Buckley's face. "Well, it's only proper, like. I'm not gonna take responsibilty for anyone's bags for nothin'. Would you?"

Jack Buckley wasn't interested in deposits, or Ollie Jenning's corrupt little pickled brain. "Where are they?"

"They never came back."

"What about their baggage?"

He nodded back in the direction of League Point. "In the barn. They've been there best part of the week now. What'll I do with them?"

Jack was already walking back to his car. "Don't touch them. I'll get Maggie to drop by for them later this morning. And get that truck taxed. Next time I'll do ye!"

A stroke of luck, if ever, he thought. Everyone knows they're missing. But not just simply unaccounted for. It seemed much worse than that. The different strands of information he had nagged him like toothache. It didn't add up. A five-year-old goes missing on a crowded beach: he could understand. A three-year-old wanders off among the aisles of a supermarket. That's fine. But three seventeen-year-olds: dropping off their luggage and disappearing into abeyance. Last seen hitching a lift.

The grandeur of the bank manager's house always left him feeling dejected. It was monumental in every way, like a Babylonian temple jutting out from the side of the small mountain. He always subliminally counted the fourteen fake oil-lamps adorning the long, twisting red-tarmacked driveway every time he called out to see Alex; and the three artificial ponds, one with a statue of a fit-looking, naked man, staring at the sky, pissing from a superbly endowed stone penis. Jack often wondered to himself whether it was the house or the penis which made him more curious. Fifty metres from the house the driveway divided. One road swept down to a lower-tier section which included a double garage, parking bay, and a set of offices. A plush brass plate bore the words: A & E KLINE ESTATE AGENTS.

This morning's visit, purely sociable, took the other driveway straight to the front door. At least Jack wanted to give that impression, as if he'd just been passing by and called in to say hello to Alex and Ethel. He hated Alex with a vengeance. He was uncouth, as Maggie would call him. But Ethel's home-cooking – especially her tea-bracks and rhubarb tarts – partly made up for her husband's ignorant moods. He parked the shabby little banger away from the huge glassed porch, trying not to pay much attention to the opulent Mercedes 300SEL to his left. A red-faced man with thinning, gelled black hair, who might have passed for tall if he hadn't been so overweight, in a snow-white bathing robe – and not much else it seemed – was already opening the door. "You're early," Alex Kline shouted, glancing at his watch. "Something wrong?"

"Nope. I had to drive into Bantry and I thought I'd stop off on my way back. Not too early, I hope?" Jack noticed how agitated Kline seemed to be.

"Early? For *me*? Never too early, Jack. Not in my game. You're just in time for breakfast. Come on in."

Jack remembered what Alex had once told him: when you can fake sincerity you know you've made it. It was clear to Jack Buckley that he was playing his own game this morning. "Coffee will do me fine, Alex." He wiped his feet. A cluster of pairs of shoes were dotted around the end of the staircase. "Kids asleep?"

"Yeah. Holidays."

"And Ethel."

"Yep. Come on into the kitchen."

No tea-brack or rhubarb tart today.

The conversation remained inconsequential for nearly ten minutes, Jack estimated, mainly about the disappointing weather, Jack's shameful little patrol car and Alex's forthcoming holiday in Australia. Then Jack's low boredom threshold got the better of him and he seized the moment.

"Alex, do you mind me asking you where you were last Saturday night?"

"Why?"

"Just wondering. Leo Hannon's car was stolen on Saturday night while he was serving behind the bar. He's not sure if whoever stole it had been drinkin' in his place. But whoever did steal it drove it into a tree on the Bantry Road, he says, not too far from here in fact." He watched Alex's reaction. None.

"You didn't hear anything round about half eleven on Saturday night, did you?"

"Like what?"

"The sound of a car hitting a tree on the road down there. It would have made a pretty loud bang, wouldn't it?"

Alex sniffed, appeared to be in deep thought for a moment. Then his eyes opened wide. "You know it's funny you say that, Jack. I heard a real loud, real long screeching noise, then what I thought was a load of milk churns falling off a lorry at about quarter to twelve on Saturday night. Like a real loud *clank*. And glass breaking. Then silence."

"Did you go out and check what it was?"

"I didn't bother. It seemed a long way off."

"Right." Jack made a few notes in the small pad and pocketed it. He finished his coffee and placed the mug in the dishwasher. "That'll do me fine, Alex. How's work treating ye?" He walked towards the door.

"Which one?" Alex giggled.

"Oh yeah, that's right. I keep forgettin' you've got two businesses, Alex. You're the Sheep's Head bank manager *and* the estate agent. Sure you must have every penny worth spending in the whole area locked up in either a bank account that you run *or* a house that you've sold."

It was clear Alex Kline didn't appreciate the sarcastic undertones of Jack Buckley's comments. He said nothing.

"I've never heard of that before, Alex." Jack stepped out into the porch.

"What?"

"A bank manager *and* an estate agent. Kinda clever, I woulda thought."

"Why?"

"Well, the way I see it, you gotta borrow money to buy a house. So, you're the estate agent who decides on the value of the land or property and then takes a commission on whatever you're instructed to sell and then organises with a local financial institution to provide the buyer with a twenty-year loan. Right?"

Alex nodded brusquely.

"Then you take off your estate agent's cap and put on

the hat of the bank manager and run in behind your lovely polished desk and interview the buyer as to their credit worthiness; 'cos you are the financial institution, Alex. And then you go off and think about whether or not to hand over the X number of thousands the buyer is hoping you'll loan to him. That right?" Jack was thoroughly enjoying his frolic.

Alex fumed and nodded again.

"Well . . . isn't that kinda cheating, Alex?"

"*Cheating?* How *dare* you? What are you accusing me of?"

Jack waved his hands. "Hey, hey, hey, Alex. How long have you and I known each other? Five years?"

Alex Kline continued to stare indignantly at the sergeant.

"I'm not accusing you of anything, Alex. All I'm sayin' is that you're kind of a God Almighty around these parts." Jack stopped smiling. "You decide who buys the land, who gets planning permission, who gets loans. And – the bottom line – who gets to live happily ever after. Basically you *are* God." Jack laughed and slapped Alex's arm. "I'm just thinkin' it's a good job I am your friend."

Alex forced a smile, then a ribald snigger.

"On a more serious note, Alex . . ."

"What now?"

Jack pulled the newspaper article from his tunic pocket. "Three boys . . . believed to be missing in the area. You didn't see three teenagers hitchin' a lift into Durrus on Saturday evening, did you?"

Alex Kline glanced frostily at the photographs. "No!"

"What am I thinkin! Sure you stayed in on Saturday.

Sorry about that. Maybe you could keep your eyes open if you're driving round sellin' anymore of that expensive land of yours." Jack swung around and picked up the size 11 leather shoe from the end of the stairs. It was caked in muck. "You really oughta get a good pair of boots or waders if you're gonna be showing prospective buyers around mucky fields, Alex. Even a cheap pair of galoshes." He dropped the shoe and doffed his cap. "Give my regards to Ethel. See ya."

Jack Buckley felt the burly, balding foreigner's eyes burning into the nape of his sweat-sodden neck as he fumbled for his car keys. He badly wanted to run his hankie across his neck but that would show Kline that he was feeling the pressure. Again silently, he cursed the little car that would take him into Leo Hannon's pub for a chat and another cup of coffee, recalling, from driving around the jurisdiction at least a dozen times in the past forty-eight hours, that Alex Kline had land for sale all right. Green fields, some of them full of sheep and the odd lonesome bull, where he'd extracted a few extra pounds from desperate farmers; but no houses for prospective buyers to view. Then again there were no buyers, not since the three mansions, as Maggie had always called them. And the mud on the shoe wasn't real muck: more a rough, gravelly mixture of greyish, caked cement, exactly what you'd find on a construction site. But not around Durrus. Apart from the new road twenty-eight miles to the east, getting closer by the week and slowly linking them with the city, there was no building taking place now. Hadn't been for donkey's years. Not since the price of land on Sheep's Head had rocketed.

4

Durrus folk knew Jack Buckley to be a fair man with an awesome temper.

"I'm not lookin' for trouble," he'd tell the occasional rabble-rouser, "but if I find trouble, I'll as sure as shit find who's causin' it." He rarely used bad language in public, preferring to save it all for his patrol car, or for when things got completely beyond his means of control, which, on Sheep's Head, was as likely as The Jessie James Gang riding into town on horseback.

A couple of women out wheeling their children waved. Three teenagers sitting on the church wall made him slam on the footbrake, another fault that needed fixing. He pulled out the dog-eared newpaper page and compared the photo. It wasn't them. He indicated and turned into the carpark behind Leo Hannon's pub. It was twenty to ten. Time for a Coke.

Martha Hannon had her back to him, soaping the counter, moving bottles and replacing them as she moved from left to right. "Hi Martha. Is Leo . . . " He stopped midstream, his mouth still open, as Martha turned to face him. She had a long gash above her right cheek. Another half-inch and she would have lost the eye. "What happened you?"

Leo Hannon stepped through the half-door from the living quarters to the bar. "Hello Jack." He tried hard to be his usual cheerful self. It didn't rub off. Martha disappeared quickly into the kitchen.

"What happened to her?" Jack asked again.

Leo Hannon seemed to ignore his question, almost not hearing it, eager to ask his own. "Listen Jack, I owe you an apology."

"Why?"

"Remember I reported the car stolen to you yesterday evening? Well, it wasn't stolen. Martha was comin' back from her bridge club in Bantry. She must have driven into a deep flood patch. Anyway she lost control and hit a tree. She reckoned I'd be furious. So she got Ollie Jennings to tow the car back here the next day with his truck and say it was stolen. She only told me late last night when I told her I'd reported it at the station."

Leo seemed relieved to have got the story across in the one breath. Almost the one sentence. "Is that what happened her face?" Jack nodded towards the kitchen. He knew she was listening.

Leo nodded. "It didn't need stitches, thank God."

"Says who, Leo? I would've thought it did!" Jack waited. "Now are you goin' to tell me what really happened?"

"I *swear,* Jack. She hit a tree. That's all. No one got hurt. Straightforward claim on the insurance. It'll be fixed up in a week."

"Where's the car?"

The small corrugated iron barn behind the pub stank of the dregs of beer bottles piled high in crates and of stale chicken shit. It was an antique dealer's delight: an old sideboard, bedroom dresser, an ancient cider-press, a woodworm-devoured teak headboard, old books in tea chests, kitchen utensils from another century, by the look of them. A stack of old, musty sofa cushions piled in the corner looked as if they had been slept on. And in the middle, the terrifying remains of what was once a black Vectra that looked as if it had fallen off the edge of the world. Jack gasped for air. "I didn't know your Martha was a test-pilot, Leo. Did she try to get this thing airborne or *what*?" He opened the driver's door. "Does she always burn out the clutch when she takes the car into Bantry?" Then the rear door. "Who had she with her?"

Leo shrugged. "She was on her own."

"Well then, Leo, she must have been driving the car from three different seats if she was on her *own*!"

"What?"

Jack beckoned Leo to the rear door, wriggling his index finger. Then he pointed. "Very simple. I'd hazard a guess and say there were two other people in the car with your Martha last Saturday night." Streaks of muck and pebbles covered the carpet below the two front seats. The same style of smutch was all over the back of the driver's seat. "It's as if whoever was sitting in the back had their shoes planted against the back of this seat, for support, I'd say, more than fun." Then he felt the upholstery. It was ripped. "So hard they tore it." He stood up and faced Leo suspiciously. "I doubt Martha would take too kindly to her friends rippin' up the seats of your nice car while she's droppin' them home."

The glow on Leo Hannon's forehead had turned to sweat. He swallowed hard and fumbled in his pockets, careful to avoid the sergeant's prying eyes.

Jack Buckley stepped out into the bright sunshine. "I hate to say this, Leo, but I think Martha's not telling you what really happened last Saturday night. Either that, or you're lyin' blind to me."

Almost quarter past eight. It had taken Jack Buckley a full head-wrecking hour to find the pocket-sized nature encyclopaedia on trees and foliage that Maggie had bought locally in Kenny's superstore in Durrus shortly after they'd both moved to the area three years ago. It was her way of switching off Jack's "bad patch" as she referred to it. While he drank himself to oblivion, ranting about how no one "gives a shit anymore", Maggie would take herself, equipped with her lexicon of greenery and leafage, up past Gerahies to Ball Alley forest and disappear into the undergrowth until such time as she could find the strength to go back to her sick partner. Now he waited for her to return from League Point with the haversacks.

The eagle caught his eye, high above Gouladane mountain, hovering with its wings spread full-span, gently rocking backward and forward, guileful and composed, as if waiting for its prey to make the first move. Somewhere, hundreds of feet below, its unsuspecting target – foraging for its own supper, thinking that *its* prey would be a pushover – was only seconds away from dying beneath the crushing claws of this huge beautiful, majestic creature. Jack wondered what the bird was thinking, mulling over its next move, like clockwork by now, but never showing its victim what its next tactic might be.

It took three hellos from Maggie before he realised she was standing behind him. "Sorry," he said, turning around to hug her. "Just watching something."

The three small rucksacks lay on the kitchen floor, reeking of Ollie Jenning's barn. Jack did a sprightly check on each one. Nothing but socks, jeans, underpants, a tiny block of marijuana, pullovers and a pack of condoms. "Poor bastards never even got to open the box," Jack muttered.

Maggie stood over him and watched him rummaging. "You're talking like they're dead."

He stopped and looked up into her face. "I never said that." He dropped the last bag on top of the others. "Come over here. I need you to look at something. They walked back out to the veranda. Maggie sat at the table, careful not to disturb the small arangement of twigs and shoots and leaves. "Is this a new hobby?"

Jack ignored the question. He pushed her book towards her. "What's this one?" he held up the longest stem.

Maggie placed the small, stiff branch carefully onto the brightest part of the table, where the light from the setting sun illuminated its needle-like stem. She thumbed through the index, turning to page two-hundred-and-ten. "I was right. It's a *picea*."

"A what?"

"A spruce pine. Any conifer of the spruce is called a *picea*. Long shoots only, see?" She demonstrated with the tips of her fingers along the stem. "Four-angled needles, and over-hanging cones. See?"

"Yeah yeah yeah . . . Go on!" Jack was like an excited child unwrapping a present.

"It's from a spruce pine." She waited for his next question.

"Does it grow everywhere?"

"No. Normally forestry plantation, where the vegetation and undergrowth would be permanently damp, and not much light getting in. That's why they grow so tall, upwards toward the light. See?"

"Forests?" He couldn't contain the enthusiasm any longer. "You did say forests, didn't you?"

"Without a doubt."

"Yeesss!" He clenched his fist, squeezing it so hard the knuckles turned a painful white, his face almost purple with the confirmation.

"Why do you need to know?" she asked softly, hoping he'd tell her. He relaxed again and watched her. She knew the detective mind was thinking again, thank God. He said nothing, just nodded in appreciation.

It was half nine when the doorbell rang.

"Damn!" Jack mumbled, munching on the beef in black bean sauce and plain chow mein that was their Friday night pig-out. It was a tradition. Jack would pick up the ingredients in Kenny's on his way home, and Maggie would cook. He finished his orange squash.

"I'll get it." Maggie was up and into the hall before he could swallow and say thanks. "Anytime after eleven?" she shouted back to Jack.

"It could be important. I'm expecting the father of one of those kids to . . . " His words stopped and fell into a hole. Leo Hannon stood, clutching his cap nervously and apologising for disturbing the sergeant's dinner.

"Sit down, Leo." Jack gestured to Maggie's chair. She told them she had to make a phonecall. "Glass of rock shandy?" he asked sarcastically. He smiled, knowing that Leo would understand the joke. He didn't seem to care. In fact he looked as if he'd just been given a prolonged electric shock. He was pale, gaunt and exhausted-looking, as if he'd just jogged five miles. Jack didn't want to rush him. Extracting information like a dentist pulls a wisdom tooth never worked. Slow coaxing was the only way. "How's Martha?"

Leo nodded remorsefully. "She's OK."

"Why did you hit her?"

He said nothing.

"She didn't crash the car at all, did she?"

"No," he whispered.

"Who did?"

"She told me I should call you. She was rantin' and squawkin', runnin' round like a headless chicken, callin' me all the names under God's heaven. I was tetchy and didn't know what to be thinkin' an' before I knew it, she was cryin' an' lyin' on the floor callin' me an evil bastard, holdin' her bloody face!" His breath shivered as he gasped hard and held it, a small dribble in the corner of his mouth, staring down at his cap now, balancing it and spinning it, making it dance on his finger. "I gave the three young lads a lift into Durrus. Invited them in for a drink. They were nice young kids. Didn't mean any trouble."

Maggie stuck her head around the door. She grimmaced, knowing Jack wouldn't want to be disturbed. "Sorry, Jack. Alfie Carruth's on the phone. He says it's really urgent."

Jack clenched his teeth. Not another bloody two-hour-long conversation with the superintendent, he thought. "Wait here, Leo. I'll be five minutes." Maggie handed him the phone. Her eyes said it all. The superintendent was not a contented man. "Evening, Alfie." Jack waited to gauge the senior man's mind.

"Jack, what the hell do you think you're doing?" the voice ripped down the line.

"Sir?" Ignorance and respect, the best form of defence.

"You paid a dawn visit to Alex Kline this morning?"

Jack could hear that Carruth was reading from notes. "That's right."

"Why?"

"Part of my investigation into the missing kids."

"He says you were asking him about cars crashing at the entrance to his driveway . . ."

"Maybe."

"*And* that you accused him, in his *own* kitchen, of a series of business and banking malpractices when it came to dealing with his clients."

"Like *what*?"

"That you accused him of conning his customers; of withholding important information from prospective buyers; of cooking the books and fiddling people's bank accounts? Sweet Jesus, Jack, what the fuck are you playing at down there?"

"I never said any such thing, Alfie!" Jack knew he had to keep his anger under wraps. There was no point the two of them bawling each other out.

"Misappropriation is a crime, Jack. It you're found guilty it'll get you a ten-year stretch. And to accuse someone of doing it you'd want to have plenty of rock-solid evidence and a damn good legal team to back you up. Especially when it's a JP you're accusing."

There was a blood-curdling silence which felt like it would last forever.

Jack felt sick, his beef and black bean talking to him. He fought for breath and strength. "Justice of the Peace," he said slowly. *"Who?"*

Alfie Carruth was somewhat more relaxed now. "Alex Kline. He was appointed this morning, it seems."

"Why?"

"It doesn't matter, Jack. The bottom line is that you're now no longer a part of this investigation."

"What?"

"I got a call an hour ago, Jack. Seemingly, Kline's been making a lot of noise about your visit this morning, to some of his government pals in Dublin. Have you any idea who Alex Kline is?"

"No. But I'm sure you're gonna tell me, Alfie."

"Formerly attached to the German embassy in Dublin, personal secretary to their ambassador, until ten years ago, when the big man resigned out of the blue. Wouldn't give any substantive justification for his sudden return to the Fatherland. Just said it was for family reasons. Within forty-eight hours he was gone. Kline stayed on but resigned as a member of the diplomatic corps. But – and this is the interesting bit – retained his diplomatic immunity."

"So?"

"It means that while he's no longer regarded as a foreign diplomat living abroad, he still retains his immunity from Irish laws and taxation. So whatever you've got a snot about, there's no point winding him up. You'll get nowhere. Just grief."

"And now he's Justice of the Peace? He's not even Irish!"

"Well, according to the man who called the commissioner at her holiday home in Ballina and bawled her out of it, he owns an Irish passport. Probably why he gave up his title."

"The commissioner rang you?"

"Yeah."

"Who rang her?"

"Alan Harrission. He's the private secretary to the Taoiseach. Alex Kline has sold some really expensive properties to a number of German businessman in the last ten years. They're all tied into this huge car tyre production plant up at Shannon Development. Girundbach GVI. Have you heard of it?"

"Yeah. It's meant to be one of the biggest factories in the country."

"That's right. Kline's saying that your accusations

could damage his reputation as an estate agent to wealthy buyers who might be considering retiring to Ireland and bringing their millions with them. Do you know how much money these people invest in this country?"

"I don't need a lecture in economics."

"Yeah, well the bottom line is that they don't need a moral lecture from some small backwoodsman; some keystone cop who might 'tarnish their ascribed characters'. His words, not mine. Listen to me, Jack, for your own sake. Leave Kline alone. If people like the Taoiseach and the Garda Commissioner have to make a choice between you and Kline, I don't see your horse crossing the line first. Take a holiday, Jack. Why don't you and Maggie head off somewhere for a couple of weeks. This'll all have blown over when you get back. Those kids'll have got pissed off runnin' away from home. Then you just settle back into your routine."

"My *routine*? Don't patronise me, Alfie. I've always been honest with you. So I want you to be honest now. What am I hitting on that all these assholes are so afraid of?"

"I don't know, Jack. And part of me is glad that I don't know. Did you ever hear of Pandora?"

"Who?"

"Pandora's box. Pandora was a big name in Greek mythology. She was given a box which she disobediently opened, and released all the ills of human life. You're sitting on a Pandora's box, Jack. Any source of great and unexpected troubles. And, let's be honest, life's tough enough without looking for more aggro. Don't you agree?"

Jack smiled. "Yeah, Alfie, you're right."

"Good boy. Pack a few things and surprise that gorgeous woman of yours. Take her camping for a few days. Forget about it all and I'll give you a call in a couple of weeks when the dust has settled. I'll organise a replacement and cover your ass from this end. OK?"

Jack sighed. "OK."

The line went dead.

Jack put the phone down. To his right, through the corner of his eye, he could see Maggie watching him, her attention divided between the television and his conversation. He ignored her and went back to the kitchen and his unexpected guest. The patio door leading out onto the veranda was open. The kitchen was uninvitingly cold.

And there was no sign of Leo Hannon.

5

Hannon's pub was unusually full for a Friday night. Saturday was traditionally the heavy-drinking night, given the respite of a long, idle Sunday morning for the men to sleep off their excesses and for the women to take the children to the eleven o'clock mass in the small church overlooking Four Mile Water and the Gaelic football grounds directly below the steep hill.

Jack Buckley had a good mind to stop his car, switch on the flashers and give every single one of them, the full length of the main street, a parking ticket. But it was just the frame of mind he was in: seething – and boiling dry by the minute. He drove his patrol Astra much slower than usual, careful not to scrape the sides of the cars parked on either side, allowing barely enough width for one-way traffic. There must have been hundreds of them. What was the occasion? he wondered. Quarter past ten. It resembled a New Year's Eve, he thought, or the first night of the annual Harvest Homecoming Festival each August, when they'd elect a Queen of the Watch, based on a tradition years ago, some hag told him, where the women would wait for their men and sons to return from weeks of hay-making, utilising every minute of good weather they were blessed with. It was one tradition that was always good for tourism, attracting the foreigners in thousands, and luring the occasional expatriate out of places like Boston and San Francisco for a few days back on the oul sod. It was Leo and Martha Hannon's big weekend each year. But tonight looked to be turning into an unexpected windfall for the two publicans, for some reason. He'd made up his mind on the journey to town what he was going to do. It was important to remain calm and dignified throughout. First, though, he had to see Leo Hannon.

He'd left his cap behind him on the back seat and wore a waist-length brown leather jacket over his official shirt, semi-casual so as not to unnerve or create suspicion. He squeezed in through the side door, the waft of body heat, a brace of perfumes and aftershaves, and alcohol, clashing with the jet of cold, dark May night air, and Martha Hannon's voice shouting *Next please*. He had his smiling, caring face on now, the look that told Durrus folk that he was only half-patrolling: the other half mingling and having a good time. He was good at lying, though. Truth was quite different. All the way into town he couldn't get Alex Kline's face out of his mind. His big fat, bloated shape, and how he ate like a pig at a trough, slobbering and dribbling until Ethel would lean across and dab his chin for him with a napkin; and how he would belch and fart liberally all night afterwards, smoking his filthy cigars and sipping his expensive Cognac; and slipping away from the dinner party and returning in his dressing-gown. Maggie asked to leave early on one occasion. She told Jack on the way home that Kline had been flashing his testicles and penis at her since he sat in the armchair near the window. Ever since that night, Jack Buckley hated the sight of Alex Kline, the man who had sold them their house, but failed to mention the reason they "got it for a song", as he put it: it had been built, thirty years before, on marshy land. There was no evidence of subsidence, but – as one surveyor told him – "Jack, it might stand for another thousand years; on the other hand it could fall into a hole in the ground tonight". He'd never told Maggie about the marshy land. The same way as he hadn't told her his reason for coming into town tonight.

Then he saw him, holding court like he always did in the far corner, and it clicked. They were all here tonight to congratulate their new Justice of the Peace – the estate agent they had all bought houses from, and the bank manager who tended to their accounts and paid their bills each month for them by direct debit, and organised the college fees each September for their sons and daughters, and who dined on the interest and the various bank charges he offset against their worth on the first day of each month – who was throwing the bar open to them tonight to win over their affections and their trust. Then they wouldn't bother checking their bank accounts with a fine toothcomb and discover the hidden charges which didn't add up, and the small deductions that didn't make sense but must have been due because Alex Kline's bank said so.

Jack Buckley stood in the shadow thrown by the giant

television screen perched overhead. He studied Alex Kline and wondered who he was. Why did a man of such worth and such wealth want to live in such a quiet, secluded part of the world? Surely he would have been better suited to one of the cities, where he could have talked in *millions* about commerce and national debts with other business tycoons. Why Sheep's Head? He looked like a lion at a cub scout meeting tonight, resplendent in his yellow linen shirt and orange cravat, neatly shaved, his small toss of hair gelled back with a generous lick of hair oil.

Martha Hannon had stopped calling *Next please*, and was watching Jack Buckley, as if she was anticipating his next move. He nodded and smiled, and shuffled towards the bar. "Can I speak to Leo for a second?"

She shook her head contemptuously. "He went out two hours ago and never came back." She carried on serving, as though her duty to the law was complete.

Jack scratched his head, trying to put a time frame on the last twelve hours. It would be important. Then without a further thought he moved quickly through the blocky crowd, away from the bar. He approached Kline from behind and tapped him on the shoulder.

Alex swung around with every intention of accepting more congratulations. Instead he froze, almost spilling the vintage Midleton whiskey.

Jack stared into his eyes until he could no longer hold his gaze without blinking. Then he smiled and held out his hand. "Congratulations are in order, I believe."

Kline relaxed with sheer relief. "Thank you," he replied warily.

"It must have come as a pleasant surprise?"

"It most certainly did, Jack. Are you going to join us?"

"Can't." He patted Alex's arm and looked him up and down. "You're lookin' terrific tonight, pal." He checked his footwear. Soft sandal-like flip-flops. Not the usual leather shoes. Still full of muck, he thought. "At least now I know where I can get any parking tickets quashed."

Kline laughed uncomfortably. "What's that supposed to mean?"

Jack extended his hand again.

Kline started to shake it until he felt its contents, a small square leather wallet. He pulled back taking the holder with him. "What's this?" he asked indignantly, studying the photograph, with its details and official logo and stamp.

"It's my badge. *I quit!*"

Kline tossed it onto the table as if he had just touched something highly infectious and dangerous. "What do you mean you *quit*?"

A curious, nosey silence was descending in waves across the pub now. "Exactly what it sounds like, *Justice* Kline." He stepped closer and dropped his voice. "Come on, Alex, don't take me for a complete fuckwit. You rang your friends today shortly after I left your house. You were worried that I had something on you. Something that might just upset your cosy little lifestyle here among all these hapless gobshites who think you are God. Or so *you* think. You think just because you buy them a few rounds of drink that they'll love you? Forget it, Alex. They'll just hate you all the more. And they'll go home tonight pissed drunk and talk about you like they talk about their next-door neighbours. I'm through with all this shite. I don't need it anymore. Maybe I'll just go camping with Maggie. Or maybe write that bestseller that I've always been tellin' myself is waiting to be written. Ye know, Alex, I reckon I've met enough corrupt people through the years to write ten novels. Maybe you could even help me with research. I'd say you'd be quite good at that. I suggest you give Alfie Carruth a call tomorrow morning and tell him that Sheep's Head needs a new sergeant because this one's just about had enough. Good luck in your new position, *Justice*!"

He walked back to the bar and placed a twenty on the counter. "A bottle of vodka please, Martha." It was a triumphant moment, he felt, as if he had just taken charge again, having stood in the wings waiting for years. Martha Hannon showed no surprise. She wrapped the bottle in a brown-paper bag. "Do you want some slices of lemon to go with that?" Her question was tinged with a slight surliness. Almost a heartlessness about her voice and her husband missing now for nearly three hours. Maybe Jack would catch up with him and they would drink this together. First he had an important matter of business to conclude, which required a clear head.

Call it luck. Alex Kline hadn't bothered to switch on the huge spotlights at the front of their house before he went in to his celebration party in Hannon's that evening. Usually they lit up the R591 for a good half-mile out of town. Tonight though the road was pitch-black, save for the occasional car returning from Bantry and the pear-shaped moon, too low in the sky and smothered behind rain-filled clouds to give any real shine.

Jack parked the car the far side of the bridge over Four Mile Water, close to bursting its banks tonight, the rain had been so heavy in recent days. The night was heavy with the scent of heather and dandelions, the grassy verges bordering the main road mulchy and unsteady. By the time he'd climbed the steep driveway and taken the avenue to the house he was sweating heavily. There'd been no need for the leather jacket, he told himself, but still he wore it to dampen the officialism of his prowl if anyone should ask him what he was about at such a late hour. It was ten to eleven. The curtains in the sitting-room were fully closed. The rest of the house was in total darkness. He was faced with a choice. He could knock and say he'd noticed the security lights switched off. Or he could just take a chance and open the front door. He turned the handle and listened for voices. It was likely, being a Friday night, the children would still be up. Then he remembered they were on holidays from school and could sleep late in the mornings. Now he was sure they were all in the sitting-room. He listened carefully. Voices. He couldn't be certain how many. But at least three. And a softer, more authoritative voice above the others. Cindy Reilly, the Kline's sixteen-year-old baby-sitter, warning them that if they continued arguing she'd call their mother and put them to bed.

He knew if he knocked he'd never get past the front door. On the other hand if he let himself in and got caught he was in serious trouble. Take a chance, he thought. He could always say he found the door open and, after all, he was in uniform. The whole exercise should take no longer than twenty seconds, he guessed.

The handle squeaked. The door was solid, well-hinged and opened painlessly. He waited a second until his eyes adjusted to the darkness of the hall and he found his bearings. It wasn't happening quickly enough, he thought. He got down on his hunkers and started to feel his way to the end of the stairs. All the shoes were still there. Small ones, high-heels, trainers. Then he felt them. Alex Kline's leather shoes, still covered in muck. He was about to stand when the sitting-room door opened, pouring brilliant white light out into the hall and up the stairs. He cowered behind the huge stairwell and held his breath, waiting for Cindy Reilly's terrified scream. The door closed again and it was dark. He nearly gagged with the relief. He picked up Alex Kline's shoes and stealthily closed the door behind him, waiting in the shadow to see if anyone might look out the window. A few seconds later, the hall light came on and two young children and their charging baby-sitter thundered out of the sitting-room and bounded noisily up the stairs.

He was about to breathe a huge sigh of relief, when the driveway was suddenly bathed in a blinding white light. Jack Buckley dived head first into the bushy hedgerow, clinging to the laces of the shoes for dear life, seconds before Alex Kline's 300SEL swept passed the spot, veering right onto the avenue that would take him to the house and his bed.

The clouds had cleared now, and the moon was higher in

the sky, giving the craggy, stoney beach at Coosbrack an animated ghostly feel. Jack Buckley had parked the car carefully at the water's edge, making sure the front tyres got wet, and packed his few belongings into the leather hold-all, Maggie's present on the day he'd joined the gym two years before. He had told her the drinking was finished and that that day marked the beginning of the new man. She smiled and said "I believe you" for the umpteenth time. Then she'd warned him that if he ever drank again she wouldn't be there for him when he got back home. He'd been to the gym once and never bothered again. Going to the gym was harder than staying off the bottle, he'd joked to her more than once. Two years, ten months, one week, three days, fifteen hours and – give or take – thirty minutes he'd been on the wagon.

He'd spread out his jacket and sat down beside Alex Kline's shoes, careful not to get them wet, watching the tide coming in around the small, helpless, drowning Astra. *"Go on, swim!"* he'd shout now and again, and laugh. It had been parked almost an hour, and already the water had filled the driver's well, dragging the heavy weight further into the doughy quicksand. He'd opened the bottle of vodka and smelt it. He'd waited a long, long time for this moment. He'd known it would come. He'd only have been fooling himself if he had believed he would never drink again. He had planned it for a night like tonight. A nice quiet beach, under the stars. Just Jack, the bottle and his thoughts, and *fuck* the rest of yis! He was calm enough now to savour it, not to gulp it down too fast and make himself sick. He lifted it to eye-level with his left hand, his arm extended, put his lips to the brim and tipped it back slowly. It filled his mouth, forcing his eyes shut, washing around his teeth, reaching the back of his neck and burning. Down, down it went, right to his gut. He could feel the electrifying hit, the sensational kick of cold, pure alcohol splashing across hot flesh. The taste was sizzling, effervescent, indescribable. He put the top back on and turned it tightly. The wind felt colder now against his forehead and throat which were burning up, his head spinning. He opened his eyes. The car was going faster now, nose down and sinking. *"Go one, fuckin' swim, Sergeant Buckley!"* He laughed hysterically. *"You rotten piece of tin shit!"*

Two hours later, all that remained was the white roof and its blue light. Jack Buckley snored peacefully as the water lapped at his feet, his arm wrapped around the two leather shoes which were so important to him. The empty vodka bottle bobbed about in a soft wave a few feet off shore. A sudden gust of cold night air made him shiver, then jolt awake. He was disorientated and frightened, wet to his thighs, then lonely, then aware of the barking dog. His head was thumping and his mouth dry and sickly sweet, his tongue swollen, as he tried to focus on the small animal jumping around at the water's edge, playfully teasing what seemed to be a huge black refuse sack which refused to budge with the current of the incoming tide. Jack Buckley managed to crawl across on all fours to the strange-looking heap. The dog ran off when it realised it had company, growling from a distance.

Jack looked at the heap. It was a sobering sight that he would never forget.

Leo Hannon's eyes stared up at the stars, bulging and terrified, as if they had almost been squeezed from their sockets. He had been dead for hours. His face was blue and swollen, his neck and belly bloated, his body surely twice its normally heavy weight. Jack felt the vodka burning his throat as he vomited across the body of his friend. He cleared his nose and mouth and sat down in the wet sand, gasping and crying. He looked for marks to the body. Nothing. It could have been a straightforward case of helpless drowning. There didn't seem to be any signs to suspect foul play.

He'd seen many bodies down through the years, some mutilated beyond recognition. But what he saw next disgusted Jack Buckley more than anything he had ever seen. Leo was still wearing the blue open-neck Thomas Burberry shirt he had on when he'd called to Jack's during supper that night . . . But now clipped to his breast pocket was Jack Buckley's police badge.

6

The hours following the dawn brought brilliant sunshine, and a hot, stifling stillness about the house, ideal for Jack Buckley to contemplate the cruel hangover he'd inflicted on his aching body. One bottle of vodka couldn't have wreaked so much damage. Yet his mind drew a blank shortly after getting Leo Hannon's body into a likely, reasonable posture in the driver's seat of the Astra to make it look like a clumsy suicide. He wished he could have been racked with guilt for what he'd done but he wasn't. Not even slightly. The small compartment inside his brain which seemed to have survived the tidal wave of neat alcohol was more concerned with getting Maggie back. He'd crumpled the letter out of anger when he'd first read it through stinging bloodshot eyes, their lids baked from lying directly under the glass conservatory roof. She'd propped it up on his chest, against his folded arms, and left. He read it again. It was tinged with her usual sarcasm.

Dear Jack,

Don't worry, I cleaned up after you during the night. It's sad when a forty-two year old policeman can't tell the difference between a sun-chair and a toilet bowl. As a result you'll need to get the carpet cleaned in the study. I tried to wake you to tell you that the police in Macroom found Leo's body in your car early this morning when the tide went out. I would have left before your escapade with the furniture only I had to pack. See Jack, I won't be coming back. You promised me three years ago you'd never drink again. In return, I promised I'd do anything to help you stay off it. You also promised we'd get married. You're a double bastard, Jack. There's only one thing sadder than a grown man pissing on his own furniture; that's when he hasn't got the courage to commit himself to the only person who ever gave a shit about him in the whole world and would have happily died for him. Not anymore, Jack. You can die all alone now. And I hope you do. Don't come looking for me.

Maggie.

It was time to crumple it up again. Aim, fire. It hit its target: the bin beside the sun-chair, which was all stained and yellow. He knew his body would survive because his aim was accurate again. But he wasn't sure *he'd* be able to survive without Maggie.

There was a soft, almost apologetic, knock at the front door.

Tourists, he thought. Then he remembered. He'd divested himself of his rank and job. He was no longer a sergeant. No longer a cop. *Oh shit!* What would Maggie say when she found out the real story. They would all find out within days, how he pulled him out to the car, into the deeper water and strapped him in. Macroom wouldn't release any information until they had questioned him first. But they couldn't question him if he wasn't at home when they called. Time to get moving. He eased himself up and swivelled around slowly as if his body was in three separate parts, like the tiers of a wedding cake, and the middle one was about to crumble. His stomach was sore, his mouth felt torched and ulcerated. His clothes were stuck to him like postage stamps and his legs and arms hurt so much he wanted to cry with the pain as he straightened them inch by inch.

The knock on the door was more urgent now.

Shit! he crackled. Please don't let it be them. He wobbled as he targeted the window to stop his fall. If they were uniformed it was a random housecall. If they were plainclothes it was a murder investigation. He peeped through the side of the warm, fresh-smelling net curtains that Maggie washed religiously every month, expecting to see two of his casually dressed ex-workmates from the Serious Crimes division in Macroom. Instead a tall, dark-haired woman stood facing the door, now and again stepping back to look up at the bedroom window.

Jack Buckley opened the door just as she was about to knock for the third time. Her knuckles were in the air. They stayed there as her mouth dropped slightly.

"Yes?" Jack slurred.

She kept staring.

He looked down at his chest and stomach. His shirt was ripped wide open, revealing a gash that had congealed messily. Then he remembered what Maggie had done to him when he had tried to explain to her hours before, in some sort of garbled nonsense, why he smelt of vodka and Atlantic Ocean seaweed.

"I'm sorry for disturbing you," was all the stranger could say, in a pronounced, well-spoken Dublin accent. She turned and walked back towards the gate.

Normally he would have just closed the door. Wrong house, perhaps. A lost tourist, maybe. "Excuse me," he called in a husky voice. She might have had a message from Maggie.

She turned around. "I'm looking for Jack Buckley. I was told he lived here." She seemed cagey now.

Jack nodded, pulling the strands of the torn shirt together. "That's me."

He wasn't sure why he had offered to make her a mug of tea. But she'd said yes. And she seemed to be enjoying it. He'd never invited a blank stranger into the house before. But this morning was different. His girlfriend was gone. His best friend was dead. And someone was trying to pin it on him. She hadn't even told him her name. And yet, she was drinking tea, cosy but watchful, as if this was a regular, every morning type of thing.

"What's your name?" He blushed. Cops always had a way of asking that question – as means to an end.

"Heather Lohan." She sipped again.

"Where are you from?" He could tell the tea was too hot. Not enough milk. It was the way Maggie liked hers.

"Dublin. I met you before," she said softly, the steam from the piping hot tea rising off her breath.

He froze. The tone in her voice told him it hadn't just been a casual meeting. It was more important. Before or after? he wondered, trying to recall faces and places as quickly as he could. Before he'd dried out? In which case he'd probably been rude to her. She had the most beautiful blue eyes, deep set. Her black hair was tied tightly back with a small band, almost painfully tight, sleek and shiny.

"Three years ago. You investigated my brother's death – Nathan?"

Jack was no good for names. Give me a face and I'll pick it out at a hundred yards, he'd always sworn. But names just collapsed into an anonymous muddle after a few minutes of conversation with strangers. *"Nathan?"*

"The hit-and-run near Drishane Bridge."

He nodded and grimaced as the throbbing headache racked his brain. "It was my first job after I arrived here." He reached out for his mug. He'd only enough milk for hers. His was still too hot. "So what brings you back to Sheep's Head?"

She shrugged. "Curiosity, I suppose."

He chanced a small sip. "Why are you curious?" He watched her eyes. They seemed to be searching him for something.

"Because . . . " She broke off and picked up her bag, pulling at its contents. She held out the letter. The envelope had been opened roughly. "This arrived at my mother's house the day before yesterday." Now she was upset. "I'd be grateful if you'd read it."

Jack took the small parcel tentatively. He opened the pages and started to read.

Dear Nathan,

It was so good to hear from you today. Your letter gives me great hope. It looks as though our search may indeed be nearing a conclusion. I had almost given up on hearing from you, it has been so long. And when I didn't hear from you after my last letter I worried a great deal about you. I could not have blamed you for quitting, especially since it is almost three years since I wrote last. You are a young man and you have your whole life ahead of you. So much has happened since our last meeting. I will be arriving in Ireland on May 18th. I will be in touch then. The Keeper's end will be our final liberation.

JM

Jack placed the pages on top of the envelope on the table and scratched his head. "Why are you showing me this?" His question sounded nasty and careless.

"Because no one else can help me."

"*Help* you? Why do you need help?"

"Because my brother died nearly three years ago. And this arrived on Friday."

"So?"

"Oh, come on! Call yourself a cop? Can you not see what's happening here?" She slammed her mug down, spilling it across the morning newspaper.

"Listen, I don't need this. I don't even know who you are. I have a few problems of my own to sort out today. And just in case you haven't heard I'm no longer a *cop*! So I *don't* need any of this detective shit! OK?"

Heather stood up and swung the black leather bag across her shoulder, knocking an ornament off the mantlepiece. "Please yourself. But I just thought you might like to know that Leo Hannon left the pub with Alex Kline and two other men last night." She walked through the front door, into the streaming sunlight, and banged it behind her.

Jack felt a surge of energy as he lunged towards the

door. He grabbed it, almost catching his fingers, and pulled it back. *"Wait!"*

She turned. "What?" she said calmly.

"Have you got a car?"

She nodded.

"I need a lift to Macroom," he said sheepishly. "I'll drive if that's OK. I'd feel safer considering there must be one or two people out there looking for me this morning."

He tried to explain to her, as logically as he could make it sound, why he had to make it look like Leo Hannon was drunk and in possession of a stolen car. Half the time, while he talked, she didn't seem to be listening. She looked left now, out the passenger window, shielding her eyes from the brilliant glare of the May sun. "Well, what else could I have done? I wake up and there's a dead body lying beside my car which is buried in three feet of seawater and sinking fast. The police would probably have arrived at any minute. It looks to them like a drunken brawl, to all intents and purposes. So I get eight years for manslaughter? Forget it. He'd been drinking anyway. So the coroner will just record suicide."

"Just like you recorded a hit-and-run in my brother's case?" She was staring at him head-on now.

"It *was* a hit and run."

"How do you know it wasn't intentional?"

"Because it was investigated thoroughly and the file is closed."

"Thoroughly? There was no investigation. Oh yeah, sure, the cops look for witnesses to an accident in the

middle of nowhere. How many people rang up to give information?"

He kept his eyes on the road in front.

"Well? How many?" she demanded.

He shrugged and shook his head.

"Nobody. I thought so. So just because nobody comes forward, you close the file. You just automatically assume that it was another sad hit-and-run and you pop the manilla folder into a filing cabinet and forget about it."

A drink was what he really wanted. It would have to wait. For all he knew they were right behind him. He shouldn't have tried to resuscitate Leo. Shouldn't have tried the kiss of life. He had been dead for ages. Putting his mouth to Leo's was like kissing a dead salmon. Now his saliva and bits of his hair and jacket-threads would be all over Leo. They'd trace it all back to him. It had been a beautifully planned, perfectly executed manouevre, whoever was behind it. And whoever it was wanted Jack Buckley out of the picture quickly and was obviously prepared to go to hell to achieve it. "Where did they go?"

"Who?" she asked flatly.

"Alex Kline and Leo Hannon, when they left the pub last night?"

"I don't know. They got into a big car and left."

"A Mercedes."

"Yeah."

Jesus, if only he could prove it. "Who is JM?"

Heather looked across at him.

"The writer of the letter," he said.

"I don't know."

"How could JM have received a letter from your brother if he was dead? Surely if they were good friends JM would have heard."

"That's my point. JM obviously doesn't know about Nathan's accident. I've never heard of JM in my life. But someone must have written to him pretending to be my brother. Why would anyone want to do that?"

"You tell me."

"To lure JM into a trap?"

"Read the letter back to me." Jack indicated and pulled into a lay-by.

Heather read each sentence slowly, looking up to see his reaction each time. He leaned forward and hugged the steering wheel. She finished reading a line from the end and studied his expression. "What are you thinking?" she asked.

"What am I thinking?" he muttered painfully. "I'm trying to figure out just how serious a mess I'm in." He sighed, long and hard.

"The woman who left your house this morning with the suitcase. Is she your wife?"

Jack cringed. "Yeah. Well, more my partner. We're not married."

"She looked pretty pissed off."

"That's kinda stating the obvious, I would have thought."

"Where was she going?"

"As far away as possible, I guess."

"Did you have a row?"

"What is this? *Twenty questions*," he snapped. "I'm sorry." He took a deep breath. "Something happened in my brain last night which I can't understand or quite take responsibility for. First I quit my job. Then I handed my badge to our new Justice of the Peace while he was celebrating with a few of his old cronies. Then I got drunk. Then I woke up on the beach with my best friend lying dead beside me with my police badge stuck to his shirt." He banged the dashboard with his fist. "Then what did I go and do? I *panicked*! I stuck him in the driver's seat in my car and let the tide come in to make it look like he'd stolen the fuckin' thing and drove it into the sea!" He sniffed hard to hold back tears. "They're never gonna believe it!"

"Why not?"

Jack turned off the engine and reclined the seat a few inches. Her voice was so soothing. He'd expected her to freak but all she seemed to do was smile. "Are you a cop?" he asked nervously.

She laughed. It was a warm mellow giggle. "Of course I'm not a cop!" She turned sideways to face him and sat back against the door. "Why did she leave?"

"Maggie? Because I was drinking."

"Did you hit her?"

"No. I've never hit Maggie. I guess I just broke a promise and it brought back horrible memories for her. I haven't drunk in three years. *My name is Jack . . . I'm an alcoholic. We love you, Jack!*" he mimicked, half singing, half mocking. He looked across at this stranger with the dark-blue eyes, set against the jet-black hair and the cheeky grin. "Do you ever stop smiling?"

"Only if I'm sad."

"You mean to tell me I'm not making you sad? You

should get together with my wife. She'd give you a dozen reasons to be sad." Jack started to smile himself. "Now look what you've done." He grinned. "I'm supposed to be worried. I'm supposed to be in serious trouble and you're making me laugh."

They both creased up.

Heather nodded to the supermarket carrier bag and the mucky boots. "They're dirtying my back seat. What are you doing with them?"

Jack started the engine again. "I need to drop them into a friend of mine in Macroom. He works in the forensic laboratory."

"A cop?"

"Yeah. He's a good friend. We were in college together. He might be able to help me."

"Who owns them?"

"Alex Kline."

"And what's in the bag?"

"Classified information. If I tell you I'll have to kill you." He looked across, expecting shock.

She balked. "Yeah, right."

"Only kidding. A handful of muck from the wheel cavity of Leo Hannon's car. It was stolen and written off last weekend."

"Where did they find it?"

"I don't know. And we may never find out now because Leo's dead. But I reckon that if the muck from the car is the same as the shit on Alex Kline's boots, well, it's a long shot . . . who knows."

"But you're not a cop anymore, are you?"

"Correct."

"So why do you want to investigate this?"

"Because I reckon I can find out a lot more about what's going on if I'm just Joe Citizen. Being Sergeant Jack Buckley has its drawbacks. You're perceived as being on the inside. People feel threatened. But not so much when you're just a bystander."

"You've lost me."

He slowed down while he looked across at her. "Are you gonna be around for a few days?"

"If you can help me."

"OK. I'll help you. Now I need to get food into me if we're gonna do a bit of detective work. I know a really nice restaurant. Do you like seafood?"

She shrugged. "Whatever. What's this Alex Kline like?"

7

Frankfurt, Germany.

Lunchtime was always busy at Frankfurter Stubb, an intimate rustic cellar bistro, with its alcoves, and waitresses in traditional German costume. *Stubb,* situated on the Am Kaiser was, for years, the haunt of local business people who liked genuine German cuisine of the highest quality, including *Grune Sosse*, Frankfurt's own herb sauce.

The small group in the corner, farthest from the milling lunchtime crowd, numbered five when the menu was accepted and passed around. It was unprecedented that these five men should be sitting at the same table. But then, the meeting was unexpected. Normally each of them would have enjoyed a glass of wine or a gin and tonic with his lunch. Not today. It was important that they got their business sorted as quickly as possible and returned to their offices and their families. Orders were taken and menus gathered.

"Give us twenty minutes before you serve."

The man with the fair hair spoke with an Irish accent.

The waiter nodded and backed away towards the kitchen.

Two of the men fiddled nervously with their napkins. Another wiped his forehead with his. The Irishman picked up the jug and poured iced water into each glass, his hand steady, his eyes composed. He could disguise his fear and anxiety, he thought, by appearing busy and in control. He cleared his throat. "It's important that we all know where we stand at this time regarding The Keeper," he said in English.

Two of the men looked agitated, eyeing each other across the round table. One of them reached for his glass. It had been almost seven years since he'd heard anything about the man they would only refer to as The Keeper.

"He is safe." The Irishman waited to see if anyone would take him up on such a general statement.

"Where is he?" the balding red-faced man with a rich German hue asked slowly, slightly unsure of his English.

"He is where he has been for almost ten years now. In a location in a remote part of Ireland. Deep in the secluded countryside of West Cork. He is known to the locals by a name which could never arouse suspicion. He is healthy and receives regular medical checks from a travelling nurse who visits elderly people in the area who are regarded as housebound."

The four men listened with great interest, as if being told about a distant relative none of them had seen for a very long time.

"Who takes care of him?" asked the man with slicked-back, black hair and a thin moustache, adjusting his cravat as if he needed air.

"A small dedicated group." It was clear he wasn't going to elaborate any further.

"Are they aware of his identity?"

The Irishman shook his head. "Partly aware. Only what they need to know. No more."

"Something has gone wrong, hasn't it?" The man asking the question appeared to be the calmest member of the group, and the oldest. He had been sitting back in his chair, silent and composed since he arrived. Now he was perched forward, determinedly interested.

"Wrong, Herr Luger?" the Irishman asked ironically.

The old German seemed indignant at the Irishman's flippancy.

"Yes, my friend. *Wrong*. You wouldn't have flown all the way from Ireland this morning unless there was a serious problem. You wouldn't have contacted each one of these busy men," he nodded to each of the guests with respect and they reciprocated the gesture, "if The Keeper was not in danger. His position has been compromised, hasn't it?"

Now the Irishman was nervous. "Of course not."

"Well then, *out* with it. You're wasting my time, friend. What's the bloody problem?"

"Three kids stole a car late last Saturday night. Now they are missing. A major investigation is being launched. Unfortunately, some of our guards are implicated. This may turn into a very embarrassing situation for all of us.

"Embarrassing?" one of the Germans spat. "Do you have any idea what the implications of someone stumbling onto this would be for your people?"

The Irishman bowed his head and nodded. He didn't want to be here today. He'd wished for years that he'd never been a part of it. That he had never agreed to be sworn to secrecy and do what he had done. He was Irish and now he felt after years of sickly worrying that he was a traitor. "I want you to take him back," he muttered. There was a leaden silence. He was terrified by what he had just said. Even the thought alone of such a outrageous demand chilled him to the bone.

The elder statesman sat back. "Let me get this right. You want us to take The Keeper back?"

"Yes."

The four men looked at each other in horror. Weakness and timidity were not qualities they suffered gladly. Luger was about to clarify his position when he felt his trouser leg being pulled discreetly. The man opposite nodded to the table close to the huge mahogany dresser. Luger twirled his fish fork between his fingers as he studied the couple who were ordering. Two of the men sniggered. Luger rapped his fork against his side plate. They regained their dignity and stopped staring.

The couple who were ordering hadn't noticed that they had become the object of attention of the next table. She might have passed for a young business executive treating her doting father to a posh lunch if she hadn't been dressed like a high-class hooker. The man she was dining with knew exactly what she was: an attractive, wealthy prostitute with more money in her bank account than he had seen in many years. She worked hard, she told him. He had found it difficult for a long time to reconcile the idea of screwing a stranger with his own idea of work ethics. On the other hand, as she explained, money is money, whichever way you choose to look at it.

For as long as he'd been brought his clothes to the small basement launderette around the corner from his bedsit, Karla had taken the two green plastic sacks across the counter, smiled and told him they would be ready on Saturday. They struck up a peculiar friendship with those few innocent words. She never seemed to feel threatened by him, nor him by her. Smiles eventually gave way to short conversations. He found himself dallying, waiting for other customers to clear off before he would hand over his bags. Then one day she said: "Hello, Josef". His heart almost stopped beating. It was his *bar mitzvah* all over again. She was German. So what. She'd found his name on a jacket he'd left in to be drycleaned. Six months they'd known each other, three since she'd explained she was a prostitute. She needed the extra money to pay for the insurance on her small launderette. The thugs threatened to break her beautiful long legs with a baseball bat and smash her face, and eventually kill her, if she didn't pay fortnightly. Josef had thought about giving her some of his money but that wouldn't have been right. She knew he was a Jew. But he was careful to make sure that was all she knew about him.

Yesterday Josef had explained to her that he was going away on business soon. It was likely that he wouldn't be returning to Frankfurt. Karla seemed devastated on hearing his news. She placed his plastic bags on the counter and took his hand. It was the most intimate they'd ever been, but seemed natural. They'd never kissed or hugged. Just talked and laughed. Two lonely strangers living off each other's energy and optimism. "Can I treat you to lunch?" he'd asked that morning as he took the small white cleaning docket. She smiled and agreed, but insisted the treat would be hers.

8

The Lobsterpot restaurant, at the top of Castle Street in Macroom, was unusually quiet. Jack Buckley had called ahead and asked for a window table. Louis Lee, Macroom's highly respected gourmet chef, laughed and asked Jack was he joking. "You can have any table you want, Jack. In fact, if business doesn't pick up in the next few weeks you can have the whole stinkin' lot!"

Jack and Heather sat at the window which overlooked the ancient walls of the town. Caesar Salad seemed like a good appetiser. But now that it was sitting in front of him like a miniature botanical wonderland he wasn't hungry anymore.

"Is it always this quiet?" Heather asked softly, nodding to the sound of Louis's loud kitchen voice shouting orders to the commis as if he was out the door with business.

Jack nodded. "Kinda. He won a television award last year. Since then there's no talking to him. His head swelled. So did his prices, through the roof; and his portions wouldn't fill your back tooth. He's talking about presidents and royalty putting this place on their list for future visits. Truth is no one comes here anymore. This is farming terrain. Big men with big appetites. None of your nouvelle cuisine. Or whatever you might call it."

"Cuisine bourgeoise?"

"Whaaa?"

"Cuisine bourgeoise. Plain cooking. A *Bourgeois* is a person with conventional values. It's French. See, in France, we'd be the *Bourgeoisie*: kind of middle-class citizens." She seemed pleased with her explanation.

"French. Eh?" Jack chirped.

Heather nodded and picked up another garlic mushroom.

"Well then, what's the French for vodka and tonic?"

Jack had bought a new shirt en route. Heather could still see spots of blood through the white fabric. "I think Louis speaks English," she said warily. "Why don't you ask him?"

Jack decided to postpone the vodka. "Tell me about your brother."

"Nathan?"

"Yeah, Nathan."

"Where do you want me to start?" She put down her fork and wiped her mouth with the napkin.

"Well, I reckon if you want me to help you, the start might be as good a place as any." He sat back and pushed the salad to the side. "Louis, a vodka and tonic, please. Easy on the tonic."

Heather placed her elbow on the arm of the chair and leaned across to the left. She seemed to be considering how she was going to start. "It's taken me three years to get to know my brother."

"But he's dead three years."

Heather didn't appreciate the interruption. "Have you any brothers and sisters?"

Jack nodded.

"Would you say you know them in the true sense of brothers and sisters?"

He thought for a moment and shook his head.

"Well then, maybe you'll understand. Nathan was always my *brother*, but it's only recently that he has become my real brother. He was always there, always doing his own thing. Studying, working, on the phone, meeting friends, the occasional girlfriend, nothing serious though. He wanted to be a writer, I remember my mother telling me. Then he wanted to be a war correspondent with the BBC. I remember she wasn't too impressed when an application form arrived from London one day marked *Foreign Correspondent Competition*. It used to piss me off how she used to mollycoddle him so much. He got a job working the night-shift with the *Herald*. Nightdesk newshound, she used to call him. She used to make him up a big pack of sandwiches before he'd go in every evening. Then she'd get up at four every morning and ring him to make sure he'd eaten them all. Then she'd have his bed ready when he'd fall in later in the morning. It used to really annoy me."

"Did you get the same treatment?"

"Did I *what*? I ended up like Cinderella. I cleaned up after him. She kept telling me he needed his rest. And when he was writing, he needed his privacy and his silence. I was just a jumped-up charwoman. I really got to hate him after a while."

"And your mother?" The vodka and tonic arrived. He ignored the bottled mixer.

Heather shook her head. "I don't think you ever really *hate* your mother. I don't think we have it in us."

"So what happened?"

"My father died. I was really close to my dad. That was the last straw I suppose. I moved out. I just had to get away from their little charade. It was making me sick. It was just unnatural. Nathan was nearly twenty-five. Yet he was being treated like a ten-year-old behaving like a grown-up, by a woman who seemed unaffected by the death of her husband or the concerns of her bewildered daughter . . . if you understand what I mean."

Jack nodded, savouring the biting blow of the first mouthful of liquid manna. If she kept going at this rate they could be here all afternoon and he could enjoy seven or eight of these. "Did he apply for the foreign job?"

"Of course he did. In fact, within a week he was invited to London and told he was already in the final ten. Within a fortnight he was down to the final three. It was a Monday when he got the letter. They needed him to start immediately. A week's notice. My mother was broken-hearted. He might as well have told her he was gay . . . Although that might have suited her down to the ground."

"Did he like his new job?"

"They were assigning him to Bosnia Herzagovina. The Croats were having their chimneys knocked off by shells around about that time. He was going out to stand in a minefield for the *BBC Nine O'Clock News* and he was ecstatic. We rang him a week later, the night before he was due to fly out to Geneva and then on to his post but a rather irate BBC person told us he'd never arrived."

"Never *arrived*? What do you mean?"

"He never showed up for the job. He just disappeared off the face of the earth. We were worried sick. Although I have to say I wasn't that surprised, the more I thought about it. Nathan was capable of anything. He was getting weirder the older he got. I suppose my mother can take a lot of the credit for that."

"So where did he go?"

Heather didn't like being rushed. "This might sound a bit long-winded, Jack. But you need to hear the whole story."

Jack checked on his vodka and tonic. Almost time for another. "No hurry at all. We've got all day."

"He turned up three months later, unannounced. No phone call, no letter. Just Nathan, complete with a beard and long hair, like he'd been living in some hippy commune somewhere. My mother never even asked for an explanation. She threw her arms around him and cried. Then she told him to tidy himself while she prepared his favourite: Shepherd's Pie. She hit me across the face when I called him a selfish bastard. I never saw him again after that."

"How long ago was that?"

"About a year before he died."

"How come he died in West Cork?"

"I don't know. He flew off to the States shortly after arriving home from wherever he'd disappeared to. He never told either of us where'd he gone, or why. I don't know where he got the money from to go to America.

Then all of a sudden money wasn't a problem. He seemed to be able to up and go at a moment's notice, or at the prompt of a phone call. He'd never say where he was going. He'd ring my mother from wherever he was to reassure her that he was OK. She'd ring me then to tell me he'd called. She started to distance herself from him at that time. I was convinced he was into drugs, transporting them from country to country. I still don't know what he was doing when he went away. But it must have had a magical appeal if it interested Nathan."

"What did your mother think he was doing?"

"Oh, typical her. She always maintained Nathan hadn't a bad bone in his body. He wouldn't hurt a fly, she kept saying. Eventually she gave up asking him. She just half-accepted that this was how Nathan was going to be for the rest of his life. A harmless drifter who was always welcome to come back home to his mammy whenever he felt he'd had enough.

"The phone calls."

"What?"

"You mentioned he'd go off after he'd get a phone call. Who was calling him?"

"He never told us. But I think it had something to do with this." She took out the letter again and opened it. "It definitely has something to do with whoever wrote this."

"How do you know?"

"I don't. But when you've absolutely nothing else to go on, at least this is a start."

Jack picked up the letter and read it through again. On May 18th, JM would come looking for Nathan Lohan.

Tomorrow week, a Saturday, would be the 18th of May.

9

Friday, May 17th – a week later – 1.25pm.

Lunchtime in the restaurant was always known as rush hour.

It was quiet now at Frankfurter Stubb, apart from the two of them, and the same businessmen at the corner table – just like the previous week, when Josef placed his hand on Karla's and told her it was time for him to go. He had some packing to do and some arrangements to finalise for his trip. He told her he was travelling to Pittsburg and the flight would take eight hours.

"I'll just pop to the ladies' room." Karla winked and smiled. "I won't be a minute."

Josef had tried to eavesdrop on the men's conversation on a few occasions, but Karla had seemed adamant to keep him all to herself that afternoon. After all they would never see each other again. If he hadn't been so much in love with Helena, his wife, he might have proposed to Karla there and then, that very afternoon. She was beautiful and needed someone she could call her own. She had told him she would give up the game if she met someone she could fall in love with and trust. Josef knew she was referring to him. He knew the opportunity was presenting itself that afternoon. She wanted to go to bed with him, even though he knew he was at least twice her age – old enough to be her father was an expression he hated, even though it was true. The temptation was so strong now, after the wine and the brandy that she insisted he drank.

Karla watched the mirror, touching up her lipstick, careful not to smudge it and get it on the tips of her snow-white teeth. She looked beyond her lips, at the cubicle door opening slowly, directly behind her. She wasn't surprised to see a tall, graceful, well-dressed businessman step out. She never turned around.

"His name is Josef. Josef Maister. He leaves for Pittsburgh tomorrow morning. American Airlines. 11.30 flight." She pulled a scrap of paper from her bag. "That's his address. He'll be back there in half an hour."

"Where will you be?"

She turned her head and stared at the frosty face. "My mother wouldn't even ask me a question like that." She took the envelope from his hand. "I take it you've counted it."

He nodded. "Twenty-thousand Deutschmarks. As agreed."

She folded the envelope and stuffed it into her bag.

"I take it you'll be at home all night."

She nodded.

"I'll call you later."

The taxi journey to Josef's flat took ten minutes. He paid in small change, trying to get rid of the coins which would be useless once he left the following morning. He would have given them to Karla only she might have felt insulted by the gesture. In the sensible part of his mind, he would make her coffee and they would talk and listen to some nice violin concerto. But the reckless side of his mind, which he had always kept strictly to himself, wanted to strip her quickly and fuck her hard. He knew, turning the key in the lock and hearing it click open, the reckless side was winning.

By the time the perculator was popping and the smell of fresh Brazilian coffee was wafting throughout the small accomodation and Josef was taking down his coffee cups from the top shelf, Karla was naked, unbuckling his belt and pulling down the noisy zip of his trousers. Her long fingers prowled hungrily until they yanked down his pants. He dropped the two cups, smashing them on the tiled floor, and, lifting her into his arms, carried her awkwardly into the bedroom, trying not to trip over his trousers which had fallen to knee-level now. They fell onto the bed and within seconds came together. They lay in each others' arms, half-sprawled, half-locked together, breathing deeply and sweating in the late afternoon May sunshine. Silently his reckless side commended himself. Not bad for a sixty-two-year-old yet secretly he longed for Helena and hated himself for what he had just done.

Neither said anything for a long time. Eventually Josef tried to estimate the time by the dullness which sat outside the window now, turning every thought of his into slow motion. It must have been close to six, he thought. "I'll miss you," he said softly, his bottom lip flicking her warm earlobe. No reply. He listened to her soft, steady breathing. She was fast asleep. He unlocked himself from under her arm and got dressed. Not much time left now, he knew he'd have to move quickly. He pulled the sheet up around her to her neck and kissed her on the cheek. He would let her sleep for an hour and then drop her home. It was better for him to pack alone. Then he would get some sleep himself.

* * *

Kranz Luger sat at his office desk overlooking Am Kaiser, having had his special guests chauffeured back to their rooms at the Holiday Inn close to the city's international airport. He was sweating profusely, his heart thumping like a bass drum: a troubled man; and he knew it wasn't the copious amounts of brandy he'd been sipping after dinner. The ghosts he had always feared might haunt him in time were filling his office space that afternoon. Only four months to retirement now. If he didn't act quickly he might never see the day. He picked up the ex-directory, direct-line phone and dialled a number.

The phone at the far end started to ring. "Yes?" was all the voice said.

Luger waited for a second, recalling the last time he'd called this number. It was almost three years he was sure. "Get me Proctor."

Another pause. "This is Proctor."

"Are you still available for work?"

"Always available, Herr Luger."

As perceptive as ever, Luger thought. And as hungry as he was perceptive. "Get a pen and take down this address quickly. We don't have much time."

"The pen has been ready since the phone started to ring."

10

"I *won't* cry!"

Maggie Flanagan thumped the dashboard and bawled her eyes out. It was a long, lonely sobbing sound, the kind that comes with too much crying, when the throat is raw and the lungs exhausted, and the eyes are salty and swollen. But only a few seagulls and mallards nestling at the water's edge on the cliffs near to Glanroon could hear. It was always quite nippy this far out along the northern side of the peninsula. The wind was a lot colder than usual this evening though, and sharper, for mid-May, the skies cloudier. A good enough reason to cry a bit louder.

"You stupid bastard!" she keened, wishing now that Jack could hear her. But, no matter how hard she screamed and shouted, she couldn't feel any badness towards him. *She* was the stupid bastard, she thought. She had never even bothered to ask why he had got drunk. And now it was all over the papers. Leo Hannon had been found dead: drowned in Jack's car. No wonder he'd started to drink. She'd tried to call the house most of the day, at random intervals from patients' houses she

had visited. They had all asked the same question: "What's wrong with you, Maggie? Something's been upsetting you, girl." She just brushed it off: "Hay fever", she told them each time. There had been no answer all day. It was unusual for Jack. He always answered any messages she left on the machine as soon as he got in. What if he was unconscious? Or worse. Dead from the drink. Choked to death on his own vomit. She hit the redial on her mobile again. Nothing. Not even his voice on the machine. All the time she listened to the dialling tone she thought about the note she'd left, propped open in the crook of his elbow, and the names she called him. Her breathing quivered as she sucked in the salty sea air and wiped away any signs that would give rise to more questions.

Harry Vogel was her last call of the day.

It was almost seven when she started the engine and drove the last mile to Harry's quaint little cottage, with the seashell mosaics – two tiny pink and purple ducks – on the front wall around each of the tiny windows, and the rusty brown cobblestones below the tiny porch, which had started to subside earlier that cold winter. But where would she go when she said goodbye to Harry? She told Jack she wanted to stay with her stepmother. But she didn't. Farthest notion from her mind. She wanted to burst through the door and throw her arms around him. Then run a nice bath for him and make him his favourite dinner. Then, while the baked potatoes took their usual sixty-five minutes, to climb in behind him and scrub his back and run her hands where he would know for sure –

no doubt in his mind – that she loved him. Always did and always would.

She parked the car and blew her nose in her last tissue. The silence after the engine died was deafening. The back wall of Harry's cottage, built on a tiny scrap of flat basalt, with a half acre of a weedy field for a back garden, looked down at the furious, heaving foam and the huge white breakers a hundred feet directly below, and out across a watery wilderness, nothing – as far as the eye could see. The blustery wind, turning south-easterly again in the last hour, chopped the surface, giving it a grey sliced ripple effect. It was always a sign of heavy rain.

The half-door was ajar, like he was expecting her. Inside, she could hear a whirring mechanism, coming and going in her ears with the swirling, dizzying wind; then the scratchy sound of the old balalaika music box, or was it a scratched record, playing her favourite air, a tune called *Love's Old Sweet Song*:

"Just a song at twilight, when the lights are low,
And the flickering shadows softly come and go,
Though the heart be weary, sad the day and long,
Still to us at twilight comes Love's old song,
Comes Love's old sweet song."

Only the tune, of course, not the words; but Maggie knew them well enough. Jack had sung them to her, softly into her ear, when he surprised her for her birthday seventeen years earlier and took her to stay in Hotel Maurice, close to the Seine's bank in Paris. And they danced as the pigeons scurried at their feet and picked at the crumbs in the gutter outside the little wine bar where she had hoped he would propose. He didn't. Not that night. Not any night, she thought. Still the tune held a certain magic.

God, how times change!

Harry must have heard her car and put the music on. It always pre-empted her visits if he heard the car in the distance. It annoyed her at first because she felt obliged to stay longer than she really wanted. He always had fresh scones baked – under a tea towel to keep them from drying out – and fresh camomile tea in the red teapot on the stove. Soon she got to enjoy her visits to Harry. Eventually she would leave Harry's cottage till last so she wouldn't have to hurry away. Jack had asked her why she enjoyed visiting Harry over and above her other Golden Oldies. The reason was obvious. He never bored her with his past. In fact, he might as well not have had any past. Life existed for the present. Add a bonus: he loved listening to Maggie sounding off about her problems. All he did was sit back in his armchair beside the giant, ancient Stanley stove and smile, his hands joined, his finger touching his chin, almost in prayer.

Maggie was convinced there wasn't an ounce of badness in him. She had often felt terrible having to leave half of one of his beautifully baked cakes on the plate: so much so that she lately started to fast on days she'd planned to visit Harry so that she would come away with a full stomach.

He hated the formalities: Are you eating from the list? she would ask him. Are you taking your angina tablets? she would say in an authoritative nursing voice. Are you getting enough exercise? You're not drinking too much brandy, I hope? He lied to all of her questions, just to get her relaxed and talking. And she knew it too. She didn't mind because she liked him just the way he was. The way he had always been for three years, ever since she'd knocked on the door for the very first time.

"How are you, Harry?" she asked, keeping her head bowed into her muffler and her red eyes hidden from view.

He stood and reached out, patting her elbows, with the big welcoming smile she'd come to adore. "I'm wonderful, my dear. Never been better," he replied in his soft Austrian accent. "And how are you?"

Maggie tried hard not to hear the imaginary words that wafted with the sweet stringed music. "I'm fine."

He waited for her to tell him. "Well! Aren't you going to get all the usual bullshit out of the way?"

"Of course."

They did.

Minutes later they were sitting, one on either side of the rumbling stove, sipping their mugs of sweet tea. Big band music – Glenn Miller – from the *BBC World Service* had broken the conversation but she knew it wouldn't be for long. She watched his head swaying, eyes closed, in time, reliving the mood of that period. She'd only known him a few years. But she loved him. Nothing sexual, she kept telling herself. It was more than that. Stronger. She often wondered on the slow drive back home at night what Harry Vogel might have been like forty years ago. Would she have fallen head over heels for him? There was a certain pomposity about him which she was sure had mellowed with the years. A quality that becomes more consuming in many of the older people she knew. Maybe it was the loneliness that had bled the arrogance dry. Whatever, she loved him for what he was now. A gentleman.

Maggie checked her watch. It was after eight. Jack hadn't answered her messages. But coverage was poor this far out onto the peninsula. So even if he had tried to contact her she wouldn't have known. She left the phone down, to her left, on the edge of the stove.

"I hate those things. So intrusive," he muttered.

"You should get one. They're very handy in emergencies."

He smiled. "Are they?"

The man sitting in front of her had become like her father. He was seventy-seven years old, but younger in appearance. At least that was what he'd told her when she was filling out his small medical record card. Despite his years, a strong rugged look about him made her feel safe and protected, exactly what she needed tonight: just someone who cared; someone she trusted because he trusted and needed her, who would sit with her and – without saying anything – make her feel that everything was OK.

Even if she knew it wasn't.

11

It was well past nine, and dusk, by the time Proctor had negotiated Frankfurt's vicious late-Friday evening traffic and arrived at Luger's house on the outskirts of the city. He parked towards the end of the long, tree-lined avenue, closest to the main road, eight doors from Luger's majestic house on Bockenheimer Landstrasse – Frankfurt's Millionaires' Row, they used to call it – once full of wealthy industrialists, merchant bankers, the odd ambassador's residence; and hidden in amongst them a few inconspicuous, rotten, high-class crooks who would never dare to shit on their own doorstep and, as a result, whose cause to live on one of Frankfurt's most affluent cul de sacs was never questioned, nor their names brought into disrepute. The truth was the police were afraid of what these people might do to their wives and children if they felt the cold wind of the law on the backs of their sweaty necks.

Luger often complained about a couple of his neighbours. Undesirables, he called them – in private of course, to people like Proctor, and others who he had sworn to secrecy. He called his small circle of friends the Klavern, after an old American folklore expression he'd come across on a trip to Idaho some years back. He never fully told his friends what the word meant. And it wasn't in any of the European dictionaries they might lay their hands on. Luger liked that, because it was another secret.

The blocky middle-aged woman who opened the door beckoned him inside. She pointed to a drawing-room across the spacious hallway. "Sit in there." She seemed nervous.

Proctor chose to stand. He strutted from painting to fireplace to photograph to mirror, where he examined his new physique. He'd made a New Year's resolution to lose three stone, get in shape, lift heavier weights, get his big muscular frame well pumped again, build up his strength and charge more for his unique work. He admired what he saw in the full-length mirror. The wall light behind his head threw a sinister shadow against his reflection. All he could see was the long dark trench coat held back to show off the thin waist complementing the huge chest and broad shoulders, and the dark growth, four days without shaving. He preferred boots to shoes, and black Calvins to neat trousers. He liked the idea of looking like a mean bastard, the sort you only see once. Then you're dead. "Not bad," he whispered.

"How's your conscience?" asked Luger, closing the door swiftly behind him.

Proctor watched him from the mirror. "*What* conscience?"

"That's what I like to hear, Proctor." Luger placed a

thin file on the table, a brand new manilla folder. The file had just been opened. "Busy these days?"

"Always busy. Always some bastard out there someone wants to be rid of." He turned a chair around and sat with his arms draped across the back. "How much?"

"Your life?" Luger waited for a reaction.

Proctor froze, almost became a helpless little dribbling baby again. "What?"

"You do this one job for me and I spare your life. Otherwise I turn you over to the authorities and tell them you've assassinated six people in four years, including a government official." He sucked on a dead cigar-butt which smelled of stale tobacco.

Proctor's eyes bulged. His face tensed.

"I'm only joking."

Proctor sat and sighed. "You're lucky you said you were only joking."

"Why?" Luger asked casually.

"I don't have a sense of humour." Proctor pulled his hand out of the long coat pocket and placed the Walther PPK pistol on the table. "I was just about to blow your head off." He licked the spit off the side of his mouth and swallowed.

Luger smiled. "Good," he cheered.

"Good?" Proctor mocked. "What's so good about getting your head blown off?"

"Not a lot. But it leads me to believe that you will do anything to keep yourself out of the wrong hands. Therefore I feel I can trust you. You're a friend."

"Money's my only fucking friend."

"Yes, I know that," said Luger, trying hard to hide his revulsion for the parasite sitting opposite him and his foul language. "But this job is bigger than you and me together, Proctor. I need to know once you leave here tonight that I can forget about what's been giving me a migraine all day."

Proctor started to whistle. *"Who wants to be a millionaire?"*

"Sit down." Luger fought the temptation to be flippant. He hated anyone who used the element of surprise to outwit their opponent and then kill them as quick without any chance of defending themselves.

"How much?"

"Two-hundred-and-fifty-thousand US dollars." Luger opened the file and ran his gold pen down the side of the long list of phone numbers and figures. "It's been lodged for you, waiting to be collected as I speak. Account number 0244753187 in Westdeutsche Landesbank in Dublin."

He jotted the number down on a scrap of paper.

"Dublin?"

"Yes. For that amount of money you will carry out two operations, swiftly and silently, as soon as possible."

"What are they?"

Luger slid another small scrap of paper out onto the middle of the smooth polished table. "Go to that address. He should be there now. He's a Jew and a major threat to our ongoing operation. No questions. No nasty punishment business. Just kill him."

Proctor studied the address. Then threw the scrap of paper into the fire. "Then what?"

"Well, you're going to have to travel to Ireland to collect your money."

"So?"

"You will remove a man while you are there. A very important, influential man who must be treated with the utmost of respect at all times, do you understand? No talking. No hanging around. Just brief familiarisation. You'll get in and out as quickly as possible."

"In *Ireland*?"

Luger fiddled with a small sachet, pouring its contents into a glass. "I've never known you to be a nullifidian," he said vainly. "Are you telling me you're not up to it?"

"Of course not." He smiled. "It's just been years since I travelled to Ireland. That's all."

"There's no room for your conscience to be getting in the way, Proctor."

Proctor was annoyed that this man doubted his capabilities. "I don't have a conscience."

"Good. Look on it as a little holiday. You'll be able to meet up with some of your old IRA friends. I'm sure they must have loads of time on their hands these days. One of them will provide you with the tools you'll need for the job. It's all been arranged. He'll meet you in Dublin." He took out a wallet. "At this address. Do this right, Proctor, and you can up your price if I need you again. You are the top cleaner in the business. Carry this off clinically and you'll have them running for fresh underwear. But don't do anything until you've heard from me. Do you hear?"

"Who is he?"

"Who?"

Proctor grinned and pocketed the piece of paper. "The man I'm going to remove."

Luger stiffened slightly and swallowed the cocktail of aspirin and milk of magnesia, shaking his head twice. He bowed his head and muttered. "Someone you don't need to know." Now, if you don't mind, I want you to leave."

Luger led the way to the front door, shielding Proctor behind him, almost holding him back, as he opened it slowly. "There's already a sleeper on the ground. You'll be contacted once everything is in place. Until you are contacted you behave like a sleeper. Lie low. Get plenty of sleep." He was about to close the door when he stopped. "Remember, I don't know who you are and you have never heard of me. You were never here tonight."

Proctor sneered. "But of course, *Herr* Luger." He stepped out into the garden and pulled his coat tightly around him. "I love a sense of humour."

* * *

It took twenty minutes to drive from Luger's stately residence to the address Proctor had memorised from the scrap of page he'd chucked into the fire. Seahofstrad, just off the busy Offenbacher, where every denomination and nationality packed into thousands of tiny box-shaped apartments and bed-sits, some of them no bigger than Luger's drawing-room.

Proctor parked the black sporty MR2 a block away, just far enough to make out his target landmark – the bedroom window on the third floor of Apt 5144. His victim was male. No other information. He would just think of him as X. Proctor locked up the car and checked the street, left and right, before moving away out into the open. He hated wide footpaths. No cover. He walked stealthily close to the wall, tiptoeing at times, keeping his nerves at bay, like he always did, by thinking of crimes his victim could have been guilty of to make him worthy of such a sudden end. A pimp? Not really. That was good money, and a comfortable lifestyle. And, let's be honest, he thought to himself, everyone got what they wanted! A child molester? *Yes!* That would do nicely for tonight. He would focus on his victim as being someone who sexually interfered with young children and deserved therefore to die. But he wouldn't think too elaborately. Otherwise X would end up dying slowly, probably screaming and arousing suspicion in the apartment building. He was surprised how quickly he was travelling. Already he was at the main entrance. Locked.

Shit!

He jabbed eight numbers at random, as if making a phone call. One of them was sure to answer. There was a muffled buzz and the door clicked open.

He watched it swing shut behind him, then pounced up four steps like a cheetah. Then another three. Then he took two at a time, his head down, until he reached the third floor.

The door of 5144 was ajar, the apartment beyond almost dark except for a faint light towards the back, in another room. He could just about make out the end of a bed and two bare feet. It could be a trap. And whoever was waiting in the semi-darkness for him would have the benefit of night sight. He eased the door forward. A slight break. No movement. The Walther was drawn, by his side, the back of his hand firmly against his leg to give his arm strength in the event of a surprise.

Nothing.

Maybe someone had got to his victim ahead of him. Maybe Luger had sent another hitman to do the job. But why? He'd never doubted Proctor. He was at the bedroom door now, his senses telling him he was alone in the apartment, except for the man sleeping on the bed, a white sheet draped loosely across his naked body. He could just make out the man's head, buried half beneath the white fabric. He checked the silencer and took a deep breath. He raised the gun, arm's length, and pointed it, exactly eighteen inches from X's head. The gun recoiled as it fired its bullet with a putting sound. The shape beneath the sheet jolted once, as if it had just received a strong electric shock, and whimpered. Then lay still. Proctor was about to fire a second shot into his victim's back but something made him hesitate. The whimper maybe. He grabbed the sheet which was covered in blood now and yanked it away from the body.

"Jesus . . . NO!" he roared. He'd never pissed himself before when it came to putting a bullet into a sucker's brain, not once in six years, or a previous ten with the French Foreign Legion. A true virtuoso, Luger had once called him. But tonight he couldn't stop pissing. Hot yellow urine soaked his black Calvin's and mixed with the dark red blood which had oozed from her head wound onto the floor. "Karla!" He dropped his gun and grabbed her by the shoulders and shook her violently.

Then he cradled her. He'd asked her to marry him three months before. She told him she would think seriously about it only if he gave up the killing job.

Proctor lay her back down onto the pillow and kissed her cheek, closing his eyes to avoid the bloody puncture hole just below her right temple. He should have been meeting her at ten for a drink, and from there a spot of clubbing. He'd looked forward to it since accepting Luger's offer. Seized with an icy determination he thought of the small piece of paper in his wallet with the bank account number in Dublin. There was still a job to be done.

He was sorry he hadn't asked Luger for a photograph or a name for his first target, the one who'd got away tonight. Calling back to the house was out of the question, he knew. He would have to explain that he had shot Karla by mistake. Luger would be livid, maybe even call off the deal. Proctor couldn't afford to do without the money he'd been promised.

Although this time it would be personal. With the anger he felt in his heart that night it would be a piece of cake finding out the identity of this mystery man. Then he would kill him whether Luger withdrew the money or not.

12

Jack looked up the driveway at the dark house. The ghostly grey reflection of the noisy branches of the twin chestnuts scooping up the wind made the place look desolate, almost weird. Maggie still hadn't returned. He couldn't remember a night when he came home and the small flickering porch light wasn't glowing. Now it was almost a week. And not one phone call. He'd been quite pleased with himself all evening that he had stopped drinking after lunch. His mouth was dry, with the taste of garlic, but at least he was sober. But why had he bothered? he asked himself now. At least he would have slept if he'd been pissed. He wouldn't have to think about Maggie, and where she might be, or what he would like to do to this young, dark-haired stranger sitting beside him if she had consented.

"Thanks for a nice day," Heather Lohan said softly. "I was looking forward to meeting you."

The engine purred, the small car rocking slightly, left to right, in the strong May storm that was brewing.

Jack noticed she was looking up the drive at the empty house.

"It must be lovely here in the winter," she said dreamily.

"It's all right. Kind of a bit of everything really. Rain, snow, fog, you name it, we get it." Just then the sky seemed to rumble loudly. "I nearly forgot . . . and thunder."

Heather seemed to freeze. "I love thunder."

"You get used to it down here." He looked back up at the house. It looked shabbier than normal, in the darkness, with the light of the moon looking like an old black and white movie on the front wall." He didn't want to go on his own. "Would you like a cup of coffee before you drive back?"

Heather considered the question. "I really should be getting back. It's a long drive." She looked at the clock on the dashboard. 10.15pm. "OK. I'd love one." She reached into the back seat and took a brown parcel from under her jacket. "I want to show you something."

They got out of the car. The central locking whirred and clicked. It was beginning to rain more heavily now, a thick Atlantic, squally shower. They ran up the driveway into the shelter of the porch. Jack turned the key and they stepped inside.

He handed her a mug. "I'll let you milk and sugar it." He sat down at the table with his. The surface was covered strategically with newspaper cuttings and photographs. "What are they?"

Heather neatly laid out the final couple of clips in chronological order. "I found these in an envelope in Nathan's room. Well, actually, my mother was about to throw them out when I called around to visit her."

Jack studied the biggest cutting closest to him. The headline was a screamer.

PASSPORT SCANDAL

"I remember that. It made big news about three years ago. Why did he want to keep that?" Jack asked.

"I'm not sure. My mother seems to think he was doing an investigative piece for *Magill* magazine. The article is dated April 12th. He was killed a fortnight later."

"So what has this got to do with his death?"

"I don't know. Here, have a look at this." She pushed another article closer to his coffee mug.

Jack read the piece quickly, then squinted for a better look at the figures in the photograph before shaking his head. "Girundbach? Isn't that the German car tyre company?"

Heather shrugged her shoulders. "I don't know."

"They set up a huge factory here in Ireland. It must be nearly twelve years ago. It made huge news because it created over three thousand jobs. Everyone down here was a bit pissed off because the original plan was that it would be based in West Cork. Then they thought about Shannon, better accesss for Germany and The States. So Shannon won out in the end."

"What do they do?"

"They make car parts for German cars."

"Why move to Ireland?"

"Tax incentives. Provided their mother company is in another country, they can repatriate all of their profits. Basically they're a wholly owned subsidiary." He could see she wasn't really interested. "This company was the toast of the Irish people when it started. It created three-and-a-half-thousand new jobs for Irish workers, and generated a billion quid in its first three years. Not bad."

"But why would a German company which had been so successful in its home base want to set up in a country with such a pathetic infrastructure?"

Jack had been wrong. This woman had done her research.

"Why didn't they set up in Turkey, or Greece? Or Baghdad, for that matter?"

"Simple. Look at Ireland, compared, say, to Baghdad. We have a skilled, plentiful workforce. We're, generally speaking, highly educated. And there are no terrorist threats like you'd get elsewhere. Anyway, if these people were involved in a passport scam, maybe it was worth it. I think I'd give a passport or two away if it meant creating three thousand jobs. Would you?"

She didn't answer, just watched.

Jack sat back in the chair and fidgeted, sipping his coffee. "Jesus, wait a minute." He went back into the kitchen and returned holding a copy of *The Examiner*. He sat down and started to leaf through the pages, faster and faster as he got towards the centre. *"Here it is!"* he said excitedly. He placed the paper down, fully open, across the table, pointing to the photograph. "Him!"

Heather was confused. "Who is he?

"Ben Roper, multi-millionaire businessman. He's the new chief executive of Girundbach Ireland."

Heather waited. "So?"

"He's the father of one of the kids who disappeared last week."

"So?"

Jack ignored her. He wasn't too sure himself what way his mind was working. But it seemed strangely ironic that her brother had kept a newspaper clip about Girundbach. And now here they were reading about the new boss of the company in that morning's newspaper.

Maybe he was wrong. What if they had been kidnapped? Roper's personal fortune was estimated at one-hundred-and-fifty-million. The kid would make the perfect hostage. A young seventeen-year-old snatched by a gang demanding a million quid. The sky's the limit. Public reaction would be incredible. The kidnappers would instantly get their money, no questions asked. On the other hand, why take three kids? You're asking for trouble. One is a handful, lugging him from safe house to safe house, from the boot of one car to another. But *three* of them? Tying them up. Untying them. Gagging them. Ungagging them. Feeding them. Forget it. It's just not on. Especially when only one of them is worth that sort of money. It would have been easier just to take the Roper kid. To hell with the others.

Jack sighed. He resorted to his old theory. They'd just taken off, probably stoned and pissed, free from exams, met up with a a couple of young ones, and just couldn't give a shit. Eventually, when the money ran out, they'd find their way home. Anyway millionaires were bound to be paranoid about kidnappers. Especially when it came to their kids.

"What are you thinking?" she asked.

She brought him out of the dream. He could hear the thunder rolling now, getting closer. She jumped as the blue streak lit up the long back garden, causing the lights in the kitchen to flicker. "You all right?" he asked.

She nodded.

The lightning streaked again. The thunder, only a couple seconds behind now, gave a long constant growl.

Heather stood up. "Do you mind if I open the patio?"

"Not at all."

She opened the two doors and stood out into the garden, under the soft canopy. It was raining heavy now. "Poor fox," she said.

Jack walked up behind her. "Where?"

She nodded to the pond.

The animal was lapping at the water with its tongue. Then the rain became too heavy and the fox made a bolt for the hedge.

Heather stepped forward and looked up at the broody sky. Within seconds, her dark hair was matted, saturated by the heavy rain. Her outfit had turned a darker shade of blue. "Jesus, you're getting soaked. What are you doing?"

"You can't catch a cold in the rain. Did you know that?" She didn't move, her eyes tightly closed, her head as far back as she could stretch, the heavy rain splashing off her face now. "Do you know what I've always wanted to do?" She tilted her head slightly right to see him.

"What?"

"Take off all my clothes and walk in wet grass during a real heavy rainstorm, and feel the cold rain everywhere on me. Just like this one."

Jack laughed uncomfortably. "You'd definitely get the

flu." The thought of it alone made him quite aroused. "Well, don't let me stop you," he said jokingly.

Seconds later, like a dream but it was actually happening, she turned her back to him and raised her wet top over her head with outstretched arms. She threw it back to him. "Here." She grinned cheekily and turned to face him, backing onto the sodden grass. She unclipped her bra as she kicked off her shoes in his direction. Her full, swollen breasts, their tight, dark-brown nipples jutting out, toppled forward, wet and shiny now. Then she lowered her jeans and stepped out of them.

She seemed lost in some sort of a trance now, her body exquisitely beautiful. She lifted her hands above her head, joining them and swept up her soaked, black hair into her fists. "Take yours off," she shouted.

Jack choked with a mix of embarrassment and excitement. "Maybe we should call it a day," he replied.

"Jack, I'd love to have you in the pouring rain. I can't make myself any clearer than that, can I?" She waited, the heavy rain teeming down her breasts and ribs in long, meandering rivulets, on down over her stomach and thighs.

He stepped forward.

She pulled him closer, tugging at his belt, feverishly pulling at the buckle with one hand, ripping at his shirt with the other. Then he could feel the heavy rain on his bare skin, freezing cold at first, but then warmer. It felt exhilarating. He threw his head back, gasping for air in the pouring spray in the pitch darkness.

Then he toppled and fell down beside her, on the

freezing wet grass. She was oblivious to him, writhing in the mud, covered in black treacly earth, her hands tugging hard at clumps of wet, slippery grass for any kind of support.

All the time the rain poured down, heavier with each minute, stinging and biting the bare flesh of his back, until he could barely hear her shouting his name. It dropped from the tip of his nose, a never-ending stream of water, onto her chin and into her mouth. Just then a huge blue flash lit up the garden. And he thought of Maggie. And he stopped what he was doing.

He made her coffee.

She cupped the mug and sipped the steamy brew, the wet strands of her hair hanging over her eyes. "It's half twelve," she said sleepily. "I'd better go."

Jack was glad she suggested it. He wanted her to go now. He wasn't sure why. But what felt good in the rain an hour before felt uncomfortable now. "I'll call you tomorrow." He hugged her and kissed her lips.

She watched him. It wasn't the way a lover would watch though, he felt. "Why did we do that?" he asked. It seemed like a stupid question.

She stood on the doorstep and kissed him again. "Because sometimes it feels good to fuck a stranger."

The rain was much lighter now.

She raised her hand to wave and walked to her car.

Then he remembered.

Jack closed the door and hurried back out into the garden, scouting around and scouring for anything they might have left behind them. There was no visible evidence in the wake of the sexual hurricane. He walked over to the pond and bent down, reaching into the water and sweeping back the colourful stones and pebbles which illuminated the bed. Underneath, chilled and inviting, was his trusty friend. He smiled as he squeezed it, licking his lips and moistening his tongue.

The last vestige of a by-gone era. The one Maggie never found during her all-night hunt to exorcise the demon and rid her house of temptation three years before. It was still there, God bless it.

A half-full bottle of Johnnie Walker Red Label.

"Ye good thing! You'll do nicely."

13

"You're very quiet," Harry Vogel said, jolting her back into the present.

Maggie forced a smile. She mustn't have said anything for at least ten minutes. She could have thought of a dozen excuses for her lack of chatter. But tonight she couldn't be bothered. Truth was, she felt like sitting here until Harry Vogel kicked her out. And she knew that wasn't going to happen. "Am I?"

Harry nodded. "For someone normally so garrulous, I would say so." The hands went under the chin again. "You remind me of my wife tonight. She was such a taciturn woman."

"Sorry?" She could see he had made an effort at ironing a shirt, probably because she was coming, and had given up. That was nice. He was in a contemplative mood tonight, she could see.

"She never spoke. So when she died I thought I would never miss her." He tutted. "Quite the opposite, in fact. I still miss her. Awful, *awful* loneliness." He sighed. "And I always thought that I would be the one to go first.

Heart attack or something dramatic. She always said that I liked to steal the thunder."

"How long is she dead?"

"They say you can tell from a person's sorrow, how well their heart mends over time. How long would you say?"

"Five years?"

He smiled wistfully. "Not bad. Does it show?"

"It was a guess." She waited. "What did she die of?"

"Cancer. Of the brain." He trembled. "Poor love. She had a terrible end." His voice rose slightly, his tone choked. "Refused a lot of medication they tried to force her to take. Instead she just wanted to come back here and be near the sea."

"Brega. That's a nice name."

"Yes, it's Austrian. From Salsberg. Mozart country. And salt mines."

"Is that where you're from?"

Harry nodded. "I wasn't there for very long. My parents were German. We moved back there when I was very young. They wanted to bring me up as a German boy." He seemed distracted. "I met her after the war. She was eighteen and very beautiful. I left Germany in 1943. It was such a different place to where I had grown up as a child. I needed a new beginning. Then I met Brega. She saved my life." He glanced across to the mantlepiece, reaching out and carefully lifting the small pocket-size frame. "This was taken a week after I met her."

Maggie took the delicate casing and studied the shot. She was extraordinarily beautiful. But she didn't smile for the photograph which seemed such a pity.

"Isn't it quite extraordinary how our parents urged us to read and learn, and develop our minds and expand our imaginations. And how we spend our childhood years packing our minds with information and education that we hoped would eventually benefit us in whichever walk of life we chose to follow. And all the wonderful books and works of genius that we read so lovingly through the years and refer back to again and again. And suddenly the cancer comes and eats your brain and turns it to mush and gives you a horrible stinking smell that follows you to the bathroom when you want to be sick from the radiation. It's not treatment at all. Torture. You rot before you're dead. The only organ in the human body apart from the soul that makes us so unique and different from each other. I find it difficult to understand how something so special is taken away from us so crudely and we can be left to die in such awful, undignified pain and misery. I cannot believe that a God exists who would allow that to happen." There were tears in his eyes. "I don't believe in God. Do you?"

His eyes were sinister, staring almost.

"Sometimes. Don't you ever?" she asked.

He shook his head determinedly. "Of course I don't." Then he mulled for a moment. "I can't afford to. Put it that way. But enough about me. You still haven't answered my question."

It was only when Maggie tried to speak that she realised she too was almost in tears. "It wasn't a question."

"Yes, it was. Why are you so quiet?"

His warm, drawing smile reminded her of her father.

"Because I left my husband some days ago. And for some reason I miss him tonight." He didn't seemed surprised, just listened after what she thought was a slight flinch. "Well, actually," she shrugged, "he's not my husband. I've lived with him for twenty-two years. I suppose that would make him my common-law husband, wouldn't it? Anyway, I just had enough." She sipped the mulled wine and wrapped her arms around her knees hugging them tighter to her. "He hasn't drunk for three years. He came home last week pissed. Falling around. Getting sick. Pissing in flower pots. It just made me mad. Reminded me of all the bad times we had. I just . . . *walked*! That's all." She felt such a sense of relief saying it that she started to laugh.

Harry Vogel smiled. "I'm glad you're laughing. It means you'll recover. Are you glad you left him?"

Maggie kept smiling but shook her head. *"No!"* She squeezed her nose, like she always did to ward off the crying. "That's the crazy thing about it. I'm not. I miss him. I don't know why. But I do." She wanted so much for Harry to do the talking for a while. To say something sensible like he always seemed to have a knack of doing. Her head was feeling a bit light. She tried to remember how many glasses of the wine she'd drunk. Five, maybe six. "What am I doing here?" She stood up and swayed. "I'm meant to be looking after you. And here I am pouring all this rubbish out to you. I'm going to have to go." She staggered, looking for her carry case.

"Please . . . sit down." His expression was still the same. He smiled. But his voice was more authoritative.

"I can't." She was slurring.

"Please!"

If the word hadn't been *please* it would have sounded like a command. She sat down again.

"I have something to tell you." He breathed deeply.

She listened, forcing her eyes to focus, pursing her lips.

"Often, during our short time here, we all do things we regret terribly. And it is by saying sorry for our actions that we learn to live with ourselves again. The ability to feel regret should not be taken lightly. I have done some things in my life that I have regretted doing. We all have. It has not been until much later, having realised the greater consequences of my actions, that I have thought to seek inner peace."

It seemed like an unusual thing for him to say. "What actions?" Maggie asked softly. He seemed to ignore the question.

"I can understand perfectly well why many people will never understand me. But that is their prerogative. They are perfectly entitled to their feelings just as I am to mine. And you are to yours."

"Is that why you can't believe in God?"

His snigger ridiculed her question. *"God?"* He sneered again. "There *is* no God. Not in the context that you were brought up to believe in. How can there be? If there was a God as kind and merciful watching over us, all loving and forgiving, why does he let atrocities happen on the scale of what's been recorded in world history?"

He was waiting for her answer. She felt uncomfortable now. This wasn't the Harry Vogel she'd come to know over the years. That Harry Vogel was an old well-informed man who minded his own business, and made apple tarts and scones, and brown bread from packet mixes he bought in Kenny's supermarket when he used to get a lift in from Leo Hannon on a Wednesday. Harry Vogel who painted portraits of the rough seas, and talked about the weather, and the stories he heard on the short-wave radio frequencies late at night, and the state of his wife's grave. She looked at her glass of mulled wine.

It was empty.

"More wine?" He smiled again.

Maggie shook her head. "I'd better be going."

"I'm just an old man living out my last few years watching the gulls and cormorants on the cliff face; spending a couple of hours sitting at Brega's grave every day; being visited by a very beautiful nurse who likes my home cooking. We all deserve to be left alone with ourselves at some stage in our lives. Sometimes we have no choice. To crave the company of others is to taunt fate, I always say. I've come to enjoy my own company now. Well, sometimes. Maybe time apart will do the two of you the world of good."

14

It was close to one in the morning when Bruno Proctor arrived back in the sedate, less frenetic, more residential streets of Bad Homburg. He removed the police *No Parking* bollard he had stolen at a rock concert the previous year and reversed the sports car into the adequate space, five cars from the door of his apartment block, as he did every evening, and popped the triangular plastic cone into the back seat. It never ceased to surprise him how the bollard remained exactly where he had put it earlier that morning. No one ever tampered with it. Not even the police. His theory was that, in Germany, with so many different police categories and graded levels, no one had a fucking clue what anyone else might be doing. To remove a police bollard might mean treading on the toes of a more senior officer who'd placed it there for a perfectly good reason.

He was about to activate the car alarm – three long beeps, three long orange flashes. Tonight he decided not to. He looked down the street and upward towards the apartment. The curtains were open, the two rooms dark. A mental precept had always forced him to check his surroundings before leaving the safety of the small gap between cars and walking out defenceless into wide open space. His army training had saved his life on dozens of occasions, like it might do again tonight. The smell of Karla's blood, sticky on his fingers now and caked under his nails like dried carbolic soap, was making him feel nauseous. He had a peculiar feeling for almost a minute now that someone had been there before him. He watched the windows again for a moment, holding his breath as if taking aim. They were firmly closed, yet the curtains were swaying as if blown by a draught. His chest tightened, his heartbeat speeding up. He took out the photo Luger had reluctantly given him when he unexpectedly called back close to eleven. Proctor told him that Karla had been shot dead before he had arrived. Luger fell back into a chair and muttered the name Proctor had been longing to hear.

Maister.

"He is running ahead of us, Proctor," Luger said with eyes that were screaming with fear and uncertainty. "He must not get to The Keeper."

The main door to the twelve-storey apartment block had been left open, swinging back and forth in the nippy night breeze. It was unusual for the old widow Fennsbeck on the ground floor not to have noticed it. The sign on the lift said OUT OF ORDER. He drew the Walther and pulled the long sleeve down over his left hand, making sure to place each foot to the extreme left or right of each step of the creaky staircase. The squeaky, unoiled sound was loud, even before he got eye level with the third floor landing.

The door of his apartment hung from its hinges like a broken jaw. A size twelve boot, Proctor was certain. Not much had been damaged, from first impressions. Then he noticed the drawers of the work cabinet on the floor, papers strewn under the table, and the scribbled message on the A4 page of white photocopying paper.

LOOK IN THE MIRROR

The only mirror was in the bathroom. The light was on. He drew the pistol to shoulder level, arm's length, and cushioned his left index finger firmly against the trigger. He stood for a moment, looking through the gaps between the hinges of the door. Seemed empty. He kicked it forcefully with his right foot and stood firmly behind the weapon.

Nothing.

Just a hastily scrawled message on the half-length bathroom mirror which ran across the head of the jacuzzi, written, he knew, with Karla's red lipstick.

If anyone is to go into captivity, into captivity he will go. If anyone is to be killed with the sword, with the sword he will be killed. This calls for patient endurance and faithfulness on the part of the saints.

Revelations, 13:10

Proctor read the scripture again. And again. Then he realised he was shaking with fear. A sensation he hadn't experienced in fifteen years. He knew this was the message he'd expected some day. Not tonight though. *Patient endurance . . . faithfulness . . . saints*. Luger had told him that Maister's greatest virtue was his patience. He was not bothered about waiting. God knows, he'd waited all these years. Tonight, Proctor sensed, the loose strands of the secret that Maister had spent years trying to solve had finally been tied up and it was time to turn it into a conundrum for the enemy.

He noticed that the lipstick started to fade on the final few words as if Maister was running out. Then he noticed the arrow below the message, pointing into the bath. He gasped. Carved crudely across the floor of the lime-green coloured jacuzzi with a knife of some sort was another message.

Dinner's in the oven, pet xxx.

Proctor froze. He had a gas cooker. The whole apartment block could blow depending on how long the gas had been left running. He sniffed deeply. No smell. If it was nautural gas, there wouldn't be a smell. The cooker was cold, the front grill flap half open. He pulled it down carefully, stooping, but leaning back at the same time, to see what was waiting for him.

It was another page.

While you've been reading scripture I've been busy.
By the time you've read this, I will have notified the
police that a bomb will explode in twenty minutes.
That gives you ten minutes to decide exactly what
to do.

Proctor ran to the window. Outside the world was fast asleep. He checked the time. 1.35am. He had been here almost twenty minutes. If the bomb was going to explode it would blow any second, he reckoned. But it was probably a hoax. Jesus Christ, the bastard was playing cat and mouse. Maister had prepared and perfectly orchestrated his game of hangman. If Proctor didn't hurry he'd be swinging from the end of a rope. He grabbed a bag from over his bed and pulled the zip hard apart, throwing in items of clothes that he would need. Then he stopped and took a deep breath. The sound of a police siren in the distance almost panicked him. He had to get out, whether this was a hoax or not. He couldn't afford to be compromised. The police would find Karla's body sooner or later and trace her identity back to their apartment. He had to get out. Head for the airport and stay there overnight. They might know his car. He would get a taxi.

A few moments later he was on the street, striding rapidly away from the approaching police siren.

* * *

Maggie turned her key in the front door. Thank God, she thought, he hadn't changed the locks. Then again, she asked herself, why should he? After all, she had walked out on him. The clock on the mantlepiece told her it was nearly two in the morning. She had walked along the strand at Goleen for over an hour after leaving Harry Vogel's house. His conversation had upset her. Maybe upset was the wrong description. More like confused.

The light in the sitting-room was still on, it's huge tangerine shade casting a warm orange glow across the room, on into the kitchen and across to the French doors. She could hear Jack snoring in the bedroom. So much for missing her. Then again, she did emphasise in her goodbye note that he wasn't to come looking for her.

Everything was exactly as she'd left it the morning before. He'd obviously been out all day and come back late and gone straight to his bed. Drinking? she wondered.

He'd left some photographs on the table, she noticed.

Black and white. Most of them quite old. Four large profile shots, all taken with different cameras, it seemed. She studied them. Young men, all fit-looking, all young and handsome. Army photos, by the looks of it and some documents half out of the A4 sized envelope, its sides partly torn through overuse, she guessed. One of the photos seemed to have been taken in the desert. One showed two of the men from the desert image at a graduation parade. The one that she picked up was the oldest. Slightly shabby and dog-eared.

The man in the photograph looked proud, almost sneering. He wore a brown shirt, with black leather buttons. Black tie. Black breeches. Black jackboots. Black tunic with four silver buttons; three parallel silvered threads on the shoulder tabs; on the left sleeve, an armband which appeared to be made up of three different colours. The buckle of his black Sam Browne belt glinted in the sunlight. Its holster held a 9 mm Luger pistol. A black cap with silver death's head and eagle. Black leather gloves. He was like a film star from a black and white war movie.

Maggie stood frozen, unaware that she'd been holding her breath, her eyes fixed on the face in the shot, the face of a sergeant from the German army, the Waffen-SS, with a swastika on his armband and his hand high in salute.

Maggie checked again for the sound of snoring. She picked up the photographs and placed them carefully back into the envelope.

She wasn't sure why she did it, but she slipped the photograph of the young sergeant into her bag.

15

Frankfurt International Airport. Saturday, May 18th

Bruno Proctor locked himself into a cubicle in the gents' toilets at Frankfurt Am Main. He checked his watch. 3.20am. He set the alarm for 5.20am, then bolstered his softish carry bag between the cistern and the wall, as diagonally as he could force it, and lay against it. He slept clumsily and uncomfortably for two hours.

From half-five, the tannoy in the gents' announced departures every ten minutes, in German first, then English. Then every five minutes. Then it became so noisy that Proctor would mutter angrily each time it spoke. *Fuck off, bastard!* he'd bark under his breath. By six he was shaving and freshening up. By six-thirty he'd booked himself onto EI 561 to Dublin, departing at 10.50am, arriving at 11.55am, Irish time. Doing so any earlier would have compromised his position if a bomb had gone off and the taxi driver had reported picking up the owner of the car and driving him to the airport. Doing so any later might have cost him his seat on the flight.

By 7.30am he was enjoying croissants and cappucinos –

five of each – in the small breakfast bar above the departures area. He had one final job to do before boarding the Aer Lingus A320. Luger had told him when he called back to his house the second time for identification, that Karla had mentioned Maister being booked onto the morning flight – American Airlines – to Philadelphia. He was not to board the flight under any circumstances.

At 10.40am Proctor took off his heavy coat and locked it in the cubicle in the gents' toilets. He walked to a secluded public telephone, rang the international operator and asked to be connected with the sales and reservations desk of American Airlines. As soon as he heard the official voice, he straightened up and closed his eyes. He shielded the mouthpiece and spoke slowly. "I will only say this once. I represent Arian Nations, and their crusade for worldwide white supremacy. We have placed a device on board one of your airplanes which is due to depart in the next few minutes. It is our intention to blow up flight AA342 to Philadelphia this morning, and we will continue our plan to seek revenge and wreak havock until you bastards stop employing mud people and nigger pilots on our aircraft. I repeat the bomb is already on board the plane." Proctor hung up immediately and walked away, shielding his face from the full view of the security camera.

It took less than a minute for the first armed police unit to arrive in the departures area. The area was sealed off. Passengers were told of a security alert and asked to be patient while airport officials carried out a routine check on board one of that morning's departures. The female voice sounded warm and comforting. "We apologise for what we expect will be a short delay and thank you for your patience." There was a pause and then the same voice: "Would Albert Dietrich, travelling to Philadelphia, please pick up the nearest courtesy telephone." It was a coded message, broadcast over the public address system to alert all security staff. Albert Dietrich was the code name for an explosive device.

Harald Buhler had just given flight clearance to the pilot of AA342. He watched as the Boeing 747 Jumbo Jet throttled, its bulbous roof reflecting the strong morning sunshine. He watched with admiration as the huge hulk edged forward, listening with a degree of envy as the co-pilot read out loud.

"V1."

Five seconds.

"V2."

The phone was ringing. Buhler cursed the interruption. He wanted to watch the Minotaur of aircraft lift into the sky. Then he wanted to say to the crew: *"Have a nice day"* in his ridiculous American accent. He grabbed the phone. "What!"

The voice was screeching. *"AA342 . . . don't let it take off. There's been a call . . . "*

Buhler didn't bother to listen to the full message. Another second and the co-pilot would call *VR*, the point of no return. Then the plane would have to lift off. It had no choice. If the pilot took it down again it would explode. Once off the ground, because of a full fuel load, it would take an hour before it could land safely. He held his mouthpiece close to his bottom lip: "AA342, we have a security alert." It was important to sound relaxed. Don't panic the crew, he thought. "Reverse throttle immediately. I repeat. You must *not* take off!"

He breathed deeply and bit his lip, leaning against the glass to get a better view of the plane as it raced towards the end of the runway. Then smoke. Then the shuddering sound of brakes. He sighed and sat down again. All in a day's work.

The passengers looked dazed and a little frightened as they shuffled back into the departure lounge twenty minutes later. All they knew was that one of the tyres under the left wing had blown out. Nothing to worry about, the pilot told the four-hundred-and-twenty-two-capacity full aircraft.

"I've never had to jump down an emergency shute for a bloody tyre before," one elderly woman muttered to her husband as they passed Proctor. He waited, watching carefully, for the man he would kill. No need for a crude, bulky weapon. Knives and guns would have been detected coming through the security checkpoint. He'd done without them for years and used his bare hands, preferring to surprise from behind. Best time to pounce was when his target was standing at the urinal, whistling while he enjoyed a good piss. Proctor would place his arm around the target's neck, forcing his head into the crook of his elbow. A swift thump to the side of the head with his free hand guaranteed a broken spine and almost instant death. No blood. Just urine, careful not to get it on his own trousers. The satisfaction of hearing Maister's neck snapping was slipping further away now. He wasn't on the first bus. Or the second. Or, five minutes later, the third.

Slowly it dawned on Proctor than the man he thought he would recognise the moment he walked into the lounge wasn't on the flight at all.

16

Cork International Airport, 9.35am. Saturday, May 18th

Ben Roper wore the looks of a man who had just suffered a bereavement. He was tall and attractive but it was clear to Jack Buckley by the way he walked through the arrivals hall that he was dogged by questions no one had been able to answer. He held a mobile phone to his ear and talked as he walked. It was a weary sort of stride, one no doubt he had become used to for over a week now.

Jack held the scribbled strip of cardboard at chest level, checking to make sure he still had the keys of Ollie Jenning's car, which he'd been kindly lent for a few days. He'd written Roper's name instead of his own. *Ben Roper.* The businessman seemed to see it but then just walked right past. He stopped and turned, his back to Jack, in heated argument with whoever he was talking to. Jack watched, craning his neck slightly to hear.

"I don't give a shit what you think. *Don't* threaten me. Of course he was old enough to go away for a weekend. What do you want me to do? Wrap him in cotton wool.

Listen. Shut up and *listen*! I'm fed up getting silly letters from your bloody solicitor. After all I'm the one who still foots the bill for all this nonsense. Hello . . . " He pressed *end* and switched the phone off, popping it into his pocket. He turned around. His paleness was gone now, replaced by a bright red anger and bulging eyes. "I'm sorry about that. I'm Ben Roper."

Jack smiled and held out his hand. "Jack Buckley." He rolled up the cardboard and shoved it into his jacket pocket. "Can I take your bag?"

"I'll carry it. It's only an overnight."

Jack nodded to the main entrance. "Planning on staying tonight?"

"Well, it makes sense. The last plane out of here is quarter-to-five."

He spoke softly and slowly, with an almost resigned tone of voice, as if waiting to hear the worst.

He was a tall man, mid-forties, Jack guessed, greying hair, receding slightly, broad. Probably played football at some stage.

"Mr Buckley, where is my son?"

Jack might as well have been hit in the face with a shovel. "Call me Jack." It gave him a few seconds. Ben Roper waited. "Let's get into the car and we can talk as we drive. We're about an hour from Durrus if the traffic's light."

The first ten minutes were spent in silence.

Jack was more concerned about his green fingertips and the small conspicuous blades of grass which were popping up all over him all morning, and still wouldn't go away. In his hair, under his shirt collar, under his arms, in his socks. The combination of the pouring rain and the pure roughness she had displayed, followed by the whiskey, had left him exhausted. He yawned and apologised. "Getting a bit of stick on the phone back there?" he said casually. He didn't want to appear too nosey.

"I'm used to it now. She rings whenever she thinks I might be enjoying myself. At lunch. In bed. In the middle of the night. First thing in the morning. In the middle of meetings."

"Your wife?"

"*Ex*-wife, actually. We're separated five years."

"Why don't you divorce her?"

"Because I'd have to give her half of everything I have, short of cutting off an arm and a leg. This way I control the purse strings. She can have practically everything she wants. Money, jewellery, nice holidays. Flash cars. Posh restaurants. I still pay for them all. But I'll be fucked if she's going to financially rape me and take half of everything I've spent the last fifteen years working for. I have very few fond memories of my wife, Jack. She makes my life hell. But at least it's partly consoling to know that everytime she reads about my success, she throws up."

Jack tittered. "Why did you marry her?"

"Because I thought I loved her. She was five months pregnant with Adam. It seemed like the right thing to do. I should have been as shrewd as you, Jack."

Jack looked sideways. "What's that supposed to mean?"

"Well, you're not married. Are you?"

"No. But how do you know that?"

"I just asked around. I thought if I was going to come down here to meet you, I might as well know a little bit about you. That's all right, isn't it?"

Jack shrugged. "S'pose so. What else do you know?"

"That you were a detective. Correction. The best detective in the business. Decent bloke. Fond of the old bottle."

Jack laughed. A sign of indifference more than anything. This man knew his stuff. Still, he wasn't going to be intimidated. The man's sensibility must be all over the shop, he reckoned. He glanced across at him discreetly. He'd cut himself shaving, just below his right ear. A touch of dandruff on his shoulder. A jacket that looked like it had been worn all weekend. A slight stench, not acute by any means; but a smell which told Jack he hadn't washed in a couple of days. Still, he seemed to be retaining great dignity in the face of adversity. God help him. He must be in hell.

"You still haven't answered my question, Jack."

Roper asked politely but his voice suggested that all time would be suspended until he got a reasonable answer, preferably the one he was looking for.

"I don't have an answer to your question."

There was silence again.

The storm had left a beautiful morning in its wake. The fields and the trees looked greener, the sky was dark blue, punctuated here and there by a great big puffy cumulonimbus. It was real May weather. "This is real May weather, isn't it?" Jack said, as if making the comment just for his own benefit.

Roper looked out to his left and said nothing.

Jack overtook the small tractor which had held them up for fifteen minutes now, and settled back into the seat for the long journey.

"I'd like a drink."

Jack almost swerved. His heart sped up. Jesus, he said to himself. "I'm sorry?"

Roper turned. "I quite fancy a nice pint of Guinness."

"Well, it's only ten o'clock." Who was he – Jack Buckley – to pass judgement. "If you can hold off for half-an-hour, I know a nice quiet little pub just outside Dunmanway." Jack was delighted. He could relax now.

"Any chance we could have that pint in the pub where Adam was drinking?"

Jack was beginning to understand his thinking. "No problem. That'll take us an hour."

Silence.

"You think my son is dead, don't you."

It wasn't even a question. "I never said that. I never assume anything."

"Not even that he was kidnapped?"

"I don't believe your son was kidnapped."

"Why not?"

"Because three people disappeared. Not just one."

Roper was waiting to hear more.

"Look, Mr Roper . . . "

"Ben . . . "

"Listen Ben, it's been all over the papers that you're a

very wealthy bloke. I don't begrudge you a penny of what you earn, or how you earn it. But you can be damn sure there are a lot of people out there who'd love to have just a teeny-weeny fraction of your fortune. And to relieve you of it as quickly and as deviously as possible."

"So kidnapping is still a possibility?"

"No."

"Why not?"

"Because this is West Cork. Because most people down here never heard of you. And even if they had, they wouldn't be able to tell your son from . . . " Fuck! He'd almost said it.

"Adam?" Roper smiled.

At least he had some sort of a sense of humour. "Ben, kidnappings on that scale happen on your doorstep. Two or three blokes who want to abduct your son do it on their own territory where they know where to hide out. Where they know they're safe. A bunch of Dublin gangsters aren't going to wait for some kid to come down to the remotest part of the country, then follow him here to kidnap him." Jack looked across at his guest. "Does that make sense?"

Roper was mulling over his answer.

"And if you don't mind me saying so, you're a bigger fish."

"What's that supposed to mean?"

"That if I was a kidnapper, I'd plump for you rather than your son. For a start, someone your age is far easier to control. You'll behave yourself if you're told to and you're less likely to try anything stupid like running away."

"How do you know?"

"Because I'd shoot you."

"And what *if* that's exactly what's happened to my son?"

"It's very unlikely."

"Why's that?"

"Because they would have had to shoot three boys, not one. That's when things turn very ugly." He waited. There was nothing forthcoming from the millionaire thinker. "I haven't convinced you, have I?"

"Maybe."

"Look. Do you think a bunch of nervous criminals are going to leave it this long before contacting you? They would've been on to you within a couple of hours. How long is it now?"

He ignored the question. "You're a good cop."

Jack decided it was better not to say anything about that. "If you like I'll book you into the Westlodge, just outside Bantry. You're about five miles from Durrus there and it's a lovely place. They've got a nice fitnesss centre and pool if you feel like relaxing for a couple of days."

"Thank you, but I've made arrangements to stay with an old friend for the duration."

"On Sheep's Head?"

Roper nodded.

"Do I know him?"

"Actually he speaks very highly of you, Jack."

"Really?"

"Alex Kline. He's the local estate agent."

Jack squeezed the steering wheel as the collar of his shirt dug into his neck and his blood ran cold, right down to the tips of his toes.

17

Almost fifteen minutes later, Jack Buckley noticed his passenger was asleep in the most peculiarly awkward way. Roper's head was still perfectly upright, as if he was keeping one eye on the road in front of him. It was an agonising slumber, by the sound of it, muttering sounds like musical notes and the odd plaintive sigh. Jack wasn't sure if he should be grateful for the time to think alone. This man was a personal friend of Alex Kline. But why should he be so concerned? Kline was a family man who loved his wife and doted over his children. He ran a reputable business, by all accounts. He was a bank manager in a rural location. Many of his customers looked up to him in the same way they might a doctor, or even a priest. They confided in him. A woman might tell him that her husband drank the money they needed to pay the mortgage. Or a man might admit to his gambling problem and Kline would arrange for a place on a counselling programme and organise a repayment scheme until the customer was back on the right track again.

"Please God," Jack whispered to the salient clear blue sky stretching out across the fields to his left, and beyond to Mount Corin which he could just about make out, "give me just one reason why I'm justified in hating Alex Kline."

No answer. God was obviously too busy cleaning up after the May storm the night before.

He tried to recall the first time he met Alex Kline.

It was the morning he arrived on Sheep's Head, and was unpacking the car. He had just turned around with a tea chest full of Maggie's old medical books buried in his gut and had almost tripped. "I've gotcha!" a big, well-overweight, balding character dressed to the nines shouted as he lunged forward and caught the box. He had the most extraordinary toothy grin that Jack could remember. Almost too many teeth to fit in one mouth. A big treble chin hung low over his starched shirt collar, definitely a size 20. And then there were his eyes. Huge bulging brown eyes, distended almost. And a great big hearty laugh, which sounded like a rolling cough as he grabbed the heavy instrument.

"You must've played rugby," were the first words Jack said to him.

"Too long ago to remember," was Kline's reply.

Maggie had accused Jack for years of being paranoid. Jack often mentioned to her that it was sad that Kline disliked him so much. Maggie laughed off the notion. "Kline is a busy man," she would explain. "He's got a lot on his mind. He probably doesn't even notice you half the time, Jack." But Jack would argue that Kline would go out of his way to avoid his company. "Maybe he's afraid of reformed alcoholics," Maggie often suggested. It was one sure way of bringing any conversation to a quick close. Jack hated to think that he was some sort of freakish side show that spiced up people's conversations at parties and the occasional official function that Kline invited them to. "Ye see that bloke in the corner holding the dressed orange? He's an alcoholic. Don't offer him a drink, whatever you do!"

His counsellor had told him to expect the occasional bout of paranoia in the early stages of recovery, as if the world and its mother had a private pass through a secret door into your mind and knew exactly what you were thinking. He got over it, like he had managed to cope with most things, but he couldn't help thinking that Alex Kline had singled him out, had always observed him in a unique way, from the moment he caught the tumbling tea chest and Jack had spotted the rugby techniques, and lately had come to look on him as different. Yes, he was a cop. But there was something more to this than just intimidation or officialdom. "Everyone has their own weakness," Jack used to say to try to explain away his alcoholism in the early days of recovery, "so what's yours?" Another foolproof way of killing a conversation stone dead.

Maggie thought Kline was wonderful, all those years back then, almost a father on loan. "Come to think of it," Jack had said to her one night, "it's strange that he married so late and fathered so many kids, so quickly."

"Jack," Maggie snapped in Kline's defence, *"the man's not some sort of stallion!"*

It used to annoy Jack that she was so close to Kline,

that maybe she was making up for some sort of absence that she had noticed in her relationship with Jack, maybe a comfort thing that only Alex Kline could give to her. He could drink, Jack couldn't. Maggie enjoyed her wines but always felt uncomfortable, almost selfish, drinking in front of the dipso, as he used to call himself. It was only natural to feel at ease drinking with another drinker. Jack had never been that sort of socialite. While everyone else drank pleasantly, and topped up their glasses at the behest of the host, Jack would work the room, as many as five large vodkas strategically placed on different tables, in varying positions around the function room. If he ran out, he'd drink anything, and anybody's. He remembered seeing Maggie, watching him from a distance, in tears one night. Then he realised he was drinking someone else's half-empty, half-stagnant pint of curdled stout which must have been sitting there for over an hour and tasted like piss. What made it more repulsive for him was that he didn't give a shit. He would drink to excel, to surpass, to feel that combustible level of numbness that only a hardened alcoholic could relate to, and then coma. "God, I'd kill for a drink," he muttered.

"I wouldn't mind one myself."

The croaky voice reminded Jack of Ben Roper, in the seat beside him. His passenger must have slept for three quarters of an hour at least. He wasn't sitting any differently to the way he slept, but now he was awake. "You probably needed that," Jack said, his way of breaking the ice.

Roper yawned. "Are we nearly there?"

"Twenty minutes." He looked across at Roper. He had closed his eyes again. Jack wanted to find out more about his relationship with Alex Kline. He probably wouldn't get another opportunity. Not if Roper was going to be Kline's guest for the term of his stay on Sheep's Head. And since Jack was no longer a cop on the case he would most likely get relegated to a position of busybody, if Kline had anything to do with it, and get shut out. "How long have you and Alex known each other?" He used Alex's name in such a way that Roper might think they were good friends.

Roper thought for a while. "Mmm, ten years, maybe more."

Jack thought back ten years to what he would have been doing, more so to get an angle on how old Roper would have been then. Kline was definitely older than this man. "Did you work together?"

Roper smiled. "No. He was my boss, I suppose."

"And now you're the boss."

"Yep. For all it's worth . . . I'm the boss."

"What do you mean by that?"

"Have you children, Jack?"

His question seemed pointed, almost poignant against the backdrop, the childhood appeal of the safe, beautiful, lush green countryside to their left, and the cold, barren, brown-rock face of the hills to their right. Bantry was only minutes away. Then, six miles further on, Alex Kline's sprawling mansion. "No. We've tried. But we've kinda given up now."

"Kinda? Does that mean that you no longer love each other?"

Jack shrugged. What kind of a conversation was this going to be? He needed information and here he was about to be lectured on life and it's ups and downs. Spare me! he almost blurted. "Where did the two of you work?" An attempt to swing the conversation back again.

"Girundbach in Shannon. Originally in Frankfurt, where the mother-company is."

Jack's mind began to race. He tried to recall the photographs. Then the newspaper cuttings. He couldn't remember if he had seen Kline's face. But then that was ten years ago. And the newspaper photos had faded badly with time. "What did Alex do at Girundbach?"

"He was one of the original directors here when the company relocated. I met him when I worked in Frankfurt."

"What was his position in the company?"

"Financial controller. Then Director of Financial Affairs."

"What was your position?"

Roper laughed quietly. "You probably wouldn't believe me if I told you."

"Go on."

"Head of the Post Room. That was in Germany. I hated Frankfurt. It was more homesickness than anything to do with the Germans. I met Kline at a function one evening. He told me I had great potential. That I shouldn't be wasting my time, that I should be planning ahead, and watching out for the right opportunities. He pointed me in the direction of evening classes. I spent my evenings and nights studying. First accountancy. Then business studies. Kline always had a kind of soft spot for me. Invited me to his house for dinner most Sundays. I ended up dating his next-door neighbour's daughter. That was twenty years ago. And we eventually got married. Me and Remy. And when Girundbach moved to Shannon, Kline asked me to take over running the day-to-day administration of the factory. Tough job considering I was in charge of two-thousand employees initially, increased to three-and-a-half within eighteen months."

Jack listened carefully, one half of his mind assimilating the information, the other half counting down the distance to his first drink of the day.

Roper continued. "But, believe me, Jack, all this pales in insignificance. I'd hand it all away if I could just know that my son is OK. Just to see him for five minutes and to know that he's safe. I'm grateful to you for giving me your time. I know you're extremely busy and this is probably only one case that you're working on, but I . . ."

Jack could tell he was on the verge of breaking down. He thought it strange that Kline hadn't told him about Leo Hannon, or the patrol car ending up in the sea, or his resignation from the force that night in the pub. For a moment Jack Buckley almost felt grateful to Alex Kline for one small mercy. It seemed grossly insensitive to steer the conversation back, yet again, but he knew he had to. "When did Alex leave?"

"Girundbach?"

"Yes."

"Eh, nearly five years ago."

"Why?"

"He was doing some work for the German embassy. Then that seemed to take a strange twist and he gave that up and moved here, I think. I haven't seen him in quite a while. He rang me when news of Adam's disappearance got out to the papers."

"What do you mean by a strange twist?"

Roper seemed to be surprised by Jack's question, as if he himself had never really given it much thought. "I'm not really sure. It never seemed to be a big issue. I would imagine he just wanted to ease back on the amount of work he'd been taking on successively over the years. Mainly because he was too busy, I suppose. Too many things on his plate. He had started dabbling in land by then. He had bought a fair slice down here here before he had even considered moving to Ireland with the company, I hear."

"How much?"

Ben Roper sighed. "I've no idea. Two thousand acres?"

The car almost swerved of its own accord. *Sweet suffering Jesus!* Jack's tongue dried up instantly and his eyes stung, they had been staring into the bright sunshine for so long.

"It seems like a lot of land, Jack, but you have to remember Alex Kline is a wealthy man. Twenty years ago, he had his money made. He was always a retiring sort of person, minding his own business, shying away from the limelight and the publicity of the papers and television. He always left that side of the business to his two directors. He was always talking about moving away to somewhere quiet. Somewhere no one would bother him."

"Who were they?"

"Who?"

"His two co-directors."

"They were the real kingpins of Girundbach. I never met them."

"Why?"

"Because when I was down in the basement sorting out all the post, they were in the penthouse making the decisions and earning the big money."

"Are they still involved?"

"No. They would have cleared off their desks nearly fifteen years ago."

"But Alex Kline would have known them. Wouldn't he?"

Ben Roper smiled. "Alex Kline would have been living in their pockets, Jack. Why do you ask?"

"No reason. Just curious, that's all." Jack would have spotted the tall steeple of the comfortable church in Durrus, like he did every day he drove back in from the city along the R591, and the scaffolding from the ongoing renovation work on the church's roof that Alex Kline, among others, had been so generous to support, and which the small committee wanted to have finished for the June Holiday Weekend, if his mind had not been trying to figure out how big ten thousand acres of prime land was. And, more importantly, how much it was worth.

They were questions he could find answers to with relative ease. But there was another question. Why, in his right mind, would a wealthy German industrialist want to buy that much land in the middle of nowhere so far from his natural home?

18

Cars and vans and tractors and bikes lined the small main street in Durrus that morning, up to the church and beyond as far as Hannon's public house. They were still there two hours later as the midday Angelus bell tolled more slowly than usual. Local businesses had shut down for the morning. The cluster of colourful buildings – eight in all – cream, pink, yellow, orange and white, all lacked life today. Clouds hung heavily on the Gearhameen hills in the distance. Tobin's family butcher shop would remain closed until two, as the small scrap of paper in the window announced. Reilly's hardware store had another message propped up in the window beside the dead wasps and the boxes of plugs with the faded red and yellow labels:

Closed until after the funeral.

No one ever knew what that meant. Tommy Reilly never decided until he could observe how upset he might become. This always differed from funeral to funeral. If he wasn't too bad he would reopen immediately after the church service. If he was slightly gippy he might have a pint or two and reopen after lunch. Considering that Leo Hannon had been a close friend no one expected the shop to open for a couple of days.

Jack Buckley cursed under his breath. An abandoned tractor, double-parked outside the church, meant that they could drive no further.

"There must be a funeral," Ben Roper said respectfully.

"Shit!" Jack remembered Leo Hannon's funeral. He started to reverse when he noticed he was blocked by a car behind.

"Whose funeral is this?" Roper asked.

"Leo Hannon, the local publican. He drowned the other night."

"You say that as if drowning's a regular occurrence. I presume it was an accident."

"Yeah." Jack was panicking. He wanted Roper to shut up and the bloke flashing at him from the car behind to vanish into thin air. *"Fuck!"*

"Calm down, Jack. I'll get a taxi if you like."

Jack cracked up laughing. "A *what*?" He slapped the steering wheel. "That's exactly what I needed . . . a good laugh."

"What's so funny?"

Jack pointed out the window. "You see this? This is Durrus. The population is one-hundred-and-fifty. Unemployment: zero per cent, or one-hundred per cent. It depends on what way you look at it. This is as rural as it gets, Ben." He pointed to the hills up the road. "Next stop, New York. There are no taxis here, Ben. No taxis, no buses, no fire brigades, no ambulances, no airports, no railway stations. In fact, you wanna know something else? You'll never find two of anything here. That's how unique we are. That's what we love about living here. There's no hurry about anything. You don't have to get out of bed in the morning if you don't want to. Why, *Jaysus*, you don't have to *go* to fucking bed if you don't feel like it! And that's why the people here love it. And you know what, it's starting to drive me fucking mad!" Jack jumped out of the car and slammed the door. "Let me buy you a drink, Ben. Welcome to Sheep's Head."

Most of the mourners had vacated the church, assembled in the cemetery, buried Leo Hannon and got their seats in the pub for soup and sandwiches inside of thirty minutes.

Jack stepped through the side door, like he had done the week before to hand his badge to the new Justice of the Peace. He checked behind him to make sure that Ben Roper was safely inside.

The mood in the pub was one of quiet disbelief and tangible numbness. Leo Hannon's loyal patronage was well represented, over a hundred mourners packed into a lounge built for no more than a comfortable fifty. Jack Buckley looked around him, studying the faces, trying to interpret their expressions. He turned to Ben Roper. "When you've known the same publican for most of your life and drunk nightly from his hands, losing him suddenly to his Maker is a bit like Noah ditching all the passengers in the Arc and telling them to fuck off and save themselves." Who would they talk to when they came in for a drink in the evening? Jack wondered. Who would lie to their wives when they rang Leo to find out "is he there?" And tell them that their dinners were in their respective bins. Not Martha. God knows, she'd shopped dozens of Leo's loyal drinkers down through the years. *And* she pulled a shite pint of stout.

Jack ignored the stares and the coughed comments. Alex Kline was standing exactly where he had shook hands with him the previous Friday night. Jack felt obliged to deposit his important passenger safely into the care of his host. God help him.

Kline turned around, holding a glass of white wine. "Ah, Jack. How are you?"

The smile and concerned tone of his voice almost convinced him that the man was genuinely concerned. Then he spotted Ben Roper.

"Ben!" he cheered, putting his glass down. He seized Roper's right hand, clasping it firmly with both of his. "How are you? I wasn't expecting you till after lunch. Have a drink."

A *drink!* Jack Buckley felt fresh and revived all of a sudden. He'd have a large gin and tonic, plenty of ice, down the hatch. Then he saw her. Martha Hannon, pulling pints, and passing bowls of soup and brown bread across the counter as if it was just another busy session. She always wore that morbid black dress for funerals; the one that made her look like Queen Victoria, as Maggie had always said, with her hair yanked back and tied up in a bun, and not a screed of make-up to disguise her harsh countenance. Today was different though, and Jack could see that plainly. The pressure was taking its toll. Every few minutes she would step through the door into the kitchen and, turning her back to the drinkers at the bar, she would wipe her eyes. "Hello Martha," Jack said thoughtfully. He tried to think of something else to say but it wasn't a time for experimenting with the sort of terms of condolence that he despised hearing other people using. He had often heard people say *sorry*. Sorry for what? he wondered. It was most definitely the one word he would not say to her today. "How are you?"

"I'm fine, Jack. How are you?"

Her voice was cold, its tone delving. Her question was more pointed than a dentist's needle. What she was really saying, he knew, was: What were you up to with my husband on Coosbrack Strand in the early hours of last Saturday morning that led to his death? In truth, if he had known the answer himself, he would have told her. "Fine," was all he could say. "A cup of coffee, please." He looked back towards Ben Roper. Alex Kline had his ear now, probably telling him what a loose cannon Jack Buckley really was and how the police were investigating him in connection with Leo's mysterious drowning at the wheel of Jack's patrol car. Just then, Alex Kline looked up and beckoned to Jack to join them. Jack was raging that Alex Kline would have noticed him staring. He picked up the mug of coffee, black.

"We got your car back this morning, Jack," Alex Kline said triumphantly.

"What car?"

"Your patrol car." Kline grinned, stuck out his chest and slurped his wine.

"*My* patrol car?" Jack wanted to run out of the pub.

He looked at Ben Roper. He was smiling too. Jesus Christ, what was all this about? "What are you talking about, Alex? I don't have a patrol car."

"Well, actually, I originally thought myself that it was beyond repair, what with the engine damage caused by the salt water. But I managed to source a second-hand engine for it in Macroom for three hundred quid." Kline put his glass down, looking quite giddy and excited at whatever was about to follow. "Here," he said, pointing to them to free up their hands, "follow me." He nodded to the side door, leading to the street and the entrance to the yard behind the pub.

Alex opened the barn door and nodded to the spot where Jack Buckley had carefully looked over Leo Hannon's Vectra only days before.

Jack gasped and felt weak.

The Astra looked brand new. On closer inspection it seemed as though someone had cast a magic wand over it and turned the clock back twenty-thousand miles. It had been to a serious panel beater, resprayed and decorated with new blue, red and yellow decals, a gleaming blue light replaced the one Jack had broken that night on the strand at Coosbrack, and the upholstery smelled of shampoo. Even the tyres had been washed and shined.

Jack reached out to touch the new trim below the driver's window, then looked back at Alex. Then at Roper, who seemed amused at the occasion. "What's going on, Alex?" Jack asked. He ran the back of his hand under his chin then across his mouth.

"I don't understand, Jack. Are you unhappy with the job on the car?"

"No, it's very nice actually, but why are you showing it to me?"

Alex appeared confused now. He laughed nervously. "Because, it's your car, Jack."

Jack slapped the roof of the Astra. "It's not *my* car, Alex."

Kline looked across at his guest. Ben Roper now seemed nervously unwelcome. "OK, Jack, you're right. In theory it's not your car, it belongs to the force. But it's your car as long as you're a sergeant here. Am I right?"

Jack felt short of breath, so much so that he held off answering for a second. It was like an intricate riddle, a trick question, with no logical answer. "I am not the sergeant here anymore. *You* know that, Alex."

Alex shook his head in mock disbelief. "I don't understand. Has something happened in the last couple of days that I missed? Are you saying that you've been promoted?"

"*Don't* play games with me, Alex!"

"Excuse me," Ben Roper said, almost apologetically. "I'll wait for you back in the lounge, Alex." When he saw that Alex wasn't acknowledging, he turned and left, closing the squeaky barn door behind him.

Alex Kline's broad smile was extinguished now; a cold, pursed-lips expression of anger remained. "What the fuck do you think you're doing?" His voice was cold.

Jack shivered. A beam of sunshine broke through the cracked corrugated roof and pointed to the spot in front of where Kline stood, making it difficult to see his eyes and mouth. "I resigned last Friday night. I handed you my badge. Remember?" He spoke quietly, yet forcefully, in sharp staccatoed whispers. "What is this charade?" He kicked one of the car's wheels. "I suppose you're going to tell me next that Leo Hannon's not dead."

"Leo Hannon is very dead. We all saw his body below in the funeral home. You saw his body the night he died."

A slight twitch of nerves. Jack buried it. "What are you talking about?" He wanted to ask straight out about the badge but knew he could be compromising himself by talking so honestly. "What are you implying?"

"Nothing, Jack. Relax." He sat back against the bonnet of the patrol car. "Leo Hannon drowned. Death by misadventure was what the coroner recorded. Check the death certificate if you don't believe me. Leo had been drinking. High alcohol level in the blood. Not a mark on his body." Alex Kline leaned back with the air of a man who had just proved an argument and was waiting now for the bet to be paid.

"How come my badge was pinned to his jacket?"

Kline studied Buckley's eyes for a moment. "What badge is this?"

"My police badge. Remember? The *badge* I gave you last Friday?"

"You didn't give me a badge last Friday."

"Jesus Christ, Alex!" Jack was fit to explode, exasperated by the mind game that Kline always loved to win, and to the best of Jack's knowledge, had never lost in all the time they had known each other.

"Look, Jack, if you don't believe me, ask Father Kerr. He told me he saw Leo Hannon last Friday night up on the rocks near Collack. If he had fallen, or jumped, the current would have taken him up past the cliffs at Glanrooncosh and onto the beach at Coosbrack. I swear to you. It's the truth, Jack."

Jack Buckley turned to leave.

"Jack."

He turned around. "What?"

"You're a good cop, Jack. We don't want to lose you here. You know how things are run and what the people are like. There's no reason why this whole nasty business can't be put behind us, and you and me get along well. Come on, Jack, you're a fair man. Don't throw it all away. You've too much to lose. Let's work together."

Jack listened to his words and watched his face as he pleaded. But he knew he wasn't pleading. He was warning Jack of what could happen. The unthinkable, Jack knew. He forced a smile. "You know, you're right. Maybe that's my problem, Alex."

"What's that?"

"That I'm a good cop." He pushed out the creaky car door and turned. "Are you around later?"

Alex nodded. "If I'm not in the bank, I'll be up at the house. I'll make sure Ethel has some fresh tea-brack waiting for you."

"Not too fresh. It spoils the taste. Where are the keys?"

Alex searched in his jacket pocket and grinned. "That's ma'boy!" He patted the sergeant on the back as he climbed into the small Astra and started the engine, forgetting Ollie Jennings' car sitting behind the tractor in the main street.

19

Jack Buckley parked the small gleaming patrol car on the exact spot, he estimated, where he had ditched it the previous Saturday morning.

The tide was well out now, almost on the turn. In the distance, out into Bantry Bay, he watched the gannet circle, hover and dive on its prey. A small herring, perhaps. Further out, the gulls squawked as they fought for the best vantage spot behind Mick Doolan's trawler, unmistakable because of the huge Irish tri-colour billowing near the stern of the brand-new vessel.

He felt he was standing on hallowed ground now, the spot where Leo had died, maybe calling for help, begging Jack to answer him as he tried to fight for his last breath. Then slowly slipping below the surface as a wave pulled him down, while his friend snored under the influence a few feet away. He shivered. The storm had brought a fresh north-westerly breeze in its wake. Despite the gusts and the racket of the birds, the place felt peaceful, offering him a brief escape back to another time and place when life hadn't been so complicated.

He wasn't sure what made him glance behind him,

back towards the patrol car. Ben Roper stood close to the passenger door, as if he was waiting for something to happen out at sea, searching from right to left, his hands pushed down deep into the pockets of his Eton jacket, pulled tight over a thick grey roll-neck sweater.

"I thought you'd be drinking hot whiskeys up at the big house."

"Gets a bit boring after two or three. I thought I might as well get a look at the beautiful scenery while I had a chance."

"Well, I suppose it loses part of its impact when you live here and you have to look at it every day of the year. How did you get here?"

"Alex's wife gave me a loan of her car. Told me the northern side of the peninsula was the most picturesque."

"Yep. She's right. It's also the most unpredictable."

"What do you mean?"

"Dangerous. Lots of cliffs, sheer drops, strong currents. You can drown very easily in three feet of water here. The currents take no prisoners. You're better off on the south side of the peninsula. Nicer beaches. Well, nicer than here anyway."

"Your friend?"

"Leo? Someone knows what happened to him. Unfortunately it's not me. So Ethel lent you her car. That was nice of her. She's an old sweetheart, is Ethel. I don't know how she stands Alex."

"He has his moments. Don't we all?"

"S'pose so."

Ben took his hands out of his pockets and cupped them, blowing hard into them. "Jack, I'll give you quarter of a million pounds if you find my son. That's confidential. No one else knows we're having this conversation, do you hear me? Not even Alex."

"Least of all Alex," Jack muttered, so low that Roper couldn't make out what he had said.

"What was that?"

"Nothing."

"Are you interested in the money?"

"Of course I'm interested in money. It's just that . . . "

"What?"

"I don't want to be getting your hopes up too high."

Roper backed away, putting his hands back in his pockets. "What's that supposed to mean?"

Jack knew he shouldn't have said anything. "Ben, I've been in this job a long, long time. I got awards for being a clever detective. For solving this and for cracking that. I'm really concerned about your son's well-being."

"What do you know?"

"I think your son and his two friends may have found themselves in the wrong place at precisely the wrong time. Has your son ever been in trouble before?"

Ben Roper shook his head. "Never. He almost used to worry me he was so mature and careful about what he did. Look, just tell me what you know, please."

"Does this belong to your son, Mr Roper?" Jack held out a carefully folded handkerchief.

Ben Roper slid the heavy contents of the hankie into the palm of his hand. He froze. "Jesus!" he whispered. He was holding a gold watch. "Where did you get this?"

"Tucked down behind the back seat in Leo Hannon's car."

20

Aidan Kerr was Durrus's Roman Catholic parish priest.

In fact he was the parish's only priest, apart from the Presbyterian minister whose church was adjacent to Aidan's and whose garden was full of slides and swings and toys for his children and a nice car for his wife; unlike Aidan's whose garden was over-run with weeds and briars, and whose house was always empty if he wasn't at home.

At thirty-nine Aidan Kerr was considered young for the position of PP. Too young, as far as some of the more conservative hardliners on Sheep's Head were concerned. It never fazed him though. He was popular with the younger people right across the peninsula, from Durrus to Kilcrohane, and on out past Drishane Bridge to Toormore, the latest venue for his Saturday night alcohol-free disco for the under 18s. This was his one saving grace from the point of view of the older parishioners, many of whom thought it disgraceful that he should jog to the church for nine o'clock Mass each morning wearing a singlet and a tight, skimpy pair of jogging knicks, and continue to wear them, and nothing else, under his vestments. The girls in the local Leaving Certificate class thought he was gorgeous. Their parents couldn't make up their minds whether to trust him or not, especially since he spoke out so liberally on contraception, divorce and homosexuality.

A few days after his arrival in Durrus, they took Jack Buckley's word for it that he was rock-solid and utterly dependable.

The message on the answering machine was received at 2.30pm. It seemed urgent and uneasy, Jack thought.

"Jack, it's Aidan. I'd really appreciate speaking to you as soon as you can. Give me a call this afternoon if you're not too busy . . . preferably to the house, if possible. Just a couple of things which happened that . . . perhaps I shouldn't . . . that I need to talk to you about. Thanks."

The message sounded slightly garbled, as if he sounded uncertain of what he wanted to say. It was shortly after three when Jack rang the doorbell. It was one of the old presbyteries, with a big, dark porch and a dull-looking door. The bell, Jack always thought, sounded like the one in the local fire station. All the time, he tried to imagine what was worrying Aidan so much. He was a calm sort of man who took all things, stressful or not, in his stride, and with a certain respectful sense of humour for good measure. That afternoon though, he sounded upset.

The door opened, the security chain still attached. The jangling sound startled Jack. "Are you hiding a woman in there?" he asked.

Aidan peeped out through the couple of inches into the afternoon sunshine. It took him a few seconds to smile and relax. He closed the door again and opened it fully, nodding to the sergeant to step inside.

"Are you all right?" It took Jack's sight a few seconds to adapt to the dark hallway. Aidan looked pale and unsettled.

"Would you like a drink?" Aidan asked.

Jack could see he had already poured a large one for himself. "Don't tempt me. I'm trying not to, and I'm not doing too well."

Aidan said nothing, just stared and waited.

"Ah, go on then. Just a small one." He sat down.

Aidan filled a tumbler half-full of neat Scotch, handed it to his visitor and sat down opposite him in front of the empty grate of the cold-looking fireplace. "You look like you've seen a ghost," Jack said.

"To tell you the truth I feel like I've seen a ghost. You didn't see a maroon-coloured car on your way up here by any chance?"

Jack shook his head, savouring the sharp, cold bite of the Scotch as it hit the back of his throat. "I wasn't really looking. Why?"

"There was a dark-coloured car, maroon I think, sitting outside the house just as I got back from the cemetery about an hour ago. A man and a woman in the front seat. They watched me drive into the garden. They waited until I got out of the car and then drove off."

"So what's the problem? They could have been at the funeral earlier on."

"I know most of the mourners. I shook hands with them. This couple weren't in the pub."

"Tourists?"

"Why would two tourists sit outside the local priest's house?"

"Loads of tourists sit outside my house. Maybe they were looking for directions."

"Then why didn't they ask?"

Jack shrugged his shoulders. "You're just not used to the tourist trail yet, Aidan. Thousands of people come down here every summer and just sit in cars and look out at the view. Often it's too bloody cold to get out of the car, so they just sit there and read the paper."

"What's so appealing about my house? Anyway they weren't reading the paper."

Jack laughed. "Of all people in this area, you are the last person I would've accused of being paranoid."

It was patently clear that Aidan didn't appreciate the levity in Jack's voice. "Leo Hannon came to me the night he died."

Jack wasn't laughing anymore. He put his unfinished drink up on the mantlepiece and stood up, his back to the fireplace. "What did he say?"

"Jack, it's important you know that he came to me in the confessional. So it must remain strictly confidential."

"*Bollox!* You brought me all the way over here this afternoon to give me that line of bullshit? Aidan, I don't believe Leo's death was accidental. Nor do I believe that he committed suicide. I will spend the rest of my life, if I have to, of the opinion that his death was planned and he was murdered." He sat down again and pulled his chair closer to Kerr's. "Aidan, listen to me, there's something very strange and very sinister going on around here at the moment. My belief is that quite a few people know what's happening but they're not prepared to talk about it. Leo Hannon came to me that night as well. But the damn superintendent rang me. By the time I got off the phone Leo had quietly slipped out the back door as if he'd got cold feet and changed his mind about whatever it was he wanted to tell me."

"What time did he call?"

The young priest sounded nervous now.

"Shortly after nine. I drove down to the pub to see if he had gone back there. No one knew where he was. Four hours later he was dead."

"Who found his body?"

"I did."

Aidan Kerr was shocked. "I thought the police found him in your patrol car. They're telling everyone that Leo was drunk and stole your car and drove it into the sea trying to kill himself."

"And what they're hoping people will believe is working. Can't you see? Leo knew something. Maybe he was coming to see me that night to make an official statement about whatever it was, but *they* got to him before I did."

"Who are *they*?"

Jack rubbed his face and reached out for his glass again. He nodded to the bottle on the table and knocked back what was left of his first.

Aidan poured him another.

"I have never seen Leo Hannon looking so scared as he was last Friday night. He was dressed up in his Sunday suit for some reason, like as if he was waiting for the devil himself to appear and frighten him to death."

"Well, someone obviously had done a pretty good job of it before he called to you."

"What do you mean?"

"He came into the confessional at half-past-eight, just after the evening Mass. I had seen him from the altar and noticed he didn't receive communion, which he always did on a Friday and Saturday nights. He knelt towards the back of the church with his head down all the time."

"So? Is that unusual?"

"Unusual? Leo Hannon never sat any further back than the fifth row. He sang and answered and generally took a very active part."

"So what happened after Mass?"

"Well . . . " Aidan Kerr sipped his Scotch and took a deep breath, exhaling it slowly, almost shivering as he bowed his head. "May God forgive me for telling you this, Jack, but I know that Leo would have wanted me to tell you. Apart from being such good friends, he obviously needed to get this off his mind. I was after hearing three confessions when he stepped into the cubicle."

"How did you know it was him?"

Aidan Kerr looked rather indignant at the question. "Because he was next in line. And also because I'm not stupid. Leo's voice was unmistakable. You should know that."

Jack nodded to him to continue. He checked his watch. It was twenty-five to four in the afternoon. Maybe this was going to be the moment when the events of the last week would finally begin to make sense.

"I could hear him coughing and clearing his throat, and shuffling around on his knees to get a comfortable spot. Then he mumbled something as if he was rehearsing. He was whispering to himself. Every few seconds he said *'Sacred Heart of Jesus I place all my trust in Thee'*. I slid the small panel back and waited for a second. There was dead silence, and it was pitch black in there. I couldn't see a thing. I started the rite of absolution and . . . "

Jack interrupted. "What did you say?"

Aidan paused. "Jack . . . please, let me be the decider of what I can and can't tell you. OK?"

"Come on, Aidan, I need to hear everything."

"Leo stayed very silent, almost deathly still for – it must have been – about three minutes before he said anything. I decided not to rush him. I could hear him breathing deeply, very unevenly, almost wheezing as he fought to get the words out. I told him it was all right, that there was no hurry, that we had all night. Then he said . . . "

Kerr put his head down into his hands and sniffed. Jack realised he was crying. He reached out and put his hand on his shoulder. "It's OK. You take *your* time." He patted him firmly and sipped his Scotch. Sweet sufferin' Jesus, he thought, what's goin' on here, for God's sake!

Aidan Kerr took out a handkerchief and blew his nose. He wiped his eyes and sniffed hard. "He told me he had done something terrible which he thought I wouldn't be able to forgive him for. But he had to come to tell me anyway in case anything happened to him."

Jack felt frozen to the seat of the wooden chair. "And?"

"I told him that anything he told me was strictly between himself and the Lord Jesus Christ who would find it in his heart to forgive anything once we were truly sorry for our sins. That seemed to help him to relax for a minute or two. He seemed to be trying to compose himself even more. I could see the queue getting longer outside the confessional and the woman in the cubicle on the other side was making an awful fucking racket. But I didn't give a shit about her." He looked up at Jack Buckley. "Do you know what, Jack. If Jesus Christ ordained me and put me in this parish for one thing and one thing only, it was to listen to Leo Hannon that night. I wanted to stick my head out through the curtains and tell the lot of them, fucking nosey busybodies, to piss off home and do something useful with their lives. Same faces, same time, every fucking Friday night. Same petty, little venial sins. 'I forgot to say my prayers, Father. I called my husband a bastard, Father'. Fuck them all, every last one of them."

Jack knew Aidan Kerr had been drinking long before he'd called shortly before three that afternoon. "So what did Leo say?" He tried to ask the question in a friendly, coaxing voice.

"He told me he had committed a terrible crime that he would go to hell for."

Jack waited, drawing out the time a little. "What sort of a terrible crime?"

"He explained to me that he had been working in the pub the Saturday night before. It was shortly after eleven and there were a few young lads from Dublin causing a bit of commotion. Then one of them broke a glass, and started giving cheek to Martha Hannon when she told them they'd have to leave if they didn't behave themselves. So Leo told them to leave."

"Did they?"

"Eventually. But it didn't end there. Leo was washing glasses in the kitchen when he heard his car leaving the carpark at crazy speed, the wheels spinning and the engine screeching. He ran out to find Tom Reilly still at the bar. Tom was going to use Leo's car to drop a couple of elderly customers home because it was raining and he'd obviously left the engine running while the ould fellas were putting on their coats."

"So what happened then?"

"Well, to be honest, it would've been easier to pull one of Leo's wisdom teeth than to get much more out of him. He started getting very upset at that point, swearing to me that he didn't mean to do anything."

"How many kids were there?"

"Three."

"How old?"

"Late teens."

Jesus Christ, Jack whispered. He had been right all along. "What happened the young lads?"

"He wouldn't tell me. All he kept saying was that they didn't mean to hurt them. He kept shouting at them to stop."

"Shouting at *who*?"

"Whoever he was with."

"So they must have caught up with the young lads who stole Leo Hannon's car?"

Aidan nodded. He was as white as a sheet now, and trembling. "He was nearly hysterical at that point. I told him he would have to go to the police. Then he started shouting at me, calling me names. I told him that I'd go with him if it made it any easier. I tried to explain to him that I couldn't just absolve him of his sins if he didn't tell me exactly what had happened. But he was incapable of making any sense by then. I kept saying that if he had committed a serious crime in the eyes of the law that God could only absolve his sins if he reported it to the police. He just kept crying, like a little child, whimpering the words, 'sweet Jesus, forgive me'." Aidan reached for the bottle, causing it to topple. Jack caught it. "A large one?"

"Please."

"What happened then?"

He pushed out the door and staggered down the side aisle toward the main door. I could hear it banging shut. By the time I got to the main gate there was no sign of him."

"Think, Aidan, did he give any clue as to who *they* were? The people with him?"

"No." Aidan nodded, staring ahead at the fireplace, cradling the tumbler of Scotch in his hand. "Maybe if I'd just blessed him and told him everything was fine he'd still be alive today. Wouldn't he?"

Jack was quick to shake his head firmly. "You don't know that, Aidan. Maybe if I hadn't left him standing in my kitchen so long that night while I took a phonecall he might be still alive. What if, what if, what if? If I got a pound for everytime I asked myself what if, I'd have retired to somewhere sunny and sandy long before now." He waited to see if there was anything else.

Aidan sighed. "There must be someone who knew what was going on inside Leo Hannon's head that night."

Jack reached out from his chair and grabbed his jacket. "I know someone who might be able to tell us."

21

Martha Hannon had her back to Jack Buckley.

He knew she was watching him in the mirror, out of the corner of her eye, as she shone the wine glasses and placed them meticulously, half-an-inch apart, on the top shelf. It wasn't often that drinkers ordered wine in her pub. But they were her friends, come to sympathise with her, so she didn't mind taking down the good glassware.

And now it was *her* pub.

Jack thought it odd that she had changed out of her black dress.

"Life goes on," she said in a resigned sort of voice as she turned around. "Is that what you're saying to yourself, Jack Buckley?" She looked up at his peaked hat, bearing the shiny badge of justice and authority. She dabbed at the counter with the tea towel. "I doubt you'll be drinking with that yoke on your head. Then again, nothin' about you will ever surprise me, Jack Buckley. You must have a lot of friends in high places."

"What's that suppose to mean, Martha?"

"I want to know what happened to my husband

above at Coosbrack last Friday night!" she bayed, poking him with her wet fingers.

It was the first time he had seen tears in her eyes. Perhaps it was selfish, but he really had believed that she would have been glad that Leo Hannon was dead. Now Jack wasn't so sure. Maybe it was the other way round, that she had made *his* life a living hell. "I don't know what happened to Leo, Martha. I'm still trying to find out."

"So why did you run away then?"

"What's that supposed to mean?"

"I saw you handing your badge to Alex Kline that Friday night. Then you got your bottle of vodka and went looking for my husband. What did he ever do to you, except feed you the alcohol that wiser folk tried to keep away from you."

"Listen to me, your husband came looking for me that night. He was deeply troubled, and, for all I know, *in* deep trouble. Who were the men in here that night after Leo's car was stolen?"

"There were a lot of men in here that night, Sergeant. The pub was packed."

"I don't mean in the pub. Who followed Leo into the carpark and went after the stolen car with him?"

"I don't know who you're talking about." She went to turn away.

Jack leaned across the counter and grabbed her by the shoulder, spinning her back and almost knocking her over. "Three teenagers are missing for almost a fortnight. They were last seen here. Your husband told me last week that they'd been drinking here that evening. I can bring one of their fathers in here now and tell him that you might know what happened to his son, since you broke the law by selling alcohol to him and his friends that night, three minors, all under the age of consent. That's a criminal offence. And I'd say, judging by the state his mind is in right now that he would go berserk." He let go of her shoulder.

She seemed to be about to say something but she quickly shut up. "I don't know who they were."

The one phone call Jack Buckley took on his mobile that afternoon, at exactly 3.45pm, when he was leaving Aidan Kerr's house, had made his day. He wasn't quite sure why, on immediate reflection, but he was certain it would show up in the scheme of things, which was progressing nicely, as an important development. He had made a conscientious decision that morning, on the way to collect Ben Roper from the airport, that he would no longer buy his booze in Durrus, or in any of the bars or off-licences in the area. He was sick and tired of the locals knowing his business. From now on, no one would get close to Jack Buckley unless he wanted them that close.

Little did he know how wrong he was going to be. His next stop was Alex Kline. He rang Ethel to check if he was there. No. He had dropped off Ben Roper and was playing golf in the garden, she told him. Ethel loved the notion of being filthy rich. She imagined it was a golf course but it wasn't. It was a tidy little green at the end of a half decent fairway. Alex used it as a driving range. It was the closest he got to his favourite sport. Sheep's Head didn't have a golf course. Nor was it likely to in the foreseeable future, since no one on the peninsula played golf.

Jack waited until Alex had hit the ball hard and given a huge grunt before he said anything. "Nice shot," seemed to be an appropriate comment even though Jack hadn't been watching the ball. It could have been a shite shot for all he cared. Two thousand acres was all he could think of.

Alex didn't seem bothered by the intrusion. "Thank you," he replied generously. "What can I do for you, Jack?" He bent to pick up the tee.

"What's your game?"

Alex spun around and stared at him. "Golf." He raised his club. "God's gift to gentlemen. You should learn how to play."

"I reckon I'm in enough trouble with God as it is."

"Oh don't be so hard on yourself, Jack." Alex held out a club. "Fancy a swing."

"No thanks. I wasn't talking about golf. And you know that. There are some very strange things going on around here, Alex."

"I know."

"Really?" Jack folded his arms and leaned back against the white garden table. "What do you know?"

Alex shoved the golf club into the caddie car and pulled out a putter, turned the two-wheel trolley and moved off in the direction of the green. Jack realised he was pulling a splinter here. He walked slowly behind Kline.

"I know you've been acting totally irresponsibly lately, Jack. But I do like you. That's why I decided to help you out."

"Help me out? What's that supposed to mean?"

Alex stopped halfway to the green and turned back. "I think it's fair to say I've just saved your bacon from your bosses." He started to walk again, more briskly now. "Your colleagues were trying to figure out why you would want to murder Leo Hannon. I convinced them it was death by misadventure, that Hannon had stolen your car and driven it into the sea after a day's drinking, couldn't get out of the seat belt before the tide came in and – hey presto – he drowned. They believed it. Case closed, Hannon gets buried. And I don't even get a 'thank you very much, Alex' from their number one suspect. That's gratitude for you."

"That's not what happened, is it?"

"I'm not interested in what you did, Jack. The case is closed. you ought to be thankful for that."

"Interested in what *I* did? I didn't do anything, Alex."

Kline stood up straight and laughed loudly. "How the fuck would you know anything? You were drunk most of that night."

"How do you know I was drunk? Did you see me lying beside the patrol car on Coosbrack strand when you arrived with Leo's body? You must have got quite a shock. It was probably you who gave me the kick in the ribs to see if I'd wake up. It was, wasn't it, Alex?"

"You're full of shit, Buckley. I should have just left you lying in the gutter, let them throw the book at you."

"Why didn't you?" Jack squatted on his hunkers and pulled at a small tuft of grass.

"Because, despite what you might think, Jack, I do have a soft spot for you. I like Maggie. And I think, it's fair to say, that most of the people in the area like you and don't want to see you go to prison. So I decided to lie for you."

It was Jack's turn to laugh. "You're afraid of me, Alex, aren't you?"

"Afraid of *you*?" he gecked. "*Ha*, I'm not afraid of anyone, Jack. In the eyes of the law I'm the most senior person in this whole area. I can click my fingers and get a warrant for your arrest. Thumbs up, thumbs down . . . wasn't that Julius Caesar's way of sparing the lives of the ancient Christians, Jack. Well, I've given you the thumbs up. So don't push it!"

"You want me back on the job so that you can keep an eye on me. Isn't that right?"

"Don't be ridiculous. If you really want out then I'll accept that. I'm not forcing you to stay. Only your superintendent can do that."

Peace settled for a few seconds.

The subject changed. Twenty questions. The time has come, Jack said to himself. "Let the games begin."

"What?"

"Isn't that what Julius Caesar used to say before giving the thumbs down?"

"What are you talking about, Jack? You're wasting my time."

"You own a lot of land around here, don't you?"

Alex thought about his question. "I have a few acres, yes."

"Two thousand acres to be precise."

"And what if I do?" Alex smiled uncomfortably, trying to concentrate now on getting the ball the four feet to the hole.

"It beats me why someone who lives in Frankfurt for most of his life, practically owns a German company that's worth millions and relocates to Ireland to set up a huge operation here, doesn't go back to Germany to retire."

"That's ridiculous, small-minded thinking, Jack. My daughter moved here and my wife wanted to be close to her. So after I set up the company, we moved down here for a quieter life. What's wrong with that?"

"Oh there's nothing wrong with wanting to live here. I think it's the most beautiful place on the planet. My compliments on your choice. But your daughter lives in Dublin. It's almost easier to get to Germany from here than it is to get to Dublin. What I'm saying is that it's odd that someone like you would want to buy up two thousand acres of wilderness on a tiny piece of land jutting out into the Atlantic Ocean."

Alex suspended his all-important shot. "What the fuck are you talking about? I'm really very relieved that I don't have much of a taste for alcohol if this is what it does to your brain, Buckley!"

"I'm not surprised you don't have a taste for alcohol, Alex. There's been so much shite coming out of your mouth for as long as I've known you, I'm surprised you can taste anything at all!"

Alex Kline bent down over the club, pretending to ignore Jack.

"You know what happened to those three boys, don't you?"

The ball overshot the green and disappeared into the lush shrubbery. But he didn't curse. He looked up, still stooped. "What are you saying?"

"I'm just saying that you know what went wrong that Saturday night after those three boys were asked to leave Hannon's pub."

Alex chortled and coughed. "I know about as much as anybody, Jack. I'm sorry I can't help you."

"Why do I think that there are quite a few people around here who know what happened?"

"As I say I wish I could be of some help." Alex walked to the shrubbery and poked at the hydrangea plant with the club.

"Recognise this?"

Alex looked around. Jack was taking his leather boot out of a brown plastic bag. "That's mine. I was looking for that. Where did you find that?" He reached out to grab it.

Jack pulled back. "I kinda borrowed it the morning I called last week."

Alex was speechless, watching his boot dangling by its lace.

"Do you know Frank Tubridy?" Jack handed him back his boot.

"Should I?"

"Maybe not. He works for the forensic division in Cork. He called me up this morning. See, I sent him a little sample of that funny-coloured caked muck on the bottom of your boot. I noticed it when I called last week. It looked similar to the mucky-shit that was all over the wheels and rear-guards of Leo Hannon's car when they got it back after it had been stolen." Jack took a small transparent plastic bag from his leather jacket. "You see this?" He took out of a prickly piece of tree sprig. "These little fellas were all over the car. Maggie says they only grow on one part of the peninsula. That's out around the Ballyroon mountains. She said it was something about the wind and the climate, and being almost surrounded by the sea. It's the only place you'll find them."

"So how does that involve me?"

"Well, I just thought that since the muck on the car and the stuff on your boots are identical that you might have been out that direction."

"I was."

Jack felt his heart almost miss a beat. He tried to hide his surprise. It was difficult. "Why?"

"Because I hunt out there most weekends."

"Hunt?"

"Shoot. Mainly wild fowl. The odd wild fox. I'm a member of Seefin Gun Club." He took out his wallet and produced a small identity card. "There you are."

"What do you shoot with?"

"Colt .22. Reliable. Pretty harmless."

"Only when it's empty." Jack glanced over the membership. "Can I see it?"

"No." He kept his back turned now.

"Why?"

"It's away being repaired."

"What happened to it?"

"The trigger was sticking."

"Painful."

"It's not of the sort of thing you try to rectify yourself if it starts acting up on you."

"Too right. Where is it?"

"Jeffersports. They're in Pearse Street, in Bandon. If you don't believe me."

Jack zipped up his jacket and nodded. "I'll let you get back to searching for that ball." He turned. "Oh, one more thing, Alex. Maybe I'm going mad. But it's worth asking anyway. What should I do if I find Leo Hannon's fingerprints on your rifle?" Jack watched closely for his reaction. The question didn't appear to surprise him. Quite the opposite, in fact.

Alex Kline was irritated more by the missing golf ball judging by the way he was thrashing at Ethel's hydrangea plants. "You're a daft, feckless bugger, Buckley. Unless you're gonna dig him up and ask him to hold it, I'd say it's very unlikely."

"Isn't it funny."

"*What?*" Kline asked, exasperated.

"In all the years I knew Leo Hannon, and sat at the bar of his pub and drank with him into the early hours, he never once told me he was a member of Seefin Gun Club."

Alex looked back at him, contempt in his eyes. "Leo Hannon wasn't a member of Seefin."

"I thought as much. I did a routine check and he's not a legally registered firearm holder." Jack stretched out his arm and slowly, revealingly, opened the palm of his hand. Five bullet shells. "They're .22 calibre, aren't they?"

Alex Kline took one look. "They are. Where did you get them?"

"They were in Leo Hannon's jacket pocket when I pulled his body out of the water last Saturday morning. Maybe it was Leo who broke the trigger on your rifle." He tried to sound slightly tongue-in-cheek.

Alex Kline whooshed first with a big gaspy breath of air, then laughed at the notion.

Jack would have believed it to be a genuine laugh if Alex hadn't tried to sustain it, and turn it into the sheepish disguise of a desperately troubled man.

22

Aidan Kerr was standing in the porch as Jack swung the car right and in through the gates of his house.

They were badly in need of a coat of paint, pretty much like the rest of the house. But they were by no means a priority. Jack was badly in need of a drink. He tried to concentrate on the radio news but gave up on the first headline. He slammed the door behind him, not bothering to lock it. "Howya," he shouted, delighted to see a friendly face.

"How did you get on?" Kerr asked.

Jack scratched his head with the halldoor key. "I'm turning up lots of stuff. Good definitive evidence. But it's not going anywhere really." He opened the door and pushed it inward. "Come in." He walked ahead and threw his jacket across the bannister.

"This must be for you," Aidan Kerr said, holding the small, neatly packaged box.

"What is it?" Jack asked.

"Don't know," Aidan replied, gently shaking it. "No name but it was in your porch." He handed it to Jack.

Jack shook it again, more vigorously this time. "No writing on it at all. No postage stamp. Unless it's medicine that Maggie ordered from Cork."

"Surely that'd have her name on it."

Jack started to peel away the Sellotape, then the brown paper. Then another layer of paper. Inside was a small carboard box, tightly closed. Jack opened it at arms' length. A small card lay on top of the jelly-foamed bag. He opened the card and read the message silently first. Then aloud.

"Whenever there is a carcass, there the vultures will gather."

Jack looked to the priest for inspiration.

Aidan Kerr looked puzzled and anxious. "It's scripture, from the gospel of Matthew, chapter 24. It deals with the beginning of the end, so to speak. What's in the box?" he asked guardedly.

Jack took the sealed plastic out, holding it between his finger and thumb, and put it on the table and started to open it out. It took a second, no more, for the two men's minds to meet. Then their eyes, and an indication of the sheer horror and revulsion both were experiencing instantaneously. Jack Buckley could feel himself starting to shake uncontrollably as he watched Aidan Kerr vomit onto the kitchen floor. Jack wasn't sure if the scream he heard was his or Aidan's. The whole room was swimming now, as he felt the surge in his own throat, a deep need to be sick himself. He held his hand to his mouth and stepped back once, then another bigger step, trying his best not to look down at the special delivery, trying to get as far away from the table as he could.

As far away as he could from the decomposing tongue.

* * *

There had been another funeral much later that day, less newsworthy, less overrun.

Nellie Fennelly had finally succumbed to pleurisy. The asthma had got the better of her since she lost her false teeth and "that bloody inhaler", as she called it, wouldn't stay steady or sit right in her mouth. "Not bad for a ninety-seven-year-old," as she often said herself.

The small cemetery on the hillside beside Doneen Pier, overlooking Dunmanus Bay, was regarded by many of the locals as the most serene and scenic spot on the peninsula. "From the earth we came and to the earth we must return," the local priest had said in his sermon as he prepared to bury another of her golden oldies. Maggie hadn't set foot inside a church for years. Ten years, she reckoned, with the exception of her best friend's wedding six months before. Normally she didn't go to funerals. What was the point? she asked herself. There was enough sadness in life without adding to the confusion. As for Mass, she just couldn't see the point. A man in ridiculously outdated clothes extolling the virtues of something that made no sense whatsoever. She would have liked to have paid her last respects to Leo Hannon, and say hello to Martha, but she was afraid she might bump into Jack in the pub, pissed and making a show of himself yet again.

She sat in her car as they carried Nellie Fennelly's

little pine coffin through the rickety gates of Verity churchyard just hours after they had dropped Leo Hannon's into his freshly dug, mulchy hole. Her husband was waiting for her in his grave. He'd been waiting for nearly twenty years, tucked away in the corner of the small triangular field, six feet under the heavy bending branches of the green willow. Now they were going to be together again.

Maggie wondered if it would be the same for herself and Jack. Who'd go first? Probably Jack if he kept up the drinking. He wanted to be cremated, he'd told her, after overdosing on whiskey. Maggie had joked that they'd have to have a fire engine on stand-by just in case they couldn't put the fire out.

It was pure coincidence that Nellie Fennelly's funeral was taking place when she stepped through the door of the church that afternoon. She hadn't been able to sleep well all night, twisting and turning, mulling over the things Harry Vogel had said, more poignant than ever now that she had seen his photograph. She'd opened the glove compartment again and studied the photo without touching it. It was definitely him. She had no doubt.

The brief ceremony was over quickly and the small crowd of fifteen – no more – had dispersed before Maggie closed the car door behind her and faced into the stiff Atlantic breeze. A man with a hunchback was shovelling clay into the grave, pebbles and stones making a crackling hailstone-like sound as they landed on the wood below. She walked past the tiny grave and on towards the bottom of the field, closest to the sea and a dying sun that was turning the low, streaky clouds orange and brown, where a man sat on the ledge of another grave, one that was visited regularly and well cared for. She knew he could hear her getting closer on the narrow gravel pathway. It didn't seem to distract him from his conversation. The weather. The boredom. It was only when she stopped that he looked up and to his right.

"The widow Fennelly?" he asked without looking at her.

"Yes," Maggie replied.

He looked up at the dark blue sky and just nodded. "Not too many of us left now," he said softly.

Maggie waited. "How many?"

Harry Vogel seemed to think for a moment. "Only four of us in our seventies. Jim Maher. Mad Mick Doolan. Sean Quinn. And me. All the others are much younger." He laid the small bunch of freshly cut daffodils at the foot of the headstone.

In memory of
BREGA HAHN
Born December 24th 1926
Died May 18th 1993

Maggie noticed the date. "This is her anniversary?"

The old man nodded. "Five years today. And it always only seems like yesterday."

"But you never mentioned it last night."

"Often I forget. Sometimes I can't remember dates. But seasons remind me well of specifics and things I should remember."

"Did she like it here?"

"Loved it." He ran his fingers across the small off-white pebbles that he had raked with the small trowel he had used to bed the potted plant of tiny delphiniums in the earth below the headstone. "They were always her favourites. They reminded her of home, she said. She was an extraordinary woman."

Maggie thought it was an especially nice way to describe his wife. "What was the one quality you always remember her for?" She could tell he thought it an unusual question.

"She had many wonderful qualities. I suppose the one I will always be grateful for was her total acceptance."

"Acceptance of what?" Maggie sat beside him, at an angle, on the narrow ledge.

He fiddled playfully now with the trowel, like a young child with the beach sand. "It's hard to define. I often wonder what it means, what it is like, to accept another person totally, utterly unconditionally, and to never despise them for any of their own qualities. Does that make sense?" He smiled at her, his thin, whispy hair flying around his forehead.

"Not really."

"You are so much like Brega, Maggie. Or perhaps, I should say, she was so much like you. You are a very unique, matchless individual, Maggie. The beauty of your qualities is that you cannot see how special, and how important you are, and have come to be, to other people. People like me, whose lives you have enriched by simply just being there.

"This man you would like to marry, who you say you have left, you miss him terribly, don't you?"

Maggie stalled for a moment, then nodded.

"Something you don't realise is how close he is to you, how much you have come to mean to him in all the years you have been together. You want him to marry you. Why?"

"I don't know. I suppose I'm getting older. All my friends are married. Well, have been married. The last one to get married last year split up four months later. But it's just for that few months, or even weeks, just to be able to experience that bond with someone you thought you could never get any closer to."

"And wreck it?"

"What's that supposed to mean?"

He shivered a little now, the sun disappearing behind the giant willow. "Sometimes we don't realise how lucky we are, and how special that other person is until they're no longer here. Don't get me wrong, Maggie. I can still feel Brega's presence around me most of the time. But the loneliness of not being able to reach out and touch her cheek, or feel her hand on your arm, or to look up from a book you've been engrossed in for hours and find her watching you, engrossed in you. They are the things I miss. And especially, listening to her breathing in her sleep late at night. And moving onto the warmth she left behind in the bed each morning when she got up to prepare the porridge. It's just not the same."

"What isn't?"

"Everything. Even the porridge is awful, the mornings I make it."

Maggie sighed. "I suppose I just want to be able to experience that elation, that excitement they have all felt wearing beautiful clothes and being driven to the church in a shiny, black car. And walking up the aisle, being given away by someone you love. Someone who cares for you."

"Who would that have been?"

Maggie smirked. "You."

Harry Vogel's face beamed. "Why, thank you. I never thought I would hear anything so nice and thoughtful again."

"Have you ever thought about getting married again?"

He laughed and stared out at the sea. "Is that an offer?"

Sometimes Maggie wondered what it would be like to marry him. He was in his seventies, she in her late thirties. It wouldn't have been so unique, so grotesque, in this day and age. Maybe around Durrus people would be shocked. But not when placed in context with the worldly scheme of things. "I know what you mean," she said.

"What do I mean?" he asked quizzically.

"That we have a good thing going. Why fix it when it's not broken. Isn't that what you mean?"

He nodded gently. "Yes. And no. I do not know this man of yours. What I do know of is what you have told me during the good times. And I think I would be right in saying there have been many good times?" He knew Maggie would nod.

She did. "Loads."

"There can be many more of those times if *you* want there to be. Why do you need a church ceremony to make you happy? I don't think you can be any happier than you were before you decided to leave Jack. Isn't that true?"

She agreed, annoyed with herself that Harry Vogel could read her mind like a textbook. "You're very perceptive."

He grinned. "I probably got that from Brega. She was the most perspicacious woman I ever knew."

"Is that why you married her?"

"We were never married, Maggie."

Maggie was instantly shocked. "But you said you were."

"Well, it depends how you see it. We thought we were. So we were. We didn't need to see some routine certificate in a frame on the wall to remind us how much we loved each other. Brega was very like you. She thought for many years, because we never married in an official capacity, that I never loved her."

"My father never married my mother." Maggie hadn't expected to say it. She was bewildered by her unlooked-for honesty. "I don't know why I said that." She had never spoken to Harry about her parents before.

"Yes, you do. You think your mother was unhappy because she wasn't married. You think that it's easier to hold onto someone you love by legally tying them into an unnatural bond."

"No, I don't."

"Were you close to your mother?"

"I never met her."

"And your father?"

"I never met him either." Maggie hesitated. "I never told you . . . I don't like to talk about it . . . but my parents lived in Germany before the war. He enlisted in the German army like all young men had to do. And in July 1942 he went off to fight on the Eastern Front where the Wehrmacht had just launched Operation 'Blue'."

"What do you know of him?"

"Very little. Almost nothing, considering he was my father."

"Which makes you German?"

"Austrian. My mother, I'm told, came from a little peasant town close to Vienna. She got work as a domestic in one of the grand, wealthy houses in Wahring, one of Vienna's wealthier sections. I read in one of her letters how she watched the Nazis order Jewish women to scrub the streets in their fur coats, then stood over them and urinated on their heads."

"Have you many letters from her?"

"They weren't to me. They were to her lover."

Harry Vogel said nothing, for a moment slightly shocked by her bluntness. "Who was he?"

"No one could tell me. My mother disappeared one year later. There was no explanation. I heard it said much later that she had become a member of an organisation that was assisting Jewish refugees to get to England and the US, and that the Nazis found out about her and shot her. The people from the house in Wahring put me into an orphanage. I was adopted by an Irish woman two years later and brought to live on a farm in north Cork, close to Mallow."

Harry Vogel was visibly dismayed. "What happened to your father?"

"I hear he was killed by the Russians."

"How do you feel about having a father who fought for Hitler?"

Maggie's expression changed from one of reminiscence, to one of horror and revulsion. "My father had no choice but to join the army. Men who didn't join the army were regarded as traitors and sent to die in concentration camps. It's a bit difficult for an eighteen-year-old fresh out of college to distinguish between practical common sense and patriotism. My father wasn't aware of what Hitler was doing to the Jews. He thought he was fighting a war for his country, just like the Americans who were taking a hammering from the Japanese, or the British bombing the Ruhr, and fighting in North Africa. When you're lying in a filthy, pissy trench holding a rifle, and hoping it's going to save your life, it's very difficult to find the time or the strength to take an interest in what's really going on behind your back, Mr Vogel!" She stood up and closed her jacket. She had never addressed him like that in the past.

"So you're saying that your father had no hand in The Final Solution?" He looked up at her, shielding his eyes from the setting sun.

"My father sounded like an honourable man, who thought he was doing his duty for his country. I'm sure he would turn in his grave if he thought anyone was casting aspersions on his character."

"I am sorry. I didn't mean to be so ill-natured, Maggie. Please don't call me Mr Vogel. We are too close for such flippancy and harshness. Let me make you a nice cup of hot soup. Or maybe a brandy and port. I would love to hear you talk more about your family."

Maggie was pleased that he had chosen to use the word family, but slightly anxious. It was a word that meant nothing to her, a word that came so naturally to others that it was commonplace. She had wanted to believe all her life that she had come from a close, loving family unit. Her problem was she couldn't. Brandy and port sounded appealing. Maggie wanted to continue the conversation.

Like never before, there was so much more she wanted to talk about.

23

The radio announcer on RTE introduced the news headlines.

Jack Buckley was surprised at how bright the night was. Ten o'clock, he thought, and he didn't need the car lights. "Almost the height of summer now," he said, trying to buoy up the conversation. "Will be in a month." It wasn't working. All he prayed for now was pitch darkness, and the cloak of secrecy that goes with the night, so that no one might ever find out what they were about to do.

Aidan Kerr sat quietly in the passenger seat, contemplating what lay ahead of them, occasionally burping from the four large whiskeys he had consumed earlier as quickly as his stomach would allow, before they had set off. All the time he struggled with his thoughts, and the gut-retching mental picture of the horrible, crudely severed remains of the tongue, which Jack Buckley had parcelled in ice and bundled into the back of his freezer. In between calling on the name of Jesus Christ, Aidan had insisted over and over that they call the police.

Jack knew better. First, he convinced Aidan after two hours of arguing that they had to find out if the tongue belonged to poor Leo. "What are we going to do? Call 999 and tell them we found a tongue in a cardboard box sitting on the porch? Things are strange enough around here without turning it into a freak show." They both knew there was only one way to establish if it was Leo Hannon's.

The car boot contained two shovels, two industrial torches, a huge sheet of black tarpaulin, and a pickaxe. The small windy road, getting duskier by the minute, would take them to Verity graveyard. Jack had to remind himself a few times to slow down. He reckoned this would have been the road the three young lads took in Leo Hannon's car that Saturday. Whatever happened out here that night was starting to unnerve him. It was imperative now that he approached this case as a professional, and not some bungling gobshite. It was also essential, he felt, as he had told Aidan Kerr earlier, that he dealt with as much of the corroborative evidence he had on hand personally. "Take it as far as we can. Then, and *only* then will we go to the police." He opened the window an inch and shivered. He could hear the strong howl of the northerly wind, which had changed direction in the past hour, and which would bring more heavy rain eventually.

"This isn't a good idea," Aidan Kerr said under his breath.

"If you say that once more, you'll be hitchin' a lift back into town." The voice of a policeman. "What has you so worried? You were the one who suggested I shouldn't come out here alone."

"Well, you need me with you. What would happen if you dug up the wrong grave? It's pitch black out here now, for God's sake."

The very notion made Jack shudder. He looked for the moon. It was behind his right ear, in its last quarter, and not yielding much light.

The radio switched off, silence prevailed now; the two men listened to the uncomfortable hum of the slow engine, and the tyres as they crunched and flicked back the loose, gravelly tarmac.

"I'll tell you what," said Jack. "We'll come back at first light. It'll be bright at five. I'll call for you and we'll get the job done in half the time." He took his foot off the accelerator. "What d'ye say?"

Aidan shook his head. He couldn't believe he was laughing. "Fuck off, ye mad bastard. You dragged me this far, we'll see it through and then go home."

The car quickened up again.

Jack watched the milometer on the dash. He wondered was this what it was like for the lads who drove the hearse, the last short distance. And what would they have been talking about? Manchester United's shite performance against Chelsea last night. Or would they have talked about the way Leo's body was discovered. And if that cop, Buckley, had anything to do with it? "Fuck the darkness," Jack said mulishly. He had always blamed it for the horrible games it played on his mind. Only another mile or so, he thought. "What'll he look like?"

"Who?" Aidan asked impatiently.

"The bould Leo." Jack's voice got higher. He gulped.

"Well, this is a gripping conversation. 'What did you do last night, Father? Watch any good videos?' 'Well no actually, I dug up Leo Hannon's body to look for his tongue'."

"Cynical bastard," Jack muttered.

"I beg your pardon?"

"See, you're OK, you've seen loads of stiffs."

"Not bodies that have drowned. Will he look bad?"

"Different, let's say," Jack said respectfully. "Decomposition differs from person to person. Leo was in the salt water for quite a while. He had consumed quite an amount of alcohol. The night was cold. He was grossly overweight. And he had probably been eating shortly before he died."

Aidan was waiting. "So?"

"Putrecine would have formed shortly after he came out of the water."

"Putrecine?"

"Did you do chemistry at school?"

"No. I read up on all that during the detective days. The smell of rotting flesh. Decay is rapidly speeded up by a process known as hydrolysis, a chemical decomposition or ionic dissociation caused by water, a process accelerated by the presence of salt in such large amounts."

"Jesus Christ, you sound more like a pathologist than a policeman. Can you not paint a more civil picture?"

"Why should I? That's life, Aidan. It happens to us all eventually. There are three things we are guaranteed in this life. Shit happens. Women fuck you up. And you die."

Aidan roared laughing.

"So you're obviously glad you don't have to share your house with a woman?" Jack shouted cheerfully.

"Sure I only have to look at you. Anyway, you don't have to be married to have a good time."

Jack's head swung hard left. He had always suspected that Aidan Kerr had a soft spot for the Kline's babysitter. Cynthia Reilly, who liked to be known as Cindy. Aidan, on close inspection, was an attractive bloke, fit and suave, a good catch for any of the throng of bored young women who outnumbered the available men on the peninsula by nearly eight-to-one and outsmarted the best of them. There wasn't a woman on the island who didn't secretly fancy him. Maggie regularly called him a red-hot hunk of burning desire. Even the old gammers often referred to him as that "nice young man".

Jack looked out at the narrow road and its hedgerows, lit up by the headlights, charging by like an avalanche of green on either side, and the few tiny moths and flies that had ventured out on such a cold night, being blown from side to side by the strengthening winds. "He'll have turned black and he'll smell awful." Jack sounded like he was transcribing Morse code. "He's been in the cold, wet ground for almost twenty-four hours by now. It'll be interesting . . . "

"Thank you!" Aidan snapped crisply. "I only wanted an idea of what to expect. Not a running commentary on atomisation."

Jack grabbed the wheel hard. *"Jesus, look!"* He nodded ahead like a woodpecker.

Aidan lunged forward in his seat, his head almost bouncing off the dashboard, as Jack slammed on the brakes.

The car could have stopped on a sixpence.

"What was that for?" That afternoon's fright was enough to last Aidan Kerr a lifetime.

Jack pointed to the car parked up ahead. "That's Maggie's."

"So?"

"What's she doing up here tonight?"

"How do I know. Maybe she's staying with a friend."

"She doesn't have friends out here." Jack nodded to the small cottage. "That's that old bloke, that doddery eccentric kind of fella, Vogel.

Aidan studied the outline of the tiny building. "He's definitely not one of ours. Any of mine get communion delivered every Sunday, and holy days. I either bring it myself, or if I'm busy, one of the Eucharist Ministers brings it. There's no one out here on my list. Are you going to go in?"

Jack contemplated the question, weighing up the political correctness of barging in on a stranger. He might be one of Maggie's patients. On the other hand, Jack gritted his teeth, he might not be as old as Aidan had claimed to suspect, and might just have taken her naked into his bed. He pressed hard on the accelerator. "Forget it," he growled.

The small car was feeling the pressure as it climbed the steep hill to the picturesque plateau: on one side of the road the small carpark, with spaces for ten cars; on the other, Verity graveyard, with its earliest occupants dating back as far as the 1840s, when the all-important potato crop failed and the first victims of the Famine were laid to rest.

There were no other cars in the carpark that night, and the picnic benches were stripped clean and frozen bare by the howling wind and the biting rain of the storm the night before.

The two men sat there quietly, envisaging what lay ahead, each reflecting privately on how he would deal with the macabre recoil of looking down at Leo Hannon's rotting corpse. Both of the front windows were open now, the wind whistling through, both of the men breathing deeply, Aidan Kerr taking one last suck off his cigarette.

"Why do you think you were sent a tongue?" Aidan asked whimsically. The question sounded contemptible, almost hilarious.

Jack stared straight ahead at the shackled, lop-sided, rusty gates of the one-hundred-year-old cemetery. "You know there are people we both know who have loved ones in there who would have us committed if they knew what we were about to do."

Aidan waited. "You haven't answered my question."

"I don't know why I was sent a tongue. Maybe Leo was talking too much. Maybe it was a message from someone who saw him coming to my house that night. Leo talked. He took the consequences. Maybe it's a warning."

"To you."

Jack stared at Aidan now. "To both of us. Maybe somebody is saying: 'Let this whole awful scenario lie.

Let people believe that it was all an accident. Then it will go away.'" Jack reached over and took Aidan's cigarette out of his fingers. He inhaled hard.

"And will it . . . go away?"

"No. It can't go away now."

"It can if we just leave it alone, and turn around here now and drive back down to our houses and go to sleep, Jack. Why are we trying to be crusaders? We don't have a clue what we're getting ourselves into. I became a priest to help people." Aidan nodded toward the graveyard. "Preferably living people. God is supposed to look after the dead ones."

Jack tutted, almost demoralised. "Aidan, let me ask you a question. Purely conjecture, you understand. Supposing someone murdered you and cut out your tongue and sent it to one of your best friends, all right?"

"All right."

"And that best friend got cold feet. And decided to throw your tongue in the rubbish bin and didn't bother doing anything about trying to find the bastard who murdered you, all right?"

"All right."

"You'd be pretty pissed off with your friend, wouldn't you?"

Aidan Kerr nodded. "Sure I would!"

"Right. Let's get the gear out of the boot."

The single grave took nearly two hours to excavate, each man taking it in turns of fifteen minutes to dig with all his strength and single-mindedness, while the other sat on the dry corner of the black tarpaulin, settling the quarried clay, wheezing and sweating, and pleading to "keep your voice down and stop cursing, or someone will hear us", while whoever was shovelling disappeared slowly downwards a little further from view with each passing minute.

Aidan Kerr sat on the canvas sheet now, pulling hard on his last cigarette. He estimated he had smoked fifteen since Jack Buckley had thrown aside the first shovelful of black earth from the newly-appointed, freshly-filled grave. It was now quarter to one. He picked at a loose bit of flaky skin on his upper lip which had been annoying him and spoiling the quality of his cigarette break all evening. He pulled it hard, felt it tear across the centre of his lip and cursed.

"What!" came the exhausted, exasperated voice of Jack Buckley, as if shouting from behind a soundproof wall.

"Nothing. Just hurry up," Aidan said impatiently.

"Hurry up? I must be down here half an hour. What time is it?"

"Almost one." Aidan Kerr prayed for another couple of minutes in the fresh air, under the starry sky, and the glassy moon which was slipping away with every minute, down towards the western horizon now, as if it were tired lighting up the hole for these two madmen and wanted nothing more to do with this crazy behaviour; as if it had given up on reasoning with them that their carry-on was futile and evil.

Any second he expected to hear the sound of metal striking wood. He hoped it would be during Jack's fifteen minutes. From where he sat now, teeth chattering and shoulders, arms and legs shivering violently, he couldn't see Jack. Just hear the bad language, and the grunts and groans, and the showers of wet, mulchy shovelfuls of thick, gooey clay that told him he was there below him.

He listened to the waves washing up on the stoney beach below the cliff, whooshing up onto the rocks and surging back. He remembered consoling Martha Hannon the morning before, telling her that Leo had simply "gone home to the Lord. No more pain, no more heartbreaking anxiety. Just peace and eternal rest". Listening to Jack Buckley cursing and swearing: *"Jaysus, Leo, you were always an awkward bastard!"* as he shovelled harder and faster, made him think that maybe Leo Hannon's suffering wasn't quite over just yet.

Aidan Kerr shivered. He felt fear now like he had never known it in all his years as a priest. He had never been afraid of dead bodies, jokingly reminding his congregation that we had more to fear from the living than the dead. The words, for the first time in his young thirty-nine years, rang true tonight as he remembered seeing the tongue on Jack Buckley's kitchen table.

Aidan trembled again, more violently this time, as he detected the sound of the shovel's metal tip striking the wood.

"Bingo!" Jack Buckley roared triumphantly.

Aidan Kerr blessed himself quickly and stood up, exercising his feet to banish the numbness in his toes.

"We're here, Aidan. Hand me down the jemmy."

Aidan did as he was instructed, relying on autopilot now, afraid that the overpowering, sweet smell of the dozens of assorted wreaths scattered around the grave would make him nauseous. Gently, he lowered the small crooked iron bar into the deep black hole. A hand grabbed it, causing him to almost lose his balance and fall in. Chancing a quick glance and holding a clump of grass, the sides of the grave were so heavy with moisture the earth started to give way.

"Jaysus, back off!" Jack shouted. "I don't want to get buried alive in here, much an' all as I liked him."

There was a waiting silence now. Aidan prayed that God might understand why they had undertaken such a despicable act and, in turn, explain to Leo that it was in his best interests to let them dig him up on such a bastard of a night. Maybe they should have waited for first light.

"Shine the torch," came the muffled command. "Down here, quick!"

Aidan could hear the jemmy running along the sides of the coffin's lid, Jack's foot sweeping the excess earth away, looking for its grip point. Stop. A loud crunch as the crowbar chipped away at large chunks of the pine wood. Then a huge breathy groan, and a loud creaking noise. Aidan couldn't bear to look down.

"Where's the torch?" Jack bellowed, under the weight of the half-open lid. A cracking sensation and it was off. Silence.

Aidan looked down from above, the cold breeze chilling his neck and back, over Jack's shoulder at the big nose protruding through a gap in the white linen, lit up now by the brilliant light of the torch. The veil was forced back now, with Leo Hannon's peaceful face, apart from his gaping mouth, in full view. Aidan watched in horror as Jack blew warm air onto his freezing cold fingers and stuck two of them into Leo's mouth. He seemed to root around for a few seconds. Then, as if he had just been bitten, he pulled away with all the force of an electric shock.

"Dear Jesus!" he blustered.

"What?" Aidan waited for the worst, most unimaginable answer he could think of.

"His tongue!" Jack struggled to say the words, as if he had been winded.

"Gone?"

Jack waited to catch his breath. He sighed slowly. "No. It's still there." He pointed to Leo Hannon's open mouth as if to reassure himself and his friend that he wasn't fantasising. He handed Aidan the jemmy and the torch, and climbed out of the grave as fast as he could. "C'mon, let's fill it in and get the fuck out of here!"

"What's wrong?" Aidan grabbed one of the shovels.

"It could be a trap. Someone could've been trying to set us up." Jack started shovelling the earth back in on top of the exposed body.

Aidan Kerr was appalled. "Jesus, Jack, aren't you going to cover him up? Put the lid back on? Treat the man's remains with some sort of humane decency, for God's sake!"

Jack kept shovelling, taking a deep breath with each load. "What did you tell me earlier, Aidan? Something about shit happening? And then you die?" He nodded down towards Leo's pale, ghostly, purple-streaked face. "He's still got his tongue. That's what we came out here to establish tonight. Now, *start* digging."

For another half-an-hour the lulling sound of the ebbing tide was interrupted by the clanking rush to return Leo Hannon's final resting place to the tranquil spot it had been prior to nightfall. The two men smoothed the topsoil, patting it at the edges, exactly as they had found it after they had lifted the wreaths to start their dig. By the time they were putting on their jackets, silent in knowing that they now knew less than when they had arrived, Verity graveyard had returned to its unchanged, sleepy necropolis. They looked around one last time to check that they were taking away everything they had brought with them, and not one thing more.

Already the birds were starting to sing.

Aidan Kerr checked his watch. Ten to four. "I'm shattered." His message was clear: I don't want to discuss this.

The sound of movement in the grass at the other side of the graveyard they simply attributed to a clever fox, foraging for food. They ignored it.

Harry Vogel stood inside the rusty, lopsided gates, where earlier there had been a long shadow, behind the bark of the elm tree. He had watched the charade since shortly after midnight, when he had seen Maggie safely to her car and decided to stretch his legs before bed.

He pulled his cap down over his forehead and decided to call it a night.

24

Jack Buckley clung to the dead-cold, shiny-white enamel of the toilet bowl, tightening his grip every time his fingertips slipped. He almost cracked his head open when the barfing started. Never been so violently sick in all his life, he kept thinking, and a whopper of a bruise above his left eye to prove how rough it had been. He sighed now, waiting for the retching to abate a bit more. Sure none of them would have sympathy for him. *"He's been drinkin'!"* was what he would expect them to say. And they would too, if they could see him now. Ah, fuck them anyway, he whispered, spitting out bits and lumps of old chewed and half-digested oddments: the contents of his belly.

He had boiled an egg after he had arrived back from the graveyard. The carton had three left in it. He should have checked the sell-by date. He might have if he had bothered to switch on the kitchen light. Instead he had relied on the light from the fridge. The eggs were rotten, and by now his stomach was in his throat. He had been kneeling in this position now for, he reckoned, an hour. It must have been nearly nine, if he could have seen the clock on the mantelpiece. He couldn't be bothered trying to focus on it. The morning traffic had started, up and down, outside the door, and the sun had been up for hours. It was nine, or thereabouts.

He coughed and closed his eyes again.

"Ye'll be grand in a few minutes," he kept whispering to himself, one hand patting the other, rocking himself gently to ease his aching stomach. Maybe it wasn't the egg, he argued. Maybe it was the delayed shock caused by seeing Leo Hannon's rotting corpse. Or maybe it was the dream. He shivered, slowly thinking back through the finer details, determined he wasn't going to forget any of it, but petrified that he should have dreamt it in the first place, considering it had really happened and that he, Jack Buckley was there as it was taking place.

It was hard to believe he had been dreaming, the scene chilling, almost touchable.

He could feel the strain in his neck from whatever way he was lying against the door of the panda car, listening to the music on the late night radio show. It was a country and western song, he remembered.

"And she believes in me, never sure just what she sees in me,
and I knew someday, if she was my girl, I could change the world,
with my little songs, I was wrong . . . "

He hummed to the music, aping the words, too late and too drunk to hit the notes; listening to the story that he was sure would never reflect his life: the truth – and he knew it – was different. This was his song. He had fucked up his whole life. And worse than that – Maggie's too.

He watched the stars, until they all seemed to be swimming above his head and making him dizzy. "Gimme a second chance," he mumbled, hoping against hope that she might tap him on the shoulder and take him home.

Now and then, for a brief respite, he'd swing the bottle upwards and take a long, deep swig of the vodka. The cut of the neat alcohol felt like it was eating into the flesh of his mouth and burning his throat, making him gasp, and dragging him back, wide awake again, for a few seconds. Then he swung the bottle and realised there was none left. *"Shit!"* He threw it, not sure in which direction. The quick loud splash meant that the tide was coming in over the beach fast. The sand around was damper. It was too cold to sit around any longer. He would go home and search for one of the bottles he was sure he had hidden years ago. Then he heard the engine. A car was approaching fast, accelerating uncomfortably quickly, tearing between gear changes. Someone in one hell of a hurry. But why? Who would be mad enough to get onto Coosbrack beach at this time of the night, unless they had been made an offer they couldn't refuse? And if they were expecting to test out the car's suspension, the heat of passion would quickly blow cold as soon as they saw Jack Buckley's police car. Jack reached out and grabbed a hold of the door sill, then the roof of the car, and pulled himself into a standing position.

The car, still a good distance away, was driving

towards him at speed. Kids out actin' the bollix on a Friday night, he reckoned. He was pissed. They were pissed. He wasn't going to let them see him in that condition.

Jack walked backwards a few steps, until he was sure they hadn't seen him. Then he turned and ran – more of a concerted stumble – towards the huge rock which marked the beginning of the estuary of the Three Little Rivers. He ducked around to the left and waited.

From where he was leaning against the huge crag, he could see his own car, its front wheels half-buried now in the soft sand of the incoming tide. Judging by the weather of the past few days it was likely to be a high tide.

The car slowed. The engine died.

Jack squinted to get a better view of its occupants. Three definitely, maybe four. Two in the back, one in the driver's seat. Maybe three in the back. He dipped his hand in the small pool of ice-cold water in the rock just below his chin and rubbed it on his forehead and eyes. He smeared more across the back of his neck and up under his hair. The inclemency of it woke him and sobered him considerably. All he could do now was to watch. He was quite insignificant by now, no matter what might have been about to materialise. If they were waiting to collect drugs, they were most likely armed.

The driver got out and stood still, watching Jack Buckley's ghostly patrol car. "He's not there," he heard him say. He didn't recognise the voice and supposed the man wasn't local. The car had a Limerick city registration. More cold water. His eyes were sore from the headlights against the blackness. *"Jack!"* the man shouted.

Nothing.

The man turned and shook his head.

Slowly, the man in the back seat, immediately behind the driver got out. He wore a long coat with a collar that obscured most of his face. He wore a tweed cap. Then another man, from the other side of the car, stood out. They all stood silently now, but someone who Jack couldn't see was making an awful commotion. It almost sounded like crying and pleading. The driver walked to the back of the car and reached in, pulling the bawling passenger out of the back seat by his hair. The man screamed with pain. *"No . . . no . . . no . . . "* he kept shouting. His hands seemed to be tied behind his back. His feet were bound, his head covered by a sack of some sort. Once out in the open and standing alone, he toppled over into the slushy sand. The biggest of the three kicked him so hard in the ribs he remained motionless until the tallest man grabbed his feet and lifted them, and pulled him into the water. He started shouting for help again.

The one in the long coat pulled the sack off his head. "We want to see the champion swimmer get out of this one." He pocketed the sack and started to laugh.

Jack's eyes opened wide. He gasped in horror. It was Leo Hannon. They were going to drown Leo Hannon. Jesus Christ. What was he going to do to save him? Then he saw the rifle. The Colt .22. The jigsaw was completing itself now. He was in control of the dream. It was too late to save Leo Hannon. Instead he was watching a replay of what he had witnessed that Friday night, of what he had been too drunk to recall immediately, or any time since then, that his subconcscious had recorded and was now feeding back to him.

The tall bloke held Leo's head under the water. Despite the small waves and the lapping noise they were making, Jack could still hear the sound of Leo Hannon's voice, and those giant lungs fighting to hold onto dear life, hoping that these bastards would let him up for air, thinking he was dead. They let him up once, after thirty seconds. The audible strength of his desperate, headstrong gasp as he filled his lungs and fought for his life was bloodcurdling.

Jack found himself shaking and crying now, whispering his friend's name over and over. He looked away, out towards Lonehore Point, wishing he could look back and find that none of it had happened. They jeered at him and called him names. They told him they were going to teach him a lesson for talking to the police. He was never going to talk to anybody again. A couple of minutes went by and then there was no more trashing about, no more loud gulps, or choking blows. No more dying pleas of help to Jesus from a drowning man.

Jack looked back now, through the silence, at the three men standing above the huge mass of Leo Hannon lying still in the shallow water. Jack wiped his eyes. He remembered Leo's boasts of how he could swim across Bantry Bay. And he did. And tonight he was drowning in two foot of water, his hands and feet tied, his head held below the surface.

The tall man shouted something as he let go of Leo's

head, and it bounced above the surface and lay perfectly still.

Jack froze. He recognised the voice. Not by the words, or by their command. He identified it by the sound. Because that was all it was: a sound, and a very distinct sound at that. A nasally noise, unclear, undefined. The cleft palate, a congenital defect whereby the roof of the mouth is left permanently with a longitudinal fissure, and the hair-lip could only mean one person: Jockey Carr.

Leo's body rose and fell now with the incoming tide, like a collapsed tent against gusts of wind, his head face down, his arms and legs outstretched once the baling string had been removed.

Jockey Carr felt his pockets, searched them, and then kicked his old friend who'd always served him a drink even though other patrons felt uneasy in his company.

* * *

Jack wasn't sure how long he had been sitting at the kitchen table when he heard the key in the door. It was a bliss he hadn't felt for days, not since he had read her note. Maggie was back. Even if it was just to pick up some of her stuff. He could barely conceal his excitement as she walked in and slammed her bag onto the worktop. Jack stood up, feeling like a big child, and knocked over his mug. "Hi," he said, trying to weigh in the greeting so it would not sound too polite, *or* too lively. The spilt coffee gave him the ideal chance to seem distracted.

Maggie's face was red. Jack knew she was fuming.

"What's going on?" she belted.

It was a loaded question. Where to start was another. "What do you mean?"

Maggie looked at him in disbelief, stripping him of any dignity and possible positive qualities he still might have managed to retain.

"I've just spent the last three hours trying to console an elderly man who watched you dig up Leo Hannon's grave at one o'clock this morning. He thinks you're some sort of monster. I had to convince him that there was a reason for it. That it was police business and obviously confidential because it was being done so late at night."

"Yeah, well, can you not give the nosey bastard something to make him sleep? Tell him to mind his own business in future."

Maggie slammed her fist hard down on the table. "How *dare* you talk about one of my patients like that. The fright alone of what that man described to me could have killed him. Are you aware of that?" She didn't wait for his answer. "Jack, please tell me: what in God's name is going on? Why were you up in Verity graveyard last night? What were you looking for? That old man said there was someone else with you. Who?" She sat down on a chair opposite, perched on the edge, shaking.

"Aidan Kerr. He was with me." Jack sighed, wondering where to start the story so that it would make logical sense. But he knew it probably wouldn't. Of course it wouldn't. It *couldn't,* for Christ sake. "A package arrived here yesterday. It's in the freezer." His fingers played with the handle of the mug while he spoke slowly and softly.

"What was in it?"

"A tongue." He couldn't bear to look at her reaction.

"*What?*"

"You heard me."

"Are you gone completely mad? Are you that sick in the head that you would think that someone around here would be capable of that? That's bordering on cannibalism, for Christ sake. There might be some strange people living out on that peninsula, Jack, but none of them are as strange as you."

"Well, what was I supposed to do?"

"Bring it into Bantry to the officers there. Or to Forensic in Macroom. Why didn't you do that?"

"Because I'm in charge of *this* jurisdiction. Not Bantry. Not Macroom."

"So you dug up Leo Hannon to see if it was his tongue?"

Jack nodded, like a sheepish imbecile. "Yep."

"And was it his tongue?" Her voice was filled with derision.

"No."

"So you just filled the grave back again and went home."

"Yes."

Maggie looked behind her, at her fridge. "Where's the tongue now?"

Jack nodded towards the top door. "In the freezer."

Maggie shivered at the notion, thought she should, then decided she couldn't. "Why didn't you ring Macroom before you went up there? At least tell them what you were doing. Why didn't you ask your superintendent buddy what you should do? Why didn't you take that – *thing* up to the police shop instead of putting it my fridge, Jack?"

"*Your* fridge? Since when did it become your fridge? You walked out of here nearly a week ago!"

"Don't you start. Do you know what's going to happen if this gets out? You're in enough trouble after what happened on Coosbrack, Jack!"

"I did *nothing* out on Coosbrack that night. I remember now what happened."

"How do you remember *now*? Why couldn't you have remembered last week?"

"Because I had a dream last night."

Maggie started to laugh hysterically. "A *dream*?" she shrieked, aping his words. *"I had a dream last night!* Jesus, Jack, I think you need to see a shrink. You're telling me that a dream is convincing you that you know how Leo Hannon died?"

"Yes. And I know who killed him."

"Did the dream tell you that as well? Jack, do you realise that what you did last night is a crime? You can go to prison for digging up dead bodies." Maggie drew back and laughed again. "What am I saying? Here I am talking to a sergeant about what's wrong and what's not wrong." She stood up and grabbed her bag. "I'm going. The only reason I came in here today was because there's still a teeny-weeny fraction somewhere in my heart that feels sorry for you. God knows why. You are an incorrigible bastard. But I still love you." Her voice jumped an octave. It was time to go. "I'll send a van to get my stuff. I have my own key so they can let themselves in." She turned, then stopped and stared at the fridge. She walked across the kitchen and opened the freezer door. She reached into the back of the compartment, over the frozen peas and the potato wedges and took out the plastic bag. "Is this it?" she demanded.

Jack looked over his shoulder. "Yes."

Maggie placed the bag on the table and unwrapped it with a certain sense of detachment about her every move. She studied the piece of frozen flesh. "A fox."

Jack thought he'd missed what she had just said. "A what?"

"It's a fox's tongue, Jack. You occasionally see them around here. The farmers hate them. They love to shoot them. Someone just decided to go one bit further with this one. That's a fox's tongue, Jack. You were wrong. Goodbye."

Jack stayed in the chair, his back to her. *"Maggie."* His voice was firm with his intent.

She stopped. "What?" she asked softly.

"Marry me?" He waited.

Nothing. No movement.

"Please?" He listened, expecting a dig in the neck, or a fist in the back of the ribs. Nothing. He could hear her turning, then walking back into the kitchen.

"You really mean it, don't you?"

"Yes." He wished her voice hadn't been so cold. "I love you. I need you. I promise I'll stop drinking if you come back."

"*If* I come back? And what happens if I *don't* come back?"

"I'll still stop."

She wuthered. "Dream on, Jack. I've stuck with you through thick and thin for twenty-two years, listening to your lies and your excuses. Waiting for you to show up for your dinner. Hoping we could do something nice like go out for a meal, or go to the cinema. You know? The kinda things other normal couples do every couple of weeks. But, *oh no*, not Maggie. She gets a phone call from the pub at closing time if she's lucky. And the slurred, gargled voice on the other end begging her to come and give him a lift home. Well, I've news for you, Sergeant. I'm outta here. I'm moving away from here. Far away. So far, in fact, you'll never be able to contact me. Get some help, Jack, before you finally kill yourself."

The front door banged shut so hard, the fridge shook on its wheels, reminding Jack of something he had to do.

25

Jockey Carr lived in a two-berth caravan close to Kitchen Cove, beside the pier in Ahakista, about five miles from Durrus, out along the Kilcrohane road. He was regarded by the locals as harmless, a bit pathetic and immature by most, unreliable and downright unsettling by a few, including Jack Buckley. Village idiot was what Martha Hannon called him for years when he picked up five pounds a night for directing cars into spaces outside Hannon's pub at weekends. That was until Leo sacked him for causing more dints and dinges during the Queen of the Sea festival three years before. Leo had tried to explain that the cars needed a couple of feet in front and behind to get in and out. Instead Jockey Carr thought that by packing them in like sardines he could make extra on the tips the locals gave him after a night's drinking. They never noticed the damage until the following morning.

Jockey always managed to outlive his transgressions. There was always someone in Durrus who had a soft spot for him. And Jockey, to give him his due, always recognised the soft touches. They were usually elderly widowed women coming from Saturday night Mass. Jockey would turn up at the church gates looking pale and miserable. He never went away with less than twenty quid. He was tall and would have been quite an attractive young man if it hadn't been for his speech defect and the famous crooked eye – his joey eye, as some of the local schoolchildren called it. Jockey used to chase them, shouting that if he caught them he would hide them up his chimney. That was when he was brought to the attention of Jack Buckley. No one knew where he came from or when he arrived in Durrus. He just seemed to be always there.

He was afraid of Jack, a man in uniform, someone who could lock him up. Yet, there was a brazen underself there, that unnerved Jack and worried him, particularly when he heard from some of the locals that he had been teasing small groups of schoolchildren while they waited for their bus in the afternoon.

Village idiot.

More like *fucking* idiot, Jack muttered nervously. He tried to remember where he had met Jockey Carr. He was some sort of stablehand wherever he was before. Hence the name. He wouldn't tell Jack his real name. It was Jockey, as far as he was concerned. *Nockey!* as he said himself. And so, Jockey Carr became Nockey Carr in private circles as people got great mileage out of vilifying and slagging the young man's disability.

Jack didn't care much about who he was or what was wrong with him. Put a step out of line and that was different. Buckley was all over him. Alex Kline's baby-sitter got the fright of her life one night when, on opening the front door, Nockey Carr jumped out of the hedge with his trousers around his ankles and started to masturbate in front of her.

Jack Buckley had called to his caravan later that night and cautioned him. Nockey Carr told him to fuck off and slammed the door. Jack Buckley created a new category for him that night: Blockhead.

He still wasn't sure why he had loaded the Biretta pistol and the Swift automatic rifle. One sat at the bottom of his jacket pocket, set away from his body across the handbrake as he drove, and weighing heavy now under the strain of the seat belt; the other was locked away in the boot. He turned left, passed Kenny's shop and the Post Office, and on out towards Ahakista, a ten-minute drive on a quiet afternoon. Jack was trying to remember as much as he could of the dream; and how something which he couldn't have verbally recalled all came back to him in his sleep. For hours now he'd questioned the validity of the images. No one, not even Maggie, as she had shown him, would ever treat the details of a dream with any sort of heavy-weight credence or serious regard. There wasn't a judge or a court of law in the country that would entertain his story, unless – *unless* – he was able to tie it in with plausible evidence. What if Nockey Carr had an alibi which would prove he was elsewhere on the night Leo Hannon was drowned? Jack was in no doubt that he died at the hands of Carr, but he also knew how easy it would be for Nockey to get some old dear to say that she had called him very late and had asked him to get out of his bed and fix a burst pipe for her. He was going to have to apply a bit of pressure, he reckoned, and make Nockey Carr, or Jockey, as Buckley – with the tiniest inch of respect – preferred to call him, sweat to prove his innocence.

Nockey Carr's caravan looked as if it should have had an *Out to lunch* sign on the door. To the untrained eye, Carr was not at home. Jack Buckley suspected differently. He knew how Nockey loved to sit inside, perfectly still, playing his little game of pretending not to be there. Then, when the kids would creep up to the window and peep in, Nockey would burst through the door and scare the shite out of them. That all stopped on further cautioning from Buckley. But Jack knew he was there today. He parked the car on the road, and walked the fifty yards or so to the modest caravan with the dainty turquoise drapes which, Jack always felt, added a more sinister depth to the man's strangeness.

He stood, well back from the door, and observed, his hand firmly clutching the Biretta pistol. The caravan seemed lop-sided, as if it had been blown over slightly and never straightened. *"Jockey!"* Jack thought he could hear music. Whatever, it was gone now. Just the silence, and the soft hypnotic lapping of the small waves behind him. "It's Jack Buckley, Jockey. I need to talk to you. I think you might be able to help me." Jack knew that Jockey loved helping people, because it usually meant he was rewarded financially for it. It worked.

The handle squeaked, then turned slowly. Jockey's gaunt face looked desperately pale in the bright sunshine. He looked as if he hadn't eaten in a week, and washed in a month.

Jack could tell he had been ill. "How are you, Jockey?"

He shivered. Then he mumbled something that Jack had to listen to carefully and then think about it. "I'm no' well, Sergean'," was what he had said.

"Have you seen the doctor?"

"Nnooo."

"Have you any money?"

"Nnooo."

It was breaking Jack's heart to think he would have to part with twenty quid and give it to this lowlife after what he had done to his friend. But then he knew Nockey Carr was as easily led aside as a stray dog.

"Here!"

The voice coming from behind gave Jack such a fright he almost pulled the gun. He swung around. It was Maggie. "*Jesus Christ*, you gave me a fright. What are you doing here?" He tried to get rid of the anger as quickly as he had recognised her.

"I followed you. I saw what you put into the boot of the car."

"Why did you follow me?"

"I don't know. Maybe it scared me to think of what you were going to do with it." She nodded to Nockey and smiled. "Hiya Nockey, how are you?"

Jack hated when the locals called him Nockey, especially Maggie. He knew she was only being friendly. It just sounded so humiliating and so crushing, he felt. "*Jockey* and I have to have a little talk." He glanced across at Maggie, where she stood on a small rock with her arms folded, signalling that she wasn't in a hurry to go anywhere. He looked back at Nockey. "Don't we?"

Nockey looked uneasy, as if he was going to run away, fidgeting with his fingers and kicking the bottom of the corrugated door. "Wha'ever 'ou say," he replied hesitantly, dropping his consonants, like he did, and talking as if his mouth was full of hot soup. There was silence for a long time then as Jack watched Nockey, who kept staring at Maggie as if he wanted to ask her something. Jack studied him, trying to sort out in his mind why he disliked this creature so much. He guessed he was about thirty, maybe a bit older, and seemed to have the mental capacity of a five-year-old who loved to pretend to be bold. He thrived on affection, but, Jack guessed, it had become a commodity that was hard-won-by and demanded big favours. He studied him harder, realising that, up until today, he had no real, legitimate reason to hate him, apart from what he had done to Kline's baby-sitter, and the upset he had caused her. He shivered and looked back to Maggie. "We're gonna go inside and have a little talk." He was telling her it was none of her business.

Maggie stepped closer to Jack and place her hand on his arm, pulling his head closer to hers, and his ear to her mouth. "This isn't Hannibal Lecter you're interviewing, Jack. He's only a little boy, remember that."

Jack could have exploded. How fucking dare she! he screamed silently. He turned and pushed her backwards, out of Nockey Carr's hearing distance, almost causing her to lose her balance. *"Who the fuck do you think you are?"* There was the soft spray of hot spit on his breath, and with it, the smell of alcohol. Each word was carefully pronounced with feeling.

Maggie turned her face away and into the wind.

He knew he shouldn't have said it. Truth was, he *had* said it. And he meant it. "I am trying to solve a very serious crime here and you are not helping one little bit. You walk into my house an hour ago, one week after walking out, to tell me you're walking out again. Then you turn up in the middle of a police investigation and try to tell me how to do my fucking job?"

Maggie stood perfectly still, her head pulled back. "Do you really think *he* is capable of doing what you think he did?" She nodded conspicuously at a very worried-looking Nockey Carr, who had stopped fidgeting and kicking now. "He is an imbecile. No one in their right minds would send him to the shop for a newspaper. He lives in a little dream world, Jack. A bit like you. Expect, in Nockey's case, his dreams are the same as a four-year-old's. Your dreams, Jack, will eventually get you locked up." She turned and started to walk up the steps to where she had parked her car.

Jack turned to Nockey. "Did you hear that, Jockey?"

He shook his head in a flustered sort of way.

"Maggie's saying you're stupid." Jack laughed.

Maggie almost lost her balance on the narrow, wooden-step ledge, she was so horrified at what she had just heard. "I beg your pardon, Jack Buckley. Nockey, I did *not* say that! He's lying."

"Yes, you did. You said he was an imbecile and you

wouldn't let him go to the shop. And for Christ's sake, *stop* calling the lad Nockey. His name is *Jockey*!"

Nockey seemed pleased at first that Jack was speaking up for him. Then he seemed confused.

Maggie turned and ran back down the steps, three at a time, her fists clenched. Jack reckoned she was about to take a swing. He took a deep breath and waited. She raised her fist to shoulder level and swung. Jack grabbed it and held it tightly.

"You bastard!" she roared.

Nockey Carr shrieked. He started to jump up and down clapping his hands, shouting: *"Bastar' . . . bastar' . . . bastar'!"*

"Now look what you've done," Jack said calmly. "You really do believe he's as thick as he looks, don't you?"

"I'm a nurse, for God's sake. I have worked with mentally handicapped patients."

Jack nodded to the jumping boy, oblivious now that he was being spoken about again. "I believe he can beat me at a game of chess. Just like I believe he drowned Leo Hannon. Just like I believe he knows what happened to those three boys."

Maggie forced a smile, as if out of sympathy. "That's why I followed you today." She dropped the smile and looked away towards the beach.

"Why?"

"To tell you that the three boys were spotted in Loughrea, up near Galway, shortly before ten this morning. A van driver picked them up and dropped them off in Eyre Square. They told him they were heading out towards Clifden."

Jack remained stoical. He was adamant he was not going to allow his disappointment to show. But why disappointment? he asked himself. If they have been seen, it means they're safe and alive. He should be pleased and relieved. He looked back towards the pathetic individual who was still waiting for something to happen. "Fancy a game of chess, Jockey?"

Carr's face lit up. *"'es, please, Sergean'!"* he answered excitedly, dropping his consonants.

Jack turned to face Maggie. "Will you stay?"

She was surprised by the request. "A couple of minutes ago you couldn't wait to get rid of me. Now you want me to stay. Why?"

"Because I find it difficult to understand a lot of what he's saying at times."

Maggie sneered. "Well, he won't be talking too much if the two of you are going to be playing chess. Unless that is, of course, you're going to let him teach you." Her voice was stinking with sarcasm. She even afforded him a gloating grin.

"I need a witness. That's why."

"Yeah. Actually, come to think of it, you're right. You are a bit short of witnesses over the last couple of weeks, Jack."

26

Two hours later.

Despite the coldness of the caravan, sparsely decorated with the bare essentials – a beer-keg for a stool, a black and white television set, a transistor, a tiny dual-hob gas cooker set in the corner and a long bench seat that doubled as a bed at night or whenever Nockey Carr chose to put his head down – and badly kept and messy, and the fading light of the late, cloudy afternoon, Jack had managed to make himself comfortable. Maggie never once took her eyes off the chessboard for the last half-hour of the game. She knew Jack was a brutal player, but she also knew that evening just how much aware of Nockey's brilliance Jack actually was. Nockey Carr was winning his third game of chess, beating Jack into almost instant submission. In his first challenge, Maggie watched Jack's best efforts. He managed eight moves, then Nockey clobbered him. Second game, Jack mustered eleven.

Nockey had said the word twice before. It was the only word spoken by him in the two hours. And he was about to say it triumphantly again. *"Checkm-m-ma'e!"* he shrilled. Jack sat back against the thin wall of the caravan and smiled. He was pleased, but for a completely different reason, as Maggie knew well. He looked across at her and his eyes spoke volumes.

Nockey started singing *We are the champions.*

Jack's gaze became more strained. He sat forward.

Maggie's concentration softened. She became nervous. Nockey Carr was a genius in his own private way. He had just proved it and embroiled himself in the events of the Coosbrack strand.

"Where were you last Friday night, Jockey?" Jack was a sergeant again, no longer the victim of Nockey's chessmen. He watched the young man scratching his odd-shaped head, his big, oblong ears jiggling at the same time.

"A' 'ome."

"You couldn't have been at home, Jockey."

"Why?" His breathing was speeding up.

"Because you were across on Coosbrack Strand with three friends of yours, weren't you?"

He didn't speak, just bowed and shook his head.

"Yes, you were. Because I saw you. You saw my car, didn't you?"

He shook his head again, more vigorously this time.

Jack produced the Biretta and placed it on the chessboard. Nockey's mouth opened wide. He froze, a long dribble landing on his baggy, dirty jeans. "Jockey, I want to help you. I want to protect you from whoever forced you to do what you did last Friday night. I know Leo was a friend of yours and you didn't mean to hurt him. I *know* that. But I have to find out why those people wanted to kill him. Here." Jack offered him the pistol. "Go on, take it. Feel it. See what it's like to aim a gun, Jockey."

Nockey closed his fingers and palm around the butt of the Biretta. He almost smiled as he sighed. He kept it at eye level and pointed it at Jack. He grinned and said something.

Jak looked across at Maggie. "What did he say?"

"He said he always wanted to be a policeman."

Jack continued to stare at her. He could see she was getting quite upset by the routine. He focused back on Carr again. "Do you like that, Jockey?"

The question was greeted with three great big nods. *"Y-yeah!"*

"That's not your first time to hold a firearm, is it, Jockey? *Nockey!"*

Nockey stopped looking at the gun, and leered now at the sergeant. Why had he called him Nockey? The sergeant never called him Nockey. It was a horrible name. *"Nnooo! No' Nockey!"* he bayed. He looked at the sergeant's hand, closed, as it slowly placed its contents on the chessboard. He counted out loud. Five bullets.

"Do you recognise them, *Nockey*?" Jack could tell he was agitating Carr by calling him Nockey. "Well, *Nockey*?"

He shook his head so hard Jack thought he was going to throw a fit.

"You put those bullets in Leo Hannon's pocket after you drowned him, *Nockey*. Didn't you?"

Head shaking violently.

"Stop Jack, *please*!" Maggie pleaded.

"You just want me to think you're stupid, Nockey. don't you? You just want me to have pity on you and to think you're too dense and clueless to be up to doing anything like that, don't you?" Jack's voice was rising steadily, becoming angrier with each question. *"Be honest with me!"*

Nockey Carr looked to Maggie for support. his eyes said: *Please stop him!*

She couldn't bear his eyes. So she looked away.

"You knew what you were doing the night you hid outside Alex Kline's house after knocking on the front door. You knew he wasn't in because you saw him down in Leo Hannon's pub with his wife. So you finished your drink real fast and ran up to the Kline's house and knocked on the front door, didn't you?"

Nockey was trembling now, kicking the beer-keg he was sitting on with the heel of his boot, fiddling with the King chessman that had just scored victory three times. But the smell of victory was dwindling fast, giving way to the smell of fear. The smell he hated. *"Naaaw!"* It was the most pronounced word he had said all day.

"And I bet you were thinking of the baby-sitter all the way from the pub to their house, weren't you, *Nockey?* Thinking of her getting ready for her bed and taking off her clothes. And those gorgeous big tits of her as she slipped down under the warm blanket, wearing nothing but a smile, eh?"

Nockey Carr was rubbing his hands between his legs now, backwards and forwards, his eyes closed.

"Stop this, Jack, *please*!"

Jack knew that Maggie was on the verge of tears now. He raised his hand, as if to say: not much longer. "Tell the truth, Nockey, you'd love to have been in there with her, under the warm blanket, feeling her soft skin, realizing that she's got the hots for you."

Nockey Carr started to whimper.

"Isn't that what you were thinking when you were galloping down the Bantry road to see Cindy Reilly? You really wanted her to invite you in that night. The house all to yourselves, the kids fast asleep in bed. No one to disturb you. And you know something, Nockey, I can't blame you. She is a beautiful young woman. How old would you say she is, Nockey? Twenty-one? Twenty-two, maybe? How old?"

"T-t-twen'y-one," he replied. "She t-t-tol' me." His fear and excitability was almost tangible now.

Jack tutted and shook his head. "Cindy Reilly is still in school, Nockey. She's only sixteen. If you were any older, I'd call you a dirty old man, and caution you. Come to think of it, I already did caution you, didn't I?"

Nockey Carr frowned and hung his head low again. "P-p-please!" he begged.

"Because not content with just talking to Cindy Reilly and doing what most decent young men might do – ask her out – you decided to give her the shock of her life. You jumped out from behind the tree in Alex Kline's front garden with your pants around your ankles. *Jesus Christ, Nockey!* Did you really think you'd get away with that? Most people go to prison for things like that."

Nockey Carr was a fumbling, blowzy, blethering wreck. Tears were streaming down his face, his chin and

T-shirt covered now in saliva as he mumbled incoherently and talked to himself.

"What would you have done that night, Nockey, if Leo Hannon hadn't caught you?" Jack waited for the reaction he hoped might come and save him.

Nockey Carr stopped crying.

The only sound to break the silence now was the occasional sniff from Maggie who sat bent over, with her hand covering her face.

"You thought no one would ever find out, Nockey. Didn't you? Leo Hannon saw you leaving his pub late that night and knew you were up to no good. Leo was your friend, Nockey. Did you know that?"

Nockey Carr nodded.

"He followed you and when he saw you running off down the dark road out of town, he jumped into his car and tailed you. He walked up the drive behind you when you knocked on Kline's halldoor. And when Cindy Reilly cried out and he saw you with your trousers down, laughing and then jumping forward to catch Cindy, he hit you with one unmerciful box to the side of the face and knocked you clean out. Didn't he?"

Nockey didn't reply anymore. He just sat and listened, and scowled.

"You would have raped her, wouldn't you?"

The gentle noise seemed familiar.

Jack thought it was the sound of rain – the resonant dripping he could hear – until he noticed the small trickle at the side of Nockey Carr's boot, becoming bigger until it was a fair-sized pool of warm, pungent urine. Somewhere in the distance he could hear Maggie whispering the name of Jesus. The piss stopped and Nockey Carr started to shake.

"Leo Hannon prevented you from throwing away your life that night, Nockey. He saw it in his heart to overlook such a heinous thing and to continue being your friend. Why? Because he was the only decent *fucking* friend you had, and he knew it. He knew how important it was for everyone to have friends. Even just one friend. He watched out for you. Gave you a few quid every week. Fed you when you were hungry. Even dropped you a few free pints in his pub despite the fact that you were bad for business. And what did you go and do? You murdered him.

"You killed him because he stopped you having what you wanted that night. He stopped you tearing the clothes off Cindy Reilly's little sixteen-year-old body and raping her. You would have taken away that little girl's innocence that night, Nockey. And then you probably would have threatened her, that if she ever opened her mouth about what you did to her you'd kill her. That way you could have had her again and again and again. Isn't that right, Nockey? And even though I find it hard understanding what you say, you would have made it very clear to her that night. you would have left her in no doubt about what you wanted. Wouldn't you?

"But, thank God, it wasn't to be. Leo Hannon got to you first. And you held that grudge against him ever since, even though he was your friend, and told everybody who was rightfully afraid of you that you were harmless. What did you do? You held his head under the water at Coosbrack strand until there wasn't a drain of life left in him, and him the best swimmer I've ever laid eyes on. How humiliating that must have been for him, to have his hands and feet tied while being drowned. And then, of course, you cut the baling twine and left him there, making it look like a selfish suicide. *Didn't you, you evil bastard!"* Jack kicked the table, sending the chessmen flying, lunging forward and grabbing the five standing bullet shells before they fell over. *"And these . . . "* Jack squeezed the shells until he could feel the metal jackets cutting into his finger joints. "You placed these on Leo Hannon's body that night, so that when the police came to fish him out of the sea the next morning, they would have found them. Isn't that right?" Jack took the cigarette box out of his pocket. He glanced around the caged confinement, then down at the trail of urine which had followed the lopsided floor to the end of the caravan and sat in a pool beside the television. "You don't mind if I smoke," he muttered, lighting the fag with a match. He inhaled deeply and held his breath. "I haven't smoked for years. Until recently, that is. Then I thought, why the fuck should I bother looking after my health? I gave up drinking three years ago because the doctor told me it would kill me. My girlfriend told me she'd leave me if I didn't quit. So I quit. And I felt great. But I wasn't happy. Far from it. I was totally fucking miserable for three years. So do you know what I did, Nockey? I started drinking again. And since you can't drink without a fag, I started smoking again. Now my doctor and my girlfriend are fuckin' freakin'. But I'm happy. And that's what counts. Why the fuck should I strive to get a clean bill of health when some raving fuckin' nutter like you can murder me in the middle of the night?"

Nockey Carr had become so calm and lifeless now, he could have been fast asleep. His head was bowed, but Jack could still see his lip twitching, from where he was sitting.

It was twenty past eight. The light was fading and the tide was in, the sound of the waves lapping against the edge of the small, pebbly beach at Kitchen Cove. Jack looked around the dingy little kip of a caravan. It was a pathetic little hovel, not fit for a dog, but suitable, he had decided now, for Nockey Carr. He only wished there was a padlock on the outside of the door.

"I used to wonder about you, Nockey, about what goes on in that grey matter up there. I used to think there was fuck all, that – God love you – you were incapable of adding two and two together. Then you made a fatal mistake. I saw you playing chess with a couple of boring German tourists a few weeks ago in Hannon's pub. They were buying you pints of cider and treating you like some sort of circus freak. And you were lappin' it up, enjoyin' every minute of it.

"I thought, 'hang on a second. This guy has it all beautifully worked out. He lets people think he's stupid. That way, no one bothers him. Everyone lets him get on with his simple life. And what d'ye know, he's running rings around them. Nockey Carr's got the last laugh." Jack started juggling with three of the five bullets. "I bet you can juggle like a circus clown as well, Nockey."

Nockey sniffed.

"Where was I?" Jack stopped juggling and straigtened up. He lit another cigarette. "Oh yeah, the bullets. Here we go, the *piece de resistance*, Nockey. You plant the five bullets on Leo Hannon's body, with his fingerprints all over them, so that when the cops eventually find the bodies of the three young teenagers who disappeared two weeks ago, and see the gunshot wounds, and match the lead with the bullets, it all points to poor old Leo who can't defend himself because he's dead.

"Leo Hannon shot them with Alex Kline's rifle which he had borrowed to do a spot of hunting. That's what the police are told. But that's not true, is it, Nockey? You were meant to leave Alex Kline's rifle into Jeffersports, in Bandon, for a repair job, but you didn't, did you? You sneakily held on to it to play with it for a day or two. You shot them in one of your mad moments, because Leo was freaking over his car being stolen because he thought you were looking after it for him. So you followed them in another car. You knew the area better than they did. Then: *Bang, bang, bang!*" Jack finished his cigarette and stubbed it out in the urine. "Isn't that what happened?"

He waited to hear a garbled answer, as usual. After a few seconds he looked across at Nockey. He was shaking his head like a nodding dog in the rear window of a car. "Well then, if you didn't shoot them, who did?"

Nockey Carr looked up and away, into the hazy blue light of the May dusk, as if recalling something to mind that he had overlooked earlier, then stared at Jack Buckley with a fearsome glower, and said, as cogently as he could manage.

"Alex Kline,"

27

Alfie Carruth's long white dormer-bungalow was like something out of a Walt Disney movie; with its lush green, rolling front lawn, bordered by chrysanthemums and wild orchids, and a small octagonal pond full of waterlilies and a water hyacinth for the goldfish; the entire two-acre setting, sitting on a hill overlooking the town of Macroom, was a scene lifted straight off a picture postcard.

Jack Buckley always asked the same question every time he had the misfortune to drive through the timber gates and up the red tarmac driveway: how was Carruth able to afford this exquisite location five years ago on a cop's salary? Jack had heard it was for sale back then. Asking price for the land, and the rundown cottage which stood on it then, according to the blurb and the photograph in the office of *A&E Kline, Estate Agents,* was eighty thousand. Carruth bought it, knocked down the cottage and proceeded to build this beautiful residence, which cost him, locals said, another ninety thousand. He wasn't getting much change from two hundred thousand pounds.

Maggie had tired of him asking the question, where did he get the money?

"He's on the same wage as I am!" Jack would protest, as they drove by on their weekly Saturday trip to the supermarket to stock up.

"Alfie Carruth doesn't drink like you do," Maggie would reply, every Saturday, somewhere between three and four in the afternoon.

"Like a fish, you mean?" Jack would argue.

"You said it," was all Maggie would say, as she pretended not to notice the beautifully kept garden that she would have killed for.

"And just because he doesn't drink as much as I do means he can buy big posh houses? Will you shut up, Maggie!"

"No, Jack. Because he doesn't drink as much as you do means he has more money to spend on nice things, like gardening, and building a nice pond for the garden. And toys and swings for the children." She nodded to the colourful array of playthings to the side of the house. "And it means they can eat in nice restaurants and go away to Dublin and London for weekends."

"You never told me you wanted to go to Dublin, Maggie. Jesus, there's seven trains a day from Cork to Dublin. You can be there in three hours. That's no big deal."

"To hell with Dublin, Jack. What about somewhere like Paris?"

"What *about* Paris? We went there for a weekend."

"*Nine years ago?* Wow, I ought to fall on my knees with gratitude. Look what they've got outside their door." Maggie nodded to her left as she slowed almost to a halt.

"Garden *fucking* gnomes. Wow!"

"Well it's a hell of a more attractive sight than a crate full of empty wine bottles and beer cans. That seems to be all that's ever outside our house."

"Oh yeah? And who drinks all the wine? Not me!"

"There's only ever one or two wine bottles; compared to twenty or thirty beer cans."

"And would you like to live with a gobshite like Alfie Carruth?" Jack always asked that question because he knew how much Maggie hated Carruth. "He's as bent as hell!" Jack would shout as the car passed the gate. "The worst cop I've ever met, he is."

"How do you know?" Maggie asked.

"Jesus, Maggie. First you say you hate him, then, in the next breath, you're defending his honour. Is there anyone in this whole world who you can safely say you've nothing good or wholesome to say about? *Anybody?*"

"Yes," she smiled. "You."

It was a conversation-stopper, worked every time. That was the last Saturday they passed Carruth's maison on their way to the supermarket. Two days later, Jack Buckley was shot and seriously wounded. It changed his life forever.

Looking up at Carruth's house now, and the dinky wall-lamp to the left of the exquisite porch and its mahogany halldoor, Jack remembered those Saturdays. They had something then, Maggie and him, a bond, or a link, that seemed to just fizzle out after the shooting. Sure, they argued. Doesn't everyone, he maintained. Jack became bitter about life in general. He started to hate everything and everybody. He went to the doctor for tablets to help him sleep. He hated the doctor. The doctor recommended a good counsellor. Jack ended up despising the counsellor. Eventually they upped and moved to Durrus, on the Sheep's Head peninsula, where life was grand and slow, and uncomplicated, and where there was very little to hate – apart from the boredom.

These days Alfie Carruth was known in public as superintendent, or Sir, as he liked to be addressed during formal occasions. He would, wouldn't he? Jack thought. He killed the car engine and stared out at the house of his boss. Carruth had been Jack's partner for a few very long months, six years before in Cork city. Jack requested a transfer, opting for a move to Macroom, to CDU, as it was known then, the Criminal Detective Unit, mainly because he could no longer tolerate Carruth's questionable work ethics. He enjoyed throwing the odd dig during serious interrogation sessions, and enjoyed "looking after" his friends by quashing fines and court summonses, in return for various favours, of course. Carruth remained in the city, studied for his exams, undertook every course he could put his name down for, and eventually ended up as a superintendent, unfortunately, in Macroom, from where, surrounded by his lush-green rolling lawn on two acres, and his octagonal fishpond beside the red tarmac driveway, he oversaw the day to day running of the West Cork police force.

Superintendent Alfie Carruth.

Sir.

Jack could never comprehend why he couldn't relax whenever he visited the Carruth's house. He got on swimmingly with Mary, Alfie's wife, and always got a smile from the kids whenever they were around. Just one of those things, a bit like visiting a distant relative one never really got to know, and didn't care much for now.

He sat in the small, colder living-room, the one used for official guests, immediately to the left of the front door. An artifical fire pretended to burn in the grate, below a mantelpiece which was almost bending under the weight of the framed photographs of children's Holy Communions and Confirmations, and a wedding photo of Alfie and Mary, looking like something out of a Kray twins' family album. Then there was the photo recording his passing-out parade at Templemore, his Ayran good looks and broad shoulders, chiselled cheeks and chin, bleach-blond hair and a forehead that reflected the light like it had been polished for hours. And a photograph of his proud mother and father, a retired sergeant, flanking their distinguished son.

Jack hated photographs, mainly because he didn't have many. Didn't have any, come to think of it. The only photographs he ever came across, rooting in drawers and on tops of cupboards, were the embarrassing kind: the stag parties – no smiling faces most of the time, just dropped trousers and bare arses, or worse. Drinking competitions, New Year's Eve parties, wedding anniversaries, the occasional twenty-first. They all had one thing in common: red eyes, pint in hand and no later recollection whatsoever that the photograph had been taken in the first place.

Jack Buckley concluded, having looked closely at all

the photographs, that Alfie and Mary Carruth were a punctilious pair of boring old tits. Given the choice, he would prefer to be his pugnacious old temperamental self any day.

Alfie Carruth closed the door behind him. He blatantly stared at the clock on the mantelpiece, immediately browbeating his guest and seizing the upper hand. A rather stiff handshake followed. "Good to see you, Jack."

Jack knew it meant quite the opposite. Alfie Carruth ran his small force like clockwork, nine o'clock and five were the perfect parameters governing his day. The occasional early morning was acceptable in extreme cases. Three or four times a year he didn't mind working until seven or eight in the evening. But tonight it was nearly half-ten and one of his sergeants from somewhere almost off the map was eating into his private time: that section of the day that was reserved for classical music and painting his Airfix planes and battleships. He wasn't offering refreshments, not even a cup of tea. "What did you want to see me about?" He didn't even sit down. He strutted up and down in front of the pretend fire, his hands clasped behind his back. All he was short of, Jack thought, was the goosestep boots. He was a perfect little Hitler, as one of his secretaries once referred to him at a Christmas party. She was transferred to Stores a fortnight later. Jack watched him, considering his few words, knowing that they would make or break the conversation, and the request he was about to put forward. The man in front of him was really two men. A caring, doting father. But between nine and five he became a bulldozer.

And Jack knew this was a sitting-down sort of conversation. He hadn't spoken to Carruth since the patrol car-in-the-sea incident, and decided tonight wasn't the best time. "I want to make an arrest, Alfie."

The senior officer sat down. "So? You don't have to get my approval to arrest someone. What did this character do?"

Jack was sucking a lozenge, trying not to smell of gargle. He breathed in and felt the vapours burning his throat, giving his voice a husky sound. "He murdered Leo Hannon."

The expression on Alfie Carruth's face remained constant. "Who *murdered* Leo Hannon?" The sarcasm was there, Jack could hear it, a front to protect the trepidation.

"Jockey Carr. He's a . . . " Jack couldn't find the appropriate words to describe the half-dimwit, half-psychopath. "He's a sad case, not fully there."

"Not *fully* there. What the hell does that mean?" Carruth's expression was menacing now.

"He gives the impression that he has the mental capacity of a five-year-old. He's a bit of a wanderer, can't talk properly."

Carruth's face lit up. "Oh, I've heard of this bloke. He lives in a little caravan down near the sea front. Doesn't he? Mentally handicapped, isn't he?"

Jack shook his head. "No, Sir, he's definitely not mentally handicapped. Anything but. I believe he's a very clever individual. He likes to give the impression that he's a bit stupid. That way people behave very charitably towards him. They give him money and food.

He gets free drink in the local pubs, provided he doesn't drink too much."

"He's not mentally handicapped then?"

"No."

"Right, Jack. So when did you qualify as a psychiatrist?"

If the question had teeth, it would have taken both of Jack's eyes clean out. "With due respect, Sir, I've been the local sergeant over there now for almost four years. I know this character quite well. To look at him you wouldn't think butter could melt in his mouth. Yesterday, he all but confessed to the murder of Leo Hannon."

"All *but* confessed? So what your saying is that you don't have a written confession?"

"No written confession, Sir. Actually, I . . . " Jack hesitated. What he was about to say would make him look more stupid than Jockey Carr. "I watched him . . . murdering Leo Hannon." He looked towards the pretend fire in the grate, a lonely false shimmering effect that carried about as much believeableness as what Jack had just said. He was looking everywhere now, except at Alfie Carruth.

"Sergeant, you're telling me you watched this man murdering Leo Hannon. That was a week ago. Why are you only telling me this now?"

Jack was very aware now that the likelihood of the conversation being taken seriously was becoming remote. "Because I couldn't remember seeing it."

"Why not?"

"Because I'd drunk so much that night I was only semi-conscious." It was quite obvious to Jack that Carruth couldn't believe what he was hearing, and even more acutely apparent that he wasn't impressed.

"So what brought it all back to you?"

"A dream. It all came back to me while I was asleep last night."

"Is this after you dug up Leo Hannon's grave?" His mood was sinister, his face glowering with anger.

Jack was shocked. It was the last thing he expected to hear. "How did you hear about that?" If Carruth had been told, why hadn't he been straight on about it earlier.

"A concerned publican's wife."

"Martha Hannon?"

Carruth nodded. "Maybe while you were down in the hole with Leo, he probably mentioned Jockey's name to you. Did he?"

Jack felt like a clown. He stood up and put on his coat. "You're not taking any of this very seriously, are you?"

Carruth belly-laughed. "Jesus, man, you expect me to take you seriously after what you've been getting up to over there on that little island of yours? You have the cheek to come in here at half-ten at night and tell me about some half-baked vegetable with an IQ of minus twenty who you think murdered Leo Hannon. Meanwhile you're running around digging up cemeteries and floating police cars in the Atlantic Ocean, and now you're going to charge some innocent half-wit who minds his business with the murder of a drunken fool who committed suicide?"

"How dare you call my friend a drunken fool!"

"Listen, Buckley. You're pushing your luck too far. If I had my way I'd have buried you by now, but despite your strange vampire-like carry-on, your people have a soft spot for you and don't want to see you let go. I'd be very grateful to them if I were you." Carruth stepped closer to Jack, a direct sign that their conversation was over. "And as for your *friend*. You obviously didn't know Leo Hannon very well. Probably drinking too much to notice."

"What's that supposed to mean?"

"*Goodnight*, Sergeant."

"A couple of things before I go, Superintendent. You'll have to hear me out or I'll be forced to lodge an official complaint. And if I don't get your full co-operation on them I'll take this all the way to the top if I have to. I know that Jockey Carr murdered Leo Hannon. There were two other men with Carr that night on Coosbrack strand. I expect you to provide me with the appropriate assistance and back-up I might require in order to find out who those two men were. Also, I want to launch a muder hunt in relation to the three missing boys."

"*Jesus Christ*, Buckley. Do you not listen to the news?" Carruth kicked the bottom of the door. "The three boys were spotted in Loughrea this morning. They're alive, for Christ's sake."

"They're not alive, Sir."

Carruth was fit to explode. "*How* do *you* know?"

"Because Jockey Carr told me, and Maggie's a witness to that."

Alfie Carruth laughed so loud he woke the baby. A

squawky wail filled the long hallway from a room somewhere towards the back of the house. "Shit, now look what you've done! I'm baby-sitting tonight, and I was hoping for a quiet night."

Jack couldn't believe what he was hearing. Here he was, after driving the forty miles to Alfie Carruth's house late in the evening, discussing a murder hunt and the considerable evidence he had spent a week amassing, and all Carruth was worried about was the kids waking up. "Are you interested in supporting me on this?"

Carruth looked at him with such contempt that Jack forgot his reason for being there. Only for a brief second though. "Well?"

Alfie smiled. The harshness and fear had vanished, almost as if he had undergone a sudden change of heart. He placed his hand on Jack's shoulder. "Jack, Leo Hannon's death was put down to misadventure. They did Martha a great favour, I think. Because even the coroner was in doubt that it was suicide. The three boys, for all we know, might be back home in Dublin tonight, in the bosoms of their families. Mind you, if they had been my sons, I wouldn't have dreamed of letting them go away on a wild drinking weekend like that until they had convinced me they had more sense and respect." He slapped Jack's shoulder. "Put all this behind you, Jack, *please*! Even if you did get a written confession out of Jockey Carr, do you think his word would stand up in court?"

Jack knew it was a perfectly reasonable question for

Carruth to ask. If only because the answer was a very definite *no*.

"Leo Hannon is dead, Jack. Nothing you or I do now is going to bring him back," Carruth's voice was filled with a false sincerity.

Jack hated it. "Don't patronise me, Alfie. I might be a bit mad at times but I'm definitely not stupid."

The compassion was gone now. "Listen to me, you stupid prick! I don't give a shit if you want to make a complete idiot of yourself in front of the people you're paid to police. But *I* will not get drawn into your hairbrain plan. You'll destroy your career if you keep going down this route, Jack. I really mean that. I will not stand for this carry-on."

"I want to investigate a series of crimes here, Alfie, and you're telling me you're not going to let me do my job; uphold justice – isn't that how you describe it when you're giving your twenty-minute talk at neighbourhood watch meetings?"

"*Uphold justice, my arse!* We're all watching out for ourselves, Jack, make no mistake about it. Occasionally looking out for each other. A good deed deserves a favour in return. You scratch my back . . . you know what I'm saying, Jack."

The smarmy undertones were back. The smug grin, the swagger.

"What the public percieves as a co-operative, endearing police force and what really goes on within the ranks are two completely different entities, Jack. Monsters, even. Take my advice. Go home to Maggie tonight and forget about Leo Hannon and Jockey Carr. They're both losers. The only difference between them now is that one of them is dead. Sometimes it pays to stick to your own depth."

"What are you saying, Alfie? That Leo Hannon didn't? What's my depth now, let me see. Directing French tourists to the Well of the Poets, or showing them where they'll get the best photographs of the sun setting over Bantry Bay, or what time the next ferry to Carbery Island is? *Bollox* to all that, Alfie. There's at least one murder staring both you and me in the face tonight, and you're telling me you won't do anything about it?"

"Go home, Jack. It's late, I'm tired and you're annoying me."

Jack turned as Carruth was closing the door behind him. "You might think I was wasting my time coming all this way over here tonight, Alfie. But now I'm more resolute than I ever was that I'm going to solve this mess. And it's obvious from what you're saying, or maybe that should be from what you're *not* saying, that I might find a few old skeletons. What d'ye think?"

Carruth gritted his teeth, closing his grip on the door handle and squeezing as he forced a smile. "'*Two men will be in the field; one will be taken and the other left.*' The choice is yours. Not all of us are forced to go down the hardship route. Why do you want to make life difficult for yourself? Life's there to be enjoyed. Do a little bit of enjoying, Jack. Don't always be lifting the carpet looking for dirt. Sometimes you might end up getting more than you bargained for. Goodnight, Jack."

The door closed and the overhead light which lit up

the lush, rolling lawn went out, leaving Jack in the darkness, very much alone. He put his hand into his jacket pocket to feel the warm handle of the Beretta Tomcat, more for reassurance, he thought, than reprisal. He froze. His pocket was empty, except for the handkerchief he had wrapped the gun in earlier that afternoon. Then he remembered.

He had handed the Beretta to Jockey Carr while questioning him in the caravan.

In the heat of the moment – the buried craving for a drink – he'd forgotten to take it back.

28

Maggie opened one eye.

It was twenty to eleven. For Maggie, this was an early hour to be in bed. The wind howled non-stop outside, like a cat in heat, screeching and yowling, paving the way for a bad storm. Nothing unusual for the middle of May. The rain lashed against the bedroom window, and with each renewed smack, she burrowed down deeper under the warm quilt. Bed was the only place to be on such an inclement night. She thought about her elderly patients and muttered a quick prayer that they, like her, were safely wrapped up, and not recklessly trying to fix a broken gutter or mend a leaking pipe. She should really have called around to them but she was too tired.

She drifted in and out of the light, restless sleep, nearly always conscious of the gentle ticking of the clock on the bedside table, and the shrieking gale beyond the closed window. Her mind seemed to pole-vault from one confusing thought to another: her petrification at the caravan incident involving Jockey Carr, the disturbing, meandering thoughts that were bombarding her mind for days now, ever since her conversation with Harry Vogel, about her real mother, and the notion that this woman who gave birth to her was somewhere out there tonight, maybe even thinking of her.

There were long periods of sleep then. Flashes of Harry Vogel sitting at his wife's grave. Images of Leo Hannon being dragged out of the water on Coosbrack strand. And all the bottles she had found stashed and hidden all over the house three years ago were lined up in front of her like the "ten green bottles standing on the wall".

Some spots of sleep were not so long. She was wonderfully warm all over, back in her own bed again. What would Jack say when he arrived home and saw her lying there? She wanted to be awake to hear his reaction, but to pretend to be asleep. They would inevitably end up making love. Was that what she really wanted? Of course it was. But what if he was pissed out of his mind? Then she would get up and go out to the other room and light the fire, and sleep in the big armchair, like she was used to doing down through the years. Give me one reason that will make me happy for taking the decision to come back, she asked herself – or her mother, if she was dead and could hear her from wherever she might be watching.

Jack. I love him.

The warm hand, still slightly wet from the rain, caught her by surprise. The duvet was still covering her, right up to her shoulders. The hand made her shiver and tingle. Then shiver again. It felt so good, slipping under her nightie and up her leg, over her hip, slowly and sensuously. And up further to cup her breast, moulding it and feeling its outline so softly. She tingled and squeezed her legs together. She wanted him to think she was asleep to see what he might do next. That way, if he thought she was asleep, she could slap his face if she wanted to, to show him that he shouldn't be taking such liberties. She wanted to whisper his name. *Jack.* She wanted to say it slowly. It felt so good. *More.* She willed him. Then she twisted lightly, more onto her back, more to enjoy the touch of his fingertips, feeling and exploring like five probes. He gently pulled her nipple.

"Aahhh."

She shouldn't have moaned. She couldn't help it. Then she smelt it. It was a stench she couldn't recall. Obnoxious, even nauseating. His breath. Like stale coffee. And salami. And beer and cigarettes. All mixed together. All the things she hated smelling. And worst of all, the same smell of urine that had made her feel sick in the caravan earlier that afternoon. She opened her eyes and she knew that this terrifying panic-stricken moment, like death, would be her one abiding memory forever.

Jockey Carr was lying on his side, his left knee straddling her left hip. Saliva, dribbling from his chin, was beginning to wet her nightie right through. He stroked her hair, back over her left ear with the Beretta pistol, his left elbow supporting his frame, while he leaned across and kissed her gently on her forehead.

"Don't shoot me, please!" she whispered calmly, trying to make it the most perfectly normal thing to say.

"I'm no' g-g-goin' to sh-sh-shoo' 'ou, Maggie," he said softly, trying to restrain his obvious excitement. "I

. . . l-l-l-love 'ou," he stuttered. "Bu' tha's our s-s-secre', OK?"

"OK. Please, don't . . . do anything, Jockey," she begged.

He seemed surprised, almost indignant. "I wou-wou-wouldn' d-d-do any'hing to ha-ha-harm 'ou, Maggie." He kissed her on the lips.

Maggie gagged and nearly choked.

"W-w-will 'ou b-b-be my girlfrien'?"

"Yes. Just don't hurt me," she wheezed, horror-struck.

Her assurance seemed to relax him. He took his knee away and sat up on the side of the bed. Maggie grabbed a clump of the quilt and pulled it, covering her shoulders and neck. "How did you get in here?" she asked, watching him brandishing the pistol.

The wind was getting stronger, lashing the branches of the old sycamore tree that stood against the back wall of the house against the bare panes of the bedroom window. Each clatter made him jump. *"Wha's tha'?"* he grunted, pointing the Beretta at the glass.

"Tree branches," she whispered, praying that he might relax. "Jockey, put the gun down, please."

He studied her, then looked down at the Beretta. He placed it low enough, and at such an angle, as to show her he wasn't going to shoot her. "I 'ave to t-tell 'ou some'hing," he moaned.

Maggie couldn't decide whether the water on his cheeks was caused by crying or by the heavy rain he had obviously been running in. His clothes were saturated, his hair soaked and matted. He looked extremely distressed. "You're all right here, Jockey. Nobody's going to hurt you," she stressed, in the hope that he mightn't hurt her. "What's wrong?"

"Wh-wha's wrong?" he snapped angrily. "The s-s-sergean' 'hinks I k-killed the t-t-three boys, I kn-know he does."

The water on his cheeks was tears evidently. More began to come now as he half-talked, half-cried. Maggie never took her eyes off the pistol for a second. "Who killed them?"

"I don' kn-know."

"But you said it was Alex Kline."

"I t-t-think it was."

"What do you mean you *think* it was."

"Tha' n-n-nigh', in the p-pub . . . " Jockey wiped his nose and sniffed hard. He rubbed his eyes with one hand and scratched his head with the other. "L-Leo's car go' stolen by the boys. M-M-Martha barred them because they d-drank t-too m-much. She told me to g-g-go ups'airs f-for Leo. By the time we go' ou' to the c-c-carpark they'd gone off in Leo's car."

"How did they get away so quickly in Leo's car?"

"Because the engine was r-r-runnin'. He was givin' Mr Vogel a lif' h-h-home."

Maggie forgot for a moment that a gun packed with a full round was sitting two feet away from her. "Harry Vogel? The old man who lives up by Verity cemetery?"

Jockey nodded and wiped his nose again.

"I didn't know he came all the way down to Hannon's for a drink."

Jockey shrugged.

"So what happened then?"

"Ano'her c-car pulled up a f-f-few minu'es la'er. Alex Kline go' ou' and opened the b-b-boo' and took ou' two rifles. He t-t-threw one to Leo Hannon and g-g-gave the o'her to the man in the b-back sea'."

"There was another man in the back seat?"

"Two."

"Did you know them?"

A branch whipped the window. Jockey jumped six inches, cocked the gun and pointed it.

"*Don't!* It's only the wind."

They were both shaking now.

Jockey Carr leaned back against the bedroom wall, cradling the gun in his lap, his legs crossed, and closed his eyes. "Say 'ou'll be my g-g-girlfrien', Maggie, please?" He opened his eyes again. They were pleading to her.

Maggie watched him carefully and nodded. "Of course I'll be your girlfriend, Jockey."

He grinned and seemed perfectly relaxed, now that she had consented. That was all he wanted to hear.

"Now tell me who the two men were."

He shook his head nervously, opening his eyes wide. "C-c-can't!" He spat out the end of the word.

"Why?"

"C-c-cos they'll k-k-kill me if I say any'hing. Tha's why I want you to b-b-be my g-g-girlfrien'. Then I kn-know 'ou'll k-k-keep it a secre'."

* * *

Martha Hannon might have closed her pub early that

night, if it hadn't been for the stranger sitting close to the fire. It wouldn't have cost her a thought to tell any of her regulars to "get off home with themselves" on such a wild night. It was well known that Martha never served late drinks on stormy nights. "The last thing I want to be is responsible for a tree falling on you after you've drunk ten pints," she'd often tell the locals. But not since Leo had died. She'd almost lost her voice, one of the men had been heard to say while having a piss up against the Gents' wall earlier that evening. "She'll probably die of a broken heart," he was heard muttering, as he buttoned up his fly.

She had watched the stranger closely since he walked in, saturated, shortly after nine. The bus had dropped him outside Bantry. He'd hitched a lift from there, he told her as he thanked her for the refreshing peach schnapps. She had spent twenty minutes searching for the schnapps. No one in Durrus drank schnapps. It was for the Germans, mainly, that she stocked it.

She studied him again now, in the quietness of the empty pub, as he smoked his pipe contemplatively. The damp fire sticks crackled under the black slack which smoked heavily and occasionally spat small red hot cinders onto the hearth. He sipped his drink, a brandy and port now, and coughed to clear his throat. Martha Hannon had remarked that he could catch an awful chill on a night like that. He simply smiled and nodded at her concern. He was a tall man, with a craggy face and thick grey hair, like you would expect of someone who had spent most of his life at sea. A fisherman out of Bantry maybe, although he didn't look local enough to be one of their own. Maybe he came from Castletownbere. Or Skibbereen. She doubted it.

It was twenty past eleven. She would be asking him to leave in forty minutes. That was if he decided to stay that long. He wasn't like the normal tourists. They arrived in couples, or packs. They would stay late into the night and get quite drunk, and sing and joke. She looked behind her at the dates on the Sacred Heart Missionaries calander. It was only the nineteenth of May. Too early for the tourists. The June Bank Holiday marked the official start of the holiday season. Almost two weeks too early. He seemed far too serious, too abstract, to be a tourist. She watched him, deep in thought, reading a small book which looked to be a hundred years old, careful to keep the loose, yellowish, dog-earred pages from falling out of their tatty cover. He hadn't once raised his head in over an hour, she imagined. It must have been nice, she thought to herself, to be sitting cosily in front of a warm fire with the wind screeching outside and a hot drink and a good book to entertain you.

Martha was getting fidgety now. She couldn't remember the last night it had been this quiet. Right now, what with the way she was feeling, she preferred a busy trade. No time to dwell on Leo's death and a tiredness, to the point of exhaustion, by the end of the night that was guaranteed to knock her out as soon as her head hit the pillow. She knew she would lie awake tonight in her lonely bed, clutching Leo's pillow, crying and wishing he hadn't died. And trying to justify why she had been so hard on him for many years. And resisting the temptation to drive out to Verity graveyard to be with him during this horrible storm. She wondered would he be frightened all on his own out there, all the time asking God to reassure her that Leo was safe and beyond pain tonight. That he wasn't feeling gallons of freezing cold rain pouring into his coffin. "Would you like another drink?" She had to say something. The silence had become too much.

"Thank you."

The sound of his voice, warm and heartening, made her feel better. "I might join you for one. It's on the house."

"Thank you." He coughed. "I'm sorry to hear about your husband."

His familiarity unnerved her for a moment, until she accepted that he was being genuine with his sympathy. "It's been a horrible week. But thank you. How did you hear?"

"The man who gave me a lift from Bantry was telling me. He also told me your husband was an excellent swimmer."

Martha placed the two glasses on the table and pulled up a chair. "He'd been drinking that night."

"Alone?"

"Possibly."

"Possibly?"

Martha knew it seemed an unlikely way to answer his question. "I hadn't seen him all evening. He was found in the local sergeant's police car when they dragged him out of the water."

"I'm sorry."

"It's in God's hands now." It was all she was going to say. "Are you from around here?"

The man with the craggy complexion and grey beard shook his head and sipped his drink. ""I'm what you might call a transmigrant."

"What's that?"

"Someone who's just passing through."

Martha laughed kindly at the notion. "No one just passes through here. People come here to admire the lovely scenery. Either that or they come here to hide. This is Sheep's Head. Next stop America."

"That's where I'm heading for. America is home these days."

"Really? I have a sister in Chicago."

"Beautiful city, Chicago. I have a brother working there. Have you ever visited?"

"*Chicago?* You must be joking. When you're a publican, you rarely ever get outside your front door. I'm lucky if I get to Dublin once a year. Not that I'm too pushed about going there. It's got very rough, I hear."

The stranger puffed hard on his pipe, the smoke from the piped tobacco filling the space above the fireplace with a deliciously sweet aroma. "You've only got to look outside your own door to see how rough life is."

She listened to him speaking so calmly, yet authoritatively, so economical with his words, talking in such a way as to make her feel so wonderfully relaxed. Almost protected and wholesome again. "So what brings you to Sheep's Head?"

He seemed to consider her question for a few

seconds, puffing on the pipe again, as if for guidance. "My curiosity, I suppose."

"What are you curious about?" Martha Hannon began to realise that his answers to her questions were guardedly brief, lacking any sort of substantial enlightenment.

"I'm looking for somebody."

"Somebody who lives here?" The curiosity was getting the better of her.

"I don't know. I've been looking for this person for many years now. Shortly I'll give up."

"Why?"

He sighed. "Because I'm tired. It's not that I'm losing interest. It's just that I am getting old now. And I would like to spend some time with my family. And with my grandchildren. They are growing up without me and that is beginning to break my heart. Have you family?"

"A son. But he died some years back."

"I'm so sorry." He waited out of respect before continuing. "I have two daughters. They live at home close to my wife in Harrisburg. In Pennsylvania."

"But you're not from Pennsylvania, are you?"

"No."

He wasn't going to tell her where he was from. That was quite clear now. He produced a small wallet from his leather hold-all. From the wallet he placed a small photograph on the table.

"Do you recognise this man?"

Martha picked up the photograph, careful not to be seen to be too eager. Of course she recognised the man in the photograph. She only hoped now that her reaction had gone unnoticed. Through the corner of her eye the stranger watched her as she studied the old black and white. She shook her head gently at first, then more thoroughly. "Never seen him before. Why do you ask?"

"I need to find him." He took back the photograph quickly, then hesitated for a moment, watching her as if, on second thoughts, she might change her mind. His disappointment, all of a sudden, was discernible.

"Why do you ask me if I know him?" Martha asked.

"Well, I suppose, someone who owns a popular pub like this would see hundreds of people passing through every week. I was just hoping that maybe you might have served him, and talked to him."

"This is a very small town, Mister . . . ?" She waited for him to introduce himself. He didn't. Immediately she felt a coldness towards him, and him to her. "This is a very small town. We have four pubs within a stone's throw of each other. Another three further out on the peninsula. During the winter months each of those pubs can calculate, almost to the nearest pound, exactly what their regulars are going to spend of a night's drinking." She nodded to the deserted bar. "As you can see, I don't think I've exactly won the lottery here tonight." He seemed to ignore her whimsey. Martha looked back at the clock over the bar. It was five minutes to midnight. "I'll give you one more if you like, then I'm planning on closing the shop."

"Thank you." He gestured to his almost empty glass. "I'll take one for the road, if that's OK?"

"Certainly," she said, picking up her empty glass. "That'll be three pound forty-five, thank you." She no longer liked him. He was an intruder, a nosey meddler, who wasn't welcome in her pub, and wouldn't be welcome the length or breadth of Durrus if some of the locals knew what he was hunting. "Why did you think I might know this man? The one in the photograph," she emphasised, trying to sound as vague as possible.

"Because he was seen drinking in here. The night the three boys went missing."

Martha Hannon almost dropped the expensive bottle of VSOP. She turned to face the stranger. "Well, in case you haven't heard, they've been found. Hitching a lift into Galway. A man in a van gave them a lift." She tried to take long breaths, knowing that her flustered state could easily give her away. "Where do you plan on staying tonight?" she asked, trying to sound pleasant and helpful.

The old man started to pack away his book and papers. "I saw a small bed and breakfast on my way into town earlier. I might try there."

"Well, you're welcome to stay here if you like. I have three spare rooms, all mod cons, that I use during the busy tourist season. It'll only take me a couple of minutes to switch on the heating and get it ready for you. Fifteen pounds a night, including breakfast. There's a bathroom at the end of the landing, hot water freely available." She wasn't sure why she had invited him to stay. "You'll only get soaked if you walk up the road on this sort of a night." Maybe out of sheer loneliness. Now that Leo was gone and the house reverberated to every move she made these past few days. And nights. The nights were the most difficult, the most soul-destroying of all. "You can have a warm bath and relax with your book. The windows are all double-glazed, so you won't be bothered by the storm." She didn't want to be alone in the house tonight, not with the storm, and the howling, whooping wind, and the loose panels of corrugated iron sheeting on the old barn flapping and banging, and the dog barking at the bleating rain.

Or maybe it was the sheer, overwhelming terror she felt when he showed her the photograph. She wasn't sure why she got such a fright. It wasn't a bad old photograph. In fact, it did him justice. Sure, she had heard all the rumours years back. But as far as she was concerned that's all they were: just rumours. For all she knew this could have been a long lost relation. She waited for him to make up his mind. "Well, I haven't got all night," she said, trying to sound a bit flippant.

He smiled with relief. "I'd love to stay. A hot bath now is very appealing. Just before I say goodnight to you, Mrs Hannon, do you know this man?" He took a larger, more recent photograph from his bag this time and handed it to her.

Martha Hannon nodded. "He's a local businessman."

He smiled as he picked up his papers and his brandy and port and followed her through the kitchen to the stairs.

29

Jockey Carr was gone when Maggie woke up with a violent shudder. She couldn't believe she had fallen into such a deep sleep.

It was exactly half past four. If it hadn't been for the stench of wet, dirty clothes, it could all have been a horrible nightmare. Carefully, she eased herself out of bed, into her slippers, and crept to the top of the stairs. The wind had died down considerably now, and, from where she was standing, small cracks of light from the May dawn were beginning to reflect off the landing wall, throwing a hazy, grey fringe around the house. She listened, her heart pounding, for his familiar heavy breathing. The house seemed empty. The front door was closed. The storm seemed miles away, still audible but in a much less threatening way.

She plugged in the kettle, still shaking, and sat at the kitchen table, listening to it picking up speed and generating noise. *Noise!* That was exactly what she needed. A distraction. A deterrent. Anything that would stop her mind from racing, from reliving the disgusting experience she had just come through. Or had she? What if she was only imagining the whole episode? From where she was sitting she could observe the damage the storm had wreaked on her picturesque back garden.

She was sure the fish were dead. The pond looked as if it had taken in five times its normal volume of water. The white bench she had painted only a week before had been blown into the pond. The colourful flowers and shrubs were beaten into masses of watery pulp and her beautiful wallflowers and creeper, just barely stuck to the wall, hung from their roots like a bunch of old skeletons. It was like as if someone had gone into the garden with a long stick and thrashed everything that was growing.

She wasn't sure how long she had been dozing. The doorbell was ringing frantically. She looked at the clock. It was just after eight. She had stretched out on the couch, a mug of tea in hand, the television on, and eventually slept for three hours.

"Anybody home?"

The voice was familiar. It was Aidan Kerr.

Maggie opened the door.

He was badly rattled and upset. *"Maggie, where's Jack?"* he blurted, gasping for breath as if he had been running.

Maggie pulled him inside, delighted to see him for other reasons. "I don't know. He didn't come home. Why?"

He didn't answer. "Have you tried his mobile?"

"I couldn't get through. I'd say a lot of the lines and the GSM towers are out after the storm. What's wrong?"

"Ollie Jennings called to the house a short while back. He was out walking his dog up around Doo Lough about seven this morning. He came across the body of a young boy washed up on the water's edge."

"A young boy?"

Aidan Kerr nodded. "That's all I know. He tried to ring here but the lines must be down. He rang my house but couldn't get through so he drove over. There are branches and broken trees and roof slates everywhere. Bad flooding as well." Aidan was shaking. "Can I make a cup of tea?"

"I'll make it for you." Maggie nodded to the chair. "Sit down."

Aidan picked up the mobile phone. "Can I try?"

"Go ahead."

He dialled Jack's number. "It's ringing," he said feverishly. "Jack, can you hear me? It's Aidan."

Jack Buckley watched as the fire tender dragged the huge tree out of the centre of the main R591 Bantry to Durrus road. Four Mile Water had burst its banks and the fields on both sides of the road were badly flooded. The road had been completely blocked by the fallen tree since before one that morning. Jack decided to stay at the scene with his blue light flashing. There was always the chance that some unsuspecting driver wouldn't see the huge tree in the deluge of rain and drive head on into it. As well as that the wide ditches on either side of the road were flooded. Five feet deep, Jack reckoned, enough to drown anyone who got stuck trying to drive around the tree. He had been sitting there now, willing himself to stay awake, for almost six hours.

He rushed back to the car and grabbed the ringing phone. "This is Jack Buckley," he shouted, above the racket of the fire engine's powerful generator.

"Jack, it's Aidan. Can you hear me?"

His voice seemed panicked and breathless. "Go ahead, Aidan."

"Jack, a body's been found above at Doo Lough. A young boy, by the sound of it."

Jack's heart sank. He'd never known his hunches to be wrong. This time, though, he had prayed his notions would be wildly inaccurate and that the sighting of the three boys had been well-judged. He had been waiting on a phonecall like this for two weeks now, begging Christ above that it would never come, but expecting it at any moment. It had been inevitable. His tiredness was gone now, as was his yearning for bed, replaced by a horrible sickly feeling of despair and anger, and an awful desire to be a million miles away.

* * *

Martha Hannon placed the plate in front of the stranger. She was still none the wiser as to who he was or what his business was about. "Mind your fingers, it's very hot." Two bacon, two sausage, a poached egg, tomato and black and white pudding. Brown toast and coffee. Great value for fifteen pounds. Martha would have given him the lot for free, including the night's accomodation if she could only have found out more about him. He wasn't being particularly co-operative, she felt, considering what she had done for him: given him shelter on one of the worst nights in living memory. She had offered him bed and board and wasn't going to just let him disappear without finding out a bit about him. Martha Hannon had a reputation around Durrus for her brusqueness. Never let it be said. "Where are you from?" she asked rather bluntly.

The man was cutting the sausage carefully, placing a sliver of the poached egg on top and dipping it into the tomato ketchup. He looked up from his plate. "Where would you say I'm from?"

She sat down on the edge on the chair opposite him, watching carefully, as she did; looking at his bushy eyebrows and thick-skinned complexion – old skin, hardened by hardship – and the steady black rings under each eye. "Germany?"

He stopped eating, almost instantaneously, and swallowed quickly, burning the roof of his mouth as he did so. "Germany? That's interesting. Why do you think I'm from Germany?"

Martha Hannon felt uneasy with his line of questioning. He reminded her of how Jack Buckley might try on his sergeant routine when he was trying to extract information. "Just the way you talk, that's all. I'm not very good at accents. It's just that we get a lot of Germans coming and going all year round. Some of them own beautiful houses dotted around the peninsula. They could be dead up there for weeks and no one would know."

He sipped from his cup of tea and stirred it a bit more. "Do they ever come in for a drink?"

"That crowd?" She laughed. "You must be joking. They arrive in here with their continental registrations, and their jeeps stocked up with Dutch beer and French wine and German mineral water. They'd knock you down on the street if you didn't jump out of their way. I don't think I've ever met a single one of them that's friendly."

"Has anyone ever met them?"

"Only if they're looking for antibiotics for the flu, or if one them needs to see a doctor. That's all."

"And who would they get in touch with then?"

"Well, we don't have a doctor here in Durrus, not since he died a few years back. If it's very serious they'll go into Bantry."

"And if it's not serious?"

"They'll ring the nurse. She's a gorgeous wee thing. So friendly and helpful. She'd do anything for you."

"So you wouldn't know any of these Germans then?"

Martha shook her head. "I couldn't tell a German from a Jew." She froze and almost apologised for what seemed to just gush out. He didn't seem too perturbed by her clumsiness. That's if he felt it was clumsiness. He smiled.

"I've never heard that expression before. It must be Irish." He placed the knife and fork down and picked up the dog-earred book again, the one he had been studying before he retired. Martha tried to see if there was a name at the top of the page, something that might give her an idea as to the man's trade. The author was Sigmund Freud. "Are you a doctor?"

"Sometimes."

"In Germany?"

"Pennsylvania. The States," he added derisively.

"What sort of doctor are you?" Her questions were bordering on impertinent now but she didn't give a damn.

"I'm a psychiatrist actually."

"I thought that. You have that look about you."

"Really? You meet a lot of psychiatrists then?"

"I've met a few." Martha Hannon had never met a psychiatrist in her life. "What area do you specialise in?"

"Well, well. We are interested, aren't we? Mental illness, some people would call it. I prefer to see it as psychoneurosis. Functional disorders of the mind in people who might otherwise be legally sane. You've heard of psychopaths, haven't you?" His question had the desired effect. Martha Hannon's face turned pale.

"Psychopaths?"

"Emotional instability without specific mental disorder. Murderers. Sexual perverts. I used to study individual cases and try to cure them."

"Were you able to cure them?"

"Not really."

She stood up from the table, draped the tea towel across her shoulder and picked up an empty bowl. "My Leo was a kind of psychopath."

He stopped eating. "Why do you say that?"

"Because he used to beat me up something awful when he was full of drink."

Martha Hannon did something then that this stranger had never witnessed before in his life. She opened her cardigan and took it off, hanging it over the chair. Then she opened the top four buttons of her plain, traditional dress until the sharp blue and purple marks stood out against her pale, soft skin. "Kicks . . . punches . . . pinches . . . fists . . . feet . . . anything that he knew would hurt me, and make me cry out, begging him to stop, he would use. Sometimes for hours." She buttoned up the dress and put back on her cardigan as casually as if she had been in the changing room of a clothes shop. "You said last night you were sorry to hear of my husband's death. Why were you sorry? I wasn't. There are nights I miss him. Today I hope he rots in hell." She said nothing else, and left her stranger guest to finish his breakfast in shocked silence.

* * *

Jack Buckley removed his cap as he waited for Alex Kline's hall door to open. It was almost nine. He had been told of the celebration Alex was throwing the night before for Ben Roper, to toast the safe return of his son. Jack had thought it would be opportune if Ben Roper accompanied him to Doo Lough, in the company of Aidan Kerr, who would perform The Last Rites on the body of the young boy. Jack had a month's salary set aside in the back of his mind, a mental wager, that it was the body of one of the three teenagers. Ben Roper could identify the body. Then they could drain the lake and recover his two mates. Then Superintendent Alfie Carruth would hold a press conference in Macroom to announce the setting up of a murder inquiry.

A very hung-over Alex Kline opened the door a squint, and shielded his eyes from the bright sunshine. "Morning, Jack." He opened the door fully, half-dressed in a vest and pants, and a pair of black ankle socks, not quite certain what to say next. "You didn't make it to the party last night?" Alex inquired, scratching his head.

Jack ignored the question. "Is Ben Roper here?"

"Yes, he's . . . "

Before Alex could finish, Ben Roper was at the foot of the stairs, pulling on a pullover, waiting with a worried look for the sergeant to say something.

"Ben, I won't beat around the bush. A body of a young man had been found on the shore of Doo Lough, towards the tip of the peninsula. I've got reason to believe it could be one of the three boys."

Roper's spirits sank visibly. His eyes filled with tears.

"Jesus Christ," Alex spouted angrily, "they were only spotted in Galway twenty-four hours ago. What's going on, Jack?"

Jack stared at Alex Kline with such contempt that the man backed off. "Ben can come in the police car with me." He put his cap back on, all the time watching Alex Kline. "Take your time, Ben. I'll wait in the car for you."

* * *

Aidan Kerr arranged to meet Jack Buckley and Ben Roper at Doo Lough. He told Maggie to stay in the car, left the engine running, and ran back into the house to collect a small plastic bottle of holy water and a thin purple stole. All the time he asked God, or whoever might be listening, not to let it be any of the three young teenagers. Odds were it had to be.

The road to Doo Lough took them out along the lush south side of Sheep's Head, ten miles of the most striking, unspoilt scenery, out across Dunmanus Bay, through Kilcrohane, hugging the steep slopes of the Caher Mountains, and on through Letter and into the Ballyroon mountains, with the rain-flooded fields and the narrow bumpy roads. From there, a short walk through long grass and marshy bog, sodden now and quite deep and unmanageable in places after the torrential rain of the night just gone.

Doo Lough was a haven of tranquillity for writers and poets, and for anyone who simply wanted to get as far away as possible from the noisy city and the pressures of life. During the winter months you could walk for miles and not meet anyone, alone with the sound of the waves crashing against the pebbly beach below the steep hills of Tooreen.

Now the summer was coming, and with it the tourists would flock to Sheep's Head, in search of a week or a fortnight when they could tell their friends they did absolutely nothing except walk along some of the fifty-five-mile-long Sheep's Head Way nature trek, or call into Durrus Tropical House where they saw fascinating insects and reptiles and exotic butterflies. Another day they might take a trip to Carbery Island to visit the seal colony and on the way back try their luck at catching a mackerel. All-day sea fishing was available to the serious angler. Or a bundle of friendly pubs for the serious drinker.

Aidan Kerr sighed. The dream seemed shattered. He loved Sheep's Head and its people and all it had going for it: the simplest things in life which made it his favourite place on earth. He loved standing up in the old pulpit in the church on Sunday morning in the summer, smiling as he looked around the packed congregation, spotting the new faces who were visiting Durrus for the first time, recognising the old reliables who came back for their fortnight or their eight weeks of the school holidays year after year, without fail, and welcoming them – genuinely – to one of the best-kept secrets in the whole country. He would urge the visitors to enjoy the peace and tranquillity "amongst stunning surroundings and friendly people" – those were the words he used every first Sunday of every summer month. Now the words "one of the best-kept secrets in the whole country" were beginning to haunt him for a different reason.

Father Aidan Kerr prided himself on his summer sermons, as he referred to them, and on the image he tried to portray, particularly to the holiday families, full of young children and their cousins and friends and grandparents. Some of them went to the caravan parks. Others, who had the money to spend and who wanted seclusion, had built their own small houses on land they had purchased from *A&E Kline, Estate Agents*, up around Gortnakilly and Glanalin, and nearer the beaches and the small stoney inlets on the south shore, close to Dooneen and Rosskerrig. Eventually when they had their children reared, they told Father Kerr, they hoped to retire to Sheep's Head. He had always endorsed how safe a place

Sheep's Head was, particularly for young families. "You can leave the engine running and the windows open here, and they'll think you're just one of the locals," he boasted from the altar to the new faces every Sunday through the summer. "Sheep's Head must be one of the safest places in the country to bring children for a summer break. The worst that can happen them is they'll fall and scratch their knees."

The congregation would always show their contentment by laughing softly.

He won them over every time. The bishop commended him on Sunday, having sat at the back of the church listening. He enjoyed when the children would shout to him from the playground in the caravan park every Saturday evening as he cycled out to Kilcrohane to celebrate mass. "Hiya, Aidan," they shouted, only to be chastised by their parents for calling the priest by his first name.

The bubble had burst. The "best-kept secret in the world" had just become a barbarous transgression. He had always urged parents "not to be afraid" to let their children enjoy themselves freely on Sheep's Head. Now, a young boy, who was still a mere child in his parents' eyes was dead. Aidan checked the milometre on the dashboard. He had zeroed it as he left Durrus. Exactly sixteen miles to Doo Lough. How was he going to explain the boy's death to the first of his visitors over the Bank Holiday weekend? What would he tell them? That the young boy wandered out of a pub sixteen miles away and slipped into a deep lake? Jesus Christ, no one *walks* out this far, never mind *drives*! Unless, of course, he was brought out here. And dumped. Then he might have slipped into the deep lough if it had been dark, and if he had wandered off the narrow road. And where were his two friends?

Sheep's Head had been unique in the statistics books up to now. Today it was only a matter of time before the country's media descended on the peninsula and changed his sermons and the way the children might say hello to him every Saturday for ever.

Aidan Kerr parked close to the rickety fence on the left-hand side of the road and killed the engine. The hearse and the police cars would need to use the small official carpark, close to the picnic benches and the neat family area where the children played in the summer while their parents admired the scenery and wrote their postcards. He opened the window and took a lungful of the fresh, raw North Atlantic wind. He turned to face Maggie, unable to recall the last time he had seen her so quiet and removed. "Are you all right?"

She nodded and shoved her hands further into the sleeves of the heavy Angora sweater.

"I think we'll wait here until Jack arrives."

She agreed and they said no more, the howling northerly wind doing all the talking now, rocking the car from side to side with the occasional gust, reminding them of its awesome power.

Aidan followed the lush green and heathery slopes down to where the edge of the land disappeared and fell away to the sea, still thrashing and white with breakers. He couldn't swim, which always kept him aware of the sea's deadly dominance and its need for respect. The sky was darkest blue, the spot where they had parked unchanged, as it had remained for what seemed like forever.

"Do you think it's one of the teenagers?" Maggie asked gently.

"Probably." Aidan tried to concentrate on a buoy marking some lobster pots he had just spotted back towards Coosbrack.

"How come someone saw them in Galway then?"

Aidan shrugged. "Mistake, I suppose." He reached across Maggie's legs and opened the glove compartment. She jumped with fright. "Sorry," he said softly. "I'm no good at this sort of thing."

"What sort of thing?"

"Dead children."

A car drew up behind. It was Jack's police car.

* * *

Jack removed the key and placed it quietly beside the handbrake as if trying to make the least amount of noise possible. Ben Roper hadn't said much since sitting into the car outside Kline's house. He admired the striking beauty of the peninsula's scenery a couple of times, muttering words like "astonishing" and "breathtaking" to himself, as the road took another sharp turn and Owen's Island and Goleen Strand both came into view. Once Jack had asked him was he OK? Roper just looked awkwardly at him, as if to say that he couldn't understand the logic of asking such a question.

Jack tried to make himself content with admiring the

scenery. But he was tired of the beautiful landscape and the endless water for as far as the eye could see. He was bringing a father to identify the body of a seventeen-year-old boy, maybe his own son, who should have returned home to his family nearly two weeks before with great stories and photographs of a weekend away with his best friends.

Instead the young boy's body was being returned to his family this gorgeous May morning by the storm which had swept him ashore.

"He couldn't swim," Ben Roper whispered, trying desperately hard to remain capable and resilient. He smiled grimly and looked at Jack Buckley for some sort of optimism.

"It mightn't be him, Ben." Jack fixed his eyes on his. Here he was, sitting in a little car on a small chunk of land jutting out into the Atlantic Ocean, a smalltown sergeant offering false hope and consolation to one of the wealthiest and most successful businessmen in the country. He couldn't help but wonder how important his money was now in the face of such unthinkable adversity.

"I know what you're thinking," Ben Roper said. "And you're right. I'd give every penny of it away this second if he would just walk up that little grassy path from that water and smile." He bent over and placed his hands up to his face and started to cry. Jack found himself stretching out and placing his arm across Ben Roper's shoulders, as the familiar, long, black estate, with the darkened windows, carefully pulled past and parked in front of Aidan Kerr's car. The pathologist, dressed in white overalls, doffed his cap to Jack and waited. Three members of a local mountain rescue crew, returning from the lake, rested at a huge rock until the party got out of the cars and organised themselves for the gruesome identification process. Jack waved discreetly to Aidan who had stepped out of his car now. Maggie was already leaning against the fence.

"Are you ready?" Jack asked his passenger, courteously.

Ben Roper buried his face in his handkerchief and nodded as he blew his nose. "My son hated going to school. I always remember him asking me before he'd go some mornings when he was nearly five: 'Dad,' he'd say to me, 'would you know I was crying?' he'd ask me." Ben Roper stepped out onto the mulchy verge, its thick tufts of grass, almost washed away by the rivers of rain pouring off Ballyroon mountains, giving way underfoot.

Jack looked back down the narrow roadway as he closed the car door. Two more cars were pulling in now. Alex Kline was parking his Mercedes. Superintendent Alfie Carruth was straightening his cap as he searched for a spot of ground to stand out onto that wouldn't dirty his shiny shoes. Jack continued to stare until he was sure that Carruth could see him looking. He watched the senior policeman with a mixture of mockery and rebuke. Carruth avoided his gaze, shaking hands with Ben Roper as he introduced himself.

* * *

Jack remained at Ben Roper's side all the way down the grassy path to Doo Lough. They hung back in the procession, allowing the mountain rescue men lead the pathologist, followed by two other police officers, followed by Alfie Carruth and Alex Kline, both deep in huddled conversation.

Jack could hear Ben Roper's voice trembling as he negotiated the difficult, slippery terrain, which became quite steep towards the final hundred metres, all the time keeping his sights level with the surrounding hills. "This is such a beautiful place," he said, almost sounding sentimental. "I suppose you couldn't really pick a more beautiful spot to die in. Could you?"

"It is beautiful," Jack replied, trying to strengthen whatever resolve and will power it was that Ben Roper was reaching out for. In the distance Jack could see Ollie Jennings, who had made the grim discovery shortly after seven that morning, sitting frozen-looking on a small rock at the edge of the lake, close to a small bundle which lay perfectly still. As they got closer Jack could make out that the small body was covered by a scanty sheet of green plastic, each corner weighted by small rocks, billowing in the stiff breeze. He shivered, begging that God in his mercy would drop a very large Scotch whiskey from the blue sky any second. He badly needed a strong drink. His mouth was dry, his lips raw against the biting cold wind. He shoved his hands deep into his pockets and looked behind to where Maggie was walking slowly, her arm linked by Aidan Kerr's.

Ben Roper joined his hands lovingly as he reached the edge of Doo Lough and the spot where the shrouded body lay.

Jack stood to his right, about four feet away from him,

and watched him. The man squeezed his eyes closed tightly, as if dragging up the force and the spirit he needed to lift the plastic and look down at the young boy's face.

The unbearable whistling and jostling of the strong, unbending northerly wind seemed to drop at that moment. The uncanny silence was almost eerie. The heat of the sun, if only for that moment, became tangible.

Ben Roper bent down, stopped for a few seconds, and lifted the green sheet. For a moment his face didn't show any reaction. Jack's hopes lifted. Maybe it wasn't his son.

The first backwash was like a sneezing, choking sound. Then Ben Roper coughed as if he was trying to catch his breath. And he started to cry. *"Oh God, Adam. No, please!"* He dived down and grabbed the young boy by the shoulders, his huge swollen neck and face horribly distorted and discoloured. *"Oh Jesus, somebody, help him! Adam, it's Daddy . . . Adam!"*

Jack got down on his knees and tried to hug the man. The way he shouted his son's name was going to live in his mind forever.

"Adam!"

The young boy's name re-echoed again and again against the hills surrounding Doo Lough and around the small valley in the heart of the Ballyroon mountains.

30

"Good days . . . bad days . . ."

Martha Hannon was trying to remember the name of the song the words came from when her lodger sat down at the counter. Good days, bad days. She reckoned it would be a measure of each individual day of the rest of her life, now that Leo was gone. Good moments and memories. And bad. There weren't many moments in the few days just gone that Leo hadn't occupied her mind totally. She had tried to dwell on his better qualities and asked God not to be too hard on him for raising his fist to her the odd time and boxing the bejaysus living daylights out of her. She never screamed or cried when his cold knuckles slammed into the soft warm skin of her cheekbones, so no one had ever heard them fighting. She was hugely proud of that quality in herself. How she had kept "that business" a secret. That way was best. She used to tell herself she could retain her pride and dignity if no one ever found out. No one was ever going to call Martha Hannon a battered wife. She always assumed afterwards that Leo had had a perfectly valid reason for hitting her. Maybe she had provoked him in some way. Maybe he was having a bad evening and she should have kept quiet. *"Whist, woman!"* as he would always say to her when they drove into Bantry together to the Cash and Carry on a Friday morning. She would never ask though, why he hit her, in case it might remind him and he would belt her again. It had to be her fault, she always concluded. "It was *my* fault!" she would insist to her friends the very rare occasion, in the early days, when he drunk heavily and the beatings were more savage and severe, when one of them might spot a bruise or a mark. That way, if it *was* her fault, his violent temper didn't make him such a bad person.

It was getting on for lunchtime.

"Thank you very much, Mrs Hannon, for your hospitality."

The lodger's voice was soft and friendly, with a tremendous, deep resonance, as if he might have been a baritone. Martha Hannon decided to wear something nice for the occasion today, knowing that her lodger would be back for a bite of lunch. She wore a cream-coloured dress with a plunging neckline – showing off her full cleavage and her milky-white skin. No sagging, no boney spots, no wrinkles. She'd retained herself well, for a woman of sixty. She cleared away the empty bowl which, barely ten minutes before, she had taken from the oven, full of piping-hot Sheperd's Pie. He was about her own age, sixty, she estimated. She was sixty-three, but she always rounded it off to the nearest ten. That way she still had another two years being sixty.

He opened a small purse and took out some brand-new currency, folded neatly, and glanced briefly at the man in uniform, sitting at the end of the bar drinking a pint and a large Scotch, who he knew was listening. "How much do I owe you?" he asked the landlady.

Martha Hannon looked him up and down. He seemed well-fed and content after a good night's sleep. She'd bump it up a few quid. "Thirty-eight pounds fifty," she declared.

He handed her three twenty-pound notes. "A little gift for your kind hospitality." He insisted she keep the change.

She responded with a narky smile. "Thank you." She was embarrassed now because she was sure he knew she had overcharged him.

He nodded to the man in uniform. "You might like to get him another drink when he's finished that one."

Martha Hannon was astonished now at the stranger's flagrant generosity. "You don't even know him."

"Well, judging by how he's dressed, I'd say he's worth knowing." He smiled and nodded respectfully to the police officer.

Martha Hannon gave a loud tutt. "You obviously *don't* know him," she crowed through the side of her mouth. "Drinking bloody day and night." She wanted to turn to Jack Buckley, now that her Leo was dead, and tell him that it was his fault that Leo had gone back to drinking in the three years since Buckley had come to Durrus. *You killed him,* she wanted to scream. *You mightn't have drowned him above at Coosbrack that night, but you as good as drowned him with drink!* And she would have yelled it there and then, word for word, if her lodger hadn't been sitting between them, and him so generous. She picked up the visitor's book and slammed it down on the bar top. "Here, sign this. All visitors have to sign before they leave."

The stranger seemed a little surprised. He hesitated for a moment, then searched for a pen.

Jack Buckley pulled a biro from his jacket pocket and politely slid it slowly down along the bar towards the stranger. "There you go," he said. "And thanks for the drink."

"You're welcome." The stranger looked at the stripes on his sleeve. "Sergeant." He signed his name slowly, checking back through some of the previous signatories. "They get quite a few people staying here, don't they?"

Jack waited for Martha Hannon to disappear into the kitchen with the dirty dishes. "Not really," he replied quietly. "I think she just adds a few names to the book now and again herself. It gets busy during July and August, but that's about it." He coughed to make sure she wasn't listening. "You know she's ripping you off, don't you?"

The stranger smiled. "So what? I enjoyed my stay."

"I wouldn't give that bitch tuppence. She's a miserable old cow." He nodded to the man's hold-all. "Just passing through?"

"Well, I was told last night that no one just passes through here."

"So who are you here to see?"

"Yes, just down this way looking for a few people from the past."

"Ancestors."

"In a manner, so to speak."

"What's their name? I might be able to help you," Jack moved his stool closer. He could hear Martha Hannon tutting from behind the kitchen curtain.

"Well, they're definitely not Irish. That's for sure."

"Ahh," Jack sighed, "well, then, I definitely can't help you. I'd say we get more Americans and Australians down here looking for their ancestors' birthplaces than anywhere else in Ireland. They all seem to think their grandparents came from Cork. Cronins, MacCarthys, Buckleys, O'Sullivans, O'Callaghans, O'Connells, we've got the whole lot of them down here." Jack held out his hand. "I'm Jack Buckley, the local sergeant around here. And you are . . . "

"Maister." The stranger shook his hand and smiled.

"Nice to meet you."

Maister watched him sip the Scotch, trying not to make his surprise look too obvious. "Do you always drink on the job?"

Jack swallowed the Scotch and cringed. "On the job, off the job, who gives a shite? There's a young kid, seventeen. We just pulled his body out of Doo Lough this morning. I'm sure he doesn't care if the local sergeant is having a couple of lunchtime drinks, does he? Anyway, we'll all be dead for millions of years, won't we?"

The stranger stood up and put on his coat, choosing to ignore the sergeant's boorishness.

"I'm trying to convince the local Justice of the Peace *and* the Superintendent that the kid's been murdered, but they're not having any of it. Picture this: a young teenager comes down here to celebrate finishing his final exams with his two mates. They all disappear after a few drinks. One of them turns up dead at the bottom of a lake at the farthest, most remote spot on the peninsula. And this *super* superintendent thinks that foul play is not an issue. He says, 'We'll wait for the results of the post mortem and then we'll decide what we're going to do.' I mean to say, how did the kid get out to Doo Lough? Did he walk out there and just jump in for a quick swim? No he didn't. He was brought out there and fucking drowned!"

Martha Hannon was standing in the entrance to the kitchen, staring in horror at her local sergeant, embarrassed for the visitor who had paid her well. "Jack Buckley, are you trying to shame us all in front of a paying customer?" She placed her hands on her hips, a sign that she wouldn't be serving Jack any more alcohol.

"What are you talking about, Martha? How am I shaming you all? *Me?* Me shaming this bunch?" He pointed to an imaginary crowd of people standing behind him. "Let me tell you something, Martha, and you can tell all your customers that I told you, like you always do so well. Someone in this town is trying to destroy the good name of Durrus. Someone is succeeding in making us all out to be monsters. Someone in this little keyhole of a corner of this planet knows what happened to those three children. And you can tell all of your customers that *Sergeant* Jack Buckley is going to find out who it is."

Martha Hannon ignored him, tutting at his ridiculous behaviour.

"Listen, pal, I'm sorry. I might be a little tipsy. I don't

mean to be so rude. I've had a horrible morning, and I just needed a few drinks to get the circulation flowing again before I continue my investigation. A father identifying his young son's body. The kid's been at the bottom of that cold lake for nearly two weeks. I just needed a couple of strong drinks. That's all. Jesus," he raged, nodding at Martha Hannon, "you come in here and spend your money on a few quiet drinks and all you get for helping to keep this pub open is abuse from the owner. I'd say your husband is having a party in Heaven every time he realises he doesn't have to listen to your ranting anymore." He knew he was very pissed so he decided to close his shirt and do up his tie. That way she might give him another drink. "Excuse me," he turned and addressed the imaginary crowd, "it's not been one of my most enjoyable days as a policeman."

"I understand. It was nice meeting you. Now if you don't mind, I have a train to catch." He nodded to Martha Hannon. "Thank you again. I hope to be back soon." He looked across at Jack Buckley. "Very soon." He gathered his paper and book, placed them in the leather satchel which he slid into the black hold-all and slung it over his shoulder, as he stepped out through the side door.

Martha Hannon was examining the guest book's most recent entry.

"Show me that!" Jack Buckley grabbed the book and turned it around. He leapt across the pub and ran out onto the main street. *"Excuse me!"* he shouted after the stranger. *"Josef Maister?"*

The man didn't show any reaction, didn't seem alarmed, at all. "Yes, Sergeant Buckley."

Jack Buckley tried to relax. He tried to make his approach seem leisurely. No slurring, no staggering. "We've been expecting you."

"*We?* Who is we?"

"Nathan Lohan's sister showed me one of your letters. In it you told Nathan that you were planning to come to Ireland on the eighteenth of May. That was last Saturday. Obviously you kept your word."

"I always keep my word." Josef Maister seemed confused. "Why was Nathan's sister showing you letters that I sent him?"

"Because Nathan was the victim of a hit-and-run three years ago."

Maister seemed to stagger for a second and almost lost his balance. "Hit-and-run? Is he dead?"

"Yes. Heather called to my house last week with a letter from you, that you had written to her brother. She asked me to read it. She thought it might make some sort of sense to me. I investigated the incident three years ago when I first moved out here as sergeant of Sheep's Head. At the time she called I was investigating the disappearance of three young boys who were last seen here in the village a couple of weeks back."

"I know. I read about their disappearance in one of your newspapers."

He seemed very shocked by news of the hit-and-run.

"So you read my letter? Do you still have it?"

"No. She took it back. But it sounded like whoever wrote to you was pretending to be Nathan Lohan. Does that make sense?"

Maister seemed deeply worried now. "Yes. He wrote

to me some weeks back. I hadn't heard from him in over three years, which is explained by his sudden death. But then, if he's dead three years, who would want to write to me pretending to be Nathan? He told me he had been away travelling and had been unable to contact me. I got such a pleasant surprise when his letter arrived, but . . . " He was completely confused now. "Obviously someone wants me to think that Nathan Lohan is still alive."

"Why?"

"I'm not sure." He looked warily at Jack. "It's a very long story, one that wouldn't interest you, Sergeant."

"Try me, please. Would you like to come back in for another drink? You can tell me all about it over a hot whiskey."

"No," he replied, more flustered now, in a desperate hurry. "Maybe another time. I must go now."

"Do you mind me asking you why you were showing Martha Hannon photographs last night?"

"Who told you about those?"

"Martha did. She might hate me, but I'm still the sergeant around here," he said uncomfortably.

"Because I am looking for those men. It's as simple as that, Sergeant."

"She said you told her you were a psychiatrist."

"Used to be."

"And what are you now?"

He thought for a moment. "Worried. *Very* worried."

"Have you been in contact with Nathan's sister since you arrived?"

The old man shook his head, as if to ridicule Jack's question.

"Why?"

"Because Nathan Lohan was an only child, Sergeant." He almost spat with each word. "He didn't have a sister. I know, because I met his mother. And whoever this Heather woman is that you refer to, whom you claim met you and showed you a letter that I sent to Nathan, she's lying to you, Sergeant. Lying through her *teeth*. She wants something from you that obviously only you can provide. If my experience of these people is anything to go by, and she sounds as if she may be connected, I would have to say you're treading on extremely dangerous ground."

Jack Buckley watched, flabbergasted and rattled, as a tense and tormented-looking Josef Maister sat into his waiting taxi and left Durrus.

31

Dinner was ruined.

It was twenty-to-ten. The lasagna was so cold now, and sunk in the middle, it smelt like wet socks. The starter, a fresh, chilled prawn cocktail with a spicy Mary Rose sauce, was lukewarm and vinegary. The candle had burnt down to little more than a pool of dirty pink wax in the saucer. She had brought it home from their romantic weekend in Paris, and bundled it away so safely that she couldn't remember where she had put it until she had found it while packing her belongings to leave him a fortnight back. Maggie, resigned now that he wasn't coming home for his dinner – a special surprise – blew out the flame, and with it, she was sure, any hope of a reconciliation.

Aidan Kerr had dropped her home after the young boy's body had been properly identified. She had asked the lad's father if he would like her to organise some mild sedatives to help him to relax. He wasn't able to answer her. Not even a "yes" or a "no". She wasn't sure why she hugged him. She wouldn't have done it a week ago. Not even a couple of days ago. Something Harry Vogel had said had touched her. He had told her that somewhere out there a woman was thinking of her: a lonely soul who might still want to put her arms around her little girl and tell her she loved her and thought about her every minute of every waking day, and, at night, in her dreams. She was quite shocked by the way he had just come out with the words. Maggie always felt that her mother musn't have given a tuppenny damn about her, if she was willing to give her away when she was so young. And she wasn't afraid to say so, even to complete strangers.

Harry wasn't a stranger. The connection between them was even stronger now, whatever might have brought it about. It was as if Harry Vogel knew that this woman was really out there, reaching out and wanting to touch the life that she had borne thirty-four years ago, and hadn't seen for all but one of those years. It was almost as if she had told him, he spoke about it in such a sentimental way.

She stared at the thin stick of white smoke rising vertically from the saucer as she rubbed her thumb and finger together. The light of the candle had kept her little dream flickering with it, that he might walk through the hall door and catch a glimpse of her wearing the sexy dress that she had tucked away years ago, after they had moved from Macroom; the one that clung to her figure and had everyone commenting on how great she looked. "Bubble-butt," Jack called her one night over dinner, all those years ago. He couldn't keep his eyes off her, accidentally spilt his drink down his white shirt, backed the car into a wall and lost the keys of the front door. They didn't care though. They just kept laughing.

Another night she had arrived back at Cork airport wearing a long waxed leather jacket and a pair of knee-length boots which she had bought in London while attending a course in senior geriatric homekeeping. She had called Jack that evening to tell him she would be arriving on the 20.20 flight from London City, and to be prepared for a surprise. Jack's eyes almost popped when she paraded into the arrivals hall, her hair in a soft bob, her new leather creaking irresistibly. She had winked at her speechless lover and handed him her bag. They walked to the car without saying a word. It was a warm night and Jack had suggested that she might like to take off her leather coat. "Whatever you say," she replied. Maggie smiled as she remembered how she unbuttoned the coat slowly, quite seductively, actually, and watched Jack's eyes following her fingers. His mouth opened wider with each unbuttoning flick. Her smile broke into a grin as she recalled the look of sheer panic on Jack's face as she slipped the coat off and stood there opposite him in a dark, quiet airport carpark – stark-naked, except for her boots. "I told you I had a surprise for you," she said provocatively.

Jack bundled her into the car. "What if they had searched you before boarding? You're *Irish,* for God's sake. What if they'd told you to take off your coat!" Jack was beside himself with pure undiluted anger. She had never seen him so mad. In a most peculiar, almost sexy, way, she found his jealousy a turn-on. Until he refused to talk to her for two days.

On the night of the second day he had asked her out to dinner. He insisted, when he called her by phone that afternoon, that she wore the coat and boots to the restaurant. And nothing else.

Maggie sniffed and smiled. In the mirror over the mantlepiece she could see the reflection of the famous waxed leather jacket which she had taken out of the back of the wardrobe immediately after preparing the main course and hung on the curtain rail. Just in case he got any ideas. The boots sat beside the fireplace, which was stoked up and blazing at half past six when she would normally have expected him to come through the door at this time of the year. It was five past ten now and the fire was pushing out its last few puffs of smoke, happy to give up; asking the same question as she was: "Why should I bother?" She poured out the last drop of wine from the bottle, her second in two hours. The heady, maggoty feeling wasn't helping. She thought initially it might make her resilient, resistant to the temptation to kill him stone dead the minute he walked through the door. Now it took her a few seconds to locate the door from where she was sitting.

She tried to rationalise her feelings, just like she tried to help her old folk patients to do when the boredom and the debilitating extent of their disabilities were outfoxing them. She sighed and took a mouthful of the wine. It was warm. Mainly because she had only rammed it into the back of the fridge half an hour ago. Then again, she mused, she hadn't been expecting to drink two full bottles of wine. Or had she?

She wanted Jack back so badly that night that she wouldn't have objected to him having a few drinks. She reasoned with her better judgement, grossly impaired now by two-and-a-half litres of Chardonnay, that maybe she could live with this fascinating, consummate human sponge. Despite his appetite for alcohol he never turned violent. He was often funny, always vivacious and eclectic, never dull.

She searched for more words that would support her argument, her disagreement with the little voice on the right-hand side of her brain that was telling her she was a fool, a precious little pillock, if she really believed that she was going to remould this man into something she could show off by simply surprising him with home-made lasagna and a sexy waxed leather coat.

Now she could see her reflection in the mirror. She brushed her hair aside and threw her head back, straigtening up and breathing in. She looked all right, even if the dying light from the fire cast a shadow that made her look old and haggard. She thought she heard his car. Then silence. The car lights dying with the sound of the engine heading further out towards Ahakista.

She remembered how excited she was at four o'clock as she wandered around the aisles in Kenny's supermart, picking the various ingredients for the dinner; checking the labels on the bottles of wine, pretending to understand the various countries of origin and why wine from Capetown tasted different to wine produced in Cape de Mar, wherever that was. She was trying hard, determined to succeed at being exquisitely happy again, intensely enthusiastic at proving to herself that the past fortnight had only been a minor glitch in an otherwise perfect relationship which had spanned twenty-two starry-eyed years. She grinned at Mr Kenny.

He scowled. "Terrible about that young kid above at Doo Lough."

Maggie nodded, determined that her spirits would not be dented. This is the new me, she kept telling herself. I'm buying dinner for *my* man. "Jack's working hard on the case," she replied.

Marty Kenny sniggered under his breath as he counted out her change. "Inspector Morse?" he poked, with a glare that told her that Marty Kenny thought little of Jack Buckley as a policeman, and even less as a human being.

Ignore it, the little voice of competent optimism told her. He's only a sad, piddling, old small-timer. She picked up her bags and walked, sparing him a smile as she left.

The new me. The new me, she championed all the way back to her car. She even gave Aidan Kerr a quick peck on the cheek as he arrived to check that the local kids hadn't stole the shrine collection money on their way home from school. He was surprised. To say the least, so was Maggie. She felt like a young woman who had just been invited out on a date by the bloke she had always fancied but never placed much hope in getting close to romantically. *That was it!* she remembered. She felt the same that afternoon as she did the night Jack had first kissed her on the lips, and the sensation of feeling the tip of his tongue against the inside of her lips. Like a small jolt of electricity, forcing her to catch her breath.

By seven, the dinner was cooked. She had lit the candle, a momento of the mad weekend in Paris. She had come home hoping she was pregnant. God knows, she prayed, if women she knew could get pregnant from doing it only once, then she would have no problem, considering they only left the bedroom to visit the bathroom. And that usually ended up in a tight squeeze behind the shower curtain. She wasn't pregnant though, and it had upset her, making her think that there was something wrong. Surely when you lose count and still nothing happens it's worth a check-up? She put off the visit to the doctor because she didn't want to be told she was infertile. At least by having unprotected sex with Jack there was always the chance that one of his little swimmers might awaken one of her little girls. The sheer expectation of good news always caused her periods to be late, heightening the expectation that the old oven was working properly and that they were in business. It was always a huge disappointment. It got so regular that Jack gave up asking. He even started popping her usual pack of sanitary towels back into the shopping trolley on Saturdays. Worse still, Maggie stopped asking why he was doing it.

Then she was sure that that was the reason why he had never bothered to ask her. All she wanted to hear, apart from the sound of a baby crying for the very first time, were the words: *Will you marry me?* She remembered how, years ago in her twenties, she used to dismiss her friends as "bonkers" for getting married. Then, as the years got on, she would point out to herself just how right she was when she would get a phone call to say that so-and-so's marriage had ended. Maybe because of violent arguments, or an affair. But at least they *got* the chance to be married. At least they had rings on their fingers, even if it *was* for only a few months. She was stuck with a bloke who drank like a fish, earned a living carrying a gun and dodging other people's bullets, was so badly paid that she couldn't afford to give her job up even if she wanted to; and she wasn't even *married* to him.

At nine o'clock, the lasanga – having tried to re-heat it – was burnt to a crisp and she had already eaten her starter. She was half-way through the first litre of wine and was admiring herself in the mirror, having tried on the beautiful peach-coloured dress she had worn as bridesmaid to Claire Shortt's wedding six month's before. She had found it in the wardrobe behind the wax leather jacket. Not only was it difficult coping with her bestfriend getting married, she nearly passed out when Claire whispered to her in the porch of the church, just as the photographer shouted *cheese*, "I'm pregnant."

Jack wouldn't marry her because she couldn't have babies. She was convinced that was the reason. But she never challenged him on it. Well she couldn't, could she? After all, he could turn around and tell her the real reason why he wouldn't marry her. Twenty-two years on, there had to be a reason, hadn't there? At least *one*!

She was drunk. *Pissed!* It was nearly eleven now and the stink of the burnt mince and pasta was intolerable. She was about to pick up the dish and throw it into his precious fish-pond when she heard a car. It was his. And she knew by the revs of the engine that he was drunk. The crashing jangle and the sound of breaking glass sobered her enough to run to the door. She opened it.

Jack was standing at the door of the car, looking over the bonnet at the dint in the front part. "Who closed the gates?" he barked.

Maggie ignored him and went back inside, leaving the door ajar.

She was sitting at the table again, the main course in its dish closest to him on the table where he could see it immediately. She could hear him shuffling slowly in behind her.

"What are you doing here?" he asked, a mixture of chuffed surprise and relief.

"I got the idea into my head that I wanted to come home to you," she answered, her back still to him, as if reading from a script for the first time.

He moved around the table where she could see him. "Good," was all he said.

"Is that all you're going to say? *Good!*"

"What else can I say?"

"You could start by explaining what kept you. I had this dinner ready at half six. It's now half past *bloody* eleven. That's five hours ago!"

"Well, if that's the case, you can start by explaining just what you're doing here. If you remember, you were the one who walked out of here over a week ago, Maggie. *You* walked out, not *me*!"

"How dare you, you bastard! You're always walking out on me. There were days you walked out of this house lately and I didn't know when you'd be back. Most couples talk to each other, Jack. They don't take each other for granted."

"Ah, don't give me that shite, Maggie. Every time we have an argument I'm taking you for granted. Isn't that right?"

"No, Jack." She stood up. "You're taking me for granted right now. Can you not see that? Just because I left you last week doesn't mean this is all over."

"What are you talking about?" He noticed the burnt-out remains of the candle, the seafood starter, the dish of cold garlic bread slices, the cauldron of spaghetti, still sitting over the steamer, and the lasagna. "What's all this for?" He glanced through the open door, into the bedroom. The wax leather coat was hanging on the curtain rail. "What are you doing?"

"I'm giving us one more chance."

"Us?"

"Yeah, us. I don't think it's all your fault. Although tonight I don't know anymore. Why didn't you call if you were going to be late?"

"Cut out the crap. I'm pissed. I was in Hannon's all day drinking. I didn't know you were going to just show up like my fairy godmother and make me dinner."

"Well, that's something you're a little short of at the moment, Jack – help from your fairy godmother. I know where you've been all day. I saw your car outside when I went down to buy the stuff for the dinner. Same spot where it was parked when Aidan Kerr dropped me home after Doo Lough this morning. Do you know what people around Durrus are saying about you, Jack?

They're laughing up their sleeves at you. Marty Kenny called you Inspector Morse today when I was in his shop."

"Well, why do you bother to shop there then if he upsets you?"

"Why *shouldn't* I shop there, Jack? I happen to like Marty Kenny, and his wife. She's one of my patients. Just like you're his sergeant. He expects more from you. He expects to feel safe when you're around. Instead, what does he get? He steps outside his shop only to be greeted by the sight of your official car sitting at the door of the fucking pub from noon till night. Why should he bother saying nice things about you? You're only a loser, Jack."

The words caught him like a blow to the gut. His woman, the only person he trusted in the whole world, was calling him a loser. "I'm not a loser. Anyway I don't give a shit what Marty Kenny says about me. If he paid more attention to his kids than he did to me then maybe his eighteen-year-old son mightn't have been arrested for selling Ecstasy tablets."

Maggie was shocked by his insensitivity. It was a trait she had only noticed lately. "You always fight like a little schoolboy when you're cornered Jack, don't you? It's not Marty Kenny's fault that his son keeps bad company. If that's the case why don't you blame me for turning you into an alcoholic?" She said nothing for a moment, knowing he wouldn't either.

It was an expression he abhorred. He hated being told he had a drink problem. He hated being asked how he was getting on by close friends, knowing that what they were really asking was: Are you still off the booze?

"That's not fair," he said calmly, his mouth dry, his voice shaky.

"Fair?" she asked, waving her hand across the cold contents of a once-romantic dinner. "Call this fair?"

He shook his head. "If I'd known you were going to be here, I would've been back earlier."

"What's earlier? Half ten?"

"No. Lunchtime. What's the point of coming back to an empty house? Of course I would've come home if I'd known you were here."

"That's just another one of your lame excuses, Jack. Just like you're going to tell me that Leo's death made you sad. So you had to have a drink. And the pressure of looking for those teenagers was stressing you out, so you had to have another drink. And digging up graves in the middle of the night made you thirsty, so you had to have *another drink*! Do you really think you're fooling me, Jack? That no one else matters except you?"

Jack sat down.

"Jockey Carr came over here last night."

Jack's eyes opened wide, his face tensed up. "What?"

"I woke up in bed and he was lying beside me stroking my face with your gun," she continued, her voice telling the strain of her horrible ordeal. She folded her finger and the palm of her hand, outstretched on the table, into a tight fist and banged it down hard on the surface, making the plates and wine glasses hop and clatter. She was shouting now, agitated and nervous. "He sat on the bed for nearly an hour, playing with the gun, playing with my clothes and my hair. Where the *fuck* were you then, you precious little waster. Call yourself a policeman?" She stood up and ran at him, thumping him hard in the shoulder and slapping his face.

Jack was thrown back into the chair. He took it head on.

"What if I had been found dead in a pool of blood when Aidan Kerr called here looking for you this morning? They'd have all thought you did it. Do you know that? That's the crazy thing about you lately, Jack. No one around here, the length and breadth of this peninsula would have batted an eyelid. They would have all have just pointed the finger at you. Just like they're doing over Leo Hannon, Jack. Do you know that? That's what all the folks around Durrus are saying. They're even saying it as far away as Bantry and Macroom. I'd say even your old mates in the force are talking about it. Jack Buckley murdered Leo Hannon. And his friends in the cops got him off, scot-free. Can you imagine how that makes people around here feel? They can't trust their own sergeant. If they think you killed Leo Hannon why shouldn't they believe you had a hand in that poor kid's death this morning?"

"Don't be so stupid!" Jack snapped.

Maggie's eyes looked through him with sheer spleen. "Don't you dare *ever* call me stupid, do you hear me? You really do think you're the only person who isn't stupid, don't you? Listen to me – for your own good. Maybe I'm wasting my time. Maybe I'm too late but you'd better hear me out." She was whispering now. "I should be dead, Jack."

Jack looked at her peculiarly. "What do you mean?"

"I believe that Jockey Carr came over here to kill me

last night. With your gun. I believe he was sent over here to make it look as if you killed me. That way whoever's bed you're ruffling would be home and dry. Shut and close case. They throw the book at you for Leo Hannon *and* me."

Jack couldn't believe what he was hearing. "It couldn't be."

"What couldn't be?" He was interrupting her and she didn't like it.

"Why would anyone want to kill you? They know you've nothing to do with my work."

"Simple. It's staring you in the face it's that simple. If they kill you one of them will eventually end up taking the rap. If they kill me you take the rap for everything. It was your gun that shot me. They can accuse you of anything they want to. Even the death of that young boy."

Jack was sweating profusely. "Who's *they*?"

"You're the detective, Jack. You find out."

32

Jockey Carr's caravan was in total darkness.

Jack couldn't make up his mind whether to knock or kick the door down. For all he knew Jockey could have been pointing the Beretta Tomcat at his forehead at that precise moment. On the other hand he could have been down in Hannon's pub scabbing free drinks off the locals who regularly bribed him with alcohol just so he would wander off and talk drivel to someone else.

Maggie wasn't taking no for an answer. She was going out to the caravan even if it meant walking. Jack couldn't decide if Jockey was there or not. Dunmanus Bay was housing rough waters that night. The fishing boats hadn't gone out from Bantry or Castletownbere all day. The high tide after the big storm meant the sea was closer to the rocks of the cove and therefore a lot louder. He tried to listen for music. Or snoring. Or anything that might give away his presence. He could rush the little shack and get blown away in the process. There was only one thing for it.

He tapped casually, three times, on the fibreglass

door. His heart jolted as the door opened out almost instantaneously. Carr's face, terrified and open-mouthed, stared down at him. The gun, Jack kept thinking. He has my gun. Without a second's hesitation he lunged forward, aiming high, and grabbed him by the neck, thrusting him backwards and down hard on his back onto the floor, winding him and almost turning the caravan onto its side. He pressed down harder on Jockey's neck until he could hear a choking, gurgling sound. *"You fucking piece of retard shit!"* he shouted, pushing the palm of his hand against Jockey's Adam's apple. *"Where's my gun?"* Jack roared, not caring who might be able to hear him.

Jockey burbled.

"Answer me or I'll break your fucking neck!"

Jockey pointed to the cooker. Without relaxing his grip, Jack felt around in the small space beside the twin-hob. He recognised the familiar shape of the Beretta and seized it. It was time to go to work. He flipped out the magazine with his thumb, just enough to check it was still fully loaded. Click. Back in. He shoved the neat snout of the pistol into the back of Jockey's mouth and lessened the grip on his throat.

"Now, you listen to me good." Jack spoke quickly and clearly. "I'm going to shoot you if you don't answer my questions truthfully. You hear those waves crashing against the rocks out there?" Jack nodded to the roar of the tide. "If I pull this trigger no one's gonna hear a thing, cos' the bullet's gonna go straight through the back of your empty head, through this filthy, rotten floor and two feet into the soft sand underneath. You play as smoothly as you played those three games of chess yesterday and you'll be able to go down to Hannon's pub tomorrow night and tell all those nice folk how much of a dangerous bastard Sergeant Buckley really is. OK? Answer simply yes or no. Is that clear?" Jockey Carr answered with a garbled *yes*, his head nodding frantically.

"Someone sent you to my house last night. Yes or no."

Jockey Carr nodded reluntantly. Standing above him now, directly behind Jack Buckley, with her arms folded, was Maggie. He mumbled and squeezed his eyes closed.

"Answer me, you fucking parasite!"

"Yes!"

Jockey Carr's reply was more like a dog's yelp.

"They didn't want you to kill me though, did they?" He applied more pressure, but not too much to distort his answer. This time Jockey Carr shook his head.

"No."

He waited for a second before asking the crucial question, knowing that Jockey Carr couldn't be trusted for anything. Carruth's words haunted him: "His evidence would not stand up to scrutiny in a court of law." Jack Buckley still needed to know the answer. "Were you going to kill Maggie?" He could see Jockey's eyes move away from his terrifying stare, to the petrified look of the woman standing closely behind him. Slowly Jockey Carr started to shake his head.

"N-n-nooo!" he stammered, adamant and decisive.

"Tell the fucking truth, you asshole!"

Maggie could see that Jack was losing control now,

fuelled by too much anger and too much alcohol. "He wouldn't have, Jack. Please *stop*!" she begged.

"You *promised*, if I let you come over here with me tonight, you *weren't* going to get involved!"

"N-n-nooo!" Jockey Carr squalled again.

Jack was getting confused. "Right let me rephrase that. Did someone send you over to my house late last night to kill Maggie?"

In the silence of the dark caravan, with the waves sounding further away now, a small beeping alarm like a sensor or a cooker timing device began to sound, scaring the daylights out of all three of them. Jack nearly pissed himself when he realised he had almost instinctively pulled the trigger. He took the gun out of Jockey Carr's mouth. "What's that?"

Jockey seemed more frightened by the irritating beeping noises than he was at the prospect of the gun being fired. He started to shake. "An al-l-l-larm," he howled.

Then it stopped. Silence. It started beeping again. "Maggie check that drawer. Careful."

Maggie opened the small drawer below the makeshift plywood kitchen dresser. The beeping got louder. "It's a mobile phone." She handed it to Jack.

Jack watched the flashing display, intermittently lighting up and going dark in time to each beep. The alarm had activated at 12.10am exactly, ten minutes after midnight. An unusual time for anyone's alarm clock to go off at, he thought. "Who do you ring on this?" He held the mobile out to Jock. "Go on, take it!" he shouted.

Jockey grabbed it and tried to shove it in his pocket.

"Not so fuckin' fast!" Jack growled. He kicked Jockey's wrist, sending the phone flying across the filthy floor. "Answer me." He slid it back to Jockey with the heel of his boot.

"I h-h-have it here in c-case any of the old p-p-people need me to call to them to do odd j-j-jobs," he said as clearly as Jack's crushing hold on his throat would allow him.

"Well, well, well." Jack looked around at Maggie. "You know who I think we've got here? I think we're talking to the original good Samaritan. Jockey-good-deeds-Carr. I suppose you'll be hoping that one of them old people will be nominating you for Person of the Year next September. And you'll be up there in one of them posh Dublin hotels getting presented with your statue by one of them famous television personalities. Won't you, Jockey?" Jack nudged him with his knee.

Jockey's eyes were beginning to water up. He shook his head. *"N-nooo!"* he squeaked.

Maggie cringed.

"Oh? I am disappointed, Jockey. What are you trying to tell me? That you don't deserve a nomination? That maybe you robbed a few quid off old Mrs Doyle when she wasn't watching you bringing in a few logs for her fire. Or maybe Alex Kline's baby-sitter would write in and tell them that you don't deserve to win anything because you exposed yourself in front of her. What would you think about that?" Jack held out the mobile phone. "Who gave you this?"

"I b-b-bought it," he yelled in agony.

Jack laughed and looked back at Maggie again. "He bought a mobile phone, Maggie."

"Stop, Jack! He's perfectly entitled to walk into a shop and buy a mobile phone."

"Of course he is. And I suppose you just walked into a Telecom branch and asked them to give you a number and set you up, Just like that, eh, Jockey? And they said, 'Of course, we'd be delighted to set you up Mr Carr. And since you don't have a job we'll let you have it free of charge! *Mr* Carr.' Is that what they said, Jockey?" Jack nudged him with the phone's rubber antenna. "Of course it's not what they said, Jockey. You have about as good a chance of having your own telephone account as you have of owning a driving licence for a fucking sports car." Jack waved the gun around the caravan. "Look at this dirty hole. He doesn't even have electricity, never mind a phone. And he expects me to think that he has a nice little neat mobile to ring all his friends on. Where did you get this? Before I arrest you for receiving stolen property."

Jockey began to choke. His eyes bulged and his face began to turn blue.

"Jesus Christ," muttered Jack. "What's wrong with him?" he asked Maggie.

Maggie knelt down. "He's suffocating. He must have swallowed his tongue." She pushed Jack aside and placed Jockey's head way back, raising his chest. She opened his mouth and searched the cavity. "His tongue's fallen way back." She put two of her finger's into his mouth and felt for the root of his tongue. "Got it!"

Jockey Carr spluttered and gasped and lay still as he coughed. And cried.

Jack studied the mobile phone. He pressed one of the buttons and the full display lit up. He counted seventeen buttons in all. If it was the same as his own – he should be able to re-dial the last number called by simply pressing *YES*. He pressed it. It beeped. A few seconds of crackly silence and it started to ring. Once. Twice. Three times. If it was similar to the model he owned, after five rings it would automatically activate the voice-mail service and ask you if you wanted to leave a message.

Four rings and the phone was answered. It was a voice he didn't recognise. It was the name that left him speechless.

"Alfie Carruth's phone. Who's calling?"

33

Two hours later.

"I want to leave here, Jack."

Maggie nestled into his shoulder, stretching out on the long couch, and tried to relax in front of the fire she had stoked up when they got back. She couldn't relax, no matter what way she sat or lay. The shock had taken its toll. She was shivering desperately, despite the heavy blanket. Still it was nice to feel his arm around her. Like old times. She watched him drinking his vodka. For the first time in years she didn't care. She could worry about that later. "Well?"

"Well what?" Jack asked pensively, his mind a million miles away.

"If I leave here, will you come with me?"

"Do you want me to?"

Her words were slow and sad. "Of course I want you to. I love you." She squeezed his arm and kissed the back of his hand.

"And would you go without me?"

Maggie thought over the words. They sounded well thought out. "What do you mean?"

He rephrased the question. "If I don't go, are you still going to leave without me?"

The notion made her flinch. Yesterday she wouldn't have given it a second thought. Come to think of it, three hours ago and she would have loved to bang the door behind her and walk away. Not now. What had happened in between was making her cling on to him for dear life. But life had to go on. And it wasn't going to continue on Sheep's Head. "All I'm saying is that I want us to make a new start somewhere else. Dublin. London. *Paris!* Now there's a brilliant idea. Let's go and live in Paris, Jack. We could have romance all the time." She sat up, looking at his thinking expression.

"And where would we both work? EuroDisney?"

"Why are you being funny? We're in serious trouble, Jack."

"No, we're *not*!"

"I want to leave. And I want to go this week, Jack. With or without you."

"What are you afraid of?" He hugged her to reassure her.

"What we know."

"And what do we know?"

She nodded to the mobile phone on the table, sitting alongside the Beretta Tomcat. "I'm afraid that Jockey Carr's going to go back to Alfie Carruth and tell him that you beat him up tonight and that . . . " She stopped, as if unsure what might happen if she continued to say what was on her mind.

"That I know that Alfie Carruth was involved in that young boy's murder? And that I'd put any money I had on it that one of the two men I couldn't identify on Coosbrack beach that night when Leo Hannon was murdered was Alfie Carruth? Is that what you were going to say?"

Maggie nodded. "Are you not afraid?"

Jack finished his vodka and leaned over to the sideboard and poured another equally generous, bolstering measure. "I'm scared shitless."

"Well then, come with me," she pleaded.

Jack sat back in the long chair and pulled her to him. "Come here to me. I wanna tell you a few things. For a start, Jockey Carr is a smalltime player in this equation, whatever that might be. He's only a gofer for the big boys. Someone who does all the dirty little scrappy jobs when they don't want to get their hands dirty. Someone they can pin the blame on if things really start getting out of hand. But it all backfired on them tonight."

"Why?" Maggie sipped her wine.

"Because whoever is calling the shots in this messy game of theirs sent Jockey Carr over here to kill you. And it makes perfect sense. I was in Alfie Carruth's house. He was on the phone before he came into the reception room, obviously to Jockey, to tell him I would be out of the way for a while. Jockey then rang him from here to let him know the house was empty apart from you, fast asleep in bed."

"How do you know Jockey rang him?"

"Because the phone rang in the hall just as I was leaving. He was only talking for a few seconds. I checked my watch. It was ten to eleven. What time was it on your clock when you woke up?"

Maggie thought hard. "I can't remember. I opened my eyes and there he was. I think it was about eleven."

"Perfect timing."

"That's guesswork, Jack. You can't prove it."

"No, you're right. We can't prove it. So we're going to have to approach it from a different direction, that's all."

Maggie was confused. "What *different* direction?"

Jack emptied the glass and braced himself. "This might sound strange. But this is my theory so hear me out. All hell broke loose when they stole Leo Hannon's car that night. They obviously did something awful to piss those people off that much that they'd follow them with weapons. I don't think they even knew what they were doing. Think back, Maggie. It was pissing rain that night. The three of them were probably sick from drinking all day. There was no way they were going to be able to walk all the way back to Ollie Jenning's barn, so they decided to hop into Leo's car. They heard the engine running, the doors were open. Leo was going to drop someone home. When he came out they were gone. Whatever was in that car Alfie Carruth and Alex Kline were guarding with their lives. So when they realised the car was gone they assumed whoever had stolen it knew what they were looking for. So they took off after them and chased them. The big difference was that the three kids hadn't a clue where they were going out there in the dark. The lads chasing them knew this area like the back of their hands. So it didn't take long to catch them."

"And they just shot them?" Maggie asked in disgust.

"Maybe not. Maybe the three lads made a run for it. Carruth's a former marksman. With an infra-red night-sight attached to a good lens, he could have taken them out at quarter of a mile. Leo obviously didn't like what was going on. He probably thought they were just going to scare the kids, fire a few shots in the air, tell them to piss off and never come back. When he realised that Carruth was shooting directly at them he decided he didn't want anymore to do with them. But it was too late."

"What do you mean?"

"Well, Leo Hannon, whether he liked it or not, became part of the horrible secret the minute he headed out after his stolen car that night."

"Would you say he was driving?"

Jack nodded. "He was the only one of the three of them who really knew the terrain. If they were going to cut the kids off and get ahead of them so they could block the road, Leo was the man to show them the short cuts. On the other hand, judging by the state of the car, they probably just ran them off the road. The kids hopped out, started running, and Carruth started shooting."

"But if they hadn't taken what was in the car, why did Carruth open up?"

"I don't know. Maybe he panicked."

Maggie was dumbfounded, lost between the pure evil and the incredulity of it all.

"Remember when I met you?"

Maggie was in a daze. "What?"

"Remember the night I first met you . . . the night you finished your exams? You were driving your boyfriend's car."

Maggie tutted. "You were on your police motorbike, pretending to be real important, strutting your stuff in your big knee-length leather boots and your helmet. You scared the shite out of me that night, do you know that?"

Jack laughed. "That was my intention."

"I'll never forgive you for that."

Jack tittered like a bold child. "And remember when I gave you the ticket for driving without your lights on?"

"Without my lights? It was ten o'clock in the middle of summer, for God's sake!"

"Dusk! It was getting dark."

"Do you know how much trouble you could have got into for ringing me up on the phone two nights later and asking me out?"

"Not at all!"

"You, Jack Buckley, were coercing a member of the public!"

"That's ridiculous. I was not."

"You rang my flat and said that you might be able to get me off the charge. And would I meet you for a drink to discuss it."

"Seemed like a perfectly reasonable request to me."

"You just wanted to get me drunk and get me into your bed."

"And I did!"

They both cracked up laughing for a minute or so, until it dawned on them that the problem hadn't gone away. It was getting bright outside the kitchen window, and Jack had to catch the lunch-time train to Dublin to attend the funeral of Ben Roper's young son. The memories and the clowning evaporated again. And all they were left with in the silent hour before the dawn was a question that neither of them were able to answer.

What was so important to Alfie Carruth and Alex Kline and Leo Hannon that they had to protect and keep secret?

"It was obviously more than their own lives were worth," Maggie said as she stifled a yawn.

"What?"

"Whatever they were trying to hide."

"You mean whatever they're *still* trying to hide. I don't think it's gone away."

"Why do you think that?"

"Because they're trying to use me as a decoy. When I showed the five bullet shells to Alex Kline that morning from his own gun, that I found in Leo's pocket on the beach that night, Kline almost pissed himself with the fright. So it was simple. They had to shoot you. That way it would have looked as if I went off my head and killed you with my own gun. Alex would have stood up in court and told the jury that I'd been drinking very heavily and came home late that night after threatening Jockey Carr in his caravan with the very same gun. Clever thinking. But it backfired." Jack reached out and picked up the mobile phone. He juggled it between hands.

Maggie was holding out, sleepy but determined. "So, what next?"

"Ah, the six million dollar question. Well, I've been thinking about the various options available to us. That's *if* you don't leave this week." He waited, hoping for solidarity.

"I'll let you know when you get back from Dublin."

"I don't like you staying here on your own. Why don't you come with me? You'll enjoy the trip."

"To a funeral? I don't think so. Anyway I have to look after my patients."

"And what happens to your patients if you leave?"

"The health board looks for a replacement. That's their problem, not mine. You never finished what you were saying. Our options?"

"Options. Not many. Only one actually. Take it to a higher level."

"Who?"

"The Commissioner."

"Jesus, Jack, now you *are* going mad."

"Why? I've met her a few times."

"I was with you when you met her. All you did was shake her hand and say hello, how are you. Not exactly first name terms, is it?"

"No. But what else do you suggest?"

"That we leave it behind us. That you and I walk away from it. Let's sell the house, go and live somewhere else for a while, *anywhere* else, until we decide what we're going to do."

"*Great,* Maggie. Sell the house and live in a shoebox, I suppose. What do we do for money?"

"We can live off the money we make on the house sale, can't we?"

"We have a mortgage to repay. Plus interest. We'll be left with a pittance after we pay off what we owe, for God's sake. Anyway why should I walk away from this? This is my job, bad and all as it is at the moment. If I walk away from this, Carruth and Kline will think I'm a pathetic coward. Carruth will still be my boss until they restation me. Kline will end up selling the house. We'll be running away from them for the rest of our lives."

"So what's the alternative?"

"I want to nail the bastards! I want to haul *them* up in front of a judge."

"Well, I'll bet you with all my life's worth, and this house, that you'll never succeed."

"I want to be able to prove unequivocally that they murdered three teenagers and assisted in the murder of Leo Hannon."

"*Three* teenagers?"

"Yes, *three*. I believe they shot dead two of the kids and buried the bodies."

"But you might never find them."

"I'm not interested in finding them just now. I will eventually. What I want to know is what Carruth and Kline were trying to protect that night, were trying to keep secret and undercover, that was so much more important than sparing the lives of three kids." Jack looked across at Maggie.

She was asleep.

He shivered as he looked out at the hazy, grey dawn taking shape in the back garden. And realised that he had never felt so alone as he did at that moment.

* * *

If Jack Buckley had chosen to go for a drive in his patrol car early that morning instead of catching a few hours sleep before heading to Dublin, he might have chosen the R591 Durrus to Bantry road. Occasionally, Jack would drive out past the Kline's house just to see who was visiting. That morning he might not have been too surprised to see Alfie Carruth's car parked outside the house at 2.30am. It was still there at 4.20am.

Ethel Kline had offered the superintendent some of her homemade tea-brack after Alex roared up to her to get out of bed and come down and make a cup of extra-strong coffee for their guest. "Have as many slices as you want. Jack Buckley loves my tea-brack," she enthused.

"To hell with your tea-brack, and to hell with Jack Buckley," she was almost sure she heard Alfie Carruth saying under his breath, as he stirred his coffee as vigorously as she might mix the dough for her tea-brack. Come to think of it, he did look a little peaky. Then she realised the time. "Alex, it's quarter past two, dear," she said in her usual emphatic way. "Is anything wrong?" The second she asked, she knew she shouldn't have.

"There are just some things that don't concern you, Ethel," he answered rather blisteringly. Now she was certain there was something terribly amiss for a whole load of reasons. Alex wouldn't get out of his bed after midnight even if the house had caught fire. Second, he always included her in business discussions. And business consumed Alex's life. And third, and most worrying of all, he hadn't called her Ethel for years. He always referred to her as dearest, or minikin, or poppet. Never Ethel. Not even in the throes of a heated business transaction would he call her Ethel. Something awful had happened. "Do you want your tablets, love?" she asked anxiously.

"Fuck my tablets," she was almost sure he said, under his breath.

The two worried men walked quickly into the sitting-room, carrying their cups, leaving the oval-shaped plate full of tea-brack slices behind them on the kitchen worktop, Alfie Carruth wearing a dressing-gown, denim jeans and trainers with the laces open and straggling. He hadn't even bothered to get dressed. "Would you boys like me to switch on the electric fire in there?"

The door banged shut in her face.

Ethel Kline tried to sleep into the early dawn but she couldn't. She twisted and turned, listening to the angry voices arguing in the room below her. She looked at her clock. Half three. Unprecedented. In the eighteen years she had known Alex he had never entertained anyone after one in the morning, at the latest. Not even Ethel. Sex had to be over by one. If it wasn't Alex would just roll over and start snoring. It was an unspoken rule that he got a minimum of six hours sleep each night.

She sat on the fifth step down the staircase now, her dressing-gown pulled tightly around her kness, and shivered as she tried to pick out words and snatches of conversation. She didn't notice her own shivering because the talk had begun to frighten her.

Her husband had always been a trusted friend of the superintendent. The senior police officer often asked his advice. Yet, tonight, he seemed to be shouting at Alex for something he must have done, Ethel reckoned. A slip-up, perhaps. An oversight? The conversation was making little sense. However she noticed it kept coming back to the same thing.

Someone, or something, called "The Keeper".

34

Durrus got a new doctor that morning.

The women, on their way to eight o'clock Mass, slowed down and chinwagged about the removal van outside Nolan's pharmacy. This was the lorry's second delivery. EVESTON TRANSPORT was written in bold letters on each side. Definitely not a Cork company, they all agreed. "British registration," the small woman with the hump muttered.

At first one of the women suggested that maybe Freddie Nolan was selling up. The others, one of them clutching her prayer leaflets and beads, rejected the notion. Freddie was Durrus, just as much as the Holy Well at Dunbeacon Castle was. Freddie was there as long as they could remember. Maybe, another one of them hinted, he's turning the upstairs quarters into holiday apartments. "Everyone seems to be doing it these days." They all gibbered again, eliminating their friend's idea unanimously. It was only a two-room apartment. "Anyway, where would Freddie live?" the woman with the beads spouted. Then they saw the surgical bed, a swivel-chair, a filing cabinet, boxes of wall charts, all coming out of the neatly packed truck. Then the bell for Mass rang and they shimmied away towards the church, full of talk about nothing in particular.

Aidan Kerr was mulling over his thought for the day, a message to send the congregation away with – that might bring some spiritual enlightenment to their otherwise dreary day. When the clock had gone off he cursed himself and lay there staring at the ceiling. The single bed was always much lonelier when he had been drinking the night before. He could still smell the alcohol on his breath, and kept swearing to himself that he wasn't drinking mid-week ever again, certainly not in Jack Buckley's company. He decided that he would put at least an extra measure of altar wine in the chalice that morning as a kind of a hair of the dog that bit him. A homeopathic dose to cure his massive hangover. Purely medicinal, he kept telling himself.

He doffed his cap to Freddie Nolan as he passed the chemist shop. "Morning, Freddie."

"Morning, Father." Freddie was unusually sprightly for that hour of the day. He raised his own cap, showing off the baldest, shiniest crown Aidan could ever remember seeing. Without the cap, his red nose looked three or four times bigger than usual. "Grand morning." He finished sticking the sign to the door of the shop.

Aidan stopped and stepped back, stooping to get a better look at the sign.

Dr JAMES MORRIS
M.R.C.G.P., M.R.C.P.I., D.C.H.
General Practitioner

"A new doctor!" he said quite spryly, forgetting his throbbing headache for a minute. He straightened up and looked at Freddie Nolan.

Nolan looked like a man who'd just been told he had become a grandfather for the first time. He was beaming airily with all the presence and spirit of someone who didn't have a care in the world. "Isn't it wonderful, Father. It's been nearly five years since we've had our own doctor down here. And to think we didn't even have to go looking for him."

Aidan Kerr was slightly baffled. "What do you mean?"

"He just arrived the other day and asked was the old surgery in at the back of the chemist still available." Freddie paused, tipped his cap and tapped his chest. "Tom Magnier, our old GP, God be good to him, I was only thinking of him last night. He was a brilliant doctor, Father, and do you know what he died of?"

"What?" Aidan knew he was going to be late for Mass.

"Choked on a turkey bone, Father. Middle of the Christmas dinner. And they were all running round like headless chickens, telling each other to ring for a doctor. And him the only doctor for miles around."

"God help him. So what did they do in the end?"

Freddie thought for a second and scratched his head. "They threw the turkey in the bin, Father!"

Aidan stared at Freddie Nolan, not knowing how to react. Then Freddie Nolan cracked up laughing.

Aidan smiled. "Where's he from?"

"I'm not sure. He mentioned some place I've never heard of."

"So he's not Irish?"

"Definitely not, Father. Strange accent. Couldn't quite put me finger on it. I was never any good at geography anyway. But a lovely man, Father. A real rich warm voice. He's due back shortly. He reckons he'll be up and running, open for business, this afternoon. You should drop in, Father. He'd love to see you."

"But sure there's nothing wrong with me, Freddie. I'd only be taking up the man's time."

"Ah now, Father, you're looking a bit peaky to me." Freddie Nolan winked and smiled. "Were you up late last night?"

Aidan said goodbye and hurried off in the direction of the church where three of the auld ones were shuffling about impatiently in the front porch waiting to say their daily good morning to the local priest.

* * *

Maggie sat outside Nolan's chemist and gulped the mineral water to try and free the pill she had taken for her hangover, now lodged in her throat. She slapped her chest and swallowed. Reluctantly, inch by inch, it went down. She would collect the repeat prescriptions from Freddie Nolan, as she did every Thursday, and head off on her rounds. She was earlier than usual this morning as she wanted to spend some extra time with Harry Vogel, and find out what he thought about her plans to go to Austria to search for her mother. She hadn't mentioned it to anyone, not even to Jack, not even spoken it out loud to herself. Even the thought of such a quest seemed utterly ludicrous. But she was going to do it, somehow or other. And she was going to do it soon. She knew when she woke that morning that her days in Durrus were finished. Life elsewhere was calling now, more urgently with each passing day.

Freddie Nolan was standing outside the door as she stepped onto the pavement. Unusual, she thought. His smile was dying to burst into speech.

"Morning, Freddie," Maggie said cheerfully.

Freddie said nothing, just pointed to the sign.

Maggie read it. She reacted as she knew Freddie expected her to. *"Brilliant!"* she yelled. "When is he starting?"

"Today."

"You must be delighted. It'll be extra business for you, Freddie."

He nodded, almost unable to contain his excitement. "I'm sure you'll be the first person he'll want to see."

"I'm sure he will." She read the details again. It was strange, she thought, that the health board in the city hadn't let her know beforehand. Then again, if he was moving to Durrus to live and was a fully trained doctor, why *shouldn't* he practice? Her suspicion slowly turned to satisfaction, some of Freddie Nolan's high spirits rubbing off on her. "It's about bloody time we had our own doctor." Then it occurred to her that she couldn't remember a Durrus doctor. None had existed in her three years there so this would be a novelty.

"And look at all those letters, Maggie." Freddie pointed to the man's credentials.

Maggie nodded. "Letters of credence, they're called."

It was the first time that day that Freddie frowned. "I know what they are. I am a pharmacist. I do have a few myself. But this man must have studied for years. Reading all of his letters is like getting your eyes checked."

"Where is he now?"

"I don't know. He arrived about seven. I was still in bed. He made some racket, kept his finger on the doorbell when I didn't answer the first time. But seems like a lovely fella."

"Is he driving?"

Freddie tutted, then waited to see if Maggie was pulling his leg. She wasn't. "Of *course* he's driving. He's a doctor, for pity sake. Where would a doctor be without a car?"

"He didn't say which way he was going, did he?"

Freddie shook his head. "Just said he was going to have a look around. There's too much moving and shifting going on here right now. He said he'd be back after all his gear had arrived."

Maggie handed him the small bundle of prescriptions, tied together neatly with an elastic band. "Tell him I'll be back. I'll need to collect those in about an hour."

She turned to walk back to her car and froze.

Jockey Carr sat on the low wall across the road, directly opposite where her car was parked. He didn't smile this morning, didn't acknowledge the sunshine, or how well Maggie looked, like he did most days. He just sat there, almost pensively, and stared. Stared until she got into the car, turned the key nervously a few times, did a three-point turn and drove out of town. In her rear-view mirror she could see that he was standing in the middle of the road now.

Watching her watching him.

* * *

Jack Buckley was surprised that Alfie Carruth hadn't called him. Not once since the boy's body was discovered in Doo Lough, removed to Bantry hospital, and taken from there to Cork airport where it was put on an Aer Lingus flight to Dublin as soon as the post mortem had been completed. Maybe he shouldn't have been surprised on second thoughts. Carruth had to know that Jack was on to him, crawling all over him like a million tiny ants.

Right now, Jack didn't want anyone to phone him. His own mobile phone remained switched off until he'd had a drink. The mobile phone he had recovered from Jockey Carr's caravan sat in a small transparent plastic bag on the dashboard. Jack popped it into the glove compartment, out of view. He questioned himself as to why anyone would want to set an alarm clock on a mobile for 12.10am at night. Answers weren't easily forthcoming this morning. His hangover was cataclysmic. He wasn't sure what the word meant but it had been used on the morning news to describe a violent coup d'etat in Venezuela the previous day. Couldn't be any more violent than the pain and torture this hangover was generating, he thought.

He picked up *The Star* newspaper in Kenny's

supermart and sat back into his car outside Hannon's pub. He checked the time. 9.30am. His train was at twenty to two. He would have to leave Durrus at eleven at the latest to make the departure time. Into Dublin at half four. Taxi straight to the church. Be seen to represent the police force at the removal of the remains. Then back to the hotel, get rid of the uniform and find a nice pub close by and drink for the night.

The front page of the tabloid carried a full-size colour photograph of Adam Roper's body, covered with a blanket, being led away from Doo Lough to a waiting ambulance. The headline was stark.

YOUNG LIFE ROBBED

Jack could feel his heartbeat speeding up. He was pleased that the editor had chosen to see the drowning as a possible murder. But he wasn't prepared for the first paragraph of the article.

"The man in charge of the search for the murderer of seventeen-year-old Adam Roper told The Star *this morning he was confident of making an early arrest."*

Jack looked up from his paper. Who was he going to arrest? He wiped the sweat away from the side of his forehead with the newspaper, folded it and put it on the seat beside him. He tried to imagine the look on Carruth's face as he closed his right eye and placed the left one, wide-open, against the night-sight, took a deep breath and held it. He was left-handed, Jack remembered, having trained on weaponry with him years ago. He was one shit-hot shooter. The kids wouldn't have stood a chance. And the fear in his eyes when he realised that Adam Roper had managed to slip through the net and run for his life. He must have run in the wrong direction and fallen into the lake.

Jack reclined his seat a little and relaxed, breathing deeply, with his eyes closed, thinking, scheming. Carruth couldn't have known that Roper had fallen into the lake. Therefore they must have thought he had escaped and managed to get clean away. Jesus, they must have been shitting themselves until Ollie Jennings discovered his body.

Unless they drowned him.

There was a knock on the passenger window. Jack Buckley nearly shot through the windscreen with the fright. It was Freddie Nolan. Jack opened down the window. "Jesus, Freddie, don't do that, you nearly frightened me half to death!"

"Sorry about that, Jack. I just thought I'd let you know we have a new doctor."

Jack looked at him, waiting to see if there was a piece of earth-shattering news about to follow. "You knocked on my car window to tell me we have a new doctor?"

Freddie nodded.

Jack leaned forward and covered his face with his hands. God, I need a drink, he said to himself. He eased himself out of the car, slammed the door and walked slowly to the side door of the pub and tapped on the window.

35

FOR SALE.

Maggie sat in the car outside the small cottage and stared at the sign. Her heart sank. It couldn't be, she kept saying to herself. She opened the window and let the stiff breeze fill the car, occasionally carrying with it the delicious smell of the sweetpea that draped the front wall of old, gentle Harry Vogel's tiny house. The morning sun shone beautifully across the small slope, right down to the cliff's edge. From where she was sitting she could see that the half-door was open. He was expecting her, being an official Thursday, even though she called to him unoffically, as a friend, everyday.

She had got up earlier than usual this morning so that she could spend a little extra time with Harry. She had looked forward to it since Tuesday, especially since she hadn't been able to call yesterday. She gathered up her things, a small bowl of casserole she had put in the oven while making the "romantic" dinner for Jack the previous night, her medical case and a small bottle of pills, *Promitine*, a light sleeping tablet, to help him relax at night.

Her enthusiasm about visiting was gone now, smashed by the sight of that bloody sign. She looked up at the board again, as conspicuously as she could, knowing he would be watching her from the window. FOR SALE.

Damn you.

She tapped on the bottom of the door, pushing it forward to let herself in. *"Hello . . . "* she crooned, as she always did, only to let him know it was her. *"Anyone home?"*

Silence.

Then she saw his feet, under the upturned ironing-board. She gasped and shouted his name, *"Harry!"* like she would call Jack's name in an emergency, dropping the bowl of casserole onto the hard stone floor. It smashed. She paid no attention. She placed her medical case to one side and pulled the ironing-board out of the way.

"I'm OK," he insisted, mumbling the words and holding his head. There was blood. Not a lot. He had obviously hit his head. She knelt down and took his hand. It was colder than it should have been for a man his age, on a relatively warm May morning. He was lying on his side. From first impressions, he had tripped, or fallen, and hit his head against the huge, solid fuel cooker. She tried to assess any obvious injuries. "I'll call for an ambulance!" she said quickly.

"No!" he urged. "No ambulance. I'm fine." He started to move his legs.

"What happened?" She was kneeling beside him now, rooting in her black bag for her stethoscope. She place it around her neck, opened the top three buttons of his shirt and listened, holding her breath, and placing a finger to her lips urging him to be quiet. "Heartbeat's OK." She took his pulse, searching to see where the blood around the base of his scalp might have come from. It seemed congealed now. "What happened?" she asked again. He was smiling now, and seemed quite relaxed.

"I was ironing my shirt, preparing for your visit. I must have tripped over the cable of the iron and hit my head." He touched the bloody spot and looked at his fingers.

"Did you blackout?"

He laughed softly to himself now. "Of course not."

Maggie couldn't understand what he thought was so funny. "You could have knocked yourself out. What would you have done then? Especially if I'd been delayed." She was becoming more and more exasperated by his negligent attitude.

He nodded to the sign outside the gate. "I suppose I wouldn't have had to worry about selling the cottage, would I?"

Maggie ignored the comment. she would deal with it later. First she had to get him into a chair, and then to the doctor. Of all days going, thank God for sending a doctor to Durrus, she said quietly to herself. She helped him gently to stand up and eased him backwards into his favourite chair. "Why don't you let me iron your shirts?"

"Because I like to be wearing them, freshly ironed, when you arrive each day."

"You old smoothie," she joked.

"Less of the smoothie," he mumbled. "I'm not completely helpless."

"Now I want you to think hard, Harry. Did you lose consciousness at all, even just for a few seconds? Because if you did I'll have to get you checked out at Bantry hospital."

He jerked his shoulders and stretched back into the chair, placing his foot on the poof in front of the fireplace. "Of course I didn't. And as for this," he pointed to the small gash, "it's only a graze. I'm not even going to bother with a plaster. Don't mention hospital or I won't talk to you again."

"Don't you be so cheeky, Mister."

"I'm going to get the doctor to check you out since you won't come to the hospital with me. I'll ask him to call out to you as soon as I see him."

"What *doctor*? I've never needed a doctor. If you're sick you go to bed. If you die they bury you. If you're dying there's not a lot anyone can do for you, whether they're a doctor or not!"

Maggie realised then that she hadn't had a chance to tell him of their most recent professional arrival in town. "I forgot to tell you. At long last, we got ourselves a doctor!" She started to clap her hands.

"Well, well, well," he said sarcastically as she checked his head wound, "that's the best news I've heard all day. What's his name?"

"James Morris."

"And where's he from?"

"Haven't a clue. I haven't even met him yet. I'm gonna call in to say hello when I get back into town. And

I'm going to ask him to call out to see you. That's a deep gash. It might need a couple of stitches."

"Well, you can give me those, can't you?"

"In extreme emergencies I can. But the book says that when a doctor can do them instead, then the doctor does them. Unless he's not available. And now he *is*!"

"If you bring a doctor up here I'll never talk to you again."

"Oh, don't be such a little cissy. Anyway there's far more important things to be discussing." Maggie knew the joking was over, the serious talking was about to start. "Why are you selling this? This is your home."

"It's not my home. This hasn't been my home for five years now. Sure, it's a lovely little house to live in. But it's not home, not since Brega died."

"But she wouldn't want you to move, would she?"

"She doesn't really have much of a say these days, does she?"

"And where will you go?"

He looked dreamily about the room, and out the window and beyond. "To tell you the truth, I haven't given it much thought. I just feel that while I have some strength left in me I would like to move on somewhere, maybe even back home. Austria is my home. I miss it terribly, especially since Brega went away."

"But surely you'll feel further away from her if you leave here. You buried her here. All of her memories are here where you are now. You'll be walking away from all of this, which was hers too when she was alive."

"I take it you're campaigning to keep me here?"

"Maybe I am. Maybe I've grown too fond of you to

imagine what life would be like without our little chats, and our scones, and our mulled wine." She stopped talking and studied his eyes. "Tell me the truth. Why are you really leaving?"

He seemed startled that she might doubt his word. "I've nothing to hide if that's what you mean, nothing to run away from, Maggie. I love it here. It's just getting a little bit too remote for me."

"Well, then, move down into Durrus. There's loads of lovely people there who'd be delighted to drop in and out on you to keep you company. We're not short of that around here, God knows."

"I know that." He sighed. "I've been thinking about this for a long, long time. It's not something I just dreamt up overnight. When I put my mind to it I tend to be a bit pigheaded. I tend to see things through. I have decided to go, so I *am* going. I hear there's been a couple of offers for this little place already. Beautiful spot to live, I have to say. Promise me one thing though."

"What's that?"

"That you'll look after Brega's grave for me. Just once a week, say hello to her."

"That won't be possible." She sat down and held his hand. He seemed hurt by her answer.

"Why?"

"Because I've decided to leave here."

"You?"

She nodded.

"Why? This is your home. The people love you around here. Many of them will be completely lost without you. You can't go."

"I'm thirty-four, nearly thirty-five. I want a new beginning. Somewhere I can go and feel like I used to feel years ago." She hoped the moment was right before saying what she really had to say. "Remember our conversation . . . about my mother?"

"Yes."

"Well, I've decided I'm going to try and find out where she is."

The old man waited until he was sure she was finished. He couldn't possibly interrupt such an important moment. "And how do you think you are going to be able to achieve that?" He spoke gently and squeezed her hand.

"I don't know. But I guess, when I look around at what's going on in my life right now, being realistic about it, I don't think it's ever going to change unless I make it change, I've got nothing to lose."

"And Jack. Will he go with you?" He pursed his lips.

She shook her head. "No, I don't think so. Anyway, part of me doesn't want him to come. I need a new start."

He smiled. "Well, why don't you go part of the way with me then?"

36

The waiting-room to the rear of Freddie Nolan's chemist shop was packed.

Most of those waiting to see the new doctor had spent the previous two hours concocting ailments and viruses that would guarantee them at least fifteen minutes each in the privacy of the hallowed, hospital-smelling surgery of the man the whole town was talking about that morning.

Ethel Kline was first in line. She sat with her bag planted firmly on her knee, refusing to engage in the idle clishmaclaver, as her husband called it, that was oozing through the walls of the room by now. She was there with a different reason. Alex had sent her, told her to get herself down to that new doctor and find out everything she could about him, "right down to what he had for his breakfast this morning". Alex maintained that if he was a doctor he had plenty of money to spend, having done his sums over his poached eggs that morning. "Cash business . . . fifteen pounds a visit. Listening to silly old twittering goosegobs like your friends down the town.

Twenty pounds for a house call. Seven days a week . . ." he shouted into his pocket calculator, punching in digits, as Ethel stood looking impressed over his shoulder. "Holy Sweet Divine . . . that's almost three grand a week he could be taking home. I've got some lovely properties that man might like to look at." He led Ethel to the front door and kissed her goodbye. "Go get him," he shouted as he waved to her.

Ethel counted eleven patients sitting around the walls of the sparse waiting-room, all looking reasonably healthy. But then who was she to criticise? They were all there for the very same reason. Still she had an extra reason to feel honoured among them. Her part-time housekeeper, Ciara MacCann, was the doctor's newly appointed assistant. Ethel remarked, to the woman beside her, on how well she looked in her starched white finery. She smiled at her and winked towards the closed door.

"Two minutes," Ciara MacCann whispered, as she put files in order and stacked them to one side. Then her phone buzzed once. The doctor would start to see his patients now. She nodded to Ethel. "The doctor will see you now."

Ethel pressed down on the handle and opened the door slowly, just wide enough to get inside. She didn't want any of the others, who she knew were all leering behind her for a good look, to see anything until she was finished her business. She closed the door behind her and waited.

He was sitting behind a desk with a full front, so she could only see him from the chest up behind a pile of papers and folders. He seemed to be making notes. He seemed tall, in his late-50s, she reckoned, with a craggy face and prominent features, and a fine head of white-silvery hair that looked – as her mother used to say – well-weathered and suffered, but still all intact. He glanced up over the rim of his half-spectacles. "Good morning. You must be, eh . . . Mrs Kline." He spoke slowly and softly as he checked the name against a file in front of him.

"That's right, Doctor," Ethel Kline replied, speaking in her swanky accent, as Alex called it.

"Have a seat." He studied the notes Ciara MacCann had given in to him. "You've a bad pain in your shoulder, Ciara has written down here."

"That's right." Ethel was a little surprised at his pace. No time for chit-chat, she thought. "Ciara's my housekeeper – part-time, of course." No response. She decided to draw it out a little. "You're welcome to Durrus. My husband is the local Justice of the Peace for this area, among other things," she gushed.

"Alex is your husband, isn't he?"

"That's right." She was impressed.

"Let me see." He closed his eyes for a moment, shoving his glasses further up onto the bridge of his nose, and then stood up, driving his hands deep into the pockets of his white coat. "He's also the bank manager, and the estate agent?"

"You've done your homework." Ethel was impressed.

He moved out from behind his desk. "Let's see what's causing this pain." Gently, he pinched the muscle above her left collar bone. "Is that uncomfortable?"

"Slightly," she answered, shivering at the touch of his strong fingers. "Your hand's lovely and warm."

He seemed to ignore her compliment. Standing behind her now, she couldn't see him, except for his hand which was slowly massaging her shoulder-bone now. "And there?"

"More so." She grimaced and shuddered to give the discomfort a bit of expression.

He walked back to the desk and sat down, taking a small blank note pad from the top drawer. "I don't think it's anything serious, Mrs Kline. Probably whatever way you've been lying on that side while you're asleep over the last couple of nights. I'll give you a prescription for an ointment. Rub it into the painful area tonight before you have a bath. It should relieve any pain you've been experiencing. Freddie Nolan should have this in stock. It's a simple remedy. If it doesn't sort out the problem, come back to me and I might send you into Bantry for an X-ray." He handed her the page and smiled.

"How much do I owe you?"

He waved his hand and started to examine the next patient's file. "First day here, so the first consultation is on the house."

Ethel appeared chuffed. "That's very good of you." She popped the prescription into her bag and snapped it shut. She watched him as he pored over the notes on the page in front of him. "You're not from around these parts, are you?" She tried to ensure that the tone of her voice was simply curious in a friendly sort of way, and not prying.

He looked up at her, over the top of those strangely eerie specs, more like lorgnettes than ordinary reading glasses, studying her differently this time, she felt. "Sorry?"

"I was just remarking that you musn't be from around here."

He smiled patiently. "You're absolutely right."

Ethel Kline wasn't one to be pushed aside by woolliness, when it came to conversation. "Where are you from?"

"Well, I'm not Irish, if that's what you mean."

He had stopped smiling now, and was gently tapping the page with the tip of his pen. "And you?"

Ethel wasn't sure what his question meant. If, that is, it was a question. "What do you mean?"

"Simple. We've got a lot in common, Ethel. I'm not Irish. Neither are you. You and your husband are German. Aren't you?"

Ethel nodded abruptly. "Originally. We came here to live years ago. In fact, it's been so long we almost consider ourselves Irish now." It wasn't the form of conversation she had expected to be having with a blank stranger.

"Alex would have National Socialist tendencies, wouldn't he?"

Ethel was beginning to feel flustered now. She wasn't sure how to react. A national what, did he say?

"I don't know what you mean." She wasn't sure if his question was meant as a compliment or a slur on her husband's character. Either way she didn't like the tone of the conversation. And yet he just sat there and stared. There was a different quality to his attitude now. She couldn't quite put her finger on it, but he was no longer a nice caring old doctor.

"If you have trouble, make sure to come back to me. Do you hear me, Mrs Kline?"

For a moment Ethel Kline wasn't sure what he meant by *trouble*. Then she remembered her pinched nerve above her collarbone. She closed the door behind her and hurried through the thronged, excited waiting-room, and on out past Freddie Nolan who was waiting to see her reaction. He remarked to one of his customers that she looked sicker now than when she had come in over an hour earlier. She appeared to be on her last legs as she threw back the chemist door and bounded down the two steep steps into the street to take a huge breath of the fresh cold Durrus air.

It didn't seem to bother her that she had left her shopping-bag behind her.

* * *

Maggie asked Ethel Kline if she was feeling all right, after watching her tumble out of Freddie Nolan's chemist. Ethel ignored the question as she wrapped her scarf high around the neck and walked past.

"Morning, Freddie," Maggie said with the usual friendly, confiding ring to her voice.

"Morning, Maggie. It's crazy in there." Freddie nodded to the waiting-room behind. "The doctor said if you called you were to go straight in."

Maggie squeezed her way through the packed storage-room, speedily converted overnight into a makeshift waiting-room, full of mothers and young children, and a handful of elderly citizens, some of them coughing and sniffing. She tapped on the surgery door and entered just as old Mick Boggan was pulling up his trousers.

The man didn't seem too put out by the intrusion. "Morning, Maggie," he breezed with a chesty voice. "The doctor says me piles are healing up, thanks to yerself and that magic cream you gave me." He stood still for a moment and broke wind. "See? I can even fart again without dying of the pain!" He laughed and doffed his cap to her. She closed the door behind him and laughed.

"Welcome to Durrus," she said to man behind the desk who seemed amused to say the least. They shook hands. "I'm Maggie Flanagan. I can see you're up to your eyes this morning so I won't hold you up. Can I invite you to dinner this evening?"

The doctor seemed staggered by the unexpected invitation. He smiled. "I'd love to. I hope I'm not intruding."

"You're not. My partner's in Dublin for the funeral of that young boy. They found his body in one of the small lakes out towards the end of the peninsula."

"I heard. You're married to the sergeant."

"No. We've been living together. But we haven't kinda got round to getting married just yet. And believe me things are complicated enough without marriage. That won't be happening, I don't think."

"What time should I arrive?"

"About eight?" She took out a small map. "Here, there's the direction to the house. It's easy enough to find. Any problems, ask any of the locals. They all know where we live."

"I look forward to it. Thank you."

* * *

Alex Kline's face turned so red that Ethel thought he was about to have a heart-attack.

He had been waiting for her in the kitchen when she arrived back from her visit to the new doctor. "Well, what's he like?" he asked impatiently.

Ethel shrugged. "He seems nice. He didn't say very much. I told him I thought I had a trapped nerve in my shoulder and he gave me some cream to rub on it after I have a bath tonight."

"Shit! You know that's not what I mean. What's he really like?"

Ethel thought about the question. "He's quiet. I asked him where he was from."

"What did he say?"

"It was a strange way of answering my question. He said 'I'm not Irish, if that's what you mean.' Then he said 'just like you're not Irish'."

Alex's boisterous excitement had settled down now into a more serious inquisitiveness. "What did he mean by that?"

Ethel ignored his question. "He knew we were both German, Alex."

"So what? There's thousands of Germans living in Ireland."

"He also knew you were a bank manager and an estate agent."

"Anybody around here could have told him that.

Everyone for miles around knows who I am. Don't tell me you're surprised at that?"

Ethel watched him as he tried to rationalise her side of the discussion. "What's a National Socialist, Alex? He said you had National Socialist tendencies, or something."

His eyes opened wide, and unconsciously she started to count the veins as they protruded around his neck, one or two of them twitching, before he opened the tight collar of the blue-striped Ralph Lauren shirt that she had bought him for his fiftieth birthday.

She wanted him to tell her, since the doctor had made it seem so relevant simply by the way he had asked her the question earlier.

Alex Kline didn't answer.

Instead he poured himself a large John Power whiskey and drank it. Neat, like she had never seen him drink it before. Then he went into the sitting-room and, as if retiring for the night, gently closed the door behind him.

Ethel walked into the conservatory at the side of the house, where a small service window looked into the spacious front room.

Alex was standing perfectly still in the middle of the room facing the large bay window, his back to Ethel, his shoulders hunched slightly, with his head buried in his hands.

She listened carefully to the muffled, painful sound of her husband crying softly to himself.

37

"Non-stop, all the way to Dublin-Heuston," the guard announced, as he collected tickets, punched them with his clipper and shoved them into his breast pocket.

Within minutes of pulling out of Mallow, the Inter-City express was speeding through dozens of tiny stations, turning them into little more than colourful blobs.

Jack washed the two Solpadeine down with a long gulp from the bottle of chilled Heineken. As the cool, refreshing taste of the alcohol rinsed his mouth and hit his stomach at breakneck speed, followed quickly by another strong gulp, his eyes watched the nun in the seat across, two up, trying hard not to stare at him. He raised the bottle to her and smiled. Cheers, he gestured. Today he didn't care. He wasn't in uniform. He was away from Sheep's Head. No one in the world knew who or what he was. Certainly not a nun.

Indignantly, her eyes went back to her morning newspaper. Jack tried to read the main headline.

BOY'S BODY FOUND IN LAKE

Search continues for friends.

Search continues. Jack pondered the words, mulling over the huge crime such inadequate clichés were covering up. Not for long, he thought. But who was going to believe him? There was no search. Alfie Carruth had said in the early radio news bulletin that he was in charge of the investigation, and was making extra resources available to the team he had appointed.

In truth, Jack knew, Alfie Carruth would search no further. Why should he? He would only end up staring at himself in the mirror. He settled back into the seat and tried to sleep.

* * *

At the same time, 2.15pm to be precise, the new doctor turned the key in the door of the surgery and stretched out on the long armchair opposite his desk. His next surgery wasn't until half-three. The travelling back and forth and overnight unloading and unpacking had taken its toll. He was shattered. He pulled the tweedy blanket up around his neck and lay on his side. Within minutes he was in a deep sleep and dreaming.

* * *

Then his whole body trembled quite violently causing him to start and look around, the cold blast of air-conditioning shooting into his face. He was back on the flight from Frankfurt again. Still dreaming. He estimated he had slept for half-an-hour. It had been a totally relaxing slumber, something he hadn't been accustomed to for months, brought on by sheer exhaustion. Inevitably, the fatigue always brought on the same dream. He checked his watch. Still over an hour into Dublin, he thought. He closed his eyes and dozed again, the hum of the jet's engines and the swish of the cool air above his head lulling him, coaxing him to recall the event just one more time before entering the final chapter. A dream, so to speak, within a dream. The same dream he had over and over. And now he was enduring it again.

* * *

It was three years earlier. He was standing beside Lake Wannsee, close to Berlin, a more flighty, nervous individual. A streak of bird shit splashed onto the brim of his hat, distracting him for a moment. He smiled briefly to himself, then sighed nervously, as it dawned on him that that was all it was. Just harmless bird shit. And not a bullet ripping red-hot through the soft-cap cloth, a hair's-breadth from his head. The sky was torquoise blue, as he searched for the bird. "Little bastard," he whispered. He took off his cap and shivered. Not your ordinary pigeon or chaffinch. He stroked it with a tissue. A hawk, or some other huge bird. The more he wiped it the worse it became. Maybe even an eagle. For a moment he wondered if there were experts locked away in some tiny laboratory who could identify a bird purely from examining its droppings. Now he knew he was going mad. He gave up and stuffed the tissue into his pocket.

He'd believed for years that it was inevitable that he would die this way, at the hands of someone he would never see. Just a fraction of a second to realise that death had arrived and his valued work would end, as quickly as he gasped for his last breath, and be forgotten. It was his greatest fear. More than anything else, he needed to finish his work. And today he knew the end was in sight. He looked at the letter again, reluctant to let it go, and then at the postbox, wondering was he in focus through the assassin's telescopic sight yet and at what moment would the hit man choose to squeeze the trigger.

All the while he could hear the persuasive voice of his mother. *Go on!* she kept saying to him. Writing a good letter is like reaching into your soul. They were her words. She always maintained you could swear by a good letter writer. She was a scribbler, as she called it, famous for her letters. Pages and pages of stories and news and scandal, which kept her up all hours of the night when the world and her children were asleep, penned to her sisters and her mother, and to anyone else who wrote to her. She was always encouraging her children to write. A good letter is always simple and honest, she'd say. Otherwise people will read between the lines. No one will trust you.

She was dead a long time now. Still, despite her early protests, her son hated writing. He could count the number of letters he had written, on one hand, insisting that information and honesty led to vulnerability. Letters left a trail, a bad smell that could easily be traced back to their source. You can't be found guilty for thinking, he told his wife. That wasn't the case with the printed word.

Although now he had no choice. Time was precious and he had been forced to write. A sealed letter was safer than a phone call or an e-mail.

He examined the envelope painstakingly, feeling its bulky contents with his thin fingers, making sure it was properly sealed. Until today only *he* knew what was going to happen. Sometimes he had daydreamed of changing the course of history, and of how the world would react to his plan. There were days he sat watching news bulletins and reports featuring heads of government and thinking how they would laugh if he had told them what he was planning; the same people who would be grateful when he had accomplished his task. But there were those who would persevere to ensure he died in the process, and in death to tell the world that he was a wandering, mentally unstable social misfit. He always remembered as a child watching the first competitor of the Olympic Games carrying the torch and thinking about how important the flame must have been, and how the runner could hold it so close to his face without burning himself. He remembered the exhausted look on the athlete's face. Yet he never stopped running because the whole world was waiting on the flame.

The envelope was his torch, being passed to the next player for consideration, a young journalist whose courage and audacity gave him strength to carry on with his search; a young man, he knew, who would certainly die soon because he had dared to get too close to the flame.

He hesitated for a moment, pulling it back, all the

time remembering the famous handshake, a pact he had made with the young reporter he had met at a convention in New York ten years before; a deal which had removed both of them from the world he'd known for most of his life – his family and his comfortable medical practice in Harrisburg, Pennsylvania, and all the trappings of success – and committed him to a life-long chase; an excruciatingly lonely existence.

The eyes of the whole world and all the ghosts from his past were watching him now. He glanced furtively over his shoulder to see if he could recognise any of them but there was no one there. If the pillion-riding gunman he had always feared was looking for his chance to kill this morning, then the crack of gunfire would ring out at any second. He waited, anticipating the hot searing pain of the bullet and which part of his body it would smash into.

Nothing.

Just two giddy young boys shouting as they tried to control their feisty kite.

He sighed, then shivered, as he felt the envelope drop out of his hand. Then it occured to him that they could have got there before him and planted one of their famous devices inside the postbox. He turned and walked quickly, resisting the driving temptation to run. He couldn't let them see he was afraid. Tiny beads of sweat freckled his temples and dampened the thin strands of hair that the cold March wind flicked into his eyes. It didn't bother him. He was more concerned now by the paranoia which fed off him day and night and made him feel nauseous that morning. He wanted to feel relief, a sense of release, but he knew that it would take more than a letter confirming what he had just been told. There was still work to be done, the most critical yet to come. And with it the forbidding uncertainty he'd expected towards the end. His life was still in danger but not for long more, he hoped. All the while his mind flitted over the letter he had written and pored over all morning, and the only other person who would ever read it.

Nathan Lohan
PO 2411
Dublin
Ireland

Dear Nathan,

I wanted to phone you with my news but feared that my apartment might be bugged. I came home unexpectedly early yesterday and found my housekeeper reading through some old letters. Thankfully they were of no real importance. The Germans, like us, have not forgotten. However their's is a different torment. I will move away from Berlin tomorrow, to a small spa town called Bad Homburg, near Frankfurt, where I have some friends. My work here is complete. I am making arrangements to travel to Ireland towards the end of the month. Perhaps our search is almost over. I pray it is.

Shalom,
JM

He strolled back up from the water's edge of Heckshorn Point, looking to his right and the popular restaurants burgeoning at a yearly rate, catering for the thousands of tourists who came every week and drove along Am Grossen Wannsee, a street lined with villas, and stopped with their camcorders to take pictures outside Nos, 56-58, the lakeside villa built in the First World War. He gazed for a moment at the statue of The Flensburg Lion looking out over the peaceful water, a reminder of the German defence of the region in medieval times. And then back in the direction of the villa where Reinhard Heydrich, and his assistant Adolph Eichmann, introduced the "Final Solution" to a dozen civil servants. The meeting brought together the two main centres in Nazi Germany.

He tried to imagine how the Minister of Transport might have reacted when told that plans had been laid for his railways and roads to carry eleven million Jews to their deaths. Heydrich's exact words were that the European Jews should "fall away".

He stood outside the villa now, watching the gardener, his wheelbarrow next to him, stooped over the small shrubbery, crudely, impatiently, clipping the weaker, dying foliage and purging the freshly turned soil of ugly impurities.

Once inside the villa, the natural light gone, he held his breath tightly to feel the stillness of the actual room, its tall picture windows looking out over the patio and lawn down to the lake. The air in the room was dead, touched by evil. It was as if the curators felt morally obliged to leave it stagnant. Despite the bright sunshine outside, and the long windows, the room remained dark and uneasy. He walked solemnly through a door into another room. A huge roll of old, discoloured margarine-yellow cloth was marked out in dozens of stars, with the word "Jude" on each one, ready to be cut out and sown on to Jewish coats and jackets. A telegram stared out at him from its glass frame on the wall. It was dated 30 July 1943, his birthday, and concerned a consignment of Zyklon-B poison gas to Aushwitz.

He had postponed his visit along the wooded shore of the Havel Chausee for many years now, despite his ongoing work in Berlin. He knew it required a special time when he could retreat into his soul to consider and regenerate. Now seemed like the perfect moment.

He strolled through the park at a more leisurely pace now, watching the young children feeding the ducks, stopping briefly to observe an elderly woman place a bunch of tulips at the cenotaph. He spotted the empty bench seat and sat down. From there he watched the small postbox in the distance and felt his heart speed up. Of course they weren't going to come looking, he tried to convince himself. He pulled out the morning papers from his jacket pocket, the *Frankfurter Allgemeine Zeitung* and the *Frankfurter Rundschau*. He rarely bought them but this morning, he suspected, they might carry news which would be useful. He was right. The tall broad-shouldered figure was on both front pages. Donald Klaus Eckler. He had announced his retirement the night before at a press conference in Restaurant Francais, at the Franfurter Hof Hotel. Its French cuisine – Eckler's absolute weakness – was among the best in Germany. And with its sumptuous golden and green decor, oil paintings, silver tableware and legions of well-trained waiters, the cost of a night's dining was beyond the means of most mere mortals. But not for Eckler. He'd invited two hundred close friends and paid the bill by personal credit card. The *Zeitung* estimated the bill to be close to twenty-five thousand pounds.

He was angry now that he had read the fine details of Eckler's extravagant night at the Hof. He tossed the papers into a lakeside bin. He had waited almost ten years for this moment, years of impatience and passionate anger that had aged him prematurely and caused him sickness and bad health; years of months spent separated from his wife and children whom he loved and missed. He had promised her over and over that this task he had set himself was almost complete, only to find that his target had once again slipped through the net. She'd never questioned where their money came from. She knew he couldn't have been producing it himself. He'd told her one night before he left her to continue his search that there were many generous friends who were looking after them, who willed him to continue the quest on their behalf too; a hunt which strengthened their once dying conviction in justice. He'd turned his back on a lucrative career because of the promise he had made to his mother some years after her death when he had become old enough to realise the significance of the past and the importance of preserving it as a monument for future generations. For years he'd been the woodsman, looking for a needle in a haystack, most of the time flying solo. Doors were slammed in his face whenever he asked the same questions again and again.

The sunshine seemed particularly warm and bright

for a March afternoon, serving to strenghten his resolve that none of what he'd been attempting to appease for ten years had been in vain. Then, in a split second, the radiant brightness was gone, the sun covered by cloud, the park darker and cold again, reminding him cruelly that for every pinhead of certitude, he would always carry enough doubt to make him hesitate and trip. He hurried back towards the main road to catch a bus to the Grunewald railway station to see the place from which Berlin Jews were deported – "fallen away" – and to stand on the platform where his mother and father and older brother all stood before boarding the train that took then to the concentration camp. And then on he went to the privacy and isolation of the seedy little apartment that had become home out of a suitcase for almost a year. He passed the postbox, just as the postman clanked it shut and swung the slack sack over his shoulder. If he had continued to the end of the article on the front page of the *Rundschau*, he would have noticed the headline beneath:

POSTAL WORKER'S BODY FOUND

And he might have chosen not to post his letter. Now he felt as though he would soon be closing the book for the last time; as though he had just started the last chapter of the most violent story he had ever read.

38

He was still dreaming. But within the dream, as always happens, he was awake.

Slightly startled, as if caught unawares, he spent a few moments sorting out his bearings. He was still on the plane, still in the air. His table-top was opened down, *The Irish Times* folded across page five, as he had left it when he'd dozed off, a complimentary edition to the business class passenger on boarding EI561, the scheduled Saturday morning flight from Flughafen Frankfurt am Main to Dublin. He raised the white window shutter, shielding his eyes against the brilliant sunshine.

Tables were being cleared by Maria who had told them on the intercom that she would be their attendant for the flight. She smiled as she stooped. "Would you like tea or coffee?"

Her eyes were dark blue, like the sky above the clouds, he thought. He smiled back. "Coffee, please." She reminded him of Helena, his wife, whom he hadn't seen now for two-hundred-and-ninety-six days; her dark, deep-set, sea-blue eyes and jet-black hair. He remembered the time and the day she'd kissed him goodbye. He'd hugged her so tightly, uncertain when he would embrace her again. He wished now he could reach into his pocket and take out their photo. The same one he'd carried for thirteen years: Helena and his two daughters, Misha and Abie, taken on their mother's thirtieth birthday. But he had conscientiously decided to send all of his keepsakes and sentimental homely reminders back home to Helena in Harrisburg in order to safeguard their anonymity. Once in Dublin, at the first opportunity, he would post a long five-page letter explaining exactly what he had been doing with his life for the last year.

Helena had asked him many times, pleaded with him on occasions, to tell her more about his work. Most times she had asked, he simply replied: "When the time is right". The time had come. She would be shocked, saddened perhaps, but – most of all – Josef hoped she would be proud of him. He felt hollow without the small snapshot, but happy that soon he wouldn't need the photograph, that when he would wake late at night, like he did so often lately that he had lost count, Helena would be lying next to him with her arm across his neck, just like before.

He'd called the Aer Lingus reservations desk at Frankfurt airport early on Thursday afternoon and told the girl his name was Don Eckler. He apologised and explained that he'd forgotten the departure time of his return flight to Dublin. She was very helpful and gave him all the information he needed, even offering to send a complimentary taxi to pick his party up from the hotel an hour before the flight. Maister was bursting with gratitude, only because he now knew where Eckler was staying. Then he rang Aer Lingus reservations in Dublin and booked a return flight to Frankfurt for the following day for himself, specifying that he wanted a seat on the Saturday morning 10.50am flight back to Dublin. It was crucial that officials at Frankfurt airport thought he was returning to Dublin and not just flying one-way from Germany.

The seat next to him was empty, the only vacant seat on the busy flight. The man sitting next to the aisle was immersed in his laptop. He'd tried unsuccessfully to engage Josef in smalltalk a couple of times before the flight took off. He quickly realised he wasn't getting anywhere. From where he was sitting Josef had a perfectly squared view of the two men in 2E and 2F. They'd spoken constantly since Frankfurt, their heads turning, nodding, shaking, agreeing. Josef was frustrated and angry that he couldn't hear the conversation, but that would have meant sitting directly behind them, jeopardising his cover, and the months of secretive checking and double-checking. They'd met forty minutes before the flight was due to depart, shook hands in the boarding area, and conversed ever since. Maister had watched them both check in. Light baggage, nothing else. The check-in attendant asked him if he had any seat preference since he was one of the first in the queue. He knew the men would be sitting towards the front of the business-class section. "Towards the middle, please," he said politely. He watched how she examined his ticket. She seemed a bit confused.

"This ticket was issued in Dublin yesterday. But the outgoing portion for the 7.00am flight wasn't checked through. You didn't fly on this flight, Mr . . . " She checked for his name. "Maister?"

"No, I didn't actually," he replied calmly. "My car got a puncture on the way to the airport and I missed the flight. I got a seat on the lunchtime flight." He hoped she wouldn't ask him the time of the later flight because he didn't know – she didn't.

The two men who sat eight rows ahead to his right looked slightly different to the photograph that had introduced him to them. Obviously they had aged. But different in another way. Here they were surrounded by people. They were true diplomats on their guard, their best behaviour. In the small black and white photograph they had been relaxing over a drink, possibly talking off-the-record, unaware someone close by had a camera.

Don Eckler sat in 2E. His companion in 2F was Alan Harrisson, private secretary to Ireland's Prime Minister, Taoiseach Joe Russell. To all intents and purposes, and to anyone else flying on EI561 that morning, they were just plain anonymous passengers.

Josef tried not to dwell too long on the last paragraph in the letter which he had transferred from his briefcase to his inside pocket once on board. Now and then, as reassurance, he felt its bulky outline. He explained that in the event of his death, Helen was to keep the small key stuck to the back of the fifth page safe. It would open a private locker at the arrivals hall in Frankfurt airport which he had made a point of renting on Friday afternoon shortly after his supposed arrival. Inside she would find a large, bulky envelope. His instructions were simple and terse: *"This parcel must be delivered without any delay to an address in Austria. 7 Rudolph Square in Vienna, to be precise. Do not post it in Germany, under any circumstances. Wherever you decide to post it, do not register it. Most importantly, don't tell anyone what you are doing, including Abie and Misha. Of course, your curiosity may wish to examine the contents of the parcel yourself. Unfortunately, by then, I won't be able to explain to you why I would prefer you not to. Perhaps my abiding fear is that once you'd read it, you too would become involved. This is purely precautionary, Helena, as I know that some evening very soon we will both be sitting in front of the log fire together, like old times, and I will be able to explain everything, if that is possible. If you cannot go to Frankfurt, representatives from Vienna will make arrangements to collect the key from you once you have written to them and mentioned my name. Keep it safe. And you. I love you, always. Josef."*

The possibility that he might never get to see them again hurt him beyond words. Then he remembered the one token he had chosen to keep. He took the crumpled, folded page from his wallet. It was an old aboriginal chant that his mother told to them when they were children.

Forever Oneness,
Who sings to us in silence,
Who teaches us through each other,
Guide my steps with strength and wisdom.
May I see the lessons as I walk,
Honour the purpose of all things.

Help me touch with respect,
Always speak from behind my eyes.
Let me observe, not judge.
May I cause no harm, and leave
Music and beauty after my visit.
When I return to Forever,
May the circle be closed and
The spiral be broader.

The intercom crackled. "Ladies and gentleman, this is the captain. Nothing serious, let me reassure you, but if there's a doctor or any other medical personnel flying with us this morning could you please make yourself known to a member of the cabin crew as soon as possible. Thank you."

Josef froze. He'd been aware for some minutes of the constant coughing towards the back of the aircraft. It had started intermittently. Eckler and Harrisson were looking towards the rear of the plane, craning and turning to see what the problem was. Josef waited, hoping there might be a nurse or another doctor on board. To volunteer would be to risk his disguise. But the young girl was crying now, gasping for air. It sounded like asthma. She was choking. Then retching. All the time begging her mother to stop the coughing. Passengers were looking at each other now and back towards the commotion in seats 18B and 18C. He though of Misha and Abie when they were young, imagining how he would feel if they were hurting and begging their daddy to take the pain away. And now his grandchildren and how they loved him. *"Excuse me!"* he called nervously. "I'm a doctor."

The young girl's face was puffed, so swollen her eyes were closed tightly. She was small, blonde and beautiful in her mother's arms, no older that six, he reckoned. She'd stopped coughing now and the blue rims above and below her lips told Maister she was choking to death. "What was she eating?" he asked her mother as he lay her on the floor between the seats.

"Yoghurt, that's all."

"Show me the carton."

The steward ripped open one of the rubbish bags she'd bundled into the kitchenette and rummaged through the breakfast leftovers. "Hazlenut delight."

The mother started to cry. "I told her she couldn't eat nuts. She must have tried mine when I went to the toilet."

"She is allergic to nuts?" he asked.

The woman nodded and sobbed.

Maister knew he had less than a minute to save her, allowing for the time she'd been convulsing. "I'll have to perform a tracheotomy. Otherwise she'll suffocate in a couple of minutes." He looked up at Maria, pale but unflustered. "I'll need a sharp knife and the toggle whistle from one of the life-jackets. And as many towels as you can get your hands on. Blankets as well. Tell the pilot we need a full paramedic crew standing by to take her directly from the plane. They'll have to administer an antihistamine and an antihypertensive immediately they get her down. Tell them to alert the hospital to have a theatre ready, that she'll possibly need a further tracheotomy. Now could everybody return to their seats please? I need as much space as possible here."

Just as he was about to make the small, neat incision in the front of her throat he woke up and gasped.

* * *

He shivered and felt the wetness of the warm sweat across his forehead and mopped it with the cuff of his white jacket. He sat up kicking away the blanket, wet now from his perspiration, and looked around at the silent surgery wondering just how long his secret ordeal was going to continue before he could finally return home to be with his family; this living hell he had perpetrated from the very start and inflicted on himself. He had no one else to blame for the fear he lived with as a constant companion, no one else he could turn to for solace or friendship until it was finally at an end, and the ghosts of the past were laid to rest.

He checked his watch.

It was 3.20pm.

39

Freddie Nolan looked pale as he shuffled nervously into the surgery, easing the door closed behind him, trying hard not to shatter the perfect silence. He coughed politely and waited for the doctor to look up from his desk. He was desperate now to get rid of the package he was holding. He coughed again. "Sorry doctor," he said quietly and waited. The doctor didn't answer, just kept his hands clasped, his arms circling a thick, grubby-looking folder which, by the looks of it, was full of old typed memos and hand-written notes and magazine articles. The doctor must have been in his sixties, if not older, Freddie Nolan guessed. He studied him from where he was standing, gazing down at his tough, tossed grey hair. And the small scar above his left ear. His bushy eyebrows twitched as his eyes scanned the page in front of him.

Shuffling from foot to foot, Freddie Nolan dabbed the line of sweat just above his own eyes and coughed again. This time the doctor looked up. "What time is it?" he asked sternly.

Freddie checked his watch. "It's a couple of minutes past half-three."

The doctor's temperament seemed to change once he realised it was surgery time again. "Show in the first of them," he muttered, nodding to the door leading to the packed waiting-room. He closed the folder carefully and packed it into the top drawer. He took a key from his white coat pocket and locked it.

"Before you start, doctor, I have something here that I think . . . " Freddie didn't know what to say. He'd never been confronted by such a revelation in all of his career as a pharmacist. He placed the neat bundle of colour photographs in front of the doctor and sat down. "I just finished developing them ten minutes ago. I've never seen anything like it in my life." He waited, holding his breath, sure that the doctor would balk in horror when he realised what he was holding.

He showed no signs of disgust – no reactions whatsoever – as he thumbed slowly through the twenty-four prints. Occasionally he would go back a few and examine one or two of them in closer detail, turning one on its side and twisting his head to see it more clearly. He went through them a second time, then a third. Then he bundled them neatly and placed them back on the desk, closer to him, out of Freddie's gazing reach. "Where did you get them?" He stared across at Freddie. The chemist had turned a deep shade of red.

"From Ethel Kline. She told me they were from a ladies' day out in Killarney. She said she took them a couple of months ago and forgot to drop them in to be developed." Freddie was stuttering slightly, swallowing some of his words. "What should I do with them?"

The doctor studied the top one again. "Well, I doubt if these are from a ladies' day out in Killarney somehow. When is she due to come back to collect them?"

"This afternoon."

He nodded as if he had just made up his mind. "Leave them with me. When she comes in tell her I want to see her. Tell her it's about her shoulder. Tell her to skip the queue and come straight in." He tapped the small bundle with his knuckles. "This is very serious." He turned the key in the drawer, slid it open and locked the photos away. "Forget about this for now. I don't want anybody to know about this. Is that perfectly clear, Freddie?" He waited for the definitive reply.

"Of course!" The old chemist kept nodding, harder and harder, to show that he meant it. "Anything you say to me is in strict confidence, doctor."

"Good." He sighed and gestured to the door. "Show in the first one."

40

SALE AGREED.

The warmth of the late May afternoon and the excitement she always felt as the days got nearer the June holiday weekend and the summer were forgotten in seconds. The sign hanging over the stoney wall quickly put a stop to all that. Maggie couldn't believe it. It took a minute to sink in. The two words, in large, thick red print, were pasted across the FOR SALE sign. The deal was done. It had only taken twenty-four hours. Harry Vogel's house was sold. He really was moving away. It just didn't make sense to her. If he had been thirty years younger she would have understood why he wanted to move on. But not Harry. He seemed so settled in his ways; so much in need of Maggie's company, not to mention her medical expertise. He'd just had a bad fall. The man should have been stretched out on a bed in Bantry hospital, under observation, undergoing tests as a result of his concussion. And what about Brega? She was buried close by. How would she cope without his daily visit? How would he cope? For Christ sake, he's seventy-seven! she shouted angrily to herself. She slammed the car door shut and kicked the gravel, whooshing it into small mounds in front of her sneakers as she walked up the small pathway to the front door. Normally it would be open. Today, however, it wasn't. Already she could feel a sense of detachment. She knocked hard, four times, and waited, anticipating whether she would get angry with him, or burst into tears. She looked around the pretty garden, and beyond to the low, broken wall of Verity cemetery, where Brega was buried. "What do you think?" She asked the question out loud. "He's leaving you, Brega. Try and convince him to stay. If anyone can you can."

"Who can?"

His voice was soft and tired, almost inaudible. Maggie turned around. Harry stood, leaning against the blackthorn stick. He smiled, more out of resignation that he was going, she knew, than the usual smile he would always give her when she dropped in most evenings.

"Why?"

"Why what?"

"Why do want to put yourself through all this, Harry? You're seventy-eight next birthday, for God's sake. Are you mad?"

He frowned. "Mad? Me? I might be a bit indecisive at the age I am, my dear, but one thing I am *not* is mad."

The gentleness was gone. It was as if he had already left on the journey without her, without bothering to consult her for her advice, without as much as a goodbye.

"I'm going with you," she blurted. She hadn't intended saying it. In fact she had decided that morning that she wasn't going. But seeing him again reminded her of all the nights she had sat with him, sharing his wine and listening to his stories about all the countries he'd travelled through and lived in. And then there were the famous people he had met and dined with. He was a nomad, a wanderer, who made her scream out and get angry with her own little insular, boring existence. She wanted out and now she was looking at her only hope of escaping.

He seemed surprised at first, as if he had forgotten their conversation. It was his invitation originally. "Why don't you come with me?" had been his words. He *had* asked her.

"Don't be ridiculous," he snapped.

Now it was her turn. "How dare you! One thing I might be is mad, but never accuse me of being ridiculous. *You* are the ridiculous one, if you must know. You can't just get on a plane at your age."

"Why not?"

He turned and walked back into the front room, lifting cardigans and pairs of trousers and folding them neatly. Two cases lay open on the long couch, close to the fire. It seemed odd to her that there was no fire lighting. She couldn't remember a day when the turf wasn't crackling in the small grate and the smoke pushing the sparks high into the chimney shaft. Maggie looked around the room. It was different. More bare than usual. Some of the pictures were missing. The frame still hung above the fireplace but now it was empty. The black and white photograph of Brega was gone. "Why are you leaving the empty frame?"

"I don't have enough room in my two cases. Anyway it's an awkward bloody thing. It just takes up space."

Maggie watched him as he grouped small items of clothing on the table and small knick-knacks and cute baubles of sentimental value on the armchair. He nodded to the old record-player. "I'd love if you would take that. I've had it for so long. It seems a shame to throw it out with the rest of the rubbish." He stroked the mahogany veneer as if it were a pet. "It has served us well over the years."

"This is all my fault, isn't it." Maggie said softly.

"What is?"

"It's all my fault that you're leaving."

Harry Vogel seemed to force a short laugh. "Of course it's not your fault." He took hold of Maggie's hands. "Without you I wouldn't have survived the last three years. You're a saint, Maggie. Never forget it. And I'm sure I speak for all of the poor people who are housebound on this peninsula. You've made my life so much happier. And I will never forget you for it." He let go of her hands and started to pack again, quicker now.

"Please let me go with you. You're going to need someone to look after you. I'm trained to take care of . . . " She stopped short.

He laughed genuinely this time. "Old people like me? Isn't that what you were going to say?"

"Well, who *will* look after you?"

"My sister."

The news came as a shock to Maggie. "You never mentioned your sister before. Where is she?"

"She lives on one of the Canary Islands. Tenerife. She married a Spaniard. A Canarian she fell in love with while she was on holiday many years ago. He died around about the same time as Brega, nearly five years ago. Or was it six? I suppose we have both been very lonely without our partners. She wrote to me last Christmas and suggested that I should come and stay with her for a while. She says the weather is beautiful there most of the year. And it would be very good for my arthritis. So I have given it a lot of thought and have decided to give it a try." He sighed and looked around the small house. "Some days I can cope with the loneliness, but lately those days are few and far between. She is nine years younger than me and will be able to look after me like you did, and remind me when I should take all my stupid medicines." He grinned and placed another pair of slacks neatly into the bottom of the second suitcase.

"What's her name?" The question seemed to confuse him.

"Who?"

"Your sister."

"Elie."

"How old is she?"

"Seventy-two."

"I thought you said she was nine years younger than you."

"She is."

"Well, that would make her sixty-eight."

He laughed mockingly at his mistake. "Ah, in that case, she's younger than I have given her credit for."

Maggie ignored the joke. "Please tell me the truth. Why are you going to Spain? You'll hate the weather. It gets too hot during the summer. And it's full of bloody tourists all year round. You hate tourists. You're always giving out about the way they break your stone walls by standing on them to get pictures of the sunsets. And they don't have Christmases like we have here on Sheep's Head. Why are you going? What's after happening?"

It was obvious he was becoming more exasperated with each question. "I've told you why. Now if you don't mind, Maggie, I don't have much time."

"When are you going?"

"Probably Saturday. Maybe sooner. It all depends."

"Depends on what?"

He seemed not to hear her question. Either that or he just wasn't going to answer it. She decided not to provoke him any further. Jack had always said that she asked too many questions for her own good. Maybe it was a quality that came with the job. Right now she didn't care. The answers she was getting to her questions weren't making a lot of sense.

"Take the old record-player with you." He kept his back turned to her.

"Can I call to see you before you go?" she asked tearfully.

"If you like."

It was Wednesday afternoon.

4.25pm.

41

The knock on the door was a polite one. None of the patients who had queued for an hour to see him knocked. They just came in according to their places in the waiting-room. He guessed it might be him. He had been expecting him since half-three. It was now almost quarter-to-five. The doctor looked at the card which he had stuck with Sellotape to the top of his diary to remind him always. "Come in." It was important to sound patient and polite.

First impressions. The man was fat. He might not have looked so small if he hadn't been so grossly overweight. Twenty stone, at least, James Morris estimated. His chin ate into his shirt collar. His trousers were baggy. And he was sweating. He held his cap and spun it occasionally on his fingers.

"Doctor Morris," he said anxiously.

The doctor nodded and pointed to the chair. "You're Alex Kline, aren't you?" he said, unlocking the drawer and placing the package of photographs in front of him.

"Yes."

Morris didn't say anymore for a moment, allowing his eyes to flit between the face of the man sitting in front of him and the small parcel he held now, firmly, in his hands. "I thought maybe your wife would drop by. I was anxious to talk to her."

"She wasn't feeling well. She asked me to drop by and collect the photos that she left in to be developed the other day. Freddie Nolan told me you wanted to see her." Alex Kline watched the doctor fingering the corners of the package. "She left her bag here this morning. She asked me to collect that as well." He took out a soft handkerchief and wiped his forehead, and down around his jaw. "I hate the heat. I don't suppose you could recommend something for it?" He laughed nervously.

"How about a cold shower?" Morris slid the package across the desk. "I think you might need one after you see these."

Kline seemed reluctant to open the paper wallet.

"Go on, look at them. Your wife left them in to be developed. I just wanted you to see them before I turn them over to the police."

Alex Kline took out each of the photographs one by one. He flung himself back into the chair. "Sweet Jesus Christ!" he mumbled. Then he took out a small bundle and shuffled through them. "Oh my God!" He loosened his tie and stood up, carrying the pictures across to the window.

"Trying to get a better look?"

Kline looked back at him. "Who is she?"

Kline didn't answer. "If you don't tell me, you'll end up telling Sergeant Buckley."

Kline rushed back to the desk and leaned across it. He looked terrified. "No please, don't tell Buckley."

"Who is she?"

"Cindy Reilly. She baby-sits for us whenever we go out at night. Sometimes she calls to chat to my eldest son. I often thought they fancied each other." He bundled away the pictures and handed them back across the desk.

"Do you not want to see the rest of them?" Morris asked rather smugly. "They'll be shown to you in court, so you might as well get used to looking at them."

"How *dare* you insinuate that I took them!"

The doctor looked at the card stuck to the top of his diary again and smiled. "I'm not accusing you of doing anything improper, Mr Kline. Relax." He gestured to him to sit down. "Would you like a glass of water?"

Alex Kline declined. "I'll kill him, the little bastard!"

James Morris frowned. "Who are you talking about?"

"It's obvious, isn't it? There's only one person who could have taken those photographs with Ethel's camera, and that's my son, Dónal."

"Dónal. Grand Irish name that. I thought you would've wanted your children to grow up with names from the *Vaterland*, good old homegrown handles like Albert, or Karl. But Dónal? I am impressed."

"I beg your pardon, Doctor Morris, I have an Irish passport which I am very proud of."

"I'm sure you are. So what makes you so sure that your son took these photographs?"

Alex Kline started to get flustered and embarrassed. "Well, I came home one night from a function we were at because I had forgotten my money and caught them in a rather compromising position."

"And what might that have been?"

"I'd rather not say, if you don't mind."

"Go on, Mr Kline, you can tell me, I'm a doctor."

Alex Kline coughed to clear his throat and wiped the sweat off his chin. "I caught them having sexual intercourse in the garage."

"And what were *you* doing in the garage?"

"I went to look for her. She was meant to be baby-sitting the children who were fast asleep in their beds, not screwing my fifteen-year-old son. It's criminal."

"And you should know, Alex, you being the local Justice of the Peace. You would know all about these things, I'm sure."

"What's that supposed to mean?"

"Nothing sinister. All I'm saying is that you would have a good understanding of the law. Isn't that right?"

Alex Kline nodded keenly, eager to accept what might be a compliment. "That's right."

"How old is Cindy Reilly?"

Alex thought for a moment. "Sixteen, maybe seventeen, I suppose." He looked down at the photos again. "Wait 'til I get him, I'll kill him."

"Why?"

"Why?" Kline's eyes were bulging. "Because if this got out I'd be disgraced, that's why! The girl's a little . . . slut. Every boy in the area's had his hand up her dress."

"So why shouldn't your son? And anyway, it's likely that she invited him out into the garage. I would have thought you'd be quite proud of your boy, Alex. After all, he's only doing what comes naturally to us all eventually. Isn't that right? I take it he's never got mixed up in drugs. He probably doesn't smoke. Most young kids think it's a filthy habit these days, unlike when you and I were young. And he's not gay." James Morris watched Alex Kline for a reaction. "Or is he?"

Kline jumped to his feet and kicked the chair back across the surgery floor. He was seething. "Don't you *ever* insinuate that my son is queer, do you *hear* me?"

James Morris reached under the desk.

Alex Kline froze, a look of terror in his eyes.

"This is your wife's bag. I'm sure she'd like to get it back. As for the photographs . . . maybe you should tell your lovely wife that they won't be ready for another couple of days."

Alex Kline grabbed the bag and walked to the door. Then he turned, just as James Morris had expected him to do from the very moment that he entered the room. The doctor looked down at the small business card again, just to be sure. "Yes?"

Kline stood motionless, breathing deeply, and stared. "Who are you?"

"I'm Doctor James Morris, General Practitioner, Durrus, County Cork. Who are you?"

Alex Kline banged the door behind him.

It was 5.15pm.

42

Alex Kline didn't take his eyes off his plate of lamb chops and mixed vegetables, roast potatoes and gravy that evening. If he did he would have to face his wife, or worse still, his son, Dónal and daughters Megan and Jennifer. He sat forward, his arms on the table, in a slumped position. It was 7.15pm. They had sat down to eat half-an-hour before.

"Alex, will you ever say something, please. You're putting me off my dinner," Ethel Kline said for the third time.

He said nothing. Just sighed.

"Kids, go on in and watch the television," she suggested, as politely as she could in the circumstances. Once the door to the TV room was shut, she banged her knife down in the middle of the table, accidentally breaking the sugar bowl. Alex watched her picking up the large pieces and placing them in a saucer beside her own plate. "What the hell is going on, Alex? You'd better tell me. Because I am sick of being taken for granted at this stage. You just seem to think you can walk all over me and expect me to smile and behave like everything's smelling of roses. Well, it's over unless you come clean and explain what's been going on around here for the last few weeks. Ever since Jack Buckley walked up to you in the pub and handed you his badge you've been behaving like someone who's been handed a death sentence. Well?" She waited.

Nothing. Not even an acknowledgement. He cradled his chin in the palms of his hands and stared at the broken crockery.

"Where are my photographs?"

"They lost the roll of film," he said sluggishly.

"What do you mean *lost*? How can someone like Freddie Nolan, the nosiest man in Durrow, lose a roll of film? He develops them himself. It's not like he gets dozens of rolls of film to develop every single day. Well? How could he lose a roll of film? He told me the pictures would be ready at half-three this afternoon."

Alex Kline slammed his fist down hard onto the table and roared at the top of his voice: *"I don't know and I don't care!"* It was the second time that day that he had kicked a chair backwards and banged a door behind him.

The hotel was called Judge Darley's, situated close to the railway station, handy for the 7.20am train back to Cork the following morning. It was only ten-to-eight and already Jack had drunk four large vodkas. He ordered a pint of Guinness and decided to drink more slowly. "Put it on Room 47 please," he said to the lounge girl with the cropped hairstyle and the gorgeous green eyes. He tipped her with a pound coin. She beamed back at him. "Thanks," she said in heavy, northside Dublinesque.

Jack watched the Guinness settle, gradually turning jet black from the bottom of the pint glass to the base of the creamy white head. The band was called Mulligan. They were playing traditional ballads and encouraging the small crowd to sing along to a song called "The Ferryman". It was a welcome end to an awful day. He had decided against going back to the hotel close to the church for a bowl of soup and a chat with the boy's family. Ben Roper had shaken his hand. He thanked him for everything he had done and said quietly that he might join him for a drink in the hotel about ten.

Still two hours to go. Jack needed to remain sober.

"Hello."

The voice was deadpan. Jack looked up and almost choked on his first taste of the stout. She looked different tonight. Her hair was shorter, slightly tossed. She wasn't wearing as much make-up. The woman who had stripped him naked and ravished him in a Force 8 storm in his back garden that night was standing at his table. Jack was speechless.

"Do you mind if I join you?"

All he could do was shake his head and free a chair for her.

"I saw you at the church tonight. I followed you back here."

Jack watched her warily. "Nathan Lohan was an only child."

"I know." She threw her jacket onto the ledge behind Jack's head.

"Why did you tell me you were his sister?"

"Because I needed an excuse to get to know you."

"Why?"

"Because I need you to help me."

Jack looked around for his own jacket. "Now you're talking sense. You *do* need help. But the sort of help you need you'll have to go to a doctor for. I can't help you." He stood up. "I'm sorry, but what happened that night was an accident. I hadn't intended it to go that way and I'm sorry if I offended you, but I would really prefer if you wouldn't follow me around anymore."

She smiled, then started to laugh. "Hang on a minute. You obviously got the wrong end of the stick here, Jack. I'm not following you for your body." She looked him up and down, then reached across and pulled at his belt. "At the risk of sounding cheeky, I think I could do a hell of a lot better than that." She sat back in the chair and picked up his pint. "On the other hand the night is still only a baby."

"What do you want?"

"Sit down. I'd prefer to wait for Ben Roper to join us so that I don't have to repeat myself."

"How did you know that Roper was meeting me here?"

"Because he told me."

The clock was chiming eight when the doorbell rang. Maggie was impressed by his punctuality. The doctor was dressed smartly in a striped shirt and tie and a lion-brown lounge jacket. He held out a bottle of wine and smiled. "I wasn't sure whether you liked red or white."

"Both actually." She noticed something different about him since she had visited him earlier that morning. "Your hair. You got it cut."

He nodded. "Freddie Nolan cut it for me."

"Freddie Nolan!" She roared laughing. "As in Freddie Nolan, the chemist?"

"As in Freddie Nolan, the *barber*, if you don't mind."

"You're a braver man than I am." Maggie said as she opened the wine. She realised it must have sounded like a silly thing to say. But she *was* nervous and eager to make a good impression. She wasn't sure why, but she was adamant she was going to get the ice-breaking business over and done with as quickly as possible. "We'll eat in about half-an-hour if that's OK with you?"

"Sounds great."

"Have a seat." She handed him a glass of wine and sat opposite, nodding to the trendy stereo unit sitting alongside the old record-player. "I hope the music's not too loud."

"Not at all. I love classical. Especially Elgar."

Maggie grinned with enthusiasm as she rolled the wine around her palate. She gulped and gasped. "Wonderful choice." She'd never heard of Elgar. "What a genius." Dangerous conversation, she thought. "Let me check on the gratin sauce." From the kitchen she could see that he was bent over the old record-player.

"Quite a collector's item. Where did you lay your hands on this?"

"An old friend of mine gave it to me as a present."

"Really. How long have you got it?"

"About three hours." She picked up her glass again and sat down. "Let me guess, you're an antiques collector."

"Not really. I'm just one of these sad individuals who

wanders round antique shops knocking expensive items over."

Maggie giggled at the notion, more so because he fitted the description perfectly. "So go on then, tell me how much it's worth."

He examined it more carefully this time. "Do you mind if I lift it up?"

"Not at all. Maybe your visit here tonight is going to change my life."

There was a comforting peace about the room for the couple of minutes he held the record-player in different positions, examining its sides, looking underneath at its velvety base. He put it down and turned to face her. He looked stern and long-faced, almost out of breath. "Where did you get it?"

"Why?" Maggie asked nervously.

"Because whoever gave this to you may not realise what they have just given away. That *thing* – now I may be wrong – is probably worth fifty-thousand pounds, Maggie."

"Why?" she gasped.

The doctor beckoned to her to come closer. He nodded to the bottom left-hand corner of the old record-player. Then he pointed, his hand shaking as the nail of his index finger traced the outline of the inscription on the tiny, rectangular brass plate.

Kurt Gerstein.

The name meant nothing to Maggie, but she tried to behave suitably impressed. "Who was he?"

Her guest straightened up and breathed in deeply, held it and sighed. "Someone we'll never see the likes of again." He walked to the window and stood gazing out at the sheep grazing on the side of the softly sloping hill close to the house, and beyond the hill at the giant setting sun, and knew that as certain as day turned to night, he was closer now than he had ever been in fifteen long years to The Keeper. His only cause for concern, which he tried to put down to paranoia, was the notion that if he felt this close to the man he'd been trying to track down for so long, there was every good reason to believe that his target would sense the danger and, like so many times before, might just disappear off the face of the earth.

9.15pm

Ben Roper folded his crombie overcoat in two and placed it behind him on a window ledge. He checked his Rolex watch. "I think this is the first time I've been early for anything in my life," he said to his two waiting guests. "Can I get you both a drink?" Jack Buckley could tell immediately that this man wasn't a regular pub-goer. The sergeant studied him as he stood looking around the lounge. He was definitely a man who could easily give himself airs in a business capacity, most likely wealthier than Jack could ever imagine. But tonight Jack knew that Ben Roper would happily hand him every penny of his substantial portion if he could have bought his son just one drink. He decided to let the woman order first. Her real name was Kate Doheny, she had told him as she sat down earlier, while apologising to him for lying. She wouldn't say much more for the hour they sat together waiting for Roper. She asked him if he liked the sort of music the ballad group was playing. She described it as "black-pudding diddle" and told him it gave her a headache. Jack told her he loved it and could listen to it all night.

"Maybe you will," was her reply.

Kate Doheny, he thought. She originally introduced herself as Heather Lohan. Why? he wondered. And what was she carrying in the tidy leather briefcase she'd kept placed firmly on her lap since sitting down an hour ago? She seemed to relax now that Ben Roper had arrived and was eager to commence whatever it was she wanted to discuss.

"Mineral water for me," she said politely and looked across at Jack.

"Large vodka and coke. Thanks."

Ben Roper repeated the order to the girl with the cropped hairstyle and sat down. He seemed remarkably upbeat and fidgety for a man who was about to bury his only son.

Jack decided to cut out any nonsense or small talk. "How do you know each other?"

His question seemed to take both of them by surprise.

"I gather you don't want to waste time, sergeant. I know you're a very busy man." The tone of her comment was dripping with sarcasm. "And Mr Roper, this must be a very difficult night for you. But I'm very grateful that you both agreed to meet me."

"I didn't agree to meet you." Jack sat forward. "We've only met once before."

"Would you like to tell Ben about that meeting?" Her voice was smug now.

Jack blushed. "I don't think it's important. Can we

just get on with whatever business we're here to discuss. I'm sure Ben would prefer to be at home tonight."

Roper perked up. "Quite the contrary. I'm glad to have a chance to get away from my ex-wife and all her relations. In fact this whole investigation is what's being keeping my sanity intact for the past fortnight." He smiled at the woman who was now Kate Doheny.

"Investigation?" All of a sudden Jack was interested. "What investigation?"

Roper looked to Kate Doheny. "I think Kate wants to fill you in on what's been happening."

Kate Doheny took her glass from the tray and sipped the fizzy water. She placed the glass on the small beer mat and sat back into her chair, still clutching the leather briefcase tightly. She glanced around to make sure no one sitting at the next table was listening. A group of five was discussing the merits of English Premiership football. The discussion had become a heated debate. Then she looked to her right. A couple were kissing passionately in the corner. It seemed safe to talk. She spoke softly but clearly.

"I work for a government agency known as CAB, the Criminal Assets Bureau. It's a small group . . . "

Jack Buckley cut across her. "I'm a policeman. I know what CAB does."

His intrusion was not welcomed. Kate Doheny ignored him. "We're a small group of investigators made up of detectives, revenue inspectors and solicitors."

"Which one are you?" Jack asked.

She didn't even bother to look at him this time. "In normal circumstances, if there could ever be such a thing in this business, we investigate tax fraud, money laundering, misappropriation of large funds, bank robberies, you name it – anything that involves criminals and money, especially money that doesn't belong to such individuals." She glanced back at Jack. Either he was bored or drunk. Or both. She continued. "This is where you get involved, Jack. I hope we're not keeping you up."

Jack laughed. "Delighted to help."

"You know Alex Kline."

Now Jack Buckley was right in there, eyes wide open, ears on fire. "Yes, I do."

"He's been under investigation for some time. Recently, thanks to Ben Roper's co-operation and assistance, the file has been passed over to CAB. And I have to say it makes for some very interesting reading."

Jack was beginning to feel quite excited at the prospect that Kline could – even if it was just a remote possibility – be charged with an offence. *Any* offence would give just cause for a wild celebration. He glanced down at the briefcase. She hadn't let go of it, still clutching it like a suicide bomber on a bus in Beiruit.

"Where are you staying tonight?" she asked Jack.

Jack blushed again. The last time she had asked him that question she was called Heather Lohan and they ended up in the long grass at the bottom of his back garden. "Here, actually. Why do you ask?"

"I've booked a small room in the Ashling Hotel. It's only a few doors up the street. If it's OK with you I'd prefer to head up there now to discuss this investigation further. At least we'll have comfort and privacy." She finished her water and stood up.

Ben Roper was already reaching for his crombie.

Jack made an effort to down the large vodka. He could feel the back of his tongue and the sides of his throat burning as he tried hard not to cough and cause it all to come straight back up. It made him think of the night at Coosbrack when he drank himself into oblivion and woke to find Leo Hannon lying dead beside him. He shivered and closed his eyes and swallowed. And swallowed again, trying to work out if this was his twelfth or thirteenth vodka since getting off the train. The pints always became too big by lunchtime. He slammed the empty glass down on the table. Who cares? he thought to himself. I've a friend who's rotten rich, who'll buy me my drink tonight. "I'm ready," he gasped.

As the party was leaving, the young lovers at the table in the corner stopped kissing. The man leaned out over the table and watched the two men and the woman as they thanked the girl with cropped hair and beautiful green eyes and handed her a twenty-pound note. Then they left.

The small room on the first floor was comfortably decorated – a rich, brown-coloured carpet against peach-coloured wallpaper and soft lighting thrown from a large table lamp in the corner opposite the television. A real fire burned in the grate.

Kate Doheny looked down onto Parkgate Street as she pulled the curtains tightly together. She sat down and started to open her briefcase.

"Can we get a few drinks up here? Jack asked eagerly.

"That's all organised," Ben Roper replied in a reassuring voice.

The two men hung up their coats and got comfortable in their armchairs.

"I met Ben Roper for the first time last July. He was financial controller at Girundbach. As you know he's now the managing director of the company which employs over three thousand people in a manufacturing capacity."

Unless the drink arrived soon Jack knew he was going to fall asleep. The fire was too warm. There was no need for it on a night like this. She talked and talked and talked, constantly looking back to Jack for long intervals as if Ben Roper had already heard it before.

"Last July Ben Roper noticed a number of inconsistencies in the company's accounts. He decided not to approach management because they appeared so outrageous that he thought he had made a mistake in his calculations. Most of the company's financial dealings are done on computer, directly via-modem, with the mother-office in Frankfurt. However the Irish plant is now considered to be more important from an export point of view. Consequently the Frankfurt operation continues to be wound down, with staff being deployed to a number of small outlets and subsidiary companies. Mainly in Germany." She glanced across at Jack as he tried his best to stifle a painful yawn. "I haven't lost you I hope, Jack?" Another stab of cynicism.

"Of course not," he muttered and stood up. "Anyone mind if I open a window?" He didn't bother waiting on an answer. There wasn't one.

"If you don't mind, I'd like to get on with this. I've a lot more you'll need to know," Kate Doheny explained.

Shit! Jack thought. Where's my drink?

"Girundbach manufactures car tyres, mainly for high performance vehicles such as BMWs and Mercedes, and for the lucrative sports car market. The company's net profit last year was thirty-four million pounds."

Jack forgot about alcohol. But only for a few seconds.

"That's almost two-and-a-half million gross margin every week. We all agree that it's a handsome turnover. Ireland was always the ideal place for the company because of our corporation tax, which is only ten per cent on manufacturing profits." She started to open the file. "This is where it all starts to get very interesting, Jack." She sat forward.

It was the first time she had called him Jack since that night in the garden.

The drinks trolley arrived.

The conversation stopped dead until the waiter had been tipped and the door closed tightly again.

"Ten years ago, the government, in order to entice foreign business to Ireland, introduced a new law. Provided their mother company was in another jurisdiction – Frankfurt, Germany, in this case – Girundbach was allowed to repatriate all of their profits without paying a penny tax to the Irish government. In other words it was a wholly owned subsidiary. We've since found out, rather discreetly from a former secretary in the Department of Foreign Affairs, that this new clause was rushed through the government chambers and made law only because Girundbach insisted they wouldn't set up here if they had to pay tax. And since more than seventy per cent of the manufactured product is exported, they're automatically exempt from VAT charges. It was the perfect deal."

"If you don't mind me saying so, in the nicest possible way, I'm getting a little bit bored with your speech. Where is this all leading to?" Jack sipped his drink and rolled his eyes.

"It's important that you hear me out, Jack. You're going to need to know all of this. And I guarantee you in five minutes time I'm going to give you the greatest shock of your career. And that's where you're going to enter the equation." She waited for him to acknowledge.

He nodded and poured another drink.

"About six months ago we received a call indirectly from Westdeutsche Landesbank here in Dublin. That's where Girundbach keep all of their accounts, even though they're based at Shannon Development close to Limerick. One of the staff, a senior manager, felt there was something wrong and told management of his concern. One of the directors of the bank contacted us unofficially. Seemingly three hundred million pounds was transferred by giro order from a bank account in Zurich into the main Girundbach account. The following day the entire amount was transferred again, this time to an account in the Banco de Bilbao in Playa de Las Americas, on the island on Tenerife. There was no reason given, other than a phone call from a woman in Frankfurt, authorising the second transfer to Spain."

Jack sneezed. "Excuse me." He rubbed his nose. "Doesn't seem unusual to me. It's probably more money than you or I will ever see in a lifetime but that's how international business is conducted, isn't it?" He glanced at Ben Roper. He seemed reluctant to comment.

"Well yes, it is how *most* international business is conducted. But – call it a hunch – we thought it was a bit sneaky. So one of our agents called up the bank in Zurich, ZBT Bank, one of the biggest in Switzerland. He identified himself and asked for more information. He was told that unless he had the account number they wouldn't be obliged by law to give him any information."

Jack nodded. "Makes sense."

"Absolutely. Though not in this case." She nodded to Roper. "Ben, maybe you'd like to take up the story from here."

"Kate rang me up and asked if she could meet me. She filled me in on everything that you've just heard. So I agreed to call up the accounts department in Frankfurt and try to get to the bottom of this. I was sure there was a perfectly logical explanation and that it was just some sort of computer transfer error. I rang our international account director. He swore he knew absolutely nothing about a Swiss bank account in Zurich. I spoke to him for about fifteen minutes, careful not to mention that CAB had got involved. He said he'd check into it for me and call me back. Later that night, about half-eleven, the phone rang. It was Franz Wirths, the account director. He sounded in an awful state, very distressed, like as if he'd just been fired. He insisted he'd spent the whole evening checking out this Zurich bank account I'd mentioned earlier. He had even phoned the Chief Executive and quizzed him about it. There was *no* Swiss bank account, he assured me quite categorically. I believed him because I worked closely with Franz during my time in Frankfurt. I told him not to worry, that it must have been some sort of account-number error. Then I said goodnight. I couldn't sleep at all that night, I remember, thinking about Franz. He had always been such a calm, controlled individual, the sort you'd like to know is flying your plane for you. Typical accountant, I suppose. But that night something had definitely happened to Franz. And I'm glad I was here in Ireland and not in Frankfurt."

"Why?" Jack asked curiously.

Roper sighed and shrugged his shoulders. "I wasn't sure then but after what surfaced shortly afterwards I'd say he feared for his life."

"What surfaced?" Jack was hungry to hear more now.

Ben Roper stood up uneasily and poured himself a large whiskey.

Kate Doheny took up the story. "It appears that Franz Wirths might have opened a can of worms that night by ringing whoever he rang." She paused for a moment. "His wife found him hanging by a rope in their bathroom shower one evening some months ago when she returned from the supermarket. Police believe it was suicide. There were no marks on his body to suggest he put up a struggle. Nothing was out of place in the apartment when she returned. However, she believes he was murdered."

"Why?" Jack was wide awake again and firing on all cylinders.

"Because he had just put a deposit on a holiday that

afternoon. The couple were going to come to Ireland to visit Ben and his son and spend a couple of weeks touring around." Kate looked at Ben.

His eyes had filled with tears. His hand shook as he raised the glass to his mouth. "They should have been arriving this weekend. Adam rang me at lunchtime on the Saturday of the weekend he was spending in Cork with his friends to tell me he had just found the most beautiful spot in Ireland. It was where Franz planned to bring his wife. Now they're both dead." Ben Roper gulped from his glass and swallowed. A fit of coughing followed. "Sorry. Let's continue, please." He sat down and caught his breath.

"CAB decided to put the Girundbach accounts under observation. The bank were very helpful, feeding us daily information on what was going in, coming out, phone calls looking for accounts information. Faxes, e-mails, cables, you name it. Anything that came from Frankfurt we were on top of it. Eventually, with Ben's help, we were able to piece together a peculiar jigsaw with a very strange shape. Money was being sent from Dublin to Frankfurt, which, as you'd expect is perfectly normal for a company that wants to repatriate its profits. However, money was then being sent back from Frankfurt, through Dublin and onto a Cork company called International Trading Services and two weeks later each amount would be further transferred to a small bank in Bantry."

Jack Buckley shot forward, almost knocking his armchair out from underneath him. "Which bank?" he demanded.

Kate Doheny smiled. "I thought you might get interested after a while. It was lodged in an account called," she read from the notes in her file, "AKE No 2."

"What does AKE No 2 stand for?"

Ben Roper spoke. "I checked it out while I was in Cork last week. I was in the bank meeting Alex's staff. I couldn't believe how one of them just opened the file as soon as I mentioned the name of the account. I presume she thought we were old work partners and I was familiar with the goings on at his bank. It was like finding the crock of gold at the end of the rainbow."

"Not for Franz Wirths, it wasn't," Jack said benignly. "What if he died because he knew too much?"

"Like Leo Hannon knew too much? Is that what you're saying, Jack?"

Ben Roper sounded as if he was teasing. It was just the sort of remark that made Jack livid. Kate Doheny intervened. "Hang on, boys. Let's not lose the run of ourselves here. We've still got a lot of major ground to cover before we start arguing trivial points." She sipped more fizzy water. "The most bizarre thing about this AZE No 2 account is that it is worth approximately seven-hundred-and-fifty thousand pounds at this stage. Three-quarters-of-a-million quid. I mean, let's be honest. Who in their right minds is going to lodge that kind of money in a standard bank account? Most people would invest it in bonds, or buy property. You're not just going to leave it sitting there for four years earning a pittance, something like three per cent. Every month fifteen thousand pounds is transferred into AZE No 2 from International Trading Services. And yet, the only amount ever withdrawn from the account is a weekly amount of one-hundred-and-twenty pounds. That's all. Withdrawn every Friday without fail."

Jack ran his hand over his cheek and stood up. "Why only a hundred-and-twenty? Why not twelve-hundred?"

Kate Doheny tapped the cover of the manila file. "That's what none of us can figure out. Maybe he's giving it to his wife every week for household shopping. Maybe he buys presents for his kids. I don't know. But it seems a bit strange that such a small, yet precise, amount is withdrawn every week on the same day without fail, from such a lucrative account that goes half way around the world before it arrives in a small town in west Cork that nobody's ever heard of. Would anyone in their right minds be cocky enough to flaunt that sort of money so publicly?"

"You might if you're the boss," Jack Buckley muttered.

"What do you mean?" Kate Doheny asked.

"Picture this," Jack mused aloud. "Let's say you're the manager of a successful rural bank, the only one in the area. You decide what loans are given out, credit-worthiness of customers, who gets a Christmas card, who gets a stern reminder when they overshoot their overdraft. *You* are the boss, not the directors of the bank in Dublin, not the customers. You. *You* are God Almighty. *You* are the high executioner. You pull the purse strings. Add to this scenario the fact that you are also the local estate agent, pedalling in property, some very nice property at that with beautiful sea views and mountain backdrops. Perfect place for wealthy writers and rock stars. You buy the land off the bloke who's too old to maintain his house or his farm and has decided to move back into the city so that his daughter can look after him. Now you decide what you're going to sell on that property for."

"What are you getting at, Jack?" It was Kate Doheny who asked.

"Alex Kline is a one-man band. He decides how he is going to operate, no one else. *No one.* He doesn't have to tell the accountants or the directors of the bank what's going on if he doesn't want to. I'd safely say that the amount of fiddling that's going on inside that building would make your eyes pop out."

Kate Doheny looked across at Ben Roper.

"But that's what I can't figure out, Jack. If he has stockpiled nearly a million pounds in a soft deposit account and he's only withdrawing a hundred and twenty quid a week for whatever, I can't see how he's breaking the law."

"Are the tax people aware of this account?" Jack asked.

"They are now," Kate replied.

"So why don't they do something about it?"

"Like what?"

Jack raised his voice with exasperation. "Like take Alex Kline in for questioning."

"On what grounds?"

"That he's embezzling money from somewhere."

"And where is he embezzling money from?"

"From Girundbach."

Ben Roper spoke up. "That's the problem, Jack. It's

not from Girundbach. Well not officially, you could say. It's from an account in Frankfurt. All we've been able to establish is the name of the bank. But they're not too happy to comply with our enquiries. Basically they've told us to get knotted when we started to ask delicate questions."

"But if the money starts its journey here, surely the people to ask are the directors of Girundbach."

"Unfortunately it's not quite as simple as that. Girundbach are not governed by Irish tax laws. Therefore they don't have to make any declarations whatsoever, apart from the salaries and wages they're paying their staff here. All their profits go directly back to Frankfurt, as I explained earlier."

"So what's all this about?" Jack looked first at Ben Roper, then at Kate Doheny.

"Anyone for another drink?" Ben Roper asked.

"No," Jack answered sternly, without taking his eyes off the briefcase which was now open, proud that, without even thinking, he'd refused alcohol.

"As I mentioned to you earlier, CAB have been working closely with Ben Roper for a number of months now. And we have unearthed something which initially shocked me so much I couldn't possibly imagine that it could be true." She looked across the room at Roper who had just poured himself an unusually large scotch. She waited for him to resume his seat. "I asked Ben, after he had told me about the death of Franz Wirths, to get me all the information he could lay his hands on about Girundbach. How it came about. Who set it up. Who initially ran it. Where the money came from. Why its directors decided eventually to relocate to Ireland." She started to thumb through the corners of documents which had been neatly packaged and paper-clipped together. "The man who established Girundbach was called Donald Klaus Eckler. He established the company in 1955 at the age of thirty-three." She handed a black and white photograph to Jack of a middle-aged, affluent looking, broad-shouldered man with a moustache. "He retired almost ten years ago, around the time that Girundbach relocated to Ireland. One month before he retired the German ambassador resigned and flew back to Bonn. He claimed his reason for quitting the position was purely personal. Although the papers had a field day. His sexuality was questioned after a number of photographs were sent to an Irish Sunday tabloid of him leaving a public toilet with a minor. He always claimed his innocence. Eventually the pressure became so bad he resigned under a dark cloud of unanswered questions."

"Where are the photographs?" Jack asked.

Ben Roper took up the conversation. "I contacted the paper in question and eventually got a telephone number for the man who was the editor all those years ago. I visited him in the cancer hospice in Rathgar, in Dublin. He's since died. But he claimed that they never received any photographs. He did a bit of his own investigating. And it turns out that the German ambassador was blackmailed into resigning."

"But how can you blackmail an ambassador into resigning?" Jack asked.

"Simple," Kate Doheny replied. "All of these people have diplomatic immunity, which makes them practically invincible in the eyes of the law of the country in which they are serving as ambassador. They basically cannot be convicted of any crimes which they may commit during their tenure. And since it's very difficult to have someone's diplomatic immunity revoked, they can just about do any bloody thing they want. Chances are they'll get away with it."

"So?"

"Well, obviously whoever tried to blackmail him had to do something that would completely destroy the man's reputation and credibility, not just in the eyes of the public, but also in the eyes of his wife and five children and the government of the country he was representing. There are a lot of crimes and convictions that most people will just tut at. Crimes that can be explained away by reminding Joe Public that there but for the grace of God go I. Like smoking the occasional joint, or having a pint or two over the legal limit when you're driving. Not exactly take-him-out-and-shoot-him territory, is it? On the other hand, what's the one sort of person that causes the greatest public outcry?"

Jack didn't answer. He simply watched her as she waited in silence. "What?"

"A paedophile. A real dirt bag. Someone, many would say, who deserves to be hanged."

"And was he?"

"A paedophile? Of course not. Ben Roper managed to talk to him the day before yesterday. He's retired now, living in a small village in the Loire region of France. He's in his eighties. He's always maintained his innocence." She stopped talking and closed the folder.

Then she looked across towards Ben Roper. "Tell him, Ben. He's ready to hear it now."

Ben sat forward in the low armchair, cupping his glass with his two hands, and closed his eyes as if to gather his thoughts. "Hermann Brandt was the German ambassador to Ireland for almost five years. He was delighted to hear the news that a company so powerful and successful was relocating to Ireland. But, as he told me in a conversation that lasted almost two hours two days ago, he couldn't, for the life of him, figure out why. And let's be honest, ten years ago, our interest rates were among the highest in Europe. Our economy was on the verge of collapsing. There was more bankruptcy being declared by otherwise successful companies, who just couldn't cope with the scalding levels of loan repayments, than at any time since the national bank strike during the summer of 1976. Brandt explained to me that it seemed like financial suicide for Girundbach to come to Ireland and offer jobs to three-and-half thousand employees when all around them hundreds of people were being laid off and made redundant. He advised the directors during one of their visits to Ireland that they should reconsider, that they were making a huge mistake as far as he was concerned. He tried to explain to them that he was familiar with the economic state of play here, possibly more so than a bunch of rich directors waving wads of Deutschmarks around a boardroom table somewhere in Frankfurt. Well, their reaction wasn't exactly the one he had expected. He was told, quite literally, to keep his nose out of Girundbach's business, that he was an ambassador, not a businessman, and that he should concentrate on wine receptions and dinner parties. Or else . . . "

"Or else there'd be a lot of trouble."

"Who told him that?"

"Donald Klaus Eckler. Girundbach's chief executive."

"So what did he do to end up being called a pervert?" Jack asked.

"Someone from the government here got on to their equivalent rank in Bonn and mentioned that the ambassador was poking around in areas that didn't concern him. You've got to remember that during a devastating time for the Irish economy this was worth three-and-a-half thousand new jobs. That looks good on paper, particularly when all hell is breaking loose around you and the government doesn't appear to be doing anything about it. Before you know it the government gets a vote of no confidence and they're buried. But, hey presto, suddenly they announce three-and-half thousand new jobs, everyone thinks they're wonderful. And the minister involved not only gets to keep his job but he also gets promoted."

"Who was the minister?" Jack asked.

"Ben Roper and Kate Doheny looked at each other uncomfortably.

"Joe Russell," Roper answered quietly.

"The Taoiseach?"

They both nodded.

Jack thought for a few seconds. "He was Minister for Foreign Affairs then, wasn't he?"

"Correct," Kate said and nodded.

"There's something else, isn't there? It's not just as cut

and dry, and as simple as that. What else have you found out? Why did Brandt really quit the job?"

"He got a private investigator to sit on Eckler, day and night, and bug the shit out of him. This bloke had bugs in his bathroom, bugs in his bed, bugs in his car, anywhere there was a phone. Brandt got reports back of conversations that were going on, often twenty-four hours a day. Conversations were frequent but too short a lot of the time to make much sense. The investigator – I think he said his name was Robert Berg, an American – was posting most of the information back to Brandt from Frankfurt for the few months he was on the case. He seemingly was building up a fairly decent dossier on Eckler's dealings. Problem was, Brandt wasn't receiving any of it. It was being intercepted, checked out, destroyed, and then bogus information was being sent on to Brandt."

"Who was intercepting it?" Jack asked.

Ben Roper's forehead shone now in the reflection of the fire. He wiped the thin film of sweat to one side. "Eckler, it turns out, is one of the most powerful men in Frankfurt. He is one of – if not *the* wealthiest men in the city. If he wants something he gets it, no questions asked. He has dozens of German police, at many levels of the force, wrapped around his little finger. The chief of police regularly attends his dinner parties. It's commonly known in the business that politicians, past and present, receive huge donations annually in return for favours. He lives in a beautiful part of the city that many residents of Frankfurt believe was financed by drugs. His neighbours are among some of most shifty and sinister people you could imagine. And yet he has nothing to do with them.

He is under twenty-four hour police guard because, he says, of the fear of being kidnapped. But it's also widely known that no one, no matter how dangerous a reputation they might have, no one would be brave or stupid enough to mess with Donald Klaus Eckler."

"But presumably Hermann Brandt did."

Ben Roper nodded and drank his Scotch, giving it a few seconds to settle.

"Yes, Hermann Brandt crossed over that hazardous, invisible line. And paid for it."

"But if he wasn't a pervert, why didn't he go to the law?" Jack asked.

"What law?" Ben Roper asked rather curiously. "I'm surprised you asked that question, Jack. You've had some grief lately yourself, haven't you? With the law? You see, Jack, it depends of course on who's involved and which party can be more seriously hurt, but when you go poking your nose into business that you're not familiar with, you're going to attract a lot of unwanted attention."

"What are you saying?" The tone of the conversation was beginning to irritate Jack.

"Let me put it this way, Jack. Germany is one of the wealthiest and most influential countries in the modern world. When Germany sneezes we all get the flu. The German ambassador is a very powerful man abroad. So when he starts shouting his mouth off about something that's perceived publicly as one of the most exciting and innovative business schemes ever to come to Ireland, people are eventually going to say, 'hang on, what's this bloke shouting about? Maybe he's right. Maybe there is something shifty about what's going on.' So he has to be silenced. So Eckler – no better man – put the word about that the German ambassador was a paedophile who liked to prey on little boys. Game, set and match. It's probably the one accusation that's impossible to refute, because, while some of your close friends might believe you, there's no smoke without fire, as you or I might say. Sure, you can stand up and say, 'I'm sorry for being over the limit and crashing my car.' Or, 'I shouldn't have taken drugs as a student.' Or 'I shouldn't have hit my wife.' Most people will forgive you eventually. But you stand up and say, 'I am *not* a paedophile.' How many people will believe you? Bingo, in one! He's history."

Jack whistled with an air of disbelief. "He must have found out something gruesome."

Kate Doheny started to smile as she waited for Ben Roper to finish. "Gruesome, you say? You wouldn't believe what he found out. I'm surprised he's still alive. Maybe that explains why he lives in France, in a house built behind fifteen-foot-high walls, and has two burly private detectives sitting outside his garden gate twenty-four hours a day."

Jack waited, knowing that it was coming, wondering in between of the rapid thumps of his heart what it was that could have been so terrible. She opened the brief case again.

"The reason that Hermann Brandt resigned was because of the private investigator he hired."

"You're going to tell me that he was the paedophile?" Jack said eagerly.

"No Jack, there was no paedophile. Robert Berg, the

private investigator, was found murdered in the gents' toilets of a Frankfurt strip club one night. No one knows how he got there. He'd been injected with pure heroin, enough to wipe out a herd of elephants apparently. The police claimed it was suicide."

"Just like Franz Wirths, my old friend," Ben Roper added.

"The coroner's report stated that he had simply overdosed while he had too much alcohol in his system."

"And did he?"

Kate shook her head. "His wife said he'd never touched heroin. Smoked the occasional joint but that was it."

Ben continued. "His wife told me he was a helicopter pilot, used to fly into Cambodia on intelligence missions back in the seventies. If you ask me, I think I'd prefer to stick my head into a lion's mouth. Anyway he was a superb intelligence gatherer until he had a nervous breakdown. When he'd fully recovered he set up his own detective agency."

"So Eckler succeeded in scuppering his efforts to get information to Brandt."

"Not quite." Ben Roper opened his own briefcase now and took out a thin, white A5 size envelope. "That was the reason his wife got in touch with me. He'd passed on copies of everything he thought he'd sent to Hermann Brandt in the post to his wife, Dixie, told her to keep them safe. He told her that if anything ever happened to him that she should pass them on to Brandt immediately."

"And did she?" Jack asked.

"Brandt told her a man would call for the papers. At

about three-thirty that afternoon Dixie Berg was making the final preparations for her husband's funeral when the man called and collected the envelope."

"Who was he?"

Doheny and Roper looked anxiously at each other. Then Ben Roper handed the envelope to Jack. "This is where we hope you can help us, Jack. He's a doctor. We need to get the documents from him quickly. CAB can't really press ahead until they have hard evidence on Eckler. We believe this doctor's in West Cork right now. He landed in Dublin recently on a flight from Frankfurt. The crew told us that he saved the life of a small girl on board the flight that morning. She'd got into some sort of serious difficulties with her breathing. That was how we knew he had arrived."

"What do mean arrived? Were you expecting him?"

"Not quite," said Kate Doheny. "He was spotted at a table in a restaurant a couple of weeks ago with a young woman. The people at the next table made for interesting eavesdropping, I would imagine."

"Who were they?" Jack asked.

"Have a look at the photo," Roper suggested, nodding to the envelope.

Jack slid the shadowy black and white snap out of the envelope. There were four men sitting at the table. "Who are they?"

"The man on the right with his back to the wall, facing the camera, is Donald Eckler. The man to his right, the left side of his face to the lens, is Karl Luger, a massively influential industrialist. He owns a bank, believe it or not. We're not too sure about the man with his back to the camera. To be honest we don't really care about him. It's the man to Eckler's left that would be of interest to the newspapers and the media here."

"Who is he?" Jack asked curiously.

"You're gonna laugh when I tell you this, Jack. That's Alan Harrisson. Does the name ring a bell?"

Jack sat back in the chair and unbuttoned his shirt collar. 'He's only the private secretary to our esteemed Taoiseach."

Jack shot forward, almost knocking his glass off the arm of the chair. "Jesus Christ, that's Joe Russell's private secretary?"

Roper and Doheny both nodded. "The one and only."

"So that means he would be representing Russell by being present at that meeting?"

"Presumably," said Kate.

"So what were they discussing?"

"We don't know. But if you go to the next photograph you'll seen a blown-up version of the man we need to talk to. The man we think is somewhere close to, if not in, your jurisdiction at the moment." Kate let him study the photograph. She seemed quite surprised when Jack's face registered a look of disbelief like she'd never seen before. "Do you recognise him?"

"His name . . . " Jack couldn't believe the face of the man he was staring at. " . . . is Josef Maister. I met him in a pub in Durrus last week."

"Will you help us find him?" Kate Doheny asked.

"Why?"

"Because he was meant to give the dossier of evidence that Robert Berg had compiled on Eckler's operation to Hermann Brandt who would then turn the information over to the German authorities."

"And why do you think he didn't hand it over to Brandt?"

"I suspect because the woman he was having dinner with that afternoon was found with a single gunshot wound to her head."

"Are you saying that Maister murdered her?"

"I doubt it. Although he might have. Because she was also seen by a member of the restaurant staff following Eckler into the gents' toilets before she left with Maister."

"So who is this Josef Maister?"

"We don't know very much about him at all. Obviously Robert Berg knew him, trusted him well enough to take the evidence he'd uncovered and deliver it to Brandt. Maybe Maister's afraid that if he contacts Brandt he could be compromised, and the German police will arrest him for the woman's murder. Or maybe not. Maybe he has his own reason for wanting to read what's in that file."

"How did you get these photographs?" Jack asked.

"They came off the video surveillance system in the restaurant. It's part of a big hotel and the security centre keeps a video record of all the areas of activity. We've got a good relationship with our German counterparts. They passed the duty manager a handful of Deutschmarks and he handed over the film."

Jack nodded to the woman sitting to Maister's right. "The girl who got whacked, who is she?"

Kate Doheny frowned. "Interesting. Her name is Nena Vlasova, a Russian. We don't know much about her except that she worked in a laundry shop six-days-a-week, and earned her money at night as a lap dancer in one of the seedy little strip clubs off Marlene. The plot thickens. She worked in the little laundry shop close to where Maister's apartment was. German police say that other staff used to see Maister in the shop once a week with his bag of washing. He'd spend time chatting with Nena. Intelligence has since told us that for the last couple of years she's been sharing an apartment with that piece of shit." Kate pointed to the third photo.

Jack was taken aback by her language. It seemed out of place in the conversation. He studied the photo. The man was stocky, but not fat. Well-built, and in good shape physically on closer examination. He had a mean look about him, sneering, almost pouting at the camera. Blonde hair, blue eyes, shoulders as broad as they come. "Who is he?"

Kate took a deep breath. "According to my contacts he's about as dangerous as they can get. His name is . . " Again she checked her file. "Bruno Proctor."

"He looks rough," Jack couldn't take his eyes off the mean, hungry expression.

"You can say that again. Bruno is a bit of a legend, you could say. He would have many fans all over the continent. He's a former commander of the notorious Badaar Meinhoff gang. They did a whole load of nasty kidnappings and assassinations, hijackings, that sort of thing, back in the late-seventies-early-eighties, until they were all outlawed. The police would like to have a chat with Bruno. Maybe get him to spend some time with them, like the rest of his life, if they could only just catch him. He's a master of identity, always managing to stay a step ahead. It's unlikely that Bruno murdered Nena. Chances are it was Maister."

"I wouldn't say Bruno would be too impressed with that," Jack joked.

"Probably not. Another reason why we'd like to have a talk with Maister."

"What do you mean?"

"Our intelligence sources tell us that Bruno Proctor boarded a flight to Ireland sometime in the last couple of weeks."

Jack wiped his forehead and stared at a worried looking Ben Roper. "Holy God. And what do *you* think is in the file?" he asked her.

She thought for a moment, then pursed her lips and blew, the same way she did that night in his back garden before she kissed him and dragged him down on top of her. "Pandora's Box . . . the curse of Tutankhamun. I haven't a clue. But whatever it is two people are familiar with its contents. And one them is dead." Doheny waited to see how he would react to such a dramatic surmise. "Are you in?"

For a few seconds Jack's mind was miles away. A hundred-and-seventy-two miles to be exact, sitting on a stool at the end of Martha Hannon's bar sipping the drink that Josef Maister had just sent down to him. Then he remembered the photos Maister had shown him. Do you know these people? he'd asked Jack. One of them was Alex Kline. The other was a photograph of an old man that queued in the Durrus post office every Friday morning to collect his old age pension. "Sorry?"

"Will you help us in this investigation?" she asked.

It seemed like such a ridiculous load of nonsense, like a story line straight out of a film about a Sicilean family called the Corleones, or invaders from outer space, he wanted to laugh it off and go back down to the bar before it closed. And he probably would have and told them not to be wasting his time if he hadn't met the tall man with the scraggy, grey hair and the piercing, slanty, greyish eyes that morning in Hannon's pub. "Yes. I'm in," was all he could find the strength to say. He had made his decision.

Twenty-four hours later, Jack Buckley would regret ever having laid eyes on Josef Maister.

It was nearly midnight on Wednesday when Jack Buckley said goodnight to them. He was due to catch a morning train back to Cork. Kate Doheny told him she would be touch and most likely would travel to Durrus within days to continue the investigation. Ben Roper told them he would make contact as soon as he had laid his son to rest the following morning.

A single light in the third floor window of the luxurious, recently refurbished block of apartments in Shrewsbury Park, just off the busy Blackrock road, burned late into the night. The four men chatted nervously since arriving in two taxis an hour before, making small talk, and asking about each other's families and each other's occupations. Listening to them, one might have been forgiven for thinking that they seemed like men who had once worked together closely, but hadn't been in contact for some time. They were each careful to gauge their questions, gentle, almost stilted, with their answers, often with long silences before asking another. Now and then, one of them would check his watch and call out the time. The others would grumble and curse.

Then a buzzer sounded. A click. Footsteps on the stairs. The door was opened for him. Taoiseach Joe Russell, Ireland's prime minister, stepped nervously into the waiting company. Introductions were brief. His private secretary, Alan Harrisson, introduced Donald Eckler, Alex Kline and Alfie Carruth to the head of government who had been enjoying a late-night drink with some close supporters to celebrate the opinion poll that would appear in the following morning's *Irish Times* newspaper. It would inform its readers that Joe Russell was now officially the most popular head of government since the commencement of the state. Seventy-three per cent of the electorate believed that Joe Russell was doing a fine job and was the only person for the position which he had held now for almost five years.

When Alan Harrisson had rung him in the private residents' lounge of Buswells Hotel, close to government buildings, on his mobile he laughed and asked him what was keeping him. "There's four pints waiting to be drunk here, Harrisson. And by the time you get here there'll be at least another four. I don't want you to be pissed in the morning. I want you fresh for the vultures on that radio show, d'ye hear me?"

Alan Harrisson could tell immediately that it was his boss, in fact, who was extremely pissed. "Joe I suggest you get some coffee into you and get your arse over to my apartment *now*!"

Russell could hear the nervous energy in Harrisson's voice. "What's wrong, Alan?"

"I can't talk over the phone. I'm in company. I'm sending a private car over for you. Tell your chauffeaur you're getting a lift home from me."

Russell laughed uneasily. "What the fuck's going on, Alan?"

"For the moment, boss, let's just say a number of old acquaintances are here from Frankfurt and they badly need to talk to us tonight." He knew he wouldn't have to say anymore.

Joe Russell could feel the thrill and the exhilaration of his most successful moment in power, that he'd waited to celebrate and boast about all day, slipping out of his hands. He didn't want to drink now. All he wanted to do was to crawl into a dark hole and die.

He almost found it hard to breathe as he looked around the room at the three men he hadn't seen for almost ten years. He thought he had looked after them exceedingly well and that, as a result, he would never see them again. But he was wrong. And, despite all his self-reassuring, something in the back of his mind – like a tiny screw that had worked itself loose and made its appliance noisy and unsafe to use – told him that sooner or later it would all come back to smother him. "What can I do for you, gentlemen?" It took all of his energy to be polite.

Eckler spoke first. "We should congratulate you, Taoiseach, on your highly commendable performance in the ratings war and your success since our last dealings with you."

Russell felt nauseous. "Our so-called *dealings*, Mr Eckler, ceased ten years ago. You got what you wanted."

"And let me remind you, Mister Prime Minister, you also got what you wanted. Do I have to remind you of how well you did out of that teeny-weeny little negotiation? You and your private secretary?" Eckler glared at Alan Harrisson with pure contempt. "I'm so glad you looked after the young lad. He was only a mere child when I last saw him. You must have great faith in him. On the other hand I suppose you would have to trust him with your life, wouldn't you?"

"What do you people want?" Russell snapped, rapidly running out of fake fondness for his unexpected guests.

"You were so kind to offer a number of my rather desperate countrymen Irish passports ten years ago and consequently give them the opportunity of starting afresh, and leaving their tormenters behind. In exchange for your guarantee of a *safe* haven, Taoiseach, I organised for a series of payments to be made into two private bank accounts totalling two million pounds. One account for you, a second account for Mr Harrisson. There is no way the authorities here will ever trace that money to either you or your private secretary. You have always had my word on that. Isn't that right?"

Russell was no longer the powerful man the people were cheering for. He wanted to run home to Kathleen, his wife. And lie in her arms and cry. And hear her tell him that everything would be all right. He felt spent, defenceless, useless. For the first time in ten years he was being reminded of who he had sold his soul to, reminded now of who he would be answerable to for the rest of his life. "What do you want?"

"We have a serious problem which could affect us all, which needs to be addressed and sorted immediately." Eckler leaned against the back of the mahogany Victorian chair and pushed it against the exquisitely varnished dark-brown dining-table. It started to creak under his weight. He didn't care. "The Keeper has been compromised. I want you to arrange to get him out of the country. He has decided that he would like to go to the sun. He has settled for a location that doesn't have any sort of domicile agreement with the Irish or German governments."

"What do I have to do?" Russell asked in a lowly, loathsome tone.

"Organise the tickets. Arrange a new passport for him. That has to be done tomorrow. Get him through airport security without any problems. He will be accompanied by a bodyguard. If anyone tries to behave silly they're quite likely to get very seriously injured."

Russell gasped. "I can't guarantee you any of those demands."

"You have no choice, Russell. Ten years ago, you undertook a commitment. You should have realised that you were still responsible for this man's welfare as long as he walked on your soil. He's still here. But only for another few hours. Now the quicker you accede to my demands the sooner you can get on with your little celebration. Bearing in mind that if you'd taken your responsibilities seriously I wouldn't have needed to come to Dublin to sort out this bloody mess."

"You rotten bastard!" Joe Russell screamed, lunging out with his hands ready to choke Don Eckler.

Alan Harrisson threw his arms around his boss from behind and pulled him backwards. "Don't Joe. You'll only make matters worse. *Stop!"* he roared above the din. He calmed him and forced him into a chair.

Eckler chuckled. He picked up a small bunch of grapes from the pear-shaped bowl in the centre of the nut-brown table and munched them, three at a time, spitting pips onto the rich expensive carpet. "You have no choice, Taoiseach. Quicker than you can tell the country how proud you are that they think so highly of you, I'll have called a contact of mine in the German papers. He's a real dirt-bag, a stinking paparazzo, who'll sell the sleazy story of the Irish prime minister who accepted big money and sold Irish passports. It would be quite ironic if your *Irish Times* was calling you a saint and my *Journal Berlin* was calling you an Irish traitor, wouldn't it?"

"What do you want?" Russell asked again.

"Oh, please, don't have me repeat myself. I think it's so unprofessional. Let me believe that I'm having an intelligent conversation with the leader of the country. Not some stupid, inept little messenger boy. I thought you left that business to your private secretary."

"Answer my question."

Eckler's glare sharpened. He took a long, sharp breath. "The passport will be made out in the name of Henry Myler. Make sure it's ready by four-thirty tomorrow evening. The airport authorities will be informed that Mr Myler will check in through the VIP entrance on Sunday afternoon. He will board the five o'clock flight to Tenerife. IB3559 and will sit in the front row. Is that clear?"

"Get out of here." Russell spat out each word, refusing to be drawn by Eckler's staring eyes.

"The superintendent will be travelling back to Cork with my good friend, Alex Kline, tomorrow evening. They will pick up your envelope from the concierge's desk at the Shelbourne Hotel, no later than half-past-five. Is that clear?" Eckler smiled and positioned his tweed cap so as to hide his hair-piece. "If you need me I'll be staying at the Shelbourne myself. I'll be flying back home at lunchtime." He frowned at Russell. "Don't fuck up."

As he stepped through the door to the top of the staircase, Eckler looked around at the pair of devastated men he was leaving behind. "Oh, I just remembered. Please do something about that police sergeant down there. What's his name? Buckley. Preferably get rid of him to somewhere he can't cause problems."

43

Aidan Kerr had succeeded in answering every single one of all of the contestants' questions on *Who Wants to Be a Millionaire?* that night. He kept reminding himself he would have been a millionaire five times over if he'd been taking part. Two hours later he was still feeling rather chuffed. So chuffed in fact that he decided to go down to Hannon's for a few drinks instead of saying night prayers. He dressed for the occasion in civvies and checked to make sure he had enough money to see him through to closing time. There was nothing that annoyed him more than having a twenty-pound note squeezed into the palm of his hand by some well-intentioned parishioner. The walk would take him five minutes at most. He opened the front door and breathed in the soft air, admiring for a moment the lateness of the daylight and the prospect of the June holiday weekend. His first sermon of the summer was approaching that Sunday. Hopefully the recent events wouldn't deter the tourists from the annual vacation on the peninsula. He'd think about what he would say to them on Saturday evening during his break from confession. Tonight though was for drinking and to hell with the hangover tomorrow. He pulled the door hard behind him. As he took his first steps down the driveway the phone started to ring in the hall behind him.

"Shit!" he shouted without looking around. It was a dilemma he hated. Ignore it and someone could die. Answer it and he could be kept talking for the rest of the night. He checked his watch. Twenty-past nine. Answer it and you'll still be in Hannon's for half-past, he told himself. He turned the key with one hand and grabbed the phone with the other.

"Hello," he said rather brusquely.

There was a long silence. Then a soft, elderly voice. "Is that Father Kerr?"

"Yes, it is. Who's calling?" He spoke now with his caring, pastoral voice.

"This is Harry Vogel, Father Kerr. We've only met once or twice. But I was just wondering if you might be available for a short while, Father."

Almost automatically Aidan started to pore over names and faces, tying one with the other, cursing this man silently for taking him away from his pint, but quietly accepting in another voice that he had no choice. He thought about Leo Hannon in the confessional that night. If only he had been more patient and understanding with the publican he might just have saved his life. "Of course I can, Harry. You just tell where you are and I'll be there in twenty minutes."

Maggie was even more impressed when her guest insisted on cleaning off the dinner table and stacking the dishwasher for her. "You'll have to give my Jack a few lessons when he gets back from Dublin," she shouted into the kitchen. She stood up and stretched, then took down two brandy glasses from the top of the teak dresser that ran the full length of the hall. "Would you like a drop of brandy, James?"

The doctor reappeared in the doorway. "That'd be nice. And, please, call me Josef." He sat down in the armchair.

Maggie looked around. "Josef? I thought your name was James." She handed him a large measure.

"I suppose I am unique. I have two names. Isn't that weird?"

"*Two* names?"

"Yes. I was born Josef Shlomo Maister. Seventeen years later I legally became James Morris."

"How?"

He sipped the brandy and swallowed it slowly. She could tell by the way he drank it that he was enjoying it while he contemplated his explanation. "I am adopted."

Maggie could feel her lips and mouth drying up quickly. "So am I," she added quickly, not wanting to distract him from the story she was sure he was about to tell. She was glad she had lit a fire that night, despite the warmer weather. She sat down in the old rocking-chair opposite him.

"My mother's name was Dora Maister. She came from well-heeled parents in Warsaw, and while she stood to inherit a lot of money from my grandfather she never made a big deal of the family's wealth. She moved to a small town called Zaklikow when she married my father.

She was a very beautiful woman, I'll always remember. Very tall. Jet-black hair and beautiful brown eyes. All of my father's friends use to comment on how stunningly attractive she was. And she had the most beautiful singing voice I have ever heard. She sang at my older brother's Bar Mitzvah and got a standing ovation. I'll never forget that afternoon. We had a lovely house, and a beautiful garden full of trees and flowers to play in. I always remember the way our house was always noisy; half of the neighbourhood played in our bedrooms every afternoon when we finished school. My father was a tailor; he made my brother's suit for his Bar Mitzvah. We were all so proud of him. I remember my father putting his arm around my shoulder and whispering: 'Your day will come, Josef. Don't be envious of your brother. He loves you.' We had such a wonderful party that evening. I was fascinated by the magician who came along especially and made my brother disappear for almost five minutes." Josef started to laugh heartily. "He put him into this cardboard box and seconds later he was gone. Then after a couple of minutes he pretended that something had gone terribly wrong. My mother went crazy, telling my father to call the police. Then a firecracker burst and my brother reappeared under the table." He sighed and sipped his brandy.

"The next day my father went to meet the owners of a huge store in Berlin, called Kaufhaus des Westens. They wanted him to make some suits for some rich customers. My mother went with him on the trip to keep him company. They brought my older brother, Chaim, as a treat for his Bar Mitzvah. Our house-maid, June Morris, minded us while they were away." Josef's voice started to tremble. He stopped talking and bowed his head.

"And what happened?" Maggie sat motionless, waiting for him to continue.

"I never saw them again. They were arrested by the Nazis. It all just seemed to happen so quickly. They were only down the road literally, having made the journey back from Berlin when they were stopped getting off the train. My mother had told us on a number of occasions that Jews were being arrested but we never thought it would happen to our family. We had many good German friends for as long as I could remember. We never fought with each other. Religion or nationality never entered the conversation. Anyway, they were told by station guards to get on another train which was sitting on one of the quieter side lines. They were then taken to Belzec."

Maggie shivered. "The concentration camp?"

Josef nodded slowly. "Very few of them on the train knew what was happening. They were simply told to get on board at gunpoint. The train would enter a small forest and stop. Then, the entire crew of the train was changed. SS men from the death camp replaced the railroad employees. Once the train entered the camp, other SS men would take them off the train. From there they were led to a barrack where they were told to undress. Then they herded them into a giant bath. I met a survivor many years later, one of only five who came out of Belzec alive. He'd met my father on the train and spoken with him. He told me once they went into the bath many of the men and some of the women understood what was happening. After undressing they were told to form two groups, one of men and the other of women and children. An SS man, with the stroke of a horse-whip, sent the men to the right or to the left. Right meant death. Left meant work. My father stayed with my mother and my brother but was kicked in the balls by this man and told to move. *'Dich konnen wir brauchen,'* he roared at my father as he dragged him off the floor by a clump of his hair. It means: 'We could use you'. My father was told to dress and to stand with the rest of the men while they watched all the women and children go into the gas chamber. They were screaming and begging and crying, the children pleading for their daddies to come and get them. My father and this other man watched their wives and children being slapped hard with a *knout* – a knotted whip – as they entered the room. Then this SS man fired a few shots from his revolver and there was silence. Then he closed the door and locked it." The tears ran down the doctor's cheeks, down onto the sides of his chin.

Maggie wiped her eyes and refilled his glass. She touched his hand. He squeezed it back.

"Forty minutes later the men went in and carried the bodies out to a special ramp. Then they shaved the hair off the bodies, which was packed into sacks and later taken away to be sold by the Germans. My father found the body of my mother and was forced to shave her hair. When he went to look for my brother he had already been taken away for burial." He took a hanky from his pocket and wiped his eyes and his nose. He tasted more of the brandy and sat back into the chair.

Maggie wanted to say something. Words were meaningless. "And later . . . your father?"

"My father. My poor, poor father. He was also Josef, which makes me so proud of my name. My father kept on working with his friend. Eventually they were separated and my father was sent to do more of the Nazis' filthy work in Auschwitz. He even survived the 'death march', as they called it, from Auschwitz to Bergen-Belsen. My father died on the fourteenth of April 1945; the British army liberated all surviving prisoners the following day."

Maggie watched him, his eyes heavy, his lip quivering each time he reached for his glass. Then she stared at the last surviving flame in the grate, fighting to stay alight.

"It is chilling to think that I begged my mother and father to take me to Kaufhaus des Westens, in Berlin, that morning with my older brother, I remember."

"How do you know all this if you never saw them again?"

Josef shrugged his shoulders. "I suppose I felt I owed it to them to keep their memories alive and make sure that people know exactly what those murdering bastards did to my family. I have spent nearly forty years trying to find out as much as I could about their last few hours together. I've tried to imagine what must have have been going through their minds, and what my mother would have been telling my brother while they were all taking off their clothes and stepping into that rotten, stinking bath. And what she might have told him to do while they were huddled together in the gas chamber waiting for the Zyklon-B gas to suffocate them. I'm sure she would have sung that same song to him that she sang to all of us to get us off to sleep at night when we were little. Once we heard her singing that song in her beautiful voice we knew we were safe, that nothing could harm us. I'm sure that's what she must have done while they waited to die." He finished his brandy. "Anyway, we were the lucky ones. June Morris had worked for my mother for many years. She was from Coventry, but had a great knack of putting on an accent and speaking fluent German if she wanted to confuse people. June knew everybody in our town. She was always meeting people and taking their numbers and offering to do this and that. She did an amazing amount of charity work. I think that was what probably saved my life. Her contacts managed to get us out of Poland. All the way across the continent she kept reminding me that my name was James Morris. She warned me not to talk; that if the Germans stopped us and questioned us, she would explain to them that I had a terrible speech impediment. I don't know how we did it but we eventually made it to England. And from there we went to live in New York. June married an American and they adopted me."

There was a long silence then Maggie stood up and coughed softly to clear her throat. "Would you like coffee? More brandy?"

"No more brandy. Coffee would be fine. But wait," he said quickly. "Please, sit down. Just another few minutes sitting here would be nice, if you don't mind."

Maggie sat down. "May I ask you a question, Josef?"

"Of course."

"Why did you come to Durrus?"

He smiled. It was obvious it was a question he had been asked already. "I came here on holiday some years back and fell in love with the place and its people. That's why."

Maggie smirked. "Nice one. Straight out of a tourist-board brochure."

They both laughed gently. "Well, that's the main reason," he said. "Why do you suspect it's not?"

"Because I checked with the local health board authority. They told me they never met you, and that you're not registered as a general practitioner here."

"So?"

"You can't just set up a medical practice wherever you decide to open your suitcase."

"But there's nothing in the rule book to say that I can't set up a medical practice in a town that's got no doctor, is there?"

"No. But you still have to register."

"Right, then I will. First thing tomorrow, I'll ring whoever I'm suppose to contact and fill out the necessary forms . . . if that makes you happy." He stood up. "Where did I leave my jacket?"

"I suppose you think I'm being impertinent, do you?" Maggie handed him his jacket.

"Not at all. I just hate fuss. I've lived most of my life fuss-free. So I suppose I just can't understand finicky people."

Maggie slapped him playfully on the shoulder. "How dare you call me finicky?" She reached up to his cheek and kissed him. "Thank you for sharing that with me tonight. I feel honoured."

"You're welcome. When something won't go away it often helps to talk to someone about it. At least that's what I tell my patients."

44

10.25pm.

The key was in the door of the little cliff-top cottage so Maggie, like she did on the rare occasion, let herself in. It was late and she had hoped during the twenty-minute drive that he might still be awake. The last person she expected to see chatting to Harry Vogel was Aidan Kerr. The two men looked deep in conversation. She took a quick step back onto the doorstep. "Oh, I'm sorry, I'll call back in the morning." As she pulled the door closed, it was Aidan's voice she recognised.

"Maggie, wait!"

She stuck her head around the door again. "Yes?" The two men sat at opposite ends of the long couch where she loved to stretch out with her wine and talk. Maybe he might let her have that as well before he left for Spain, she thought cheekily. "Well?" she asked again. They both seemed reluctant to say anything. Harry stared at the fire and Aidan tapped his empty coffee mug, as if both men were hoping that the other one would do the talking. "Is someone going to say something?" Maggie asked impatiently.

Aidan looked across at the old man. "Harry? Will you tell her, please?" he implored.

Maggie was worried now. "Jesus, lads, will one of you say something, for God sake." She sat down at the small table and concentrated on Aidan. "If it's that he's leaving, I know all about that, Aidan. I've tried to change his mind but he's not having any of it. I've tried to convince him that he won't like Spain. It's too hot and full of bloody tourists. But he still won't listen. And if it's about his fall, I told him I wanted the doctor to take a look at it but he told me he'd never talk to me again if I brought a doctor out here to see him. So there."

But that wasn't it and Maggie knew it, simply by watching the two of them. Aidan was preoccupied with something else. Something a lot more serious by the sound of it. "Please tell me, one of you. What's wrong?"

"This man tells me he's your grandfather." Aidan Kerr kept his eyes on the empty mug as he said the words slowly.

The old man looked back at the priest, as if disgusted that he had let her know something that had been a secret for so long.

Maggie laughed, then she stood up and crossed the room to where the record-player had resided for all the years she had called to see him. "Don't you think that's a bit of a sick joke, Harry?" she said in a bull-headed sort of way. She turned around so that she could see him – or at least the back of his head. "I suppose you're ashamed to face me. Are you?" She looked at Aidan. "I told this man in confidence that I wanted more than anything in life to find out who my mother was. And to meet her and talk to her if she's still alive. Very few people knew about that. I'm not ashamed that I'm adopted. It's just that I find it really difficult to cope with the fact that my mother may be somewhere out there and I don't know whether she's alive or dead. Or whether she cares half as much about me as I do about her. And you," she shouted, pointing at Harry Vogel, "you decide to concoct some cock-and-bull story about being my grandfather. Been drinkin' too much wine again, Harry?" She threw the handful of paper tissues she'd carried during her drive to the cottage in his direction.

No one spoke for a while.

"I'm going," Maggie said sharply.

"Don't!" Aidan was insisting. She looked back at him. He was pointing to the mantelpiece. Pointing to an small, old, discoloured black and white photograph of a man and woman. The man was standing beside the woman with his arm around her shoulder, bending down as if to kiss her on the cheek. Maggie picked it up. She waited for one of the two men in the room to tell her who it was. The old man sitting closest to the mantelpiece spoke.

"That's your mother. The photo was taken in 1967. You were one. Your mother had contracted tuberculosis and was sent to a sanatorium near Salzburg. She died two weeks after that picture was taken."

Maggie couldn't take her eye off the woman in the picture. She smiled at the camera. It was such a beautiful smile as if she was smiling especially for her daughter. "Where was I at that stage?"

"You were taken into care until they were able to find parents to adopt you."

"And why couldn't you have adopted me?"

The old man raised a hand to his forehead and squeezed his eyes closed. His face was contorted, almost painfully, his fingers stretched until they turned red and his knuckles pure white. "Because I was away a lot of the time. I travelled a lot on business."

"And why couldn't Brega, your wife, have looked after me?"

The old man just shook his head and ran his hand up and down his face.

"Are you really my grandfather?"

He nodded and took the hand away. "Yes," he whispered.

"*Are you?*" she yelled.

"Yes!" he said, more coherently this time.

"Then tell me, where have you been all my life?"

He sat back in the comfortable chair now and joined his hands. "Looking for you."

"Why?"

"Because I made a promise to your mother that I would always look after you, even if I couldn't be with you. I would always make sure you were safe and well."

"And how long have you known that it was me you were looking for?" Her voice was etched with both disbelief and bitterness now.

"For some years. I saw you on the television the morning Jack Buckley was shot in Macroom during that botched bank raid. I knew the minute I saw you and heard you talking to the interviewer that it was you. I had an idea you were living in this part of the country but I never seriously believed I would ever meet you."

"But you did."

"I did."

"And why didn't you tell me who you were? More bloody importantly, why didn't put me out of my misery and tell me who I was, and who I belonged to?" She was in tears now, crying as she tried to speak. "Why did it have to be such a secret?"

He shook his head again and sighed. "Because I was on the run. I couldn't afford to compromise my identity." He sniffed and coughed, leaned forward and put his hands over his head. "I suppose I didn't want the world to know that you were my granddaughter."

"Were you ashamed of me?"

"Never, never, never. Quite the opposite. I just couldn't have coped knowing that my granddaughter was ashamed of me. That was the only reason why I stayed away from you and kept my distance. I swear, Maggie, I wanted so much to tell you every time you called. I wanted so much to hug you and tell you what your mother was like and how much she loved you for the short time she had you. That is the truth."

Maggie wiped her eyes and looked behind her at Aidan.

The young priest seemed to comply with everything he had just heard. He nodded. "I believe him."

It was after midnight when Maggie got home. All the way back she had wished that Jack could have been waiting for her when she got there. Aidan Kerr had offered to drop in for a while until she had relaxed, but then she would have had to keep talking about the revelations. And he would have kept convincing her that the old man was telling the truth. She didn't need to be told that. Something inside told her it was true; that he was the father of her mother. She poured out the remainder of the brandy and sipped it, staring into the grate at the dying embers of the night's fire, trying to recall as many of the conversations she had enjoyed in Harry Vogel's company over three years, and wondering would she have been as honest with him if she had known he was her grandad. A part of her wanted to believe him so much. Another side didn't want to have to endure the pain of having to re-adapt her life to accommodate someone who was never there for her even though he could have been. And what had him on the run? She remembered the evening he had told her about the time in his life he wanted to put behind him and forget forever. Maybe now he had done just that.

She walked to the front door and put the chain across the lock. She checked the table to make sure her car keys were lying somewhere she would see them the next morning. Then she noticed it. The answering machine had recorded one message. What if it was from the old man? More likely from Jack, she thought. She pressed play and waited for a voice.

The young girl on the tape sounded distressed and very upset. She fought to catch her breath before leaving a message. Maggie was willing her to speak.

"Hello Maggie, this is Cindy Reilly. I need to talk to you. I hope you'll be able to meet me after school tomorrow. I must talk to you. I'm pregnant . . . "

45

She had tossed and turned for most of the night. Then, just as she lapsed into a deep, exhausted sleep, the room began to light up and the birds took up their positions in the branches of the chestnut tree directly over her bedroom window. It was the sort of dawn she'd loved since arriving on Sheep's Head – a brilliant, blinding sunshine, bursting with new life but yet silent in all its glory, that made her want to be up and about before six, before the rest of the world could claim a part of it.

But not that morning.

All through the short few hours of restless sleep, her mind continued to digest and regurgitate the events of the night before, over and over, like a scratched record would repeat the same line, again and again. She could see him sitting close to the fireplace, his head buried in his hand, his elbow resting far out on his knee. "Why couldn't you have taken care of me?" The question was always the same. Though each time she asked it the voice inside her head sounded different. She had spent time looking in the mirror at the foot of the bed, having opened the French doors out onto the small balcony so that she could listen to the soft breeze in the trees at the bottom of the garden, and to the sound of the birds each time the breeze died down. She tried to imagine what sort of a woman her mother might have been, and why this man who claimed to be her grandfather hadn't mentioned her father.

Maggie gave the mirror a dismissive stare. "He's not my grandfather," she said to her reflection, as if challenging her image to argue the point further and prove her wrong. "That could be any woman in the photograph. Any of his girlfriends." She kicked at the quilt, tossing it off her legs so they could breathe and cool down. "But why would he want to pull such a sick hoax and still manage to sound so convincing and genuine?" The face in the mirror began to annoy her. She threw the small teddy at her reflection, forcing the mirror to tilt back and away. The soft breeze felt warm as it forced the creaky doors wide open slowly and filled the room. She glanced at the clock on the bedside table.

9.30am.

Out onto the side of the bed. She finished the mug of coffee. It was almost cold now with that mucky taste that made her wonder why she drank so much of the damn stuff in the first place. It was going to be a strange day. She knew that, from the moment she had poured a brandy for the doctor the night before. Maybe even a day that would change things forever. She wasn't sure how, but already things were different. Life was throwing up a whole bundle of new expectations. In the space of a fortnight, an old man had become her grandfather; a mysterious doctor had arrived in town overnight, and within twenty-four hours was giving the impression of a man who'd lived in the village most of his professional life. And then there was Jack. Poor Jack, some of the town's older folk would say to her when they met her in Kenny's supermarket, or when she would call to them with their medication. "How's poor Jack?" they'd always ask, tossing their heads, or nodding and smiling, in that scornful way that she'd come to despise. What they were really saying to her was, "Is Jack still on the bottle?" Or, "How do you manage to put up with that oul' piss artist of a man of yours?" Yet they were the very same people who would wake him at four in the morning and ask him to come out because they heard someone prowling around the farmyard, or trying to rob their lives' savings from the copper kettle on top of the fridge.

Maggie always defended him. No matter what had happened the evening before, no matter how much he might have had to drink, she always took the side of Sergeant Jack Buckley, championing his honour and his virtues. People in glass houses shouldn't throw stones, she used to remind the denouncers. They'd just tut and walk away. She would have loved to have spilled the beans and let them blab to each other to their hearts content about the real problems on Sheep's Head: three cases of child sex abuse, and that was only within the past month; there were reports that drugs were being sold at the teenagers' disco in Kilcrohane that previous Saturday; one well-known resident had admitted to Jack only the week before that he had given his wife a terrible beating in full view of their five children. The list was building by the day. And the list always ended up on Jack's desk. Poor oul' Jack, as the oul' ones liked to call him.

9.45am.

Time to get moving, she thought. A call to the doctor to let him know about the phone message from Cindy Reilly. She'd have an hour to get her hair done, then across to Schull to collect Cindy. After that, that day's diary page was blank. Better that way, Maggie thought. She wasn't sure why.

WET PAINT

The sign hung on the door handle. Maggie wasn't sure if it referred to the door or the walls. It was the walls. The surgery looked bright and well-organised, the combination of the smell of fresh emulsion and the new creamy-orange colour making it less clinical and far more pleasant and homely.

Josef Maister – she preferred that name: it had more warmth and depth to it – stood at the filing cabinet trying the prise open the top drawer with a coat hanger in the absence of a handle. "Good morning," he said in an exasperated voice.

"Good morning. It's a beautiful day, isn't it," Maggie gushed excessively.

"Is it?" he asked without looking around. "I forgot to notice." He thumped the drawer and it opened. He smiled. "If there's one thing I've no time for, it's petty, piddling, parochial small-talk. Unless, that is, you're paying fifteen pounds to see me." He continued to grin. "Having said that, I thoroughly enjoyed dinner last night. You make for lovely company, Maggie. Thank you again."

She was about to say "you're welcome." She didn't get a chance.

"What can I do for you?" he asked, turning his attention now to the row of marked files and records in the top drawer.

"I got a phone call last night from a young girl. Her name is Cindy Reilly. She lives locally."

"And?"

"She didn't say much, except that she's pregnant. She sounded quite upset on the phone. Said she'd like to see me after school today."

"How old is she?"

"Sixteen, almost seventeen."

"I'm not surprised she's upset. She's probably suicidal. Do you know her well?"

"Not really. I gave a talk to her class a few months back. Told them about unwanted pregnancies, contraception. All that sort of thing. Then I invited them to ask me questions."

"And did they?"

Maggie coughed. "One of them did. Shay Sullivan."

"What did he ask?"

"Can blowjobs make you pregnant?" Maggie waited to see how the doctor would respond.

He raised his eyebrows and held his breath for a moment.

"You know," Maggie continued. "Up to a few years

ago, I thought that blowjobs were strictly administered by people who worked in glass bottle factories, making beautifully carved crystal by twirling a long pole."

Maggie laughed.

Josef Maister didn't. In fact, he seemed indignant at her reaction. He opened the second drawer which was cluttered with small packages and envelopes. He took out the photographs and handed them to Maggie. "I wasn't going to show these to you until I'd let your husband see them. But since this young woman has contacted you, perhaps you should see them now."

Maggie opened the colourful wrapper and took out the photographs. Her eyes opened wide. Cindy Reilly was performing a striptease act for whoever was taking the pictures. Eventually she lay across a bed and pouted, and stretched, and blew kisses, and squeezed her breasts, and fingered herself with her head thrown back. Twenty-four different poses, all revealing, all well-choreographed by the look of it. Maggie gasped. "Jesus Christ, where did you get these?"

"Freddie Nolan."

Maggie looked at Josef Maister in horror. *"Freddie Nolan?"* She winced at the notion.

"Well, actually, Freddie developed the film. He was quite shocked when he realised what the roll was turning out, considering that Ethel Kline had only dropped the roll into him that morning. He showed them to me. I said I'd keep them and pass them on to the sergeant." He took them back from her and bundled them into the envelope. "However, if, as you say, she's nearly seventeen, there's no offence committed here, is there?"

Maggie was speechless.

11.35am.
Maggie cursed herself. She was half an hour too early. She'd tried to take her time between Durrus and Schull, a whole hour to kill on a journey that would normally take twenty minutes. She tried to remind herself how beautiful the hills looked now that summer had arrived early, and how lucky she was to have a job that took her out into the most picturesque scenery in the world, and how their German and American tourists would simply kill to take a slow, comfortable journey like this on a morning when the sky was dark blue and the sun was so hot that she had to open all the windows.

But she couldn't remind herself. All she could think of was Cindy Reilly. And her baby. And the photographs. And Ethel Kline's camera. And how none of this was making any sense whatsoever.

The examination classes were being released a week early, to give them time for revision before the tests started on the Wednesday after the June holiday weekend.

Maggie railed at the notion of revision on a beautiful day like today. And the forecast was for more good weather. She remembered her own 'free week' years ago, before her Leaving Certificate exams, and how the weather was like today's; and how she spent all the time she should have been revising plotting ways of getting off with a local garda called Jack Buckley.

WELCOME TO SCHULL, the sign said.

Maggie parked outside the old convent. Not too close

to the main gate to attract attention from the other pupils or from the teachers leaving for their lunch break, and not too far that she might miss Cindy when she walked out with the rest of her classmates. She turned off the engine and opened her bag, pulling out a small square mirror, just big enough to see her fringe. She growled. Eileen Power had made a pig's ear of her hair. She'd explained to the stylist that she was giving a talk to a class of sixteen-year-olds and wanted to look reasonably trendy. Looking in the mirror she felt like she had just stuck her finger into a wall socket.

At first there was a trickle of grey pullovers and wine-coloured skirts. Then a bell rang and they all started to pour out into the wide yard and out onto the main road. Maggie waited, holding her breath, hoping that she wouldn't have to get out and shout to her, or wave. She knew it would be the last thing Cindy wanted if she was with a group of friends. Then, as quickly as they poured out the door, they were gone. In through hall doors, up side lanes, and onto coaches, waving and shouting that they'd ring each other before Saturday night.

"Damn!"

Maggie slapped the steering wheel. She'd obviously missed her in the crowd. She started the engine again and waited for a second. What if this was a hoax? she asked herself. Couldn't be. Somebody winding me up? Don't be ridiculous.

She heard a door close, the familiar sound of the main entrance to the convent slamming shut in the brisk southerly breeze. And there she was, on her own. She swung her bag across her shoulder and plodded towards the main gate, her head bowed, her long blonde hair blowing loosely, swirling around her face and her neck. She was a tall girl, five-ten maybe, Maggie guessed, who could have passed for eighteen or nineteen. She looked up as she got to the gates. Maggie flashed her headlights and Cindy waved back. Maggie could see why the boys would fall at her feet. She must have been the most attractive girl in the whole of the south-west.

If only she could have kept her attractiveness at a distance. Cindy had a reputation Maggie was only too aware of. She had often overheard the boys talking about her and what she did to so-and-so when he had walked her home from the disco.

Cindy didn't bother with the teenage disco in Kilcrohane anymore. She'd graduated to Hannon's pub on a Friday night, and the occasional Saturday when she wasn't baby-sitting for the Klines. She knew she'd get bought drink if she sat at the bar and chatted to Martha Hannon, or the sergeant if he was in for a few. One night Jack saw her chatting up a German tourist at the bar and caught them later having sex in his German-registered car outside the town. Her mother had died almost eight years ago and her father didn't seem to care where she was or who she was with. From the age of ten she looked after herself.

Maggie leaned across and opened the passenger door. "Hi ya," she said cheerfully.

"Hello," Cindy replied ruefully, as she struggled to get her bag onto the back seat.

"Finished school for good, I see," Maggie said, trying

to buy a bit of time but remembering what the doctor had said about small talk.

Cindy Reilly just nodded and stared out the window ahead of her. "Where are we going?"

"You tell me."

"Anywhere quiet. I just need to talk to someone before my head explodes." Her voice got softer and trembled.

Maggie patted her hand, noticing the teardrop about to escape from the corner of the young girl's eye. "Do you want to go for a walk?"

Cindy Reilly shook her head.

"Well," Maggie was thinking as fast as she could, "we could drive down to the beach and sit in the car. I often do that when I feel my head's about to explode."

She agreed.

Maggie killed the engine and opened the window wide, listening to the splash each wave made as it crashed up onto the small, deserted pebbly beach, then back into the swell, dragging the small stones and shells as far as it could until the soft sand beneath started to dry and stopped them in its path and held them, until the next, bigger wave crashed in and pulled them a little further out again.

She turned down the radio.

Silence, apart from the gulls away out in the distance where the surface of the water sparkled like a shower of diamonds, fighting for the prime spot behind Ger Sullivan's bright red trawler as it rounded the head and motored into Dunmanus Bay.

"How do you know you're pregnant?" Maggie asked.

"Because I'm three weeks late."

"It could be because of all the pressure you're under with the exams starting next week. That often prevents your period happening when it's supposed to."

"Don't patronise me."

Maggie decided it was best to let her do the talking. "Sorry. I didn't mean to sound patronising."

"I got a pregnancy-detector kit when I was Cork yesterday. I took the day off school. I was throwing up all morning so I got one of the girls to ring in for me. I went into a toilet in a pub and did the test. It was positive."

Maggie was impressed and relieved by how level-headed the young woman seemed to be. Then again, she had to remind herself, maybe it hadn't sunk in just yet. "Who's the father?"

Then it all seemed to fall apart. Cindy's hands started to tremble. She put them up to her face and started to cry, so loud and so uncontrollably that Maggie didn't know what to do or how to react. She put her arm around Cindy and tried to hug her. The young woman's whole body was shaking violently now. Maggie just rocked her, whispering to her that everything would be OK. Ten minutes later she had relaxed considerably.

Maggie took a deep breath and watched Cindy as she dabbed her eyes with the sleeve of her uniform.

"I'm sorry," was all she kept saying.

"Why are you sorry, Cindy? You haven't done anything wrong," Maggie urged.

"Everything would have been still OK if I hadn't been so stupid."

"What do you mean?" Maggie took her arm away and sat back.

"That night in Hannon's." She was trying hard now to speak without crying. "When the three boys went missing. I was there." She seemed reluctant.

"And?"

"I'd been drinking with them since about five o'clock. My dad had asked me to get some meat for his dinner. I suppose I was just pissed off running around after him, cooking this and cleaning up that, and ironing his shirts and doing his washing. Something just snapped inside me that evening. I remember going out the front door. I called him a lazy, selfish bastard as I was slamming it. I even gave him the two fingers when I saw him looking out the window after me. 'Don't be long,' he shouted. Well that was when I decided not to bother getting him his dinner that evening. He was just in from work and he'd left his wallet on the kitchen table. He told me to take enough for the messages. I took sixty quid and headed into town. That was when I met the three lads from Dublin."

"Where did you meet them?" Maggie didn't want to rush her.

"They were sitting on the small wall across from the church. One of them called over to me. The other two started to whistle." She smiled a little. "I suppose I'd be lyin' if I said I didn't like the attention. You don't meet too many nice blokes your own age in a place as small as Durrus. Occasionally you might meet the odd lad at the Westlodge in Bantry. But they only run discos a few times a year."

"The Dublin lads. What were they like?"

"They were OK. They'd been drinking for most of the afternoon. One of them, the nice bloke, told me they were camping over in Ollie Jenning's field, on the other side of the peninsula. And they were looking for a way of getting back to the campsite before it got dark. I told them that Ollie usually drove through Durrus in his creamery truck about seven most evenings and that he'd give them a lift. He always called into Hannon's for a drink on his way through so they decided to wait in there."

"So that was the first time they'd been in Hannon's that day?"

Cindy nodded. "They told me they'd been on a pub crawl in Bantry since lunchtime and hitched a lift from there. They invited me in for a drink. So I went with them. And had a drink. And another. And another. Eventually I lost count of how many drinks I'd had. I completely forgot about my father and his dinner, until Martha Hannon told me that he was on the phone in the bar and wanted to talk to me. I ignored her and let him ring back four times. I picked up the phone and told him to fuck off with himself and hung up."

"What time was this at?"

"I don't know. It must have been nearly eleven."

"Was the pub busy?"

"Yeah, I think. I was pissed at that stage."

"And what about the three lads?"

"I think they'd drunk themselves sober by then. I remember they were singing songs." She smiled. "They started to sing "Roll with it" by Oasis. They were really noisy and out of tune. Completely all over the place. One of them got up on the seat and started to clap his hands. I remember feeling a bit sick when I looked up at him. I must have started swaying because the nice one of the three asked me if I was OK. He said I should get some fresh air. He offered to come out with me in case I fell. I must have been locked cos' I remember a table falling over and glasses breaking. I could hear a commotion and him apologising as he helped me towards the side door. The place was just spinning."

"What was his name?"

She stopped for a moment. "Adam. He was really nice."

"He was the one they pulled out of Doo Lough, wasn't he?"

She nodded and seemed to be getting upset again, clutching and squeezing the small ball of paper tissue she had in her hand. "Yes."

"Do you want to tell me what happened?"

"It was beginning to rain. We were standing in the carpark waiting for the others, talking about music and what bands and singers we liked. I told him I loved Robbie Williams and that he looked very like him. He laughed. Then it really started to rain. I knew me da was gonna come looking for me at any minute. So I said we could shelter in the old barn behind the pub where all the empty kegs are stored. I think the night air might've made me drunker but there was just something nice about being with this bloke, just the two of us talking and having a laugh."

"And what happened then?"

"He put his arm around me and kissed me. It felt nice. So I kissed him. Then he opened the top I was wearing and started kissing me there. He said we should lie down in the corner where there was a whole load of old seat-covers from the pub. Anyway one thing led to another."

"And you're sure he's the father?"

Cindy stared at Maggie. "I'm not finished yet. I have to tell someone what happened," she snapped.

"What happened?"

"We were putting our clothes back on when all this commotion and shouting started in the carpark. Adam started to curse, saying that it was his two mates. They were yelling and screaming at Leo Hannon. Adam thought they must've been thrown out because all we could hear them shouting at Leo was, 'It wasn't our fault'. He told me he'd see me the next day. I gave him my phone number which he said he'd put into his mobile phone. Then I heard a car revving like there was no tomorrow. Adam's two mates started screaming out his name. When he went out into the carpark, they were sitting in Leo Hannon's car yelling at him to get into the back of the car. He kept saying no, telling them that they were mad, pleading with them to get out of the car before someone called the cops."

Maggie felt a bit sheepish. "And where were *the cops?*"

"He was sitting at the bar drinking his vodka."

Maggie thumped the wheel and cursed. "So what happened then?"

"They told him that if he didn't get into the car they

were going to drive off without him and leave him to face the music. Then one of them shouted that he'd have the walk back to the campsite in the pissing rain. That changed his mind. He asked me would I go with him."

"What did you say?"

"I begged him not to be so stupid. That Leo Hannon would understand that he had absolutely nothing to do with stealing the car. I should've gone with him. He'd still be alive today if I'd gone in that car."

"How do you know?"

"Because little did I know what had just happened."

"What?"

"Martha Hannon had come out into the carpark looking for me. Seemingly my father had arrived into the pub. He'd gone mad, as if he was possessed. He demanded to know where I was, screaming and shouting about what he was gonna do to me when he got me home. Anyway Martha must've seen us in the old barn and she went back in and told him I was out in the barn with one of those Dublin lads and there were clothes all over the place. He went berserk and came out and grabbed me just as the car sped off. He slapped me across the face and pushed me backwards onto the ground. Then he called me a slut, 'just like your mother', he roared. I froze. I still don't know why I said it to him. I suppose I was afraid he was going to kill me with his bare hands."

"What did you say?"

"I told him . . . " Her voice dropped, almost to a whisper. "I told him I'd been raped."

Maggie was still trying to take it all in. She tried not

to show any sign of shock or revulsion. "OK," she said softly, more as a stopgap than a sign of her approval. "But he didn't rape you, did he?"

"Of course not! If anything I'd say I led him on. I just wanted to spend a bit of time with him. I didn't realise it was going to end up like this." She pointed to her stomach.

"What did your father say?"

"He was stunned for a few seconds. Then he helped me up off the wet ground and attempted to hug me and tell me that everything would be all right. Then it was like he just exploded, as if a bomb in his head had been detonated unexpectedly. He started to jump up and down and kick the wall of the barn, and scream his head off, fuckin' and blindin' everything and everybody. I tried to get him to calm down but he just knocked me out of the way away, only this time it was like I didn't exist. He was running around in circles, shouting my mother's name. Then he started screaming for Leo. After a few minutes Leo came out with the old man, Harry Vogel. When he realised his car was gone he started to shout and curse. I heard him say something about documents for Harry being in the car."

"What did Leo do?"

"He hurried the little old man back into the pub and told Martha to get him a hot whiskey, that he'd make sure that he got home OK but that he'd have to wait until someone else gave him a lift. He came back out and started to talk to my father. I could tell they were planning something. The two of them spoke quietly but so quickly, and the looks in their eyes scared the daylights out of me. I could hear them mentioning names. They talked about Jack. Then they mentioned Alex Kline. They mentioned the documents. Then my da told me to get into the jeep and wait for him. I should have walked away. I'll never forgive myself for what happened after that. Before I knew it one of them was on the phone talking to Alex, arranging to meet further out past Toormore. They were reckoning that the boys might try to get back to the campsite but Leo Hannon doubted if they'd be able to drive properly after all the drink they'd had. Then I started to cry and my father walked across to me and punched me in the stomach. My father said to Leo Hannon, 'I'm gonna murder those little rotten bastards.'"

"Why didn't you run back into the pub and tell Jack what was happening outside?"

"Because my father pulled me back up off the ground and marched me over to his jeep and pushed me inside and locked it."

"What did he do then?"

"He and Leo went back into the pub and came out a few minutes later with Jockey Carr. The three of them sat in the front seat and my father drove that machine so hard I thought I was going to throw up all over the place. Three times I could hear Leo Hannon screaming out, *'Jesus Christ!'* when my father narrowly missed trees and walls. He was out of his head with drink."

"Did he catch up with them?"

"They made this plan to cut them off before they took the right turn to Ollie Jenning's farm. But they must have got lost and ended up on a dirt track in Dale Mill forest.

There's only one road in and out – it's the same road. So they got caught. I tried to tell my father that I hadn't been raped, that I'd lied to him because I was afraid of what might happen. But he didn't seem to care. He stayed on the phone talking to Alex Kline who must have been following them in his car. When they got to the clearing in Dale Mill, Alex opened the boot of his car and handed out guns. He had some kind of automatic weapon himself. They pulled on balaclavas. I started to cry and my father pointed one of the guns at me and told me to get back into the jeep. I remember they got the boys out of the car at gunpoint."

Maggie watched her for a few seconds, staring out at the small lapping waves, and beyond at the red trawler, which was only a dot now, as it rounded Crook Head. She was almost in a trance now, as if she'd gone over the events that night in her head, again and again, until they no longer registered any emotion, or any reason to be upset. "What did they do to them?"

"I don't know. I watched them from the back window of the jeep. Their hands were tied. Leo Hannon seemed to be talking to them. Then they turned and started to run. But the men didn't chase them. They seemed to just let them go. Then they huddled together and two of them had a smoke. My father was swigging from his hipflask. Then they all seemed to look at their watches and walked out of the lights of the two cars and followed them. I could hear gunshots a few minutes later. Then the men returned to the clearing and we all drove home."

"Did your father say anything to you on the way home?"

Cindy nodded. "Yeah. He'd look into the rear-view mirror every few minutes and shout, *'Slut!'* Eventually I put my hands up to my ears so I couldn't hear him anymore. I woke in the back of the jeep a few hours later when it started to get bright. The bastard just left me there outside our house, probably hoping I'd freeze to death, after all the times I've put him to bed, and made his dinner, and washed and scrubbed his clothes. No more."

Maggie was shaking. Her nerves were shattered. She gripped the steering wheel with her left hand and closed up the window with the other. "Do you think they . . . "

"Shot them? Is that what you were going to ask? Of course they shot them. Why didn't they come back if they were all right? Why haven't they been seen if they're still alive?"

"But they found Adam. He hadn't been shot. He drowned."

"Maybe he wandered into Doo Lough. Maybe he thought he was running the right way to get away from them. They hunted them down and killed them like dogs would tear a fox to shreds. I think that's what happened, Maggie."

Maggie reached across and took her hand. It was frozen and trembling.

Maggie reached into the glove compartment and took out the picture package. "Who took these photographs?" she asked gently.

Cindy Reilly just looked at the package, not bothering to touch it or its contents. "Alex Kline. Last weekend while his wife was away in Killarney with her friends.

They'd gone to stay in the Gleneagle. He asked me to baby-sit. He came home early when the children were in bed. He checked to make sure they were asleep and then came downstairs. He told me he needed me to come down to his office with him. I told him I didn't like leaving the smaller children on their own. He said it was all right because Dónal was in the house. He'd hear them if they woke up. When we got down there he locked the door and took a camera out of a drawer. He told me to lie on the couch and to take off my clothes slowly, 'Just like you did for that little Dublin gutser', he said, watching me through the camera. I told him to fuck off. He warned me that if I didn't do what he told me that he'd tell my father that I'd slept with half of the men in Durrus. So I did it. I took off all my clothes. Real slow. Gave him one hell of a sexy strip show, so I did. He was nearly coming in his pants, giggling and dribbling he was."

"How did they end up in Freddie Nolan's chemist?"

"I knew he'd bring them into the city to get them developed, or give them to one of his estate agent friends, the bloke who photographs the houses for him. So I called to say hello to Ethel the next morning when I knew he'd be gone to work. It was unlikely that he'd take the roll with him in case it fell into the wrong hands. Ethel had left her roll of film from her weekend away sitting on the kitchen worktop. I remembered where Alex had left his camera. So while she was dropping the children to school I took the roll of film out of his camera and swapped it with hers." She grinned, obviously pleased that her plan had worked. "And made sure to remind her to drop it into Nolan's chemist. She didn't know that Freddie had his own dark room so she was delighted that she'd have them back so quick."

"What if Freddie Nolan had just given them back to Ethel that afternoon when she called to collect them?"

"Pretty much the same thing that's happening now. I reckon she would have taken them to the police. But I'm glad she didn't."

"Why?"

"Because she would have taken them to Alfie Carruth, the superintendent. But he's Alex's best friend. So it wouldn't have got any further."

"How do you know they're best friends?"

"Because he practically lives in the house when Ethel's not there. And if he doesn't come to the house he rings Alex on his mobile and arranges to meet him in real out-of the-way places."

"How do you know?"

"Cos I've taken a few calls. He always sounds as if it's an emergency. Lately he's been ringing at all hours. Whenever I baby-sat he'd ring at least once. One night he rang five times, asking each time when they were due back and where had they gone and to make sure to give Alex the message if he called."

"Would you like to see these men prosecuted in court?" Maggie sat shivering in her seat, hardly able to believe – and wanting to repudiate – what she'd just heard.

Cindy Reilly had no hesitation. She nodded frantically.

"It means your father will go to prison as well.

She kicked the dashboard and threw her head back against the seat. *"Yes, yes, yes!"* she kept saying, over and over again, until the tears came again and she started to sob uncontrollably.

46

Jockey Carr should have been conspicuous by his absence around the small winding streets of Durrus all that morning. It was unusual for no one to mention him, but the town was immersed in speculation. The question on everyone's lips: who was the father of Cindy Reilly's baby? Not that any of the old dears on their way to Mass that morning were in the least bit surprised. She was asking for it, one of them blethered. And they all agreed. What turned the topic into bait for real discussion though was the connection with the teenagers who had disappeared some weeks before. Rumours were rife that the three boys had left Hannon's pub with her that night after she dared them to steal a car from the carpark. The car had been spotted heading in the direction of Blairs Cove, a popular late-night spot for lovers, by Ollie Jennings. Once there, on the secluded beach, surrounded by the rocky sloping cliffs, they took it in turns to rape her. The suggestion was touted that they hadn't disappeared at all. Two of them had gone into hiding, shortly after their friend accidentally waded into marshy land, and on into Doo Lough, and drowned while trying to get away from Cindy's father who was chasing them later that night. Now the police wanted to question his two friends. They knew that the stories were untrue but at least the latest rumour would discount the notion of a murder having been committed right on their own doorsteps.

It was some weeks since that night in Hannon's, and, while the rumours surrounding the events of that night became more convoluted by the day, no one in Durrus was any the wiser about what really happened.

The one person everyone suspected knew the truth hadn't been seen in twenty-four hours. Alex Kline had called to Jockey Carr's caravan at Kitchen Cove shortly after nine the previous day and told him he had thirty minutes to pack a few things. When Jockey asked why Alex Kline told him it would be better for all of them if Jockey went home to his mother for a few weeks until the whole drama – as Kline referred to it – blew over.

"You're an easy pick for the rumour-mongers, Jockey," Alex explained to him.

What he was really telling him was that he was too much of a liability to have around right now. Jockey knew what he was saying in a roundabout sort of way. Then he said something very strange.

"It would be too easy to accidentally compromise ourselves right now."

Jockey had to think about the words. He wasn't stupid. But he still had to break down such a huge mouthful of big words. Accidental meant you didn't mean it. Compromise meant something like shame.

"Shame on you!" his mother used to shout from the bottom of the stairs. It didn't make much sense. Shame was like disgrace. His mother told him that his father had brought shame on the family when he had left them for a young one who worked in the local pub. But it wasn't an accident that his father left his mother for another woman. Therefore shame can't be accidental. Or can it? Was Alex saying that Jockey has caused some kind of disgrace. Surely not. Alex was Jockey's friend. He was beginning to feel sick at the thought of disgracing his friend. And whatever he had done wasn't an accident, as his father had proved all those years ago.

He sat in the front of the car, contemplating what he should do to win over his friend again. Alex had been so good to him down through the years. He got him the caravan. He gave him money. He convinced Leo Hannon to give him a job stacking the shelves in the pub before opening time every second morning. He even forgave him for what happened with Cindy Reilly the night he jumped out from behind the bushes.

By the time they arrived at the superintendent's house he was feeling sick. He didn't know Alex was going to stop here. He assumed he was going to drop him off at Mallow and then drive on to Dublin for the funeral of the boy who drowned.

"Wait here," Alex snapped as he slammed the door shut and hurried up the fancy driveway.

Jockey could feel himself twitching, then shaking, with nerves. He hated Alfie Carruth. He had overheard the superintendent calling him some horrible name one day. "That spastic retard," he called him. Alex told him to keep his voice down. He liked Alex.

There was no more talking in the car once Carruth had told Jockey to "get into the fuckin' back" He didn't argue with him. He just sat there and wondered what his mother would say when she found out he was home. He'd given up phoning her lately because she insisted on treating him like a bloody child. "F-for G-G-God's sake, Ma," he'd plead, "I'm thir'y-one." It was no good. Jockey was convinced she was ashamed of him, and the only way she could deal with her shame was to make believe she was talking to a five-year-old. And since shame wasn't accidental, he gave up calling her.

He was glad to get out of the car because all he could see for the whole journey, whenever he forgot and looked, was his own reflection in the rear-view mirror. He hated looking at himself.

"I'll call your mother when the time is right. If anybody contacts you, call me before you talk to them. Won't you?"

Jockey nodded, swinging the rough, grey post sack that Alex had given him to carry any belongings over his shoulder. He wasn't sure who would want to contact him but he nodded anyway.

The car sped away.

Jockey leaned against the high wall under the railway bridge for a few minutes to make his plans. Then he threw the sack over the wall and followed it, climbing on up the steep slope onto the gravel beside the railway tracks. It was exactly as it had been all those years ago when he used to walk home from school along the railway line. He'd sit and wait for the 2.30pm from Cork, on its way to Dublin, knowing that his father was at the controls of the locomotive. He'd wave to his dad as the train rounded Copp's Bend. Then his father would toot the horn three times and stick his head out the window and wave. Jockey was a hero at school. Having a father who drove the Cork to Dublin express meant the other kids didn't slag his hair-lip anymore. If only he had stayed with his mother, everything would've been OK. He was sure of that.

Jockey looked behind him. He must have walked nearly half a mile. The station seemed tiny. Passengers on the platform waiting for the 13.40 to Dublin looked like dots. The sun glistened on the shiny tracks. The sign in front of him made him shiver. COPP'S BEND. Just like old times. He threw the sack away onto the grass verge and stood silently, swaying back and forth on the huge wooden sleeper. Then he heard it, just like his father had taught him to listen for: the fizzle, as he called it. The 13.40 was on its way. Then a vibration in the sleeper. About a mile, no more. He looked to his right, down below, at the sleepy bungalow with the smokey chimney. His mother would be expecting him. Always lighting the fire, she was. Even in beautiful weather like this. He was sorry now that he had called her. Sorry to be coming back. She was too bossy. Aul' bitch. He remembered how she'd stand at the bottom of the back garden and shout up to him on the grassy slope: "Jockey Carr, get down off that railway track or I'll come up there with your father's trouser-strap." The other boys would snigger and say things behind his back while he shouted back down to her. She made a show of him. Aul' bitch.

Glancing back to his left, over his shoulder, the town centre. The Mallow cops hated him, gave him shit at every available opportunity. He remembered then it was one of the reasons he'd left.

The vibrations underfoot were stronger now. He could hear the rumble of the huge locomotive in the distance. He clawed back the mulchy gravel with the sides of his shoes and dug his feet in under sleepers. He wasn't sure why he was so excited. He pushed his Doc Martins in as far as he could until his toes ached. Then he bent down and gathered the gravel in around his heels until he felt the damp earth through his socks.

He estimated the train would come out of Copp's Bend at sixty-five miles per hour, a blind bend onto the straight, and then drop its speed on the final mile into the northbound platform of the station – its final stop before Dublin.

He checked his footing. Rigid. Immobile. Stuck. There was no way that the force of impact would throw him aside now; no way the driver would have even a fleeting chance to lift off the deadman's handle. The rumble started to boom, louder and louder. Why was it called the dead-man's handle? the other kids would often ask him after he had charged them all a three-penny bit each for the honour of climbing up onto the bank and getting a wave from his father. They could jeer him all they liked, but when it came to trains Jockey Carr was a mastermind.

Then it occurred to him that he must have looked like

a railway engineer to the people on the platform, in his orange luminous jacket. He waited now, wondering what it would be like to stare into the eyes of the terrified driver as he tried to stop the train. By the time their eyes would meet, he'd be less than a hundred feet away.

And in those few seconds, while he bathed in the warm sunshine from behind, he wondered why he had to be the one who ended up with such a shit deal out of life.

The train was a lot closer than he had first thought. The huge orange and brown locomotive's three-thousand-horse-power engine dragged its thirteen-carriage load screaming out of Copp's Bend.

Jockey smiled for a split second when he realised his father could see it was him. He tried to shout something at him. Jockey waved just as the horn blew for what seemed like forever.

Then everything went dark.

47

Twenty-four hours later, as the 13.40 express thundered by on the railway track close to the small bungalow, Jack Buckley politely accepted Rosie Carr's offer of brandy in his tea.

Something very strange had happened him earlier that day. The 09.00 Dublin to Cork had pulled into Mallow, as scheduled, at 11.05. It normally stopped for five minutes to pick up passengers travelling to Cork, who were coming from the Kerry stations that were served by the Tralee to Dublin express. That morning however the train was still sitting at Platform 2 twenty minutes after arriving in Mallow. Jack decided to stretch his legs. The platform attendant told him the news. He collected his bag from where he'd been sitting in the second carriage and headed for Rosie Carr's.

The clock on the wall ticked slowly as the whole world seemed to stand still. A couple of rays of late evening sunshine stretched across the floor to where the old dog lay on the mat. With every few minutes, Rosie would start repeating herself.

"I shouldn't have been so hard on him. If I'd only treated him like a real son he'd probably be still alive."

"How's your husband?"

"I hear they had to sedate him below at the infirmary. God love him, it must've been a horrible sight to come around that corner and see your only son standing there beneath your own train engine. And to drive over him, and there nothing in the whole wide world that God could do to prevent it. Still, that's what he gets for walkin' out on us and shackin' up with that little miserable whore all those years ago."

"Is that his?" Jack asked, pointing to a shabby, brown wallet sitting beside a watch and a pair of shoes on a ledge below the table under Rosie Carr's cup of tea.

Rosie nodded. "I gave him that for his sixteenth birthday. I'm surprised he hadn't lost it by now."

Jack picked it up slowly, careful to show respect as he unclipped it and opened it out. Everything appeared to be intact. A dog-eared photograph of his father, Jack presumed, standing in front of a locomotive. Another photo of Cindy Reilly, obviously taken in Hannon's pub. A picture of a young Jockey Carr sitting on a horse. A ten-pound note and a Miraculous Medal. A scrap of paper was wedged in between the silk lining in the wallet's back compartment. Jack unfolded it. It contained a message and some numbers scribbled in childish handwriting: *NLP286*

The first thing that came to mind was a car registration. Jack tried to figure out which county was denoted by the letters NLP. He had learned them all by heart as part of his police training. There was no county in the Irish republic represented by the letters NLP. Maybe it was a British registration.

A couple of lines further down the page was filled with numbers and letters. Mainly numbers.

TDS40031308722

It made no sense whatsoever. An international telephone number perhaps. "Do you mind if I take this with me, Rosie? I'd like to show it to someone."

The old woman just nodded, head bowed, and sighed. "He always wanted to be a postman when he was small. He loved calling to the old people, seeing if they needed messages from the shop. Why did he have to do it? Why couldn't he have talked to someone about it, whatever it was that was troubling him so much."

Jack patted her shoulder, kissed the crown of her scalp, and let himself out. As he folded the piece of paper carefully he noticed it, in Jockey's familiar childish scrawl. Four words written on the other side of the page: *An Apple a Day. Macroom Library.* And underneath, six digits that made Jack Buckley feel weak as he felt the blood rush from his head: *AKE No* 2.

No one paid much attention to the two young men working on Durrus's street-lights in the town centre that afternoon. The storm the week before had damaged two of the main lights and Jack Buckley had assured Freddie Nolan that the lights – in particular the one directly over the chemist shop and surgery – would be fixed before the holiday weekend and the start of the tourist season.

Aidan Kerr was on his way into Nolan's to buy batteries for his Dictaphone so that he could rehearse his holiday-weekend sermon for tomorrow night and listen back to it for any weak points. A mixture of common sense, fruitful wisdom, a sprinkling of comedy and a quick lash of theology always went down well with both tourists and locals alike. He was mulling over a funny story he'd heard on the television some weeks back that he felt would be ideal to open the Saturday evening sermon with when he realised just in the nick of time that he was about to walk under a ladder. He stopped and looked up. A young blonde man in white overalls was attaching something to the bulb on the inside of the huge lamp frame at the top of the pole. He looked down and stared at Aidan.

"Afternoon," Aidan shouted up the ladder. "Glad you were able to get them fixed before the busy weekend."

The blonde lad continued to stare down at the priest. He didn't answer, didn't alter his expression, just stared and chewed gum. Then Aidan noticed the other man, a darker, bearded, older one, sitting behind the steering wheel munching a cheese and ham roll. He stopped chewing when he saw Aidan and just stared, his jaw dropped low, his mouth – full of Kenny's smoked ham, four slices for a pound – wide open. Aidan felt uneasy. Ignorant arseholes, he muttered to himself and walked around the ladder and into Freddie Nolan's chemist.

"Afternoon to you, Father," Freddie said cheerfully.

"Howya, Freddie. There's one weird pair of electricians out there."

"You're telling me, Father. And they've parked their

van in the doctor's space. He's due back any minute for half-three surgery. He won't be too pleased. What can I do you for?"

"Give us two batteries that'll fit this thing." Aidan placed the Dictaphone on the counter.

Freddie picked it up and studied it. "What do you use this for, Father?"

"Practising my sermon for tomorrow night. Hard to believe that I still get nervous after all these years."

"How many Masses have you celebrated now, Father?"

"One-thousand-eight-hundred-and-seventy-three, Freddie!"

Freddie Nolan's mouth dropped open. "Merciful hour! Haven't you got a great memory."

Aidan Kerr roared laughing. "I'm only joking, Freddie. Sure I lost count within weeks." He took the batteries and handed over three pound coins.

"Forget it, Father. I like to think I'm contributing to a lovely homily at the summer Mass tomorrow night."

"That's decent of you, Freddie. Thanks. See you later." Aidan doffed his cap and turned, walking straight into the doctor as he stepped out of the shop. "Afternoon, Doctor."

The doctor ignored him and hurried past Freddie Nolan into the surgery. "Call me the minute the nurse, Maggie, gets here. I don't care if there's someone with me. Do you hear me?" He didn't wait for an answer, as he slammed the door behind him.

Jack Buckley spent an hour searching in the section marked, NUTRITION & HEALTH. Two rows of shelves, four deep. Eventually the softly spoken assistant asked him if she could help. Jack thought about what he was going to say for minute, studying the small page he'd taken away with him from Rosie Carr's. "I'm looking for a book."

She fluttered her eyes and smiled. "You've come to the right place."

"At least I think it's a book. I just don't know if I've got the right title."

She logged on to the computer. "Maybe I can help you. What title do you have?"

Jack looked down the page. "Eh, this might be it. *An Apple a Day*. Does that make sense?"

She typed in the title. "If we have it, it should be listed here." She waited for a result.

"Here it is!" she said pleasantly. "You're absolutely right. It is called *An Apple a Day*, compiled by Winifred Tomley. She's a child psychologist apparently. She compiled this series of short stories by authors. It's a children's story book, basically. You'll find it in the children's book section." She looked closely at Jack.

He'd started to blush now. "Children's section?"

"That's right. That's the name you gave me."

Jack decided to try a different angle. "Did you ever notice a tall guy in here, tossed, scraggy kind of hair, spoke with a bad stammer, sometimes hard to understand? His name was Jockey."

Her eyes lit up. "Jockey Carr? Yes! He used to come

in here most Saturday mornings for an hour, sometimes longer. He'd browse through some of the stands, maybe log on to the Internet if one of the computer terminals was free. He seemed quiet enough. Why do you ask?"

"He died tragically in an accident yesterday. This was in his wallet." Jack held up the scrap of paper with the scribbled book title written on the back. "Could I have a look at that book, please?"

"Sure. I'm sorry to hear that. Sit down over there and I'll see if I can find it for you."

Jack sat at the table closest to the window, the soft afternoon sunshine filling the small cubicle. Perhaps in the circumstances it was normal to feel bad, he told himself. Jockey brought his own fair share of trouble on himself. But realising now that he really was just a child at heart, Jack felt that he had betrayed the young lad, that he hadn't taken enough interest in his welfare. He was always ready to run him out of the town's pubs, and to warn him that he would lock him up if he caught him hanging around the local national schoolyard at playtime. Yet he was never prepared to think that maybe Jockey was just short of a few friends. Desperate to think that all he could find to do on a Saturday morning was to catch the bus, or hitch a lift, to Macroom and sit in the library for two hours reading kids' books.

"Here it is. Sorry it took so long to find. Someone must have misplaced it. It was on the wrong shelf." The young librarian placed the compendium of short bedtime stories in front of him. "Call me if you need me."

"Thanks." Jack gazed at the cover for a moment

without touching it. Then he opened it back. He took out the page and checked the numbers scribbled here and there. He looked down through the list of contents. Page 286. Out of curiosity, he ran his finger underneath, then back towards the name of the story. "Peter Postman," it was called. Jack was becoming more and more confused by the minute. He read the first few lines of "Peter Postman".

"Peter Postman lived in a small town in the country, Every day he delivered letters and parcels to small cottages and villages in his little red van. Sometimes he delivered meals to the sick and pensions to the old if the weather became too bad for them to make the journey themselves. Everyone loved Peter Postman. They were always happy when they heard him knocking on their door."

Jack yawned and shrugged, slamming the book shut. He walked back over to the counter and handed it to the librarian. "Thanks, but obviously it's the wrong book." He smiled and walked out into the warm, welcome sunshine, scratching his stubbly chin, more confused now than ever.

48

Maggie felt slightly uncomfortable. She drove slowly out past Kitchen Cove, sweeping to the right and up the steep hill, along the narrow, sand-swept road hugging the Kitchen Strand. Her passenger hadn't spoken once since she had collected him, at his urgent request, from his surgery. She could hear him telling Freddie Nolan to explain to his patients that he had to nip out for half-an-hour on an emergency. She couldn't understand what all the urgency was about. Harry Vogel's grazed forehead was healing nicely. She had been checking it herself on a daily basis. Then suddenly, at half-two that afternoon, she received a call from Josef Maister. He sounded upset, told her he would like to take a look at Vogel's wound. She agreed, mainly because the doctor wasn't taking no for an answer. She looked across at him again. He was deep in thought, his mind a million miles away. "I don't know what all this fuss is about. Harry Vogel is making a full recovery. You're wasting your time coming out here. You should be back looking after your surgery." She waited for him to say something.

Nothing. Not as much as an expression. He just stared ahead, clutching his medical bag on his lap.

The sun, sitting low in the sky, obscured her vision each time the road straightened, and began to irritate her. "Shit!" she shouted, flicking down the narrow sun-shield above her head. She looked to see if he was using his. He wasn't. Yet he didn't seem too bothered by the unbearable glare of the evening's sunshine.

"You prescribed Rohypnol to the old man." He didn't bother to look at her as he said it. She knew, by the tone of his voice, that he disapproved.

"He was suffering from bad insomnia. He hadn't been able to sleep for nights, he told me. He asked for something to help him relax after he hurt his head. He said the pain was unbearable."

"Well, now you have your answer. I simply want to make sure that he hasn't had any negative reaction to the drug. Personally I don't recommend anyone to take Rohypnol. It can cause blackouts and bouts of sleepwalking. That's not a good idea when you live on your own so close to the sea."

Maggie felt dumped, the same as she used to – years ago in college – when a lecturer would criticise her essay or her answers to questions. "Well, he seemed all right to me when I visited him yesterday." She decided that she would end the conversation. Who does he think he is? she asked herself. Here he was, not a wet day in Durrus and already walking on toes. She didn't look at him for the rest of the short journey, but could tell by his movements that he was getting increasingly more fidgety as they got nearer the cottage beside Verity graveyard. She pulled in onto the small patch of gravel directly outside the gate.

"We're here," she said, looking around curiously. Something was missing. Then she noticed what it was. The sign that had hung over the garden wall for a week now was gone. She waited for him to get out. He seemed reluctant to move. "What's wrong?"

He shook his head and opened the door slowly, stepping out into the warm sunshine and the distant sound of the sea, its waves crashing against the rocks, below Verity hill. He waited for her to lead the way.

Maggie hoped that Harry Vogel wouldn't be furious with her. "Under no circumstances, *no* doctor," he'd warned. She turned the key in the door. She gasped at the sight that greeted them. The room, only the night before furnished and cosy, was completely bare, stripped of everything except his old familiar armchair, and a small side table that might just accommodate a pot of tea and a plate of sandwiches.

"Harry!" She tried to call without appearing to shout or sound alarmed at the sudden emptiness of her favourite little house. There was no answer. She took Maister's arm and pulled him into the room behind her. *"Harry!"* This time she shouted.

The toilet flushed towards the back of the house and a soft voice answered. "I'll be there in a moment."

Harry Vogel walked through the kitchen casually, glancing down once at his trouser belt to make sure he had the buckle in its usual notch. He spoke cheerfully. "This is a nice surprise. I wasn't expecting you today." He looked up and froze, his voice continuing to echo around the hollow, wooden sitting-room for a second after he had stopped.

The distant waves below Verity Hill sounded much closer now that there were no material items and furnishings to insulate the dainty cottage. The fire wasn't lit. It was cold now, colder than Maggie had realised.

She watched her old friend grow paler and paler. He wasn't looking at her. He seemed hypnotised by the tall man who stood inside the door now.

"I didn't know you were bringing somebody to see me," Harry Vogel said, once again without looking at her.

Maggie tried to dissolve his concern. "This is the doctor I was telling you about, Harry. He arrived in Durrus a couple of days ago."

"I *told* you I didn't want to see a doctor." His reply was curt, almost ungracious.

Maister spoke before Maggie had a chance to introduce him by name. "I asked to see you. Maggie told me she administered Rohypnol for your insomnia. I don't personally like the drug so I wanted to see for myself that you were OK."

"Well, I am OK. Thank you." He spewed out the words angrily, antipathy heavy in the air, and nodded to the open door.

Maggie was visibly shocked. "Harry, what's wrong with you?" she asked, concerned that she had never witnessed him in such a nasty mood before. He was starting to shake now. He reached for his blackthorn stick and banged it on the hollow floorboards. "Leave this house now." Spittle rested on his chin and on his pullover.

Josef Maister remained calm throughout, never once reacting to the harshness of the confrontation. Then he smiled almost benevolently. "I've seen all I need to see." Then his expression changed. He looked stern and aggressive again, the way he'd looked during the car journey from Durrus. "Take me back to my patients." His order was delivered boldly. He backed towards the door, watching the old man as he fumed and fumbled. As he stepped through the door, the sun at his back stretched his shadow forward, creating an eerie silhouette, almost ghostlike, so that Maggie could no longer see the expression on his face. He continued to glare at Harry Vogel. "The old record-player gave you away."

Josef Maister walked back to the car and waited.

Maggie, confused and upset by his childish, cantankerous behaviour, as she saw it, was about to ask the old man if he would like a cup of tea.

He raised his walking stick and, with a desperate roar of bloodcurdling anger, smashed it down on the small, delicate-looking three-legged table, reducing it to rubble. "Why did you let him see it? It was for your eyes only!" he shouted. A small tear hung below the eyebrow under his right eye, as his lips quivered, head nodding helplessly.

Jack Buckley squatted uncomfortably next to the toilet bowl in the small cramped bathroom. He held the vodka bottle high enough, upside down, so that he could watch it emptying and hear the loud, splashing fizz of the alcohol as it started its journey into the sewers where it belonged. Each time a bottle emptied, he pressed down hard on the handle and shivered as he listened to the cistern emptying its load. I'm finished with you. I'm-finished-with-you. I'm – finished – with – you, he kept repeating, in different tones, in different mock voices, over and over again – sometimes shouting, sometimes speaking softly – as if he was talking angrily to a real person: someone he'd known all of his life – someone who'd been his best friend through good times and bad – telling them now, categorically, unequivocally, that the relationship was over. They were bad news. The trust and the love were gone. So were they. They were not going to feature in his life again. Then he did the same again, this time with the Scotch, watching the water in the toilet turn golden-orange in colour, imbibing the rich smell of the twelve-year-old malt, then flushing, and watching for three seconds as the water turned clear again. The cistern refilled and the toilet turned quiet again waiting for its next dispatch. Red wine. Maggie's red wine. Jack didn't care. It was still alcohol. And he would drink anything if he was forced to. Port. Brandy. White wine. Sparkling wine. Tack. All of it, just tack. He knew Maggie wouldn't mind. Jack reckoned she might, in contrast, be quite proud of her man. She would arrive in from work that evening to witness a new page being turned. He'd go back to the gym at the Westlodge in Bantry the following morning. He'd stay in and watch television with her, highlighting the programmes on the television page that he knew she would like to watch. She'd like that. And then he had the ring.

He looked up at the windowsill. It was still in its box, open and sitting proudly, reflecting the soft evening sunshine in its cluster of five diamonds. "Will you marry me?" He grinned. Suddenly the absence of alcohol wasn't so hard to take. He was going to ask his long-suffering girlfriend to marry him. She'd probably faint. Then they'd celebrate with a toast. *Shit!* he shouted into the pot as the last dregs of a bottle of Harvey's Bristol Cream turned the water creamy-brown. Then he resolved the dilemma. He'd go one further and show Maggie that he was serious about giving up the booze. He'd let her raise a glass of champagne, while he clinked her glass with a Britvic orange juice. It didn't seem so hard, once he dwelled on honeymoons and holidays, and on how much better their love life would be. For a change he might even be able to impress her for the first time in years with a decent hard erection.

Alcohol. His secret friend and his silent enemy. *Good luck!* he shouted as he pressed down sharply, with all his strength on the handle, and listened to the cistern empty the last drop of alcohol he could lay his hands on into the gutter.

The doorbell rang. *Jesus!* he shouted with a mixture of nervous energy and excitement and expectation. He stood up and tossed the last bottle into the green refuse sack, knotting the top of it as quickly as he could. *"Coming!"* he called excitedly, at the top of his voice, trying to imagine what her reaction would be when he popped the question and produced the ring. She was early. She told him before he left for Dublin that she wouldn't be home before seven that Friday evening. He arrived back in Cork at three, called into the jeweller's and had the ring picked out and paid for in ten minutes.

He rushed through the kitchen, checked to make sure

everything was suitably tidy. Don't give her a chance to criticise. Sweep her off her feet. Watch her jaw hit the floor. Get the most affectionate hug in history. Live happily ever after. It seemed a bit daft. But for the first time in his life he wanted it – needed it – to happen.

He opened the door, about to smother her in kisses.

The blonde-haired man and his bearded companion seemed puzzled, almost nervous, by his obvious enthusiasm.

Jack paused, stopped smiling and apologised. "I was expecting someone else." He looked more closely now at the two men. Tourists, obviously. Friday evening before the holiday weekend and the rush, no doubt, had started. He'd stroll up the town tonight, maybe take the patrol car to let the visitors know who he was, and see the hundreds of foreign registrations and strange faces walking leisurely, finding their bearings. A holiday weekend without booze, he reminded himself. Yep! So far so good. "What can I do for you?" he asked pleasantly, expecting one of them to produce a map from his haversack and ask directions to the pub, or, if they were genuine tourists, directions to one of the old fort mounds out towards Toormore, or Coosbrack.

"We're from the electricity board," the blonde one explained monotonously.

The phone rang.

"Hang on there for a minute." Jack pushed the door over and ran back to answer it. "Hello."

"Jack, thank God you're back." It was Maggie, her voice filled with urgency. "Can you meet me in the doctor's surgery immediately?"

Jack thought for a moment. The two men from the electricity were still waiting at the door. "Yeah, I'll be over in five minutes." He put the phone down and returned to the front door. "You fellas come on in. I'm gonna have to rush out for a while. Someone in the town needs to see me urgently. Will you be all right working away on your own?"

The two men glanced at each other and nodded. "No problem," said the bearded one. He spoke, Jack thought, with a northern accent. Donegal maybe. "If you need me, here's my mobile number." He scribbled the digits on the back of an old bar-food menu he'd picked up in Hannon's and gave it to the bearded one. The blonde man had already started to check appliances. "Just pull the door behind you when you're finished. All right?" Neither of them bothered to answer him. Jack assumed they were keen to finish as quickly as possible and get away early for the holiday weekend. Then something occurred to him. "Who told you to call here?" he asked.

The blonde man turned around to face him. He put his left hand in his overalls pocket as if looking for official identification, or maybe a calling card. "We're checking all of the older houses in the area following the storm last week. Some of the houses are still without electricity. We think there might be some sort of intermittent fault that's preventing the power from being fully restored to the whole town. We've installed a new transformer above at the power station beyond the Cove. We want to make sure the wiring is OK."

Jack watched him, listening to his most bizarre accent. He was completely unfamiliar with it. He must be from the continent. Then he noticed how blonde his hair was. Not bleached, but bright, bright blonde and perfectly set in what was once a crew cut. The hand that remained free was as big as a shovel. He was tall and broad, his arms packed with lean muscle, like someone he was reminded of years ago, someone sent to train a new bunch of army cadets. "Have you fixed the street-lights that were out?"

The blonde man nodded. "They are all functioning properly."

"Great. We're expecting a lot of strangers in town this weekend. No point them all wandering around in the dark." Jack nodded, tapping the front-door window. "Just pull it closed when you're leaving if I'm not back."

49

Aidan Kerr reckoned that an extra hundred chairs should do it.

He'd borrowed them from the National School, offering to collect them at half three as soon as school business was complete, and the teachers had left for the holiday weekend. He was sorry now that he had offered to collect them. He'd lifted eighteen stacks of five and his back and shoulders were killing him. Still it would be worth it, he kept reminding himself. Mass on the Saturday of the holiday weekend was his favourite ceremony of the year. The church was always thronged. The local school choir sang. And, for a change, he got to speak to a bunch of strangers who were visibly enjoying themselves because they were on their holidays.

Aidan had had the daft notion a few weeks earlier of having the Mass late on the Saturday night. "How late?" Jack Buckley had asked him.

"Ten o'clock," Aidan suggested, knowing that he had already decided that it would be at ten. Jack mulled over the notion for a day or so and agreed to it. It would be advertised as a family occasion. At least it meant that the pubs in Durrus would remain quiet till half past ten. That was the sergeant's thinking.

Aidan had made sure to cycle around the caravan sites and the seven bed and breakfasts, and the six self-catering areas, and on into O'Sullivan's, and The Long Boat, and Ivo's, and Suzanne's, and Blair's Cove restaurant and the Bay View, and one or two other eating-houses, and finally on out to Sheep's Head Café, which had just opened for the season that very afternoon, to remind their patrons that this was an ecumenical service with a difference. Bring the family. Martha Hannon described to a small group of Dublin visitors drinking in her pub that afternoon her outrage when she saw the posters, advertising a raffle with free entry for each family in attendance at church that evening. The prize was a mountain bike. The cartoon depicted Moses cycling down the side of Mount Ararat on a mountain bike, carrying the tablets of stone bearing the Ten Commandments, strapped to the crossbar.

Aidan stood at the altar and admired the view: rows and rows of empty seats, bathed in warm June holiday sunshine, smelling of varnish and detergent. The weather forecast was promising. Bed and breakfasts were booked out solidly for weeks in advance and, already, he could hear the traffic building on the street outside as the tourists arrived for his favourite weekend of the year. He smiled and shivered in anticipation of what the next forty-eight hours might bring, and the memories he would be left with to talk about in Hannon's during the cold, winter months long after the tourists had packed up and gone home.

Maggie rang once on the doorbell and stepped back from the door. She hoped Cindy Reilly might answer, so that she would have an opportunity to talk to her again for a few minutes. She'd discussed their conversation earlier that day with the doctor. He suggested that she should urge Cindy to go to the police.

Maggie could detect a blurred shape through the opaque glass window approaching the hall door. The door opened. A small rotund man with a red nose and strands of black hair greased across the centre of his head, from left to right, stood looking at her. She was about to introduce herself.

"What d'ye want?" he shouted.

Maggie stood speechless for a moment. "Mr Reilly, I'd like to speak to Cindy, if that's all right."

He sneered at her. "It's not all right. She's making my dinner. Then she's getting a lift into Cork to visit her aunt for the weekend. She's goin' away for a few days." He went to close the door.

Then Maggie did something she would never have had the courage to even contemplate before. She stepped forward, up one step, and jammed her foot into the closing door. It opened again. "You're not welcome here, ye nosey bitch," Tom Reilly snapped. "Your sort is only good for causin' trouble."

"I'm not here to see you, I'm here to see your daughter." Maggie watched in disbelief as Cindy Reilly came down the last few steps of the stairs, behind her father, and gently pushed him aside. Her cheek was swollen and badly bruised. She had a small cut below her right eye which was squeezed shut. She said nothing, nodding to her father and signalling to him that she wanted him to go inside. She stepped out through the porch and walked away from the door, as if she didn't want him to hear what she was about to say.

Maggie was stunned. "What happened you?" she asked softly.

"I slipped this morning. It's nothing. It looks a lot worse than it is." Her eyes filled with tears as she checked to make sure he wasn't listening at the door. Her breathing trembled as she bit her lower lip.

"He did that, didn't he?" Maggie tried to hide her anger. She couldn't. *"Bastard!"*

"Look, I've got to go back inside. I have to make him his dinner." Cindy started to move slowly back towards the door. "I won't be talking to the police like I said I might yesterday."

"Why?"

"Because I don't want to."

"But, Cindy, you said you wanted to see these men in jail. If you don't make a statement they all just get away with it. If you saw them chasing those three boys you have to go to the police and tell them. Jack will be home shortly. I can arrange for the two of you to have a confidential chat. No one will know that you said anything. I swear. Just tell him what you told me yesterday. *Please?"*

Cindy shook her head. "No!" Adamant.

"Why did he hit you?"

"Because he came in drunk last night and I didn't have any cheese in the fridge for his supper. So he dragged me out of bed and kicked me. Then he pushed me down the stairs."

"And the baby. You'll have to get yourself checked out if he pushed you downstairs, Cindy. I'll give you a lift in now. The doctor's still there, and Jack is meeting him so you can tell them both what you told me. Will you?"

Cindy started to cry, in soft breathy gulps, the tears streaming down her face. She turned her back to the house. "I . . . lost the baby this morning. Half five. I didn't feel well. The pains kept getting worse all the time. I sat on the toilet and started to bleed."

Maggie put her arms around the young girl and hugged her, kissing her head and reassuring her that she was going to be all right. But she knew deep down that she wasn't going to be all right. Maggie glanced up above Cindy's head, to the curtain that had just moved in the front bedroom window. Tom Reilly was watching, cursing her she was sure. *"Please, come with me now,"* Maggie begged in whispers. *"You'll be safe, I promise you I'll look after you. You can stay with me, in our house! He won't be able to touch you. He'll never lay another finger on you, I'll make sure of that . . . "*

Cindy didn't wait for Maggie to finish. It was as if she could feel her father's piercing eyes from the window above her. She stepped back, wiping her eyes, and smiled. Then she went inside to make her father his dinner, like she did every evening after school, and shut the door behind her.

50

The ad looked like any other. It appeared in the Evening Echo that Friday afternoon.

UNBEATABLE VALUE – TWO SEATS TO TENERIFE

Seats only. Owner unable to travel due to sudden business commitment. Travel outbound from Dublin this Sunday. Great value. Call tonight, after 6. Durrus, Cork 027 343622.

Alex Kline had collected the neat brown envelope containing a brand-new passport in the name of Henry Myler, and two tickets to Tenerife, flight number IB3559, departing Dublin on Sunday afternoon, from the concierge's desk of the Shelbourne Hotel. Donald Eckler had been talking by phone to his people back in Frankfurt well into the early hours. He called Alex and asked him to join him in his room. Alex put on a hotel dressing-gown and hurried across to room 264. It was a beautiful foolproof plan, Eckler gushed, complimenting himself on his own astute brilliance. He sipped the most expensive brandy and smoked the biggest cigar that room service could provide and talked. And talked more.

"Every special branch detective and customs officer

will be on the look out for this man called Henry Myler on Sunday afternoon, Alex. You know that, don't you?" Eckler chortled and spat out a thread of tobacco.

"How do you know?"

"Because that pathetic little man who calls himself a prime minister doesn't have a leg to stand on. He should have known ten years ago, when he agreed to this deal, that something like this would inevitably happen. And now that it has, he's afraid that his perfect little corrupt world, that no one in the entire country knows about other than that other rotten little vermin, Harrisson, is going to fall apart at the seams. So what does he do?"

"What?"

"He prepares a passport for our man and provides two tickets to get him out of the country as quickly as he can. But then does a U-turn and decides to stake out the airport on Sunday and wait for Henry Myler to come along with his new passport, heading off to his new life in the sun. A detective walks up to him, slaps a pair of handcuffs on him and arrests him. They throw him in custody for a few days until they can figure out what to charge him with, and – what do you know – the country hails Joe Russell as an even bigger hero than he already is, according to the headline on the front page of *The Irish Times* this morning. He tapped his cigar on the photograph of Joe Russell, under the headline: RUSSELL REIGNS SUPREME.

"Isn't that putting our whole operation at risk?"

Eckler tutted at the crass stupidity that Alex Kline was demonstrating. "Do you really take me for a complete idiot, Kline? Do you really think I spent ten hard, lonely years in the French Foreign Legion to end up handing myself over to the international authorities? You must be mad, Kline."

"So why did you demand a new passport."

"Decoy. You will ring the *Evening Echo* first thing this morning, as soon as the offices open. Quote the ITS VISA card number and tell them you need to put an ad in their classified column this afternoon. Stress you want the early edition. Here's how the ad is to be worded. I've arranged for the passport to be processed overnight tonight. It's the least that Joe Russell can do for us. It'll be ready for collection at ten tomorrow morning." He handed the wording for the classified advertisement to Kline. "Read that properly. Offer the tickets for fifty quid each. You'll have the phone lines reaching meltdown. Let's be honest, who's going to turn down an opportunity of two weeks in the sun for a hundred quid?" He laughed.

"What happens then?"

"All you've got to do is sit by your phone until you get a buyer. I don't think you'll have to sit there for long. Then we just carry on with our original plan. The Keeper leaves the country while the keystone cops arrest and question a couple of innocent sunseekers who were minding their own business and saw an ad in the paper."

Alex Kline stood up and cheered. He crossed the room and shook Don Eckler's hand.

"A brandy to toast our good fortune," Eckler suggested.

"I don't normally, at least not this late, but tonight I'm going to break out," Kline replied, grinning like a Chesire cat.

Alex Kline sat watching *Nationwide*, wondering if the small holiday weekend festival that the town's committee had organised for the influx of the first of that summer's tourists would get a mention. It did. He wallowed in the familiar sites and streets around Durrus, broadcast tonight for all to see on national television. He sighed and stretched out across the long settee. He was quietly looking forward to a restful weekend. No work on Monday. Plenty of prospective buyers to show around the numerous properties for sale over the coming weeks as they all settled into their caravans and holiday homes. And now he had sold another property. The cottage hadn't taken long to sell. Soon he could relax, the past banished, and no fears of the authorities, or the locals, ever finding out who had been occupying the cottage until now.

The time had come to wash his hands of it all, thank God. He wouldn't have to look after their money any longer, even though they paid him well to say nothing. All he asked for now was an easy life. A spot of fishing, shooting on a Sunday morning, and his favourite stool at The Long Boat on a Saturday night.

He checked the time. It had taken him only four hours to get back from Dublin, and that was in heavy traffic. He estimated he had taken over fifty calls with offers to buy the tickets. He sold them to the man from Bantry who'd offered him three hundred pounds. *Three hundred!* He couldn't believe his luck. What a nice little earner for just sitting beside the phone. The buyer's name was Manning. He said he'd drop by around seven to collect them. It was just after half seven when the doorbell rang. Alex Kline decided to let Ethel answer it.

She poked her head in the door. "It's the man about the tickets."

Alex stood up and stepped into his slippers. He pulled up his tie-knot and checked his hair in the mirror over the mantelpiece. He pretended to be singing a song as he stepped out into the hall and opened back the door. The man seemed well-dressed, as if he was on his way to something more important. "Mr Manning?" Alex asked pleasantly.

"Andrew's the name. And you're?" He extended his hand and smiled.

"Alex. It's not really important. I'm literally just doing this as a favour for a client of mine. He was meant to be heading out to Tenerife on Sunday. But he got a call this morning saying he was needed on important business in New Jersey. So that's where he's going to be for a few days. It'd be a terrible shame to let them go to waste."

"I see." Andrew Manning took a wallet out of his pocket. "Cash?"

Alex Kline beamed. "Fine."

"Three hundred?"

"That's what we agreed on." Alex held the white envelope and watched him count out the money in twenties.

"Two-sixty, two-eighty, . . . three hundred." He handed the bundle of purple-coloured tender across and took the envelope with his other hand. "Thank you *very* much, Mr Kline."

Alex grinned as his eyes poured over the tender. Then

it occurred to him that the man had called him Mr Kline. "How did you know my name?"

The man who had just purchased the airline tickets stiffened, opened his jacket and took out a small wallet from a lower, more inconspicuous pocket. He presented Alex with a small laminated identification card. "My name is Detective Sergeant Andrew Manning, Mr Kline. I'm head of the Fraud Squad with overall responsibility for Cork city and county. I'm placing you under arrest on suspicion of receiving and trying to sell stolen goods. You have the right to remain silent. But I would like to remind you that anything you might wish to say will be taken down and may be used against you as evidence in a court of law."

Alex Kline felt as if he was falling backwards, fainting, feeling colder and colder. He tried to say something, to tell him that he was making a mistake, that he was talking to a highly respected Justice of the Peace. He was about to say it but then his words became frozen, put on ice, by the sensation of cold steel clicking tightly around warm flesh. He had been handcuffed. The humiliation. There were two others in suits waiting for him outside. He sat into the back seat of the Mondeo and moved right over to the right to let the man he was handcuffed to slide in beside him. One of the others slammed the door.

The car sped down the drive. He turned around, craning his neck, to see his wife and children standing motionless in the porch. Not even a wave, he thought. But then he stopped thinking about his family and turned his thoughts to what had just happened. Eckler, he whispered, you bastard!

51

The two men worked gingerly.

Each knew exactly what he had to do, but was, at all times, aware of how equally crucial the other's input was in ensuring the overall success of the operation. One per cent error meant total failure. The old record-player was almost ready to put back on the sideboard. It was imperative that nothing was out of place. A small film of dust was to be left untouched. No fingerprints – nothing that might compromise.

The bearded man checked his watch. "7.15," he muttered in a weary voice. "We're here too long. We must leave now. What if someone comes back and asks us why we're still here?"

The blonde man tried not to get annoyed by the older man's impetuosity. He needed to remain calm and level-headed. He was almost finished. "Five more minutes."

"You said that half an hour ago."

The blonde man stalled. "Shut up, or I might just blow the two of us up."

The bearded man scratched his chin as he looked over

his colleague's shoulder at the mass of coloured wire. "Are you sure you know what you're doing?"

The blonde man looked up indignantly. Then he realised the question was intended to be a joke. It lightened an otherwise sombre effort. He held his breath and used the pliers to draw the exposed copper wire from a red cable through a tiny hole at the end of a short thin metal strip, a blade from a man's disposable shaver. He secured the wire in place by knotting it around the thin blade twice. Gently, he squeezed the free end of the blade in between the old rusty spring that kept the turntable buoyant, directly below the centre spindle of the player. He repeated the process with a blue cable, easing the second blade into the coil of the spring, a mere fraction of a centimetre below the blade attached to the red cable. Finally, with breathtaking accuracy he replaced the spring mechanism which, when started, released the old vinyl LPs, allowing them to drop down onto the turntable. "Now it's time to see if it works."

He placed the turntable back in position, partially raised, thus causing it to drop harder, to ensure the device would be effective. He placed an old John McCormack LP onto the stacker, locked it in place, took a deep breath and pressed the button marked *play*. "Watch what happens here," he instructed his colleague. "The LP will drop down onto the turntable. Watch what happens to the two small metal strips when the weight on the turntable increases."

They both waited. The blonde man checked to make sure the bearded man could clearly see what was happening.

The bearded man's eyes opened wide. "When the LP drops onto the turntable, the increased weight caused by the longer drop makes the tips of the metal strips touch together."

The blonde man smiled, rewarding his student with a pinch on the cheek. "Next time they touch, the red and blue wires will be connected to the explosive. When they touch they will complete the bomb's circuit. And this place will just be a green field with a big deep hole in the middle of it."

He completed the job by separating the two metal strips again, positioning them so as to create a centimetre's space between them. Then, daintily, as if putting the finishing touches to the icing on a four-tier wedding cake, he attached the red and the blue to the detonator, clicked the switch so that a small red light started to flash, and, warily, lowered the mahogany casing down over the record-player's ancient electrical equipment.

52

Jack Buckley stepped into the surgery.

The doctor stared up at him from behind the desk. For a split second Jack thought he was dreaming. He gaped at the man who refused to take his eyes off him despite the heated conversation he was engrossed in on the phone. "What do you mean he's gone away for the weekend? He's expecting an urgent call from me. He told me he would make himself available no matter what hour of the day it was." Jack listened to the distant tone of what seemed like a manic voice on the far end. The doctor continued to stare, his eyes wide open, cold and filled with fear and anxiety. "Jesus Christ, man, get him on the phone *now*! Do you hear me? We could all be dead tomorrow." He slammed down the phone and rested his head on the desk. "I don't believe this is happening," he said.

"Would somebody mind telling me what's going on around here?" Jack tried to inject an air of authority into his question.

The man looked up, weary and spent. "What would you like me to tell you?"

"Who you are for a start. You're not a doctor. What are you doing here? What do you want from us?"

The man sat back in the wooden armchair and twiddled his thumbs. "That's three questions, Sergeant."

"Cut out the bullshit, or I'll arrest you."

The old man laughed hysterically. "Arrest me? Oh, yes, please. *Please!* Arrest me, sergeant. Lock me up in the cells for the night. That way I might be safe." He laughed some more and then stopped and closed his eyes, tilting his head back and rubbing his right shoulder. "Let me answer all three of your questions. Then I'm sure you'll have three more to ask. And three more after that. My name is Josef Maister. I am a medical practitioner, a psychiatrist actually, by trade. For the past almost twenty years I haven't done much medicine. Instead I've devoted my time to looking for a number of men. Three in all. Recently, almost two years ago, I discovered that two of them were dead. One of them was knocked down by car driven by a drunken driver as he left a rather expensive restaurant in Acapulco, in Mexico. No one was ever arrested for the hit-and-run incident. The other man died screaming in a Cape Town hospital in South Africa. He had stomach cancer. This afternoon I found the third man." He eased the chair back onto its hind legs and started a swinging motion.

"Are you some sort of private detective?"

"No. I told you what I am. Let me ask you a question. If you discovered that your mother and father and your older brother had been murdered, and you found out the identity of the man responsible for killing them, you would track him down, wouldn't you?"

Jack Buckley nodded unreservedly. "Naturally."

"Well, sergeant, that's what I started to do twenty years ago. What I've wanted to do for a lot longer. But I knew I couldn't just walk out on my family. So I worked hard and saved the good money I earned from my medical position and invested it and bought a nice house. And when I was sure they were well cared for, I set out on, what I can only describe as being, a very lonely road."

"This man – did he murder your family?"

"I have no doubt in my mind whatsoever that – yes – he murdered my family." He took something out of the drawer. It was a crumpled photograph. He tossed it onto the table without losing his balance on the chair. "Where did you get this?"

Jack stepped forward and picked it up. It was one of the photographs the woman from CAB had shown him the night she called herself Heather Lohan. "The woman who pretended to be that young reporter's sister showed it to me. She was here a couple of weeks ago, asking me to look into her brother's death."

"I've already told you Nathan was an only child."

"I *know* that. It turns out now that her name is Kate Doheny. She works for the Criminal Assets Bureau. They're investigating misappropriation of funds – huge amounts of money – at the Girundbach company in Shannon Development. Seemingly hundreds of thousands."

"I know all about Girundbach, sergeant. If I were to

tell you exactly what's been going on at Girundbach, you wouldn't believe me."

"Such as?"

"The reason Girundbach came to Ireland was because they did a deal with a number of government personnel."

"Tax incentives?"

"My arse, tax incentives!" Maister threw his head back and laughed loud. "Ten years ago, the directors of Girundbach set the ball rolling to get a number of German citizens out of Germany. These men were wanted for . . . crimes against humanity. I think that's the expression they use these days. Girundbach was established back in 1955 by three men who, rumour had it, financed the birth of the huge tyre-manufacturing company with money that had been stolen from the Jews, between 1938 and 1942, and hidden in a Zurich bank account. Almost twenty million pounds is the figure that my people believe was in that account. That's nearly fifty years ago. Can you imagine what twenty million is worth today? Probably billions, sergeant. What happened shortly before the Girundbach company was conceived is confusing. My sources eventually discovered how these three men ended up together. They were all members of the French Foreign Legion."

"But that doesn't make them criminals."

"Of course not. What if, though, they were all criminals before they joined the ranks of the Legion? Back in those days, I'm not sure about now, anyone could join the Foreign Legion if they were crazy enough. Go into any French police station, pick up an application form, fill it in and send it off. A couple of months later you touch down in Corsica and join up. It was a safety-net for them. One thing you are never asked about when you apply to join the Legion is your past. You could have a criminal record the length of your arm and suddenly, one week later, you're a soldier."

"And had they?"

"What?"

"Criminal records."

"Yes."

"Who were they?"

"SS Captain Franz Stangl, Commandant at Treblinka concentration camp. Stangl perfected the art of pumping carbon monoxide through pipes into the gas chambers. By October 1942, Stangl was boasting publicly about how it was possible to kill between 12,000 and 15,000 people a day. He was knocked down in Mexico."

Jack pulled across a chair and sat down. The doctor appeared not to even notice.

"Second was Hermann Dolp, a commandant at Belzec. He died of cancer."

Jack noticed how the old man was finding it increasingly more difficult to describe the threesome. "And . . . the third?"

Maister sighed. "Yes, the third. His name is Heinrich Vogelmann, next in command to Kurt Gerstein, the chief of the Waffen-SS Technical Disinfections Services. One of his jobs was to co-ordinate the disinfection of large piles of clothing coming from the victims of the death camps. Later Vogelmann was transferred to

Belsen, where he systematically lined up the prisoners and made them walk to their deaths. He might beat them, occasionally whip some of the naked women. One survivor told me how he would never forget Vogelmann's genial smile and how he always joked with the other Germans. He was a master of deceit, even among his own people. He seemed to love his work. And it paid off. Most of the top members of the SS paid tribute to him, often visited his camps and spent time chatting with him."

"Did he kill your family?"

Maister smiled sympathetically. "Thank you, Jack, for putting it like that. That's precisely what Vogelmann did. He murdered my family: my mother, my father and my older brother." Maister nodded to the photograph Jack was putting back on the table. "That's Heinrich Vogelmann. Rank: Technical Disinfections Systems. Army number, 40031308722."

Out of morbid curiosity, Jack took out the scrap of paper that he'd been checking in the library that afternoon. He shuddered with the pure shock as he checked back through the eleven numbers. He placed the piece of paper on the desk in front of Maister. "What were those numbers again?" he asked as he slid the page under his nose.

Maister's eyes flitted back and forth a couple of times. "Where did you get this?"

"In the wallet of a young boy who threw himself in front of a train yesterday."

"Who?"

"You wouldn't have known him. Jockey Carr was his

name. Young kid, lived rough. Had a lot of problems. I think it was the company he kept."

Jack's mobile phone started to ring. He pressed *receive*. "Yes?"

"Jack, this is Kate Doheny. About the weekly withdrawals from the bank in Durrus?" Her voice was lit with fiery excitement.

"Yes?"

"It was withdrawn every Friday by a Jockey Carr."

"Jockey Carr? What the fuck would he be withdrawing from an account that's got three-quarters-of-a-million quid in it for?"

"Because there was a message on the computer file from the manager of the bank instructing the teller to debit the account by that amount every Friday and hand the amount to Jockey Carr. He then acted as a sort of messenger by lodging it in an account in Durrus post office. Jack. *Jack!* Hello . . . "

All Jack could think was the story from the library book about Peter Postman. "Hello . . . I'm still here. What was the name of the post office account?"

"Hang on . . . "

Jack could hear pages rustling frantically at the far end, a number of voices muttering to each other feverishly.

"Here it is. The account is held in the name of . . . Vogel. A Harry Vogel."

Jack forgot to say goodbye. He pressed end and slumped down into the chair.

"I could have told you that for nothing, Jack. Saved you all the extra work. Girundbach paid millions to persuade a number of top government officials here to give Vogelmann an Irish passport and a complete new identity. His problem was he was a cocky old bastard. Never thought he'd be caught. Even dared to live under the noses of the German authorities for years after a file on him was sent to their Director of Public Prosecutions. He joined the Foreign Legion in 1955 with his two comrades. Managed to stick it out for ten years. In 1965 he went to Argentina. Couldn't stick the heat or the food. Missed Europe. Missed the company of 'real' people as he called them. All the time a small group of people were managing to keep him out of the hands of the authorities and, more importantly, the press. They would have had a field day. They were known as the Klavern. It's an old American mid-west folklore expression favoured by the Ku Klux Klan to describe one of their small active service units. No one understands the word, so no one asks any questions. Anyway, Vogelmann told them that if they didn't find him another more acceptable home base then he would take his chances and head home to Germany, where now he wouldn't stand a hope in hell of getting away with the crimes he had committed."

"So how did he end up in Ireland?"

"The leader of the Klavern – Donald Klaus Eckler is his name – approached a member of the Catholic hierarchy here in Ireland back in the late sixties. You must remember that the Nazis had many sympathisers in the ranks of the Catholic Church. The Archbishop at that time was a loyal supporter of a man called Lefebvre, the former Archbishop of Dakar. He claimed that Rome was no longer the true church because they had abandoned the Latin Mass and introduced the changes that followed Vatican II. In many ways they sympathised with the plight of the Nazis who were on the run from the law. So many of Lefebvre's supporters helped them to hide. However it wasn't that simple. You couldn't just be seen to be offering asylum to a man who was involved in the murder of 600,000 innocent people. So the priest involved went away and had a chat with his brother who was a big shot at the Department of Foreign Affairs back then. He told the Minister about the offer that was on the table. Not surprisingly, the man in question organised quite a handsome deal, turning himself and his secretary, and the priest, into very wealthy individuals. One of the conditions that Vogelmann was granted secret asylum and citizenship was that Girundbach relocated to Ireland. At first Eckler thought this was some sort of political joke. He laughed it off, telling the minister involved to 'get a life'. Then he realised it was anything but a joke. He had no choice but to agree to the demand since – and once again we're back to the realms of conjecture – Vogelmann's money, or at least the money he had robbed from the Jews, was used to finance Girundbach."

"So how long has he been living under my nose?"

"Many years. Before that he spent some time in France. He couldn't stay there long though. In fact he can't really stay anywhere too long these days. I often wonder if he'd prefer to lie down and die now. Because he knows I'm only an arm's length behind him."

"Does he have any children?"

"No. There was always some suspicion as to the pureness of his background. Hitler hated anything other than pure Aryan qualities. Blonde hair, soft milky skin, broad features, rugged good looks. Unfortunate for Vogelmann, he was lacking in one or two of these departments. Questions were asked when he applied to join the SS. Investigations were carried out and one source suspected that his grandmother might have been Jewish. The only condition that he was allowed to join the ranks of the SS was if he agreed to undergo a vasectomy. He did. So he couldn't have any children, could he?"

"Where is he now?"

"He's in a small cottage beside the rundown graveyard on the road out to Doo Lough. Your partner took me out there today. I told her I needed to examine a gash on his head. Seemingly he fell and hurt himself while drunk some nights back."

"Does he know who you are?"

Maister felt he could afford to smile now. "Oh yes, Vogelmann knows who I am. I tried to nail him down in France, I was too late. I tried to catch him on his way back from Argentina, as he went through Kennedy in New York. He managed to shake me off there too. But not here. He knows I'm here now. He knows he can't run anymore."

"So why are you sitting here? Why don't you go up to the cottage and arrest him?"

Maister sighed. "I thought earlier I could have done just that. After I left him, I came back here to make a phone call to my people in Austria. I am part of an international organisation based in Vienna. I needed to confirm a number of things with them, then let them inform the German authorities who have been searching for Heinrich Vogelmann ever since he left Argentina. Normally the German authorities would get on to their Irish counterparts and organise back-up for me."

"Well, I can help you."

"Thank you, Jack, I hope you can. But I fear it's not going to be that straightforward unfortunately. I got back here for my surgery session today at half three and came face to face with a man I wasn't expecting to see here in Ireland. A man called Bruno Proctor. He is a former head of Badaar Meinhoff, and one of the deadliest terrorists it's been my displeasure to ever meet. He has been sent here to get Vogelmann out of the country alive. Believe me he will stop at nothing to ensure he succeeds."

"This man, Proctor, are you telling me he's here in Durrus?"

Maister laughed synically. "*Here?* He's masquerading as an electrician, fixing street lights and checking electricity supplies."

Jack stood up, fear creeping through him. "Describe him?"

"Blonde hair. Like I say, as Aryan as they come."

"I left him checking the electricity at my place before I came over here to see you. Quick!" Jack picked up the mobile phone.

"Who are you calling?"

"Bantry police."

"What are you going to tell them? That there's a Nazi hiding in Durrus, and that the man fixing the street-lights is here to pick him up?"

Jack stopped dialling. The likeliness of the duty sergeant in Bantry believing the story, or acting on it, on the eve of the busiest holiday weekend of the year seemed remote, now that he considered it. He pressed *end* and sat down.

"Maybe now you can appreciate the dilemma we have on our hands."

"Why is he checking the electricity?"

"I dread to think. But you say you left him behind in your house this evening?"

Jack nodded. "There were two of them. The other man had a beard. I think his name was Ali. Why?"

"They're preparing to lift Vogelmann. I don't know how they're going to do it. My people will notify the authorities, airport security, ferry terminals. Anywhere he might squeeze through."

"Why now?"

"Why not. The busiest weekend of the year, Jack. It's the June bank holiday. More strangers in three days than you'll get all year. No one will notice him leaving."

"Will he leave?"

"I reckon he'll try. I'm going to try and arrest him tomorrow morning. He collects his pension, as he calls it, from the post office every Saturday morning at eleven. He normally gets a lift down to the town, collects his money, buys a few groceries in the supermarket, then has a Gaelic coffee in Hannon's before disappearing back to his cottage for the week."

"How can you just arrest him?"

"Anyone can arrest him if they can prove in a court of law that he's committed a crime. I don't think I'll have any problem proving that."

53

Jack Buckley and Josef Maister stood nervously at the top of the driveway, staring at the front door. The white Ford Transit was gone. The house seemed empty. Neither wanted to be the first to enter.

"You know what this bloke's capable of, Maister – you turn the key."

Josef Maister shook his head definitively. "That's just it. I *don't* know what he's capable of."

"Well, at least you know him better than I do. I've never met him, and hopefully never will."

"I'm not turning the key."

"Right." Maister took a pound coin from his pocket. "We'll toss for it. Heads, you open the door. Tails, I'll do it."

It landed on the gravel. Tails.

"Shit!" Maister muttered. He took the key from Jack and walked calmly to the door. He inserted it, mumbled a prayer to his mother, and turned it.

Jack shivered and closed his eyes.

Silence.

When Jack opened his eyes, Maister was grinning proudly. "What did I tell you?"

The house had a peaceful, summer's evening, kind of air about it. Long rays of sunshine stretched from the top windows of the patio doors, through the kitchen, into the sitting-room.

Maister looked at Jack. "What do you think?"

"What do you mean what do I think?"

"Well it is *your* house, Jack. I wouldn't be familiar with anything. Does anything look out of place? Anything moved from one spot to another?"

Jack's eyes scanned slowly, identifying items of furniture, acknowledging their regular positions in the familiar shape of the room. "Everything seems fine."

"Everything *can't* be fine, Jack. He wasn't here to check the electricity. He was here to carry out something, because he was told where you lived, and that was where they sent him."

"Who's *they*?" Jack asked nervously.

"The Klavern. The people who look after Vogelmann. No matter where he is around the world, they know exactly how he is, and how he can be contacted, and who to keep an eye on that might compromise his safety or confidential location."

"Maybe they were just searching the house."

"Maybe. Check upstairs."

Five minutes was all it took to convince Jack that the house was safe. "I can't see anything," he said confidently as he got to the end of the stairs. Josef Maister was looking at the old record-player.

"I wonder where that came from?" asked Jack.

"Vogelmann. Maggie told me it was a present from him. That's what gave him away. Maggie invited me over to dinner last night. The minute I saw it I knew I was in the right place." He pointed to the name etched on the small silver plate in the corner of the old wooden structure. "Kurt Gerstein was Vogelmann's commandant. He obviously gave this to him as a present. It's ironic to think that after fifty years on the run, this heap of shit is what destroys his cover in the end." He studied the LP sitting, ready to drop, on the spindle. "*The Merry Widow.* It was Hitler's favourite." He was about to twist the *start/play* button when the telephone rang.

Ethel Kline was in tears, so upset she could barely talk. "They've arrested Alex, Jack. Can you do something for him? Anything."

Josef Maister accompanied Jack Buckley to Macroom police station where they were holding Alex Kline for questioning. En route, they stopped off to collect his Indapamide tablets from Ethel for his high blood pressure.

The interview room was sparse, quite cool for the mild night they were enjoying, but comfortable. The detective who identified himself as Andrew Manning was heading up the questioning session when Jack arrived. He introduced Maister as the local doctor. Manning asked Jack to step out into the corridor for a minute. Once Manning was sure they were beyond hearing distance he began to speak quietly.

"Jack, he's coming out with some very strange stuff in there. He's now said he's not going to say any more until Alfie Carruth gets here. He's on his way. Said he'll be about ten minutes. Can you hang on?"

Jack agreed.

It was 8.15pm.

The holiday weekend had just begun.

Four men sat facing a very perplexed, very reddened-looking Alex Kline. He washed three Indapamide capsules down with a disposable cup of cool water and tried to relax.

"Recommencing our questioning session with Alex Kline. This is DS Andrew Manning. I'm joined by Superintendent Alfie Carruth and Sergeant Jack Buckley."

Josef Maister sat behind the three police officers.

"Now, Alex, can you explain in your own words how you came to be in possession of the travel tickets made out to Henry Myers."

"Last night Alfie and I were in Dublin. We met with the Taoiseach and his private secretary, Joe Russell and Alan Harrisson. Also at the meeting was a man called Don Eckler. He's the former owner of a huge tyre-production company called Girundbach. He told Joe Russell that he wanted to get a man out of the country. This man had received an Irish passport in exchange for big money ten years ago."

Alfie Carruth squeezed his hands to stop them trembling. He tried hard not to cringe at the revelations.

"What's this man's name?" Manning asked, as he checked to make sure the tape machine was recording the conversation.

Alex Kline looked agitated, more nervous with each question, his fate more hopelessly sealed, he knew, with each answer. "We weren't told. We just referred to him as The Keeper."

"What did that name signify?"

"I don't know. We were just told his name was The Keeper."

Manning seemed amused at the direction the answers were leading. "So you met the Taoiseach to see if you could get two plane tickets for a man called The Keeper so that he could go to Tenerife. Is that right?"

"That's right."

Andrew Manning opened an envelope and took out a purple-coloured passport. "We sent Superintendent Carruth over to your house half-an-hour ago to see if we had left anything behind. And he found this." Manning opened the passport. "It's a false passport for a Henry Myler. It doesn't have a photograph of Mr Myler. Why is that?"

"Because there is no such person as Henry Myler. The man that was leaving the country was calling himself Henry Myler. The Taoiseach agreed to get him a new passport so that he could leave the country under a different name."

"And why would he want to do that?"

Alex Kline searched the familiar faces behind the table for a bit of friendly support. All he could see were looks of shock and disbelief. "Because . . . he's wanted by the police."

"Who is?"

"The Keeper. He has to stay on the run. He runs the risk of being caught if he stays in any one place for too long."

"And how old is The Keeper?"

Alex was beginning to look a bit sheepish now. "Late seventies, I think."

Manning switched off the tape recorder and sat back against the wall. "Hang on, let's get this straight. You're telling me that an old man in his seventies called The

Keeper is on the run from the authorities and is being aided and abetted by the Irish Taoiseach who's providing a couple of plane tickets to a holiday resort in Spain and a forged passport."

Alex Kline looked down in disgust and nodded his head. "I knew you wouldn't believe me but it is true. Isn't it, Alfie?" He looked to his friend, the superintendent.

Carruth just tutted and stood up. "Alex, have you had some sort of nervous breakdown this evening? I've never heard such utter rubbish in all my life." He turned to his colleagues. "I'll leave you gentlemen to it. I'm off to officially open the Durrus bank holiday festival. It's a shame that you're not available to officiate, Alex."

Andrew Manning stepped out after Carruth. "Alfie, can I have a word?"

"Sure."

"What's all that about?"

"I haven't a clue. If I were you I'd throw the book at him. I can't believe that a man in his position would be so bloody stupid to think he can dabble in selling forged passports and not get caught. What do you think will happen to him?"

The detective shrugged. "Well, he'll lose his business interests for a start. The bank will fire him. The auctioneers and valuers institute will strike him off. They don't want someone who sells forgeries selling property at the same time. And as for Justice of the Peace . . . forget it. I'd say he'll get a two-year sentence, partly suspended.

Alfie Carruth walked out of Macroom garda station that night, careful not to let anyone see the broad smile on his face.

It was 10.15pm.

54

It was after midnight when Jack turned the key in the hall door. *"Maggie!"* he shouted. There was no reply. He checked the bedroom to see if she was asleep. The bed was empty.

Jack felt shivery, even though the heat of the night was annoying him. Bloody DT's setting in, he thought. Jesus, I'd kill for a drink. He couldn't believe that he hadn't touched a drop of alcohol now in almost twenty-four hours. He felt the outline of the engagement-ring box in his jacket pocket for support. If he could get through the next forty-eight hours of the holiday weekend – along with whatever other surprises it might throw up – he was certain he would never drink again. All the time all he could think of was vodka. He'd drink it neat now if someone would just put it up to him. "Distract yourself," he said aloud. *"Where are you woman?"* he shouted impatiently. All he wanted now was to hear her saying yes. *Yes I'd love to marry you!* Just to watch her slide the ring on her finger, to see her stretching out her hand to admire the small, neat cluster of diamonds.

"Jesus, what am I going to do with all this extra time?" He felt giddy, fidgety, nervous. He was sweating, yet he was quite cold. He opened the front door and closed it again. Then he spotted the record-player. He looked at the red label of the LP sitting, lined up, on the steel spindle, waiting to drop down onto the turntable. The little dog looked into the horn of the gramophone. *The Merry Widow*, he remembered Maister had said. Hitler's favourite. What sort of music would Hitler like? he wondered. *Start/play.* It was the middle knob. A small red arrow signalled to the right. Turn it and the whole system cranks itself up, he assumed. He placed his finger and thumb on *start/play* and was about to turn it when he noticed it. The white page folded in two. It was Maggie's favourite writing paper. His heart sank for a moment. Maybe it's not bad news, he thought. He opened it and moved into the light from the tall lamp-stand.

Dear Jack,

I hope you had a good trip and you're home safely by the time you read this. I know you'll probably be annoyed, but I've decided to head up to Donegal to spend the holiday weekend with my cousin. I've had such a terrible week. Nothing seemed to go right. To be honest I'm sick of that place with all its bad news. So I felt that I needed a break.

Hope you understand. I'll call soon.

All my love,

Maggie.

Jack was gutted. He rolled the note into a tightly squeezed ball and flung it at the record-player It hit the turntable and bounced onto the floor. "You could've asked me if *I* wanted to go with you, ye bitch! I don't drink anymore. I did all this for you. And what about *this*?" He plucked the tiny engagement ring out of the box and threw it at the curtains. He could hear a muffled clink as it hit the floor. He slammed the door so hard behind him the record-player shook on the sideboard.

It was 12.10am.

Hannon's pub was quiet.

Martha was reminding anyone she saw putting on a coat that she had managed to obtain a late licence for the holiday weekend. Jack was relieved that she was still open. Aidan Kerr sat at the end of the bar chatting to Cindy Reilly. When Jack noticed the state of her face he decided to leave the two of them to their conversation. "A bottle of vodka, please, Martha."

She frowned as she put it up in front of him, then a litre of white lemonade and a jug of ice. Finally a saucer of lemon slices.

Someone started to whistle behind him, in the dark corner. Jack tried to ignore him, downing mouthfuls of vodka, the first couple neat, straight off the neck of the bottle. Then the whistling got irritating. Eventually Jack looked around to show he was downright pissed off with whoever was trying to annoy him. Aidan was gone. He couldn't even remember him saying goodnight. Cindy Reilly was still at the end of the bar chatting quietly to Martha Hannon who was sitting on the stool beside her now. No one else left, Jack thought, except the stranger in the corner who wouldn't have been so irritating if he could only have whistled in tune.

Cindy muttered some sort of a goodnight as she

passed Jack and was led to the side door by Martha Hannon who reassured her that everything would be all right. The whistling had stopped now. Jack looked around. The stranger was gone, crept out without as much as the sound of a footstep. Jack began to worry. He left the vodka behind him. "I'll be back for it," he said to Martha Hannon. "Which way does she normally go?" he asked quickly about the route Cindy Reilly usually took home. Martha pointed to her right.

Jack walked quickly. Past the school up to the left, on past Kenny's supermarket and right. The young girl was standing with her back to the wall pleading with the blonde man who was pinning her to the cold surface between his outstretched arms.

"My father will be wondering what's keeping me," she said.

"Your daddy won't mind if you're a few minutes late, will he?" Proctor said slowly in the cold tone of his deep voice. He opened the top button of her shirt and placed his hand onto her right breast. "Oh yes, it's beautiful," he moaned.

"Please, don't!" Cindy begged.

"Let her go."

The unexpected intrusion startled Proctor. He took his hands away and stepped back, allowing the girl to get away from his grip. She started to run. He turned to face Buckley. Then he stepped off the kerb onto the narrow street and headed for the road out towards Four Mile Water, whistling the same piece of music over and over.

Jack waited until he had disappeared into the warm night's darkness before heading back to Hannon's to retrieve his succour.

55

All things bright and beautiful, all creatures great and small,
All things wise and wonderful, the Lord God made them all.

Saturday morning, at last. A long stream of sunlight, deflected by the stained-glass window above the children's choir split into a dozen different colours and shone down radiantly on the spot on the altar where he stood with his arms outstretched. Aidan Kerr could feel his heart pounding with excitement, spiritually fulfilled and full of the joys of the summer that had well and truly arrived in his beloved Durrus that Saturday morning. He couldn't think of anywhere else he would have preferred to be that day except the exact spot from which he was speaking at that moment. Martha Hannon had added an extra measure of starch to his alb the day before so that it would look snow-white. He couldn't resist wearing it at morning Mass that morning. He'd told himself to keep it clean for the big gig later that night – the holiday weekend Family Mass – but admiring it earlier in the sacristy he just had to try it on.

"Before the final blessing," he said, glancing around

the church at some of the new faces who'd come to Mass that morning, "I'd like to thank the children's choir who are rehearsing for our special Midsummer's Night Mass tonight. And I'd like to remind you all that it's a family occasion. And if you come as a family you're automatically entered in a draw after Communion for a mountain bike." He waited for a reaction from the small congregation. He was disappointed when there wasn't one. "Remember, friends, this is the start of the summer. Enjoy yourselves. And if I can be of any help to you while you enjoy the beauty and the wonderful facilities at your disposal here on Sheep's Head, don't hesitate to call." He smiled. "The good news for all of you hoping for some sunshine this weekend is that there'll no shortage of it, I'm reliably informed. Dougie Sullivan, our resident weather expert told me this morning that the swallows are flying very high the past few days which is a sure sign of good weather. So, with a bit of luck, this might just be a weekend that we'll all remember for a long, long time." He raised his right hand. "Father, Son and Holy Spirit. Mass is ended, go in peace."

As luck would have it, within hours the holiday was about to become unremittingly etched on the minds of everyone who lived in or visited Durrus that June weekend.

It was 10.45am.

Jack Buckley eventually found the ringing phone. He had dumped his trousers on it a few hours earlier, at half four, once he'd managed to strip for bed and crawl under the duvet, drunk and miserable. "Hello." His voice had dropped at least an octave. His nose was blocked, his throat badly clogged up.

"Jack, it's Josef Maister. You don't sound well. Have you the flu?"

"No. I just need some sleep. Call me later."

"To hell with sleep, Jack. This is all about to happen in the next hour or so."

Maister sounded adamant. What made matters worse, he sounded disgustingly fresh and wide-awake. "What's going to happen?"

"My people called from Vienna. We've been given the go ahead."

"For what?"

"To arrest Vogelmann."

"Who's going to arrest him?"

"You are. I will briefly read out the charges and you will handcuff him and bring him to Bantry where he will be held in a guarded cell like any arrested suspect would be. Arrangements are currently being made to extradite him to Berlin, where our people will oversee the final stages of the operation and hand him over to the German authorities."

"So what are we waiting for?"

Maister breathed heavily into his phone. "There's a slight problem. Not so much a problem as a snag, let's just say. Vogelmann has to identify himself before he can be arrested."

"What?" Jack yelled. "That's crazy. Why would he do a crazy thing like that?"

"No point being pessimistic in this game, Jack. I've waited nearly twenty years to nail him. Another few hours, another day or maybe two, isn't going to make much difference. Here me out on this. I visited the post office earlier this morning. Nancy Hegarty – she's the post-mistress – dropped by the surgery yesterday. I had a good chat with her. I asked her who collected Vogelmann's pension for him. She told me that normally during the winter it would be delivered to him, but only after he had signed the book and given authorisation in writing to whoever was collecting it for him. During the good weather, he normally got a lift down to collect it himself. I'm going to sit outside the post office for a while this morning. It opens in twenty minutes. Stays open till one. It'll be worth the two hours."

Jack sighed. He felt putridly ill. "And I suppose you want me to sit with you."

"I need you there. It's a long shot. He may not turn up at all. But it's worth remembering that he's a cheeky old bugger. He might think he's going to get away with it."

"What time is the Justice person arriving at?"

"Connor Colbert is his name. He's due any time now. I'll see you in the bar at Hannon's in ten minutes."

The phone went dead. Jack dropped the receiver and staggered headlong into the bathroom where he dutifully threw up into the sink.

By 12.55pm Josef Maister had cursed more in two hours than Jack Buckley reckoned he could have managed in a week. The man from the Justice department just coughed each time Maister cursed Heinrich Vogelmann. Then, just as Nancy Hegarty was about to turn the *open* sign around to *closed*, Josef Maister was out of the car and standing in the post office doorway.

He slammed the wall with the side of his fist and hurried back to the car, leaving a very worried-looking post-mistress behind him.

"What happened? Did she say why he didn't turn up?" Jack asked.

Maister turned in his seat in order to stare straight at Jack. "She did. And you're not going to believe it. Guess who collected his pension for him at ten to nine this morning before she'd even opened the shop?"

"Who?"

"Maggie."

"*My* Maggie? That's impossible."

"That's what the post-mistress told me."

"Maggie's gone to Donegal to visit her cousin for the weekend. I have a written message at home that she wrote yesterday evening before she left."

Maister was furious. "Don't mess me around, Jack. Nancy Hegarty swears that Maggie arrived into her shop this morning at ten to nine to collect the old man's pension. She explained to Nancy that she was doing his shopping early for him and she needed a few quid. Nancy says she hasn't seen her in such good form in a long time. She stayed chatting for a couple of minutes and left."

Jack cursed. He stepped out of the car without an explanation.

"Where are you going?" Maister shouted.

"Kennys."

Lunchtime on Saturdays was Marty Kenny's busiest time. The queue was eight deep at the single checkout. Marty froze when he saw Jack asking to be excused as he jumped to the top.

"Marty, I need to talk you," Jack said firmly.

"Jack, not now. I stopped selling cider to the kids two weeks ago. I swear. I told you I would and I stuck to my word. I'm not ever . . . "

"Forget that. That's not what I'm here for."

The women in the queue looked around at each other and started to whisper, shocked at the sergeant's outburst.

"Was Maggie in?" Jack asked. His fast-fire question demanded a rapid answer.

Marty thought for a moment. "No."

"Are you sure? What time did you open at?"

"I opened at eight like I always do on Saturdays. She wasn't in. I'd have remembered."

"She was in the post office about nine . . . maybe a few minutes before?"

Marty shook his head. "Definitely not. Didn't see her."

Jack returned to the car.

He sat in and slammed the door. Then he kicked the dashboard. The Justice man coughed again.

"She didn't buy any messages. Marty Kenny said she wasn't in at all this morning." He tried to reason with the confusion, to think logically. The headache was making him feel nauseous again. "I can't figure it out. Why did she leave a note saying she was going to Donegal if she was seen in the post office this morning?"

"Are you sure the note was in her handwriting?" the Justice man asked.

"Of course it was *her* handwriting."

"OK," Maister said, sounding relaxed again, let's not lose our heads. It's still early days. Let's assume that Maggie went to Donegal this morning and that was why she collected Vogelmann's money so early. Maybe she already got in his messages yesterday."

"There's only one way to find out, isn't there?" Jack said.

"Drive up to the cottage." Maister replied. It was more an instruction than a suggestion.

Sunshine and hangovers was a toxic mixture. Jack melted in the heat of the car, gasping for breath each time he closed up the window, and trying to keep the sweaty hair out of his eyes and face every time he opened it for fresh air. He couldn't remember the last time he'd seen the sky so blue. He wanted the drama to end so that he could crawl into a dark room and die for a few hours.

Josef Maister thought differently though. The glint of the sun across the soft swell in the bay was exhilarating. Further out the blue deep took over for as far as the eye could see, right out to the horizon, where the sea met the sky in a greyish, blue haze. He thought of his family beyond the sea and prayed he might see them soon, maybe within days if all went according to plan. Unfortunately the plan was already beginning to go badly wrong. Although he knew it he tried not to dwell on it. They pulled into the small, stony parking-space outside the cottage beside Verity graveyard.

Jack reached into the glove compartment and discreetly removed the pistol, hoping that the Justice man hadn't noticed. "Just in case," he whispered to Maister.

The cottage was empty. A deserted air about it made Josef Maister even more anxious.

"Is he gone?" Jack asked.

"From here?" Maister looked around the hollow cottage. "Maybe. But he's still somewhere on the peninsula."

"How do you know?"

"There is only one road in and out of this area, isn't there?" Maister enquired.

"The R591," Jack confirmed.

"Good," he said with a certain relief. "I've got two men sitting at the junction where the R591 joins up with the Bantry Road. They would have contacted me if they'd seen anything. I've another man watching the intersection for Schull. Nothing so far from there either. "

"So where is he?" Jack asked.

Josef Maister afforded a smile. It was all he could manage for the moment. "I've been asking that question for years, Jack. Heinrich Vogelmann has spent most of his life avoiding justice, skipping countries, and steering clear of the likes of you and me. The woman who told you she was Nathan Lohan's sister?"

"I remember."

"Nathan Lohan was a close friend of mine. I suppose I feel partly responsible for what happened to him. I got him interested in my work, hunting down these vicious murderers. He got caught up in it and started to research it. Investigative work, by its very nature, is addictive. You tend to take awesome chances, sometimes with your life, just to move on a couple of inches further in what you're searching for. Three years ago I am convinced he discovered Vogelmann was living here. And he paid for his snooping with his life. Some price, isn't it?"

Jack shuddered. "Are you prepared to go that far?"

"And risk losing my life? I don't think so. Because then I would be of no use to any of my people. I'd prefer to stay alive. That way I can wonder about Vogelmann and how he is spending the last few years of his miserable life behind bars in a German prison." He sighed. "But then maybe we're already too late. Again."

"And you told me I shouldn't be pessimistic?"

Maister smiled, like a father being cajoled by his young son. "Sometimes, Jack, I get tired of trying to be optimistic. Sometimes I like to be a pessimist. That way my heart beats more slowly, and I sleep more comfortably." He walked back towards the car. "There's not a great deal we can do now for the moment. We're playing the game under his rules until such time as he decides to show his face. Go home and get some sleep. I'll call you if I need you."

"What are you going to do?"

"I've a few phone calls to make to some people who are expecting to hear some good news from me. I'm going to have to disappoint them, albeit temporarily I hope. Maybe when all this is over, Jack, I'll bring my wife back to this beautiful spot and you can show us around."

"I'd love to."

Jack Buckley knew without a second thought that

Maister didn't mean what he had just said. Something told him at that moment, once all this was in the past, that he would never meet Josef Maister again.

8.30pm

Bantry Fire Station.

Duty Sergeant Bob Willis answered the emergency call. "Hello, fire brigade."

"I'm calling just to let you know that the small cottage beside Verity graveyard out on Sheep's Head is ablaze. I've just come in from that direction, and I had to wait till I got home before I could ring. It seems like a very bad fire."

Bob Willis was about to ask the caller for her name and telephone number when the line went dead.

9.25pm.

"Oh no!"

Jack flung the small clock on the floor and bolted out of the bed. He checked that the pistol was still under the pillow, where he'd placed it carefully under a towel that afternoon before he went to sleep. He couldn't believe that he had been out cold for over six hours. The only consolation was that he felt fresh. Fresh enough for another drink. He sat on the small stool at the foot of the bed and struggled with the socks, trying to recall what was planned for that night. Midsummer's Mass at ten. It'll be packed, he assured himself. So the pub won't be too busy. Not till eleven anyway. He decided against wearing the tunic. Too official. It was summertime. Families were holidaying together. Create a relaxed atmosphere. That way they'll like you from the start. "To hell with them," he mumbled, pulling at the sock caught in his toenail, "I don't give a shit it they don't like me. I don't particularly want to see too much of them." He checked the answering machine. *Please!* he prayed. *Let her have called!* He closed his eyes and made a deal. *Right God,* he whispered, *if she's left a message, I'll go to the Midsummer's Mass. If she hasn't, I go to the pub!* He opened his eyes and waited before looking down at the message-counter.

No messages.

His heart sank. Even before he picked up the car keys he was already sitting at the bar, telling Martha Hannon how well she looked, pouring his first drink.

9.43pm.

Aidan Kerr wished the choir good luck and told them he'd buy them each a bottle of coke and a packet of crisps in Hannon's if they performed well. He pounded down through the twenty-four steps from the gallery to the porch, three at a time, just in time to welcome the first of the congregation. Ollie Jennings and his wife shook hands with their parish priest.

"You might like to bring something up in the offertory procession, Mrs Jenning."

The woman with the huge hat was flattered. She thanked him and moved inside.

Ten minutes later he started to vest himself, occasionally stopping to peep out through the small slit in the velvet curtain that closed off the sacristy from the altar. At least two hundred, he assured himself, almost ready to burst with the excitement and anticipation of having a full church for the first time in almost ten months.

He was about to place the chasuble over his head when it occurred to him that the second row was empty. He'd called to Ethel Kline the night before after she'd phoned him in a terrible state to tell him that Alex had been taken away by a bunch of detectives. Aidan spent almost an hour at the house with her and their children, reassuring them that they had nothing to worry about, that it would all be resolved in a matter of days when they realised they'd made some terrible mistake.

Despite all his reassuring, Aidan Kerr was concerned. Ethel had made him a promise that, no matter what might happen, she would be in the second row of the church with her children, holding her head high for all to see.

He checked the clock. It started to chime ten bells. The second row remained empty. There was something wrong. He knew that. But he had a congregation waiting for him. And tonight was more than just Mass. It was Show Time! He pulled back the velvet curtain and glided out underneath the bright lights.

"All things bright and beautiful, the good Lord made them all."

56

10.02pm.

The tall man sitting on the armchair nearest to the door waited restlessly until Ethel Kline had stopped crying, through the gag tied tightly around her face, before he spoke. He knew why she was crying. He had told her when she opened the front door, about to leave for church, that he would blow her fucking head off if she didn't do what she was told. He'd have to use a more calming routine if he ever tried this again.

Her hands were tied together tightly. The gag – a long strip of hospital gauze tied right around her head – kept her jaws apart, forcing her to gasp long breaths slowly and regularly. The children lay on their sides, also gagged, hands and feet tied, on the mat in front of the fireplace.

He'd told them as soon as he had tied them all up that his name was Ali. He was sorry now that he'd used his real name. He hadn't intended to but it just popped out. The balaclava, apart from irritating his beard and making him unbearably itchy, was making him feel very claustrophobic. From where he sat, on the edge of the chair, he could see Ethel Kline quite clearly, but he had to take his eyes off her and drop his head down if he wanted to check on the two girls and their teenage brother.

The boy, the eldest, Ali reckoned, seemed hypnotised by the weapon in his lap. He was shivering with fear, Ali guessed. He nodded. "You look like a good boy."

The young boy left him in no doubt that he was very well-behaved by nodding repeatedly.

"How old are you? Fifteen?"

Dónal nodded again.

The doorbell rang. Ali waited. It rang again. And again. He stood up slowly, walked backwards to the door, checking through the magnifying eyepiece in the centre of the heavy door. "Who is it?"

"Dan."

Ali opened the door back fully, remaining out of public view by standing behind it but careful not to take his eyes off the hostages in the sitting-room.

Another smaller man, also wearing a balaclava, led the stooped elderly man the children knew as Harry upstairs. Ethel Kline whimpered again when she saw the grip the man had on Harry's arm. "What do you want to kidnap him for? He's only an old man. He's never harmed anyone," she pleaded, mumbling through the gag.

Ali raised the AK47 and pointed it towards her. *"Shut up! We'll be gone in twenty minutes!"*

"Twenty-six, to be precise," the man called Dan said from the top of the stairs.

"Where's Bruno?"

"He's gone to collect the minibus. As soon as he gets here I'll go on ahead with the van to light up the airstrip."

10.16pm.

Cindy Reilly passed the small intersection in the Klines driveway, where the road split, one way for the office, the other for the private residence. She'd just heard, twenty minutes earlier, that Alex had been arrested. Secretly, she was both pleased and relieved. However she still had great affection for Ethel and a crush on Dónal. Aidan Kerr had suggested to her in Hannon's the previous night that she should call to see Ethel. She would appreciate seeing a friendly face considering what had just happened to Alex.

The house seemed quiet. Then again, it was festival weekend. The Midsummer Mass was underway, the pubs would be packed by eleven and a disco was organised in the marquee in the yard of the National School for midnight. All she had to do now was to convince Ethel to allow Dónal to go to the disco.

It had become a tradition down through the years that she never rang the doorbell in case the baby was asleep upstairs. Each night she baby-sat, she peeped in through the curtains of the sitting-room first and then rapped three times on the window. She bent down to see who was inside. At first she couldn't figure out why Dónal and his sisters, Megan and Jennifer, were lying side by side on the rug, facing away from the television. Then she saw the gags, and then, only inches away from her to her left, the black mask and the rifle.

10.19pm

Jack Buckley squeezed the engagement ring between his finger and his thumb. She hadn't left a contact name.

Not even a number to call, to see if she got there all right. But she hadn't gone to Donegal, had she? "I'll have another, please, Martha." He pushed a handful of coins over to her side of the bar and took back a large vodka. This one he'd drink neat. It was lovely to have the pub all to himself. He'd be gone before the crowd arrived.

10.20pm.

"We like to pride ourselves here on Sheep's Head on the importance of the family. We're a rural community at the best of times, so we tend to rely on each other for support and friendship. And it's always a pleasure, when the midsummer holiday weekend comes around every year, to see so many of you coming back to spend your free time with us." Aidan Kerr discreetly checked his watch, pinned to the lectern in front of him. He'd spoken for exactly five minutes. Precisely as he had rehearsed it, eight times that afternoon. One more minute should do it. "We like to think we're a crime-free community, with a good relationship with the men and women who uphold the law on our behalf. I know you'll be able to relax and unwind over the next couple of days. And, of course, as I always say on this very special occasion each year, this is one of the safest locations for children anywhere in the country. Don't forget, by the way, we'll be having our raffle before the end of tonight's celebration."

He nodded to the organist and invited the offertory procession to move forward.

57

10.22pm.

Eddie Malooly was leaning against the side of his Volkswagon Caravelle enjoying a ten-minute break, a quick cigarette and a cup of coffee from the steaming hot flask his wife, Mary, had made up for him before he left Toormore that night. He had just dropped off six teenagers for the bank holiday disco in the Westlodge hotel, half a mile from Bantry, and was heading into Durrus shortly to pick up another group. He inhaled the cigarette and gazed up at the stars, counting five, then turning slightly and counting three more. He was convinced he had spotted the North Star. "There y'are, I got ye," he cheered.

He was about to stub out his cigarette with the heel of his shoe when a voice behind him said, "Excuse me."

Eddie turned around expecting to see someone he knew. All he could see were two eyes staring out between two long slits in a black balaclava. The man was dressed in heavy combat style. He was carrying what looked like a particularly lethal weapon. He spoke with ease. "I need to borrow you and your bus. Listen carefully, my friend. You will not get hurt if you follow my instructions to the letter. If you don't you'll be dead before you realise what happened."

Eddie wasn't sure why he wasn't frightened. Perhaps it was the confidence this man showed. Eddie, a former soldier who'd served three terms in the Lebanon, knew he was looking into the eyes of another serviceman. "No problem, pal. You just tell me where you want to go and I'll make sure you get there."

Bruno Proctor nodded to the taxi. "Get in. Start it and drive to Durrus. Remember I'm going to be sitting on the floor behind you. Drive as you would always drive. Do you wear a seat belt?"

"No."

"Then don't wear one tonight. Don't try anything to attract attention. Because if you do I'll kill you and whoever you start to talk to. Clear?"

"Clear."

10.26pm

Cindy Reilly was hysterical by the time she reached the gates of the church. She sat on the wall crying, trying to catch her breath, after running half a mile in less than five minutes. She thought she was going to faint.

Josef Maister came down the hill from the direction of the National School, smoking his pipe, wondering where the man he'd spent fifteen years searching for, full-time, had disappeared to that night. Vanished into thin air. He entertained the notion that maybe he was watching him right at that very minute. Maybe he was lying in a dug-out waiting for the town to retire and then make his escape with the help of Proctor. It might be best, Maister said to himself. Then there would be no likelihood of any innocent bystanders getting hurt. He stood directly opposite the big, old church now, packed to its rafters this evening, lit up brilliantly, inside and out, the organ booming against the sound of the choir. The music soothed him, as he listened to the children singing inside.

"Doctor."

Maister spun around. The voice sounded weak, barely audible, and very distressed. The young girl was slumped over, sitting on the small wall to the left of the church's main gate. He pocketed his pipe and ran across the road. *"Cindy!"* She startled babbling. It was impossible to make out what she was saying. Then he understood as she caught her breath a few times.

"The Klines' house . . . a man with a rifle wearing a mask . . . Mrs Kline and the children are tied up . . . "

Maister pulled out his mobile as he started to run back towards Hannon's. He dialled 999.

It was 10.30pm

"And the winner is . . . " Aidan Kerr stood on the highest point of the altar and proudly held up the winning ticket before reading the name of the winning family written on the back.

There was a whistling sound, like the fizzling noise a firework might make before it expires. The lights in the church flickered for a few seconds. Heads looked skyward. Aidan took his eyes off the number and looked at the lectern light to his right. It seemed to shimmer, its glow vibrating.

Then the whistling stopped and, a second or two later, darkness descended. Complete and utter darkness. Aidan couldn't see the tip of his finger or the colour of his ticket. A power cut, he thought. *Thank you, God,* he seethed. "Please everybody, don't worry, the lights will be back on shortly." But they couldn't hear him because the microphone was dead. A soft disturbing hum of noise was slowly giving way to a nervous, high-pitched fever of confused voices and calling names.

Aidan eased his way towards the front of the altar, careful to feel his way down the three steps. Odd, he thought, that the street lamps outside weren't throwing some light into the dark church like they did the odd night he came in late, in the pitch blackness, to be alone with his thoughts. Then he realised that the street lights had also died.

Josef Maister tripped and fell in through the side door of Hannon's. He was gasping for breath. *"Jack!"* he shouted.

Jack was busy dialling numbers on his mobile. "This is some bloody power cut. I can't get through to anybody on this."

Josef Maister grabbed the phone and slammed it down on the counter. *"This is not a power cut. Can't you see? It's happening. This is how they planned it. The entire area has been paralysed."*

A voice yelled in through the side door. "All hell is breaking loose down in the church. The lights have all gone out and there's a stampede going on to get out onto the road."

"Jesus Christ," Jack thought he heard himself saying. It all seemed like a horrible nightmare.

Martha Hannon seemed unaffected. She stood behind the bar calmly, lighting candles. Striking a match, lighting a few . . . blowing out that match . . . striking another match.

Jack looked at Maister. "What are we going to do?"

"Cindy Reilly has just come back from the Klines' house. She said she was able to see them all tied up inside in the sitting-room. There was a masked man with a rifle sitting in the corner. I reckon it's got something to do with Vogelmann. But not for much longer. You better get down to the church. I'll get up to Klines' and see what I can do."

"Here, you might need this." Jack handed him the Biretta pistol. "Only point it if you intend to kill with it."

10.35

Eddie Malooly swung the big Caravelle through the gates of the Klines' mansion and accelerated up the long driveway, veering right for the private residence, aware all the time that the man hunched behind his seat had the barrell of a huge, deadly kalashnikov rifle pointed at the back of his head. He slowed down to signal to his passenger that they were coming to a halt just in case he got the wrong impression. "Right, we're here," Eddie said gently.

"Thank you," the kidnapper replied calmly and politely. "Wait here. If you try to drive away or run, I'll still be able to shoot you at half a mile."

Eddie sat trembling in the seat. He turned up the heat, but that made the burning need to answer a sudden call from nature that he'd been planning to respond to back in Bantry all the more necessary. He squeezed his knees together and turned the switch from *hot* to *cold*. Then it occurred to him as he looked around the spacious car parking area at the front of the house that he was a sitting duck if anything went wrong. If the police swooped – he had no doubt whatsoever – he wouldn't survive for more than fifteen seconds. He started to pray out loud to Saint Jude, the Patron Saint of Hopeless Cases, and guessed it would end one of two ways: Eddie Malooly would be the toast of every pub in Bantry before the holiday weekend was over, or Eddie Malooly would get the biggest funeral the town had ever seen.

The scene in the area directly in front of the church was one of sheer chaos in the inky black darkness, lit up now by the blue flashing lights of the Bantry fire engine which had been returning from the Verity cottage fire when Durrus was thrown into darkness. Children screamed for their parents. Mothers repeatedly called out names. Men tripped over each other as they grabbed the arms and shoulders of small children, turning them around to check if they were their own.

Aidan Kerr stood on the top step, visible only because of his white starched vestment, pleading with the huge milling crowd, to calm down, that power would be restored any minute.

Jack got to his car, halfway between Hannon's pub and the church grounds, only to realise it was jammed in and completely unmoveable, one side by a camper van, on the other by a mobile chip shop.

Two fire fighters were trying to reassure an elderly woman that her husband was going to be fine. A third administered oxygen to an old man sitting on the low wall who'd got caught up in the rush to get out of the pitch black church and tripped, falling down the steep steps.

Jack leaned against his car and cursed. How was he going to get out to Klines' house, a mile out the R591. Then it struck him. The mountain bike!

Eddie Malooly couldn't remember the last time he prayed. Now he was able to recall all the short prayers he'd learned off as a small child. As each one came to mind, he said it in a low voice, offering each one up for Mary, who was probably sitting at home now watching *The Late Late Show*. He was glad now she hadn't come with him for the company. He'd suggested dropping her in Durrus for an hour and collecting her later after one of his last return trips. His heart pounded as the side door of the Caravelle minibus slid back gradually on its well-oiled rails.

"Turn on the full beams," the voice whispered quickly.

Eddie did what he was told.

The front of the palatial house lit up brilliantly.

Whoever had opened the door was crawling into the back of the minibus on his elbows and belly. Eddie put his gloved hands down between his legs to warm them and stop them from shaking.

"Eddie, it's me!"

The whispering voice was more familiar now. "Doctor, is that you?"

"Yes. Don't look around. Keep the full beams on. That way they can't see what's going on in the minibus if they're checking from the house. Whatever you do, Eddie, don't move. Stay exactly as you are."

"Jesus, Doc, what's going on?"

"I don't have any time to explain, Eddie. But we're both on our way to hell if they catch me. If we're careful this might work. If you do exactly as you're told I'll buy you the most expensive bottle of champagne you've ever drunk."

"I don't drink champagne, Doc. It gives me terrible wind. Either way, I feel a lot better now you're here."

"Listen carefully, Eddie – where can I hide in the van so they won't see me?"

"Right at the very back, Doc. The fella who came back here from Bantry with me was crouched down behind me. If he does that again he'll be able to see you unless you're right at the very back under the seat. There's a long blanket back there. Drape it down over the front of the seat and tuck it in under it."

"Was he armed?"

"Yes, Doc. It was an AK47 he was carrying. As cool as cucumber he was too. He even said thank you to me when I told him we were here."

"How many more of them are there?"

"I'm not sure, Doc. The door of the house was opened by another fella wearing a balaclava. They left the door slightly open and I could see them goin' upstairs."

"That means there's probably three of them. Two upstairs. One downstairs in the sitting-room with the family. That makes four if they've got Vogelmann in a room upstairs."

"Who?"

"Doesn't matter."

"They're coming down the stairs, Doc. *Quick!* Under the back seat and make sure the blanket is well draped down in front of you."

Josef Maister took up his position in the cramped space under the back seat. He could smell alcohol and feel a chilly sensation as the wet floor of the minibus soaked through his jacket and made contact with his skin. He shivered, as he turned to lie on his right, his head jammed against the driver's side of the bus, the Biretta pistol nestled against his right shoulder, pointing a fraction of an inch away from his ear.

Then it all started to happen in seconds.

The sliding side door crashed back. Maister guessed the noisy clanking sounds were the various weapons being loaded on before the passengers boarded. From where he lay, he watched for the number of feet. Two. Two more. Then two more. Then further up, in beside

Eddie, another pair of feet. There were four of them, as he had predicted. The sliding door slammed shut. There was a short silence while the hijackers familiarised themselves with the cramped surroundings of their transport.

Maister breathed deeply, slowly, careful not to let an inhalation catch on his dry, nervous breath. He closed his eyes for a minute to recall a fast relaxation technique he'd been taught many years ago. Tense all of the muscles in your body for twenty seconds, he thought, then gradually let them relax, imagining them all loosening and unbending from head to toe. Then he began to consider the possible logistics of what lay ahead. Maister had no idea where the minibus was going to, or how long he'd have to endure this discomfort. And, more unsettling still, what would happen when they arrived at their destination.

A voice started to speak.

Maister recognised it immediately. It was Bruno Proctor. He was obviously in command of the operation. This worried Maister greatly.

He spoke in German. "May I just say, Herr Obergruppenfuhrer, on behalf of your many supporters and comrades back in the Vaterland, how great an honour it is for us to rescue you from this perilous situation. Let me assure you that you are safe in our hands tonight. And within fifteen minutes we will have you safely out of danger."

The next two words, spoken by a very frightened Heinrich Vogelmann, sickened Josef Maister.

"Heil Hitler," he said in an anxious tone.

"Drive!" Proctor shouted into the front seat at Eddie Malooly.

"Where to?" Eddie asked politely.

Maister was relieved at Eddie's expedience and, more important, his prudence when it came to unnecessary chatter.

"The old airstrip along the beach, close to the hotel where we met."

Eddie nodded and turned out onto the R591, almost knocking Jack Buckley clean off the mountain bike. He opened the window to check for any oncoming traffic and immediately recognised Jack climbing back up onto the saddle. "The airstrip close to the hotel. Fine," he shouted as if simply repeating the instructions he'd been given. He knew Jack was within hearing distance. He could only pray now that the sergeant had heard him.

Jack tried to calculate how long it would take him to get to the airstrip on the bike. Twenty minutes, maybe. Too long. Then it occurred to him that Alex Kline's Mercedes was probably sitting outside the front door. He took a deep breath, dropped the gears into second and peddled with all of his drunken strength up the driveway to Klines' hall door.

Josef Maister listened closely to the conversation that was taking place. The voices spoke now in hushed tones. Proctor did most of the talking.

"We will come to the junction with the main road in less than one minute. There are two men sitting in a purple-coloured Renault Laguna at the corner, their car facing us as we go to turn left. Herr Obergruppenfuhrer, I will ask you to crouch down behind the driver as we pass them. *You!*" He poked Eddie with the tip of the barrel.

"Yes?"

"What is your name?"

"Eddie."

"Eddie. Have you a wife and children?"

"Yes, I do."

"Well, Eddie, if you follow my instructions carefully you will see your wife and children again, very soon. Then, in years to come, you will be able to tell your grandchildren how you came to the assistance of one of the sole surviving members of the Third Reich. I'm sure they will be impressed by that. What do you think?"

Eddie shrugged. "Maybe they will."

"Maybe?" He poked him harder this time. "What kind of an answer is *maybe*? Have you any idea who is crouching on the floor behind you? Do you read the history books? This man is famous. Where I come from he is one of the most respected and revered people in history."

Eddie didn't answer.

Maister listened carefully, trying to breathe in a relaxed way, worried now that the conversation could get difficult.

"You are a soldier, Eddie. I am right?"

Eddie nodded. "You're right."

"Are you not going to ask me how I knew you were a soldier?"

"How did you know?"

"By the way you looked at me, and at the rifle I was carrying when I met you at the hotel."

"You've used one of these. Yes?"

"Yes, in training. Not in combat."

"But you've been in combat?"

"Yes, I have."

"Who did you fight in combat, Eddie?"

Maister squeezed his eyes closed and prayed with all his heart that Eddie wouldn't mention where he fought. His prayer didn't work.

"I fought with the Irish Defence Forces in the Lebanon."

"Ah!" Bruno Proctor cheered. ."You fought the Arabs?"

"Shot one of them dead, actually. Injured five of them. They would have killed half of my battalion if I hadn't shot them. Those Arabs, most of them are mad bastards. They'd scare the shit of you. I'd have killed a lot more of them given half a chance."

The conversation died. Silence, apart from the chugging sound of the engine, and the squeaking of the chassis as the minibus slowed down as it approached the junction. "Ali, take off your balaclava, quickly. Hand me your rifle. Eddie, this man is a tourist. You are simply dropping him into a pub in the town. Then you are returning to collect more children to bring them to the disco. Is that clear?"

Eddie nodded.

"If you try to give any sort of indication that something is wrong to these two men up here, I will shoot you in the back of the head and then I will shoot them. Is that clear?"

"Yes."

58

Jack Buckley had never driven an automatic before.

He slammed on the brakes as he reached the bottom of the long driveway and threw the huge car into the turn, the back kicking out as he pounded his foot down hard onto the accelerator. He'd freed the Klines and told Dónal, the eldest, to check the phones every few minutes to see if power had been restored. As soon as he got a dialling tone he was to ring 999 and tell the police what had happened.

Jack checked his watch. It was almost eleven o'clock. He studied the mobile for coverage again. Nothing. Whatever Proctor and his people had done, it was nothing short of pure genius.

Eddie Malooly stopped and wound down his window.

Josef Maister held his breath. From where he was lying, the entire right side of his body almost completely numb by now, he could see Vogelmann's small arse as he crouched down below the back seat, and Proctor's heavy frame leaning down hard against him to prevent him from coughing or moving. Another man, Dan, lay in a foetal position beside Proctor. Ali sat up front beside Eddie Malooly.

"Evening, lads," Eddie said cheerfully.

"Evening," a voice replied outside the driver's window. "We hear there's been a power cut in Durrus. Do you know what's happening?"

"Nope, not a lot. I've just come from there a few minutes ago. Everything seemed fine. I'm just dropping this lad into town. He's going to sample one or two of the local pubs. Aren't you?" Eddie looked at his passenger and smiled.

Ali nodded once.

"Where are you from?" one of the men asked.

"Buncrana," Ali replied.

"OK. Have a good night." The man who'd spoken to Eddie gave him the all-clear and waved him on.

Josef Maister could have reached out and touched the tangible air of relief in the minibus.

"How far more?" Proctor was speaking again. His voice sounded more urgent now.

"Five minutes. Straight, main road for a mile, then a turn up here to the left. That'll take us down a narrow road for about half-a-mile, then a right, across a bumpy forest track, down the hill and we're practically sitting on the airstrip. Why do you want to go to the airstrip?" Eddie asked.

There was no answer.

Maister could sense some sort of movement, as if Proctor was searching for something. "You'll have to pull in here, Eddie, just for a minute."

"OK," he replied obligingly.

Maister could feel the minibus drawing to a gradual standstill.

"Thank you," Proctor said. "Now get out."

Maister closed his eyes and prayed again. There was a deathly silence among the passengers. He could tell by the darkness all around outside that they were still somewhere remote, nowhere near a town, or somewhere that might have been more convenient for Eddie.

"Out? What about my bus? I have to pick up eight kids tonight and drop a whole load more of them home later. You can't take my bus. Please?"

"Get out, Eddie!" Proctor was giving him a military-style command now. "You obeyed orders from your superiors in the past. Now I suggest you obey this one."

Eddie did as he was told. The driver door closed. Then the sound of the sliding side door opening up and a gust of cold night air filled the warm interior. Maister was very concerned now. He could hear the sound of the rifle being carried away from the bus. Then the sound of a distant voice shouting, almost crying, some yards away from the back of the bus. Then two loud, pumping gun-shots.

"That's for the poor Arab you shot, you stinking piece of Irish shit. The Arabs were the only ones who showed my people any decent support when the rest of the world denounced us and and called us mad. They gave us masterful weapons. They sheltered a lot of my comrades when the rest of the world wanted to kill them. And you call them mad. Goodbye, Eddie."

The sliding side door closed. Proctor climbed into the driving-seat now and steered the minibus out onto the main road to complete the short journey. "Soon we will be able to relax, Herr Obergruppenfuhrer. Soon."

Jack jammed on the huge brakes, the car screeching to a halt at the corner of the main junction. The two men ran across the road to the Mercedes.

"Which way did the minibus go?"

"Towards town," one of the suited men shouted.

They were heading for the airstrip. "Ring 999. Get every available police car out to the old Bantry airstrip. Tell them the men are heavily armed, extremely dangerous. We need back-up quickly."

Jack became distracted by something behind him – not at road-level, more above him. He looked in his rear-view mirror to see what the noise was. It sounded like a tractor, or some sort of high-powered vehicle that was much bigger than his car, slowing down behind him. The road was pitch black, apart from the red glow his tail-lights were throwing out behind the car. "What the hell . . . "

Then one of the two men looked up at the sky.

Jack got out of the car. *"Jesus Christ!"* he whispered. The small plane, its red and white landing-lights flashing, seemed to be dropping lower and lower as he watched. It shot over the car with a noisy, shuddering *vroom*. It couldn't have been any higher than a hundred feet above him. "The airfield, quick!" he shouted, jumping back into the car. "Are you two armed?"

One of the men pulled back his smart jacket, revealing the Uzi machine gun hanging off his right shoulder.

"Get into the car," Jack shouted.

Maister's body ached so badly now – every bone in his body begging him to move, even just one inch – that he grimaced with acute pain each time the bus turned or shook as it raced down the stony, narrow dirt tracks towards the airfield. Then he heard it. It was a plane. *Of course!* he reminded himself. The perfect escape. A private plane in the middle of the night, flying low enough to avoid the radar pick-up of air-traffic control at both Shannon and Cork.

He expected to hear a cheer any minute. None came. Then Vogelmann, for the first time since seeing him face-to-face in his small empty cottage the day before, spoke. The voice was chilling, the message even more disturbing. "I want balaclavas removed and dispensed with. I want all weaponry out of sight. The young woman must think that you are all just assisting me in my departure. I have convinced her to come with me. I don't want her to see any of this. Is that clear?"

"Yes, of course, Herr Obergruppenfuhrer. She will simply assume that you are her grandfather as was agreed previously. He turned briefly to the other men. "Do you understand that?" he asked them.

They assured him that they did.

Maister watched from behind the blanket as the

minibus disgorged its passenger onto the noisy airstrip. Luggage was unloaded with military precision and the sliding side door slammed shut. Once the inside light had gone out, Maister felt more at ease, but crippled from the pain caused by the cramped conditions he'd endured for almost an hour now. He waited to make sure no one was going to return. As the voices gradually faded into the distance, he eased himself out from under the seat and sat up, stretching each limb slowly and rubbing legs and ankles to speed up the circulation. He peeped up over one of the rear passenger windows. The small group huddled at the side of the disused, derelict airstrip, a few bags by their side, while Proctor approached the open door of the plane. He reckoned, with the noise from the propellers, that no one would hear him sliding back the side door. He waited for Proctor to board what he thought looked like a small eight-seater twin-prop, sitting opposite the derelict green corrugated-iron hangar, before gingerly stepping out into the stiff breeze of the night. He was glad he had worn his black coat now. It gave him some cover, making him difficult to spot in the darkness. He held the Biretta tightly and waited. He anticipated that it would all be over in a matter of minutes. Unless he acted, Vogelmann was gone once again.

Maister crouched down, his tall frame easily visible if one of the small party waiting to board the plane looked around. He tried to identify each of them with the voices he remembered from the minibus. A woman had joined the company now, which surprised him. Obviously she was the woman Vogelmann spoke so sternly about. She turned around.

Josef Maister couldn't believe what he was witnessing. His heart sank. Maggie stared curiously at Eddie Malooly's minibus as if she had just recognised it sitting at the side of the strip and was wondering where Eddie himself was. Maister's enthusiasm suddenly deflated. Maggie's arrival had just turned his plan into an almost impossible task.

Proctor stuck his head out the window and called the two men towards the plane. It was clear now that none of them was brandishing a weapon. Vogelmann had insisted that the weapons disappeared. Clearly they had.

Maggie was alone with Vogelmann now at the side of the airstrip. She put her arm around him to warm him and whispered something to him.

Maister was confused. They seemed to talk quietly to each other now. He knew this was his last chance, his final opportunity. He decided to seize it and take the risk. He started to move forward slowly, careful at all times to check that the three men were still on board the plane. He moved faster now, closer and closer to the old man and the young woman, huddling together in the stiff breeze with their backs to him. Now he could hear them talking as he quickened his pace even more. She was telling him that it was the smell the receding tide leaves behind it, the time when they collect the seaweed, in black buckets and bags, for sale in the town each morning. Maister raised the Biretta as he slowed again and then stopped. The gun was a mere twelve inches from the back of Vogelmann's head.

Josef Maister stood silently, waiting for one of them to turn around and find him there, watching the door of the plane anxiously, knowing that one of the men would step out at any second and see him holding a gun.

It was Maggie who turned around first. *"Josef!"* she said, clearly shocked by the gun in his hands. "What are you doing?" she asked as Vogelmann turned to face him.

"I've come to arrest this man," he said calmy, shuffling slightly left, in order to get Vogelmann directly between himself and the door of the plane, the ultimate line of fire.

"Why?"

"Maybe he'll tell you why. Where is he taking you?"

"To Spain. He's my grandfather. I only just found out the other day. I'm going with him."

Maister laughed at the notion. "*Grandfather?* How can he be your grandfather when he's never had any children of his own?"

"But he was able to show me a photograph of my mother!"

"That wasn't your mother, Maggie. That could have been any one of a million women he had his picture taken with when he was in uniform. Do you really want to know who this man is? His name is Heinrich Vogelmann. He was one of the most feared men in the early forties. This man murdered Jews . . . *my* family. That was his job. I've been searching for him for almost twenty years. He's been living here pretending to be a doting old widower for a long time now. That's the way most of the Nazis who've never been caught spend their last few years. No one really bothers to take any notice of them. Why? They just behave like you'd expect your grandfather to behave. I suppose he tricked you into believing that his late wife is buried here? Did he? Don't believe anything he tells you. He's told the same lies everywhere he's hidden since being run out of Germany by his own people. Isn't that right, *Harry*? Arrogant bastard, aren't you? At least most of your colleagues were intelligent enough to change their names when they went looking for new identities. But not you. No, you just decided to simplify your name. Slightly gung-ho, I always thought."

"Why don't you put the gun down and walk away, Maister?" Vogelmann asked.

"And throw away twenty years? I could have been at home with my wife and family all that time, enjoying their company and being a proper father. Watching my children grow up. And my grandchildren. But no. I decided to come looking for you, Vogelmann. I felt it was the least I could do to appease the deaths of my mother and my father, and my brother."

"I don't know what you're talking about."

"Oh, I think you know all right. Why don't you tell Maggie the truth? Tell her who you really are. Tell her why you've spent most of your life on the run. Buenos Aires, France, Cape Town, and now here. Where are you running to next? Spain?" Maister smiled and shook his head. "I don't think so. You've reached the end of the road."

"You won't get off this airstrip alive tonight, Maister. I think you know that."

Maister watched the door of the plane. "Well, if I die, you die too."

"Maggie!"

The shout caught them all by surprise. It was Jack's voice.

Maister glanced back to see Jack running towards the three of them. Two men were following him. He couldn't decide if they were Jack's men, or more of Vogelmann's supporters. It became too confusing at that moment to keep command. "No, Jack! They're all armed! Get back."

He felt a hand on the gun, pulling it from his grip, amazing strength for a man so old, but a man who was determined to save himself at any cost, no matter what it was going to take.

Vogelmann was raising the gun. He fired, hitting Maister in the left shoulder. The thrust and thump of the bullet crashing into him sent him flying back, and down onto the ground.

Vogelmann started to run, hobbling towards the plane, screaming in German at the top of his voice. *"Bruno, quick! Bruno, quick!"*

Maister's tried to stand up. He couldn't move an inch, as if he had been nailed down.

Bruno Proctor couldn't hear the commotion above the roar of the twin propellers. He had no idea what was taking place outside. All he could hear was his name. He stepped out onto the top rung of the small ladder. As he breathed in the cold night air, and shielded his eyes from the gale-force blast of the propeller, there was a quick burst of automatic gunfire. Bruno knew immediately it was an Uzi machinegun. *"Police!"* he shouted back into the plane's cabin. He picked up the AK47 and slung the strap over his head. From where he cowered inside the door he counted four people running in one direction, towards the plane, one running away towards the oncoming blue flashing lights, and a body on the ground. Since he couldn't decide which of the four aproaching was the Obergruppenfuhrer, and fearing that he may have been shot, he took aim at the small figure running away. He checked that the weapon was on semi-automatic and fired a quick volley of bullets.

The body dropped in a heap and lay still.

* * *

Jack Buckley froze, his legs almost giving way underneath him. He watched Maggie collapse as she ran towards him. He thought she'd tripped or winded herself. He dropped down beside her to help her up. *"Maggie, are you OK?"* he roared above the din of the engines. She didn't answer. Then he noticed Maister lying close by. *"Get an ambulance, quick!"* he shouted to one of the two men.

He looked around, noticing that the sound of the plane was different now, as if it was revving its engines. It was moving slowly. The small frail-looking individual was trying his best to reach the small rung-ladder at the door of the plane. Two men were leaning out, beckoning him, stretching out their arms to grab him and pull him on board.

Jack grabbed the Uzi and sprinted out onto the craggy jet-black airstrip, running along the wide white line to maintain his bearings. *"Stop! You're all under arrest!"* he screamed. He raised the Uzi, changing it from semi- to fully-automatic and pointed it at the plane. The hail of bullets ricocheted off the side of the plane and the tip of the wing with a hollow tin-ringing sound. Vogelmann disappeared in through the door. It closed and the plane picked up speed, turning and accelerating, its red and white lights flashing. Jack continued to run, pumping out as many rounds of gunfire as he could before his finger slipped off the trigger. Then nothing. The magazine was empty.

He tripped, tumbling facedown onto the hard cold stony concrete. He could feel the blood, mixing with the sweat on his face and forehead, and then he could smell the stale vodka above the smell of the burning rubber of the planes tyres and the freezing-cold tarmacadam, as he raised his head and watched the plane get smaller, and faster. And quieter. Then it lifted gracefully off the ground, tilting precariously to the left. It pointed towards the starry sky and quickly became nothing more that a red flashing light, followed by a white flashing light. Until the white flashing light was no bigger or brighter than any of the millions of stars that shone down on the peninsula that Midsummer's night.

Then there was only silence.

* * *

Josef Maister assured the paramedic in the ambulance that he didn't need oxygen, urging him to spend as much time as he had helping Maggie. Jack sat at the base of the stretcher, watching her pale face, cut and bruised from where she'd toppled onto the cement after three of Proctor's bullets had hit her. He listened to the siren, and hummed her favourite song to her, *Love's Old Sweet Song*. He sang the words softly, as he squeezed her fingers and rubbed heat into the back of her hand. The oxygen mask meant that he couldn't see most of her face. "Thank God, she's alive!" he said to the paramedic, and started to hum again. Then he noticed that her eyes had opened. She smiled a little and squeezed his hand. He leaned forward and lifted the oxygen mask and kissed her.

"What happened?" Her voice was so weak, it was hard to hear the words.

"You've had an accident. You're going to the hospital."

"Will I be OK?"

Jack kissed her again, this time on the lips. They were colder than he could ever remember them being before.

"Of course you will. You'll be just fine. I'm going to nurse you better." He patted her face and wiped a tear as she closed her eyes. She squeezed his hand again as he slipped the engagement ring onto her finger. When she felt the cold circular band, and realised what he was doing, she grinned.

59

Verity graveyard was packed that morning.

For the first time that year there was no breeze, no roar off the sea at the bottom of the hill, no gulls squawking; just a warm calm silence that Maggie used to say she missed. "Do you remember the weather in the old days, Jack?" she'd regularly ask on the wet, dreary winter evenings when they'd be driving back from the supermarket in Macroom with the week's shopping on the back seat.

Jack watched as the four men lowered the small coffin into the neat hole in the ground. He wondered where she was now and whether she liked her engagement ring. She smiled so she must have been saying "yes", he kept telling himself over and over.

Aidan's few words were fitting. Every now and then he'd stop to blow his nose, each time his voice would get too high to continue and then he'd cry a little. "I suppose it's only fitting that our dear Maggie is laid to rest here among all the people she looked after so wonderfully and so unselfishly for years . . . "

* * *

The hospital returned her clothes and her belongings a few days later. Jack folded them and – he wasn't sure why he did it – put them neatly into the drawer at the base of the dressing-table where she had always kept her summer things. She would have roared laughing if she had walked in at that moment and caught him folding clothes and putting them away neatly, he thought.

Then he found it. *To Jack.* A letter sealed in a small, dainty lilac-coloured envelope with a tiny brown bear in the corner, pinned to the wooden panel above the dresser mirror. He opened it slowly, careful not to tear it.

Jack,

I'll probably be gone by the time you read this. I'm sorry I had to lie to you. Although considering how many lies you told me over the years, I must be entitled to the occasional one or two. You're probably asking, 'Why did she go?' I went because I was tired, Jack. Tired of us, tired of trying and not getting anywhere, or getting anything in return. Eventually it all became too much. The old man tells me he's my grandfather. I don't know if he's lying. To be honest I don't care. He's the only person in this whole world who's ever made me feel really wanted, really needed. He's asked me to go with him. I know he needs someone to look after him. But so do I. And he looks after me in a special way. He looks out for me. And I need that.

All it would have taken was for you to ask me to marry you, Jack. Then I would have known that you really loved me. I want a new start, Jack. And I don't think you're ever going to give me that. So that's the reason I decided to go. Maybe someday I'll check with you to see if you've changed your mind.

I'll always love you,

Maggie.

Jack placed the note on the dresser and walked back into the sitting-room. He picked up the newly opened bottle of Smirnoff vodka, raised it above his head and flung it with all of his strength at the wall above the fireplace. It shattered into hundreds of tiny pieces.

* * *

Frankfurt – three weeks later.

It was almost half three in the afternoon when the blonde-haired man turned into Seahofstrad, just off the busy Offenbacher. He'd been walking for almost half an hour and the dead heat of the city was annoying him. He just wanted to pick up his car and head out towards the suburbs. He wasn't sure where he would go. He thought about crossing the border into Austria – a day's drive maybe – the following day. Maybe not even as far as Austria. He might just park up for a couple of days in the southern part of Hesse, where his mother came from – close to the Rheingau vineyards on the east bank of the Rhine. Spend some of the money he had been paid for a successful mission. Book into a nice spa and pamper himself for a few days. Sounded nice. But not tonight, he decided. Tonight he would blow some money. Maybe lots of money. He would book into a hotel in the Hauptbahnhof, within walking distance of the Kaiserstrasse red-light district. A quick shower and a change into something light and comfortable. He would book a table at Buffalo, on the Kaiserhofstrad. It was his favourite steakhouse whenever he was in town on business, much favoured by GIs and their families. So he should blend in well with his cropped hair and tall, broad frame. Then he might check out Helium, on Bleidenstrad. A trendy bar, full of singles waiting to be picked up. If he wasn't lucky there he always had the brothels of Kaiserstrasse to fall back on later in the evening.

He could see it from fifty yards, the stylish black MR2, his trusty little sports car, exactly as he'd left it three weeks before. He walked around it. No tickets. No clamp. He was looking forward to driving it again. Maybe he'd trade it in for a newer model when he got across the border. Why not a brand-new model? After all, he was a wealthy man now.

He took the keys out of his pocket as he stood towering over the driver's door. He looked left, then right, then inserted the long key with the black marker attached. Then he looked left again. There was a man at the top of the street, wearing a cap. If it hadn't been for the cap, Bruno Proctor felt he might have recognised him. He looked more intensely now. The man's arm was in a white sling.

Proctor turned the key.

The man at the top of the street jumped back at the sheer pounding strength of the explosion's recoil. He could feel the intensity of the boom right through to the very core of his stomach. He turned and walked away and hailed a taxi for Frankfurt Am Main airport, from where he would fly to Vienna having collected the package from the private locker at the arrivals hall in Frankfurt which he had rented on the Friday before his trip to Ireland.

Once in Vienna, later that evening, he would make two postal deliveries. The first was to the night-editor of *The Irish Times* – a parcel containing photographs and a indisputable documented account of how the head of the Irish government, Joe Russell, had accepted one-and-a-half-million pounds to hide a Nazi war criminal, Heinrich Vogelmann, known as The Keeper, a reference to his habit of wielding a whip to control his victims like caged animals, in a small town called Durrus, in West Cork. He expected it would make front-page news within forty-eight hours. He also planned to fax copies of the document to the editor of the Frankfurter Allgemeine Zeitung.

The second, a smaller parcel with a letter attached, was for Helena, his wife. In it, he wished her a happy birthday. He told her he loved her and explained to her, again, why he wouldn't be coming home just yet.

His work required him to travel on unexpectedly to a small town called Pico Teide, in the shadow of Spain's highest mountain, on the island of Tenerife, where the man he was searching for had been spotted tending a grave in a small cemetery beside the monastery of Santa Bella Maria. He had been seen by an elderly Jewish woman the previous evening in a restaurant called Little

Italy, in the quaint fishing village of Los Cristianos, enjoying his pasta and garlic bread, and sipping a German beer. She recognised him immediately as Heinrich Vogelmann.

Josef explained to Helena that the man would be expecting him sooner or later. Then, at last, his business completed he would be able to close the file and come home to her for good.

* * *

Durrus – that same afternoon.

The doorbell rang.

Jack opened it, expecting to be confronted by more well-wishers, more friends, who just wanted to tell him how much they missed her. They had been calling for almost a month now. Instead it was a couple of German tourists, wanting to know what time the ferry would be leaving for Garnish Island, and could the sergeant recommend a good bed and breakfast for a few nights. He just smiled at them and closed the door.

He stood at the window and watched them walk back down the drive, occasionally glancing back at the house, discussing, no doubt, the rude reception they'd just received, puzzled as to why he had never answered them. He would leave here in a day or two, as soon as he could sort out the business with the solicitor, and Maggie's belongings, and his money, and get a replacement sergeant. He'd travel if his finances were healthy enough. He didn't know where, not that it mattered much anymore. Anywhere, once it was far away from Sheep's Head, and the awful memories he knew this place would hold for him for the rest of his life.

He walked across the room to the record-player, gathering dust now, and changed the LP. He perched it on the steel spindle above the turntable, locking it in place, while humming the air in anticipation of John McCormack's familiar voice. The first track on Side 1 was her favourite song. He remembered the words he'd sung to her that night in the ambulance as he put the ring on her wedding finger.

"Just a song at twilight, when the lights are low,
And the flickering shadows softly come and go,
Though the heart be weary, sad the day and long,
Still to us at twilight comes Love's old song,
Comes Love's old sweet song."

He smiled softly as he turned the small, ivory knob on the front of the record-player – the one in the middle marked *start/play*, with the red arrow pointing clockwise – and listened to the old mechanism whirring as it came to life. Then he watched as the spindle clicked, releasing the big old, dusty vinyl LP. He raised the bottle of vodka to his lips as the big black disc dropped down onto the turntable with a heavy thud.

Published by Poolbeg

DARE TO DIE

By

GARETH O'CALLAGHAN

DETECTIVE GUNNED DOWN IN COLD BLOOD.

A 42-year-old detective was shot dead early last night in a vicious attack during a north London drugs bust. Detective Sergeant James Grant was gunned down in a dark alleyway at point-blank range from behind . . .

Frank McCabe wasn't looking for trouble when he struck up a conversation with pretty, sparky Jamie Carroll one rough night on a car ferry. He had enough on his mind – he was heading for the most important interview of his life, one that could make him manager of the Clover Tap pub in Highbury.

Nor was he looking for trouble when he lent half an ear to the incoherent monologue of a down-and-out who has witnessed a murder . . .

Then Frank puts two chance remarks together and becomes one of three men, entangled in a bizarre plot, who are trying to reach Jamie Carroll.

ONE OF THEM WANTS HER DEAD.
AND ONLY ONE OF THEM CAN SURVIVE.

ISBN: 1-85371-635-9